THE LOST CHILD

Also by Anne Atkins

Non-Fiction

SPLIT IMAGE – MALE AND FEMALE AFTER
GOD'S LIKENESS

THE LOST CHILD

Anne Atkins

St. Martin's Press ⚑ New York

THE LOST CHILD. Copyright © 1994 by Anne Atkins. All rights reserved. Printed in the United States of America. No part of this book may be used or reproduced in any manner whatsoever without written permission except in the case of brief quotations embodied in critical articles or reviews. For information, address St. Martin's Press, 175 Fifth Avenue, New York, N.Y. 10010.

Library of Congress Cataloging-in-Publication Data

Atkins, Anne (Anne D.)
The lost child / by Anne Atkins.
p.   cm.
ISBN 0-312-14006-1
I. Title.
PR6051.T49L67   1996
823'.914—dc20   95-46792   CIP

First published in Great Britain by Hodder and Stoughton

First U.S. Edition: April 1996

10   9   8   7   6   5   4   3   2   1

For Serena and Bink

Acknowledgements

I would like to thank my mother and father for giving me a happy childhood. And Serena, Bink, Alexander and Benjamin – and Lara – for giving me lots more. And Shaun, for giving me Serena, Bink, Alexander and Benjamin.

I would also like to thank Gina Pollinger and Sue Fletcher for helping me with the book, Faber & Faber Ltd for allowing me to quote from T.S. Eliot's *The Waste Land*, John Murray (Publishers) Ltd for allowing me to quote from John Betjeman's *A Russell Flint*, HarperCollins Ltd for their kind permission to quote from *Two Million Silent Killings* by Dr Margaret White, and Marcus, formerly of Heffer's Children's Bookshop.

It has been stated (as is customary at the beginning of books) that all the characters in the following pages are purely imaginary, and that any resemblance to any real person, alive or dead, is purely coincidental, etc, etc.

However, I find that one of the people in this book bears such a striking similarity to someone I know – shining, as he does, like a good deed in a naughty world – that I find it hard to believe the resemblance is purely coincidental.

They say you only begin to appreciate your parents when you have children of your own. Now I have: so perhaps I do. Maybe then this book is, in part, a tribute to them.

More and more countries are afraid of the child, more afraid of babies than they are of bombs and guns.

Mother Theresa of Calcutta

PREFACE

This is a true story, or so I believe. As I've lost touch with the person who told it to me I've been unable to verify it, but perhaps eventually some reader will recognise herself, or another will be reminded of someone he knows, and word will get back to me about how it really happened.

It was told to me one evening in early summer – it must have been May – three years ago. I was speaking at a branch of an organisation called Christian Viewpoint, somewhere in the depths of Hertfordshire: my geography is hopeless, and all I remember about the place was that it was a lot further away from home than I'd anticipated when I accepted the invitation! Towards the end of the evening there were questions from the floor. In response to one of them the president, who was chairing the meeting, told the story in this book. She described the makeup of the family, the kind of open, modern, friendly people they were, and one particular decision that they took together. That was all. Or almost all. The only other thing she added was that when they made the decision one member of the family, the youngest, had demurred. And that one person fascinated me. I asked the president to find out everything she could about the story, and its source, and let me know as much as possible. She must have written and thanked me for my talk, but apart from that I never heard from her again.

The only driving I really enjoy is late at night, on my own, along deserted country lanes, with the beam of the car shining up on the looming trees and lighting up the bends in the gloom. That night, as I drove home, this story grew and grew on me. It continued to grow on me over the weekend. By the time I woke up on Monday morning I felt as if this family – with its life, its members, and its history – was urging itself on me, driving me into my study to write down its story. And that one, lone, tiny, dissenting voice at the centre of the story seemed to me like . . . oh, I don't know: like a bright song in the darkness.

That was in the summer of 1990. And of course I was only told the story as far as 1990. What happened, and will continue to happen, after that is only speculation . . .

Anne Atkins, London, 1993

CONTENTS

THE LOST CHILD

1 May, Saturday, Parsons Green

I wonder, if I asked you to think of the most terrifying dream
you ever dreamt, wouldn't you go back to your childhood?
Some nightmare you had years ago? That feeling of being
paralysed and unable to run, like a small animal caught in the
headlights of a car; the fire, or the flood, or the frightening
creature closing in on your corner; the wave washing over your
head and sucking you under the sea? Those horrors which
haunted us when we were little.
   I had a dream last night. A childhood dream.
   And then this morning, bright May morning, I woke like
Juliet on her wedding day, sun in the window, birds outside,
early roses scenting the air, and I ran down to the park and
wandered over the bridge and strolled along the river bank
past the boathouses and down Riverside Walk, to see what I
often dream of: wildflowers in the middle of London. Waving,
dancing, shouting their brilliant colours at the Swiss-blue sky.
Michaelmas daisies, buttercups, shivering skinny grasses.
Occasionally, here and there, the splash of a poppy: bright as
blood; beautiful as paint dabbed by a careful artist. (And, yes,
thank you: I am aware Juliet never did wake on her wedding
day. Or only briefly, in the dark of the tomb.)
   As I meandered along the bank, through the prickly stalks
and the scattered sprays of colour, and watched the water
slapping the boats as they carried their traffic to and fro, I
thought how little, in some ways, it must have changed since
Henry VIII went upriver from Whitehall to Cheyne Walk
to see Thomas More, and it was fields and meadows and
country lanes all the way. *Painted all with variable flowers.*
Still the same pungent, fresh smell of river; still the same
delicate flowery overtones of elder. Still the same clouds of
forget-me-nots: seeming so tiny and fragile, but fitter to survive,
in the end, than office blocks and paving stones. And they
say there are salmon again in the river, fighting their way
upstream at the moment, apparently, to spawn in Henley and
Oxford. Though of course I saw none.

13

Then silent, statuesque, a solitary swan drifted past
regarding me warily from out of a dark black eye.
Sweet Thames, run softly till I end my song.
I used to love that line as a teenager, dipping and coming up
again as it does amongst Eliot's more stringent modern verse. I
was doing *The Waste Land* for A-level. And then when I read it
in Spenser it was such a disappointment: the swans painted on
to wooden water; the girls solemn and posed, not shrieking with
laughter and pushing their sisters into the water as they should
have been; and the Thames itself sluggish and turgid and slow
– no ripples or giggles or waves dancing in the sun.

I know, I know. It's hardly a day for dawdling by the river
with a slim volume, etc. With my house full of packing-cases
waiting for me. Nevertheless I stayed by the river for over an
hour, listening to the waves lapping the shore; making a detour
via Bishop's Park; taking a ride on the new little river bus
which goes up to Chelsea; dawdling along the Embankment;
poking my nose over the houseboats and musing on what kind
of life they have in there, behind the bright, cheerful washing
hung out to dry (very cold in winter, they say); watching the
ungainly cluster of herons plucking at the rich pickings of eels
spewed out of Chelsea harbour.

I finally arrived last night. I could have done so weeks ago.
The house became mine in early April. Perhaps I delayed
because of memories I didn't know I had: haunted by another
move years ago; feeling sad, without knowing why, at
something I thought I'd forgotten.

Even now I have a vivid image in my mind – and I'm not
sure how much of this is memory, how much imagination – of
a six-year-old girl holding a red and white rag doll as big as
herself, sitting on the bare floorboards of a new house while the
tears rolled down her face and splashed on to the wooden floor.

Strangely enough then, as now, I thought we were leaving
Poppy behind when we moved house. Perhaps that was the
reason for my loneliness, rather than my illness and my
disappointment over that business at school. And of course
as it turns out it'll be this move, twenty years on, which will
really be my parting from Poppy.

I was changing to a new school after Christmas, so the day
of the move was to have been my last day at school as well as
my last day in our old house in Clancarty Road. This was pure
coincidence: we were only moving five minutes' walk away
to Perrymead Street, so I didn't have to change schools for

geographical reasons. But my brothers' prep school in Battersea
had started up a pre-prep department, and my parents chose
that time to send me to join them. I don't know why. I was
very excited about it: they kept telling me what a grown-up
school it was, and I had seen the glossy prospectus, showing
a wide range of happy, intelligent-looking children – canoeing
and playing the violin and riding ponies and learning judo and
taking part in the school play – and it did look good. As it
happens it was years before I got in a canoe, never learnt the
violin, didn't see a single pony, and my next few years were
wretched, with the bullying and the conformity and the hours
of homework. Luckily I wasn't yet aware of that, or I would
have been even more unhappy that day we moved house. And
neither were my parents: they wouldn't have put me through
that particular misery if they had known what it would entail.
The other? Well, that was different.

It was the last day of term at my old school. There was
going to be a concert, then a Christmas party, and finally a
sale in aid of some charity. And after school I was going home
with a friend for a night or two while my parents got the new
house straight, the house in Perrymead Street. My brothers
were also staying with friends. And – great thrill – for my last
day at school I had been picked to read my own composition
in front of the parents at the concert. This was a great honour,
and all my classmates were most impressed. I had written a
poem about the angel Gabriel, and it was thought to be the only
'homegrown' piece of literature good enough to be included:
everything else was from the Bible or Dickens or the English
Hymnal. My mother and father had promised to abandon
Pickfords and the packing for the afternoon, and be there.
And I had set off that morning for school with my bag packed
for my stay at Ella's, and my hair washed and combed and
struggling out of a French plait, ready for my performance.

But when my parents turned up at two o'clock I was lying
on the sofa in the headmistress's tiny office with my hands
in blisters and my mouth so painful I couldn't even whisper
that I wanted a glass of water. I can't remember the name
of the illness now, but it was the human equivalent of 'foot
and mouth' so there was the added humiliation of having a
disease which is supposed to be caught by cows, as well as the
devastation of missing the concert and my stay at Ella's and
the end-of-term Christmas party.

The rag doll was bought by my father, to comfort me, at

the sale of goods already on exhibit in the school hall. She
only cost a pound, she was nearly as bit as I, and she had a
lovely cheerful red and white face. I have her still, though I've
forgotten her name. (It couldn't have been Poppy, too, could it?
On account of the large, bright red spots all over her clown-like
costume? No, I don't think it could have been.) Anyway, she did
her best to cheer me up that day.

When we got to the new house in Perrymead Street, that
afternoon, the removal men had gone. They were due to unload
properly the next day, so all they had taken out for that night
were my parents' bed, the kettle, and a few kitchen basics.
When I was shown my new bedroom there was nothing but the
bare and dusty floorboards: no curtains, no bed, no rug on the
floor. Only my new rag doll and the gas fire on to warm me up
and my tears falling on the floor while I put my sore fist into
my even more painful mouth and couldn't even speak.

It was the doll that I dreamt of last night: a child was
holding that very same red and white doll. Obviously the jolt
of moving house again had brought back an old childhood
nightmare. In my dream I knew that the grown-ups wanted the
doll; they explained it patiently; they said it was for my good;
they knew I wouldn't like giving it up but they were sorry they
had to have it. 'It'. They always called her 'it'. And I knew, as
certain as certain could be, that they were only going to throw
her away because there was no room for her any more. The
new house was too small. Or too smart. Or something. And I
backed away from the adults and held more tightly on to the
doll, and the adults got nearer and nearer and became more
and more ugly and started to turn into monsters ... And then
I woke up in a cold sweat in the middle of the night, asking
myself why on earth I live alone?

I must say, when I moved in yesterday evening and again
saw almost nothing in my bedroom except the shiny-brown
floorboards – though this time because I have no furniture of
my own, not because I have too much to move in one day – I
did hesitate on the threshold for a moment.

But only for a moment. I don't feel the same helpless kind of
pain I felt then. Perhaps just because it's not helpless any more.
This time I'm not a child; I am in control; I choose to move
house. I feel a great sadness, but I know it's the right thing to
do.

It *is* a goodbye. We won't ever share a house together again, in
the way that we have for the last twenty years, on and off. And

shared our lives, and our work, and everything. Perhaps it was
because I was moving out that I finally agreed to write about it.
After all, my publishers have been asking me to talk about
Poppy for several years now. A completely different kind of
book. The first I shall be doing on my own, without her. An
end to our partnership. Of course, until now I've always said
no. Not just for the obvious reasons, either; not just for the
reasons to do with Poppy herself, and my relationship with
her. But all the others too. After all, it's a story about all of us.
What will my parents make of it? And the rest of my family?
We never talk about what happened that summer. And then
if I break with Poppy herself, which is the last thing I want
to do but which seems inevitable...

(And I notice, turning back to my first sentence, that I still
write to her, still address her as 'you', still talk to her as if she
were still there.)

Oh, well. New house, new book, new life. And new diary, *ici
voilà.*
New me. Independent, brave, alone for the first time. And yet
I'm not a loner at all, and can't quite think how I'll cope. Not
that I won't eat properly, or I'll be frightened by a creak on the
stairs, but who will I talk to at two in the morning? Because
of Poppy, I never had the companions I would have wanted
otherwise: a kitten, a dog. I loved animals, but Poppy took their
place, and I simply played with her instead.
Which I now believe, looking back on it, was what happened
with boyfriends I tried to have. Trouble was, however much I
liked them, however much I fancied them even, most important
of all however good they were to me as friends, they could
never compete with Poppy. I might talk to them, but I
could never say as much as I could say to her. I might be open
with them, but they never understood me as well as she did.
Any love affair was doomed to failure; although to be honest I
didn't try very hard. I already had the best friend I could want.
Perhaps now would be the time to get the puppy my
parents should have got me when I was ten. What? A
labrador? A spaniel? Those were the days when people
had those extraordinary breeds: Pit-bulls and Dobermanns
and Rottweilers. I can hardly remember what they looked
like now, but at that age I was taught to recognize them a
mile off, and never go any nearer.
Anyway, mid-morning, I walked back from Chelsea through

the Harbour, along the New Kings Road, towards my new home. And of course when I reached Perrymead Street I forgot what I was doing and turned left by mistake as if for the old house, and was halfway along the road before I had to tell myself I don't live in Perrymead Street any more. Now it's my parents' house again, not mine and Poppy's. You live in Parsons Green now, I said to myself, as if I were addressing a child. And Poppy? Poppy doesn't live here any more.

I suppose it's good that they've moved back into London. The country never suited my mother: she couldn't be doing with all the busy commuters combined with the slow pace of life and everyone going to bed early. And it's good for them to be near one of us, at any rate, what with both lots of grandchildren hours away, in Norfolk and India. So if ever I have a family myself (some chance), well, here they are, and I've always believed in extended family and grandparents on hand and all the things industrialisation temporarily did away with.

When I realised that I was halfway down the wrong street I went on anyway, past the old house in Perrymead Street, then past the older house in Clancarty Road (older to me, I mean), and on into South Park, and I took a walk round it, as I often do. The Toddler Park is still there, though far quieter than when we were little; and the nursery school is still in that funny little hut, though now it only has a handful of pupils. And I sat in the calm May sunshine which, I had realised for some time, wasn't nearly as hot as it looked, and I shivered on a park bench and watched a couple in their sixties go past hand in hand but walking far too quickly. Where are they rushing to? I wondered. And then five minutes later saw them rush past again, going in the same direction as before.

By the time I strolled home – 'home'? is this really my home? – it was late morning, I think. My watch is still in a packing-case somewhere. The occasional bus rumbled past; a strapping, handsome young man, presumably a nanny, was on the Green playing football with a little child; the French café was open with one or two brave customers sitting out in the half-hearted sunshine; and the Green itself warm with the memory-jerking smell of cut grass.

And now, as I sit here, I hear the clop of horses going steadily past what is now my house, and I strain out of the window to see whether it is the Shires from Young's Brewery, or a solitary mounted policeman; and I can't see either. But the latter, I think: the hollow, comforting sound is too bright

and quick for the two heavy Shires. I love this view from my
new study over the Green, with the happy London plane trees
shedding their bark over the Georgian houses opposite.

And I do love my new house: empty as it is; lonely as it is.
Even with the ghost of a sad and bereaved six year old sitting
on the bare floorboards after a different move. After all, here
I am, at my age, successful and all that rot, blah blah, and yet
I've never had my own house. Yes, it really is mine, in the way
that my parents' was theirs. In fact more so: theirs belonged
to the Abbey National or the Halifax or whatever it was for
most of the time. I know, I know, nobody buys houses any
more and it won't be worth tuppence in five years' time and
all that went out in the eighties, but I couldn't resist. It was
very important to me, somehow.

I put the kettle on and found a teapot from the packing-case
in the kitchen, and wandered out into my very own garden.

There's something pink and very fragrant and beautiful
hanging over my neighbour's wall and dripping scent into the
air by my French windows. I feel as if it ought to be called a
May tree, but know it isn't because I know what a May tree is.
This is in fact far prettier than the dirty white of the May; in
keeping with that sort of fresh early-summer loveliness which
gives way so quickly to the brash blooms of June.

I put my face into the white and pink star-shaped flowers
and took a deep smell. It was a bright, slightly bitter smell;
sharp; a smell to wake you up. I leant against the wall and
turned my face to the sunshine and bathed in the warmth
and the tastes and the sounds of spring. Sparrows arguing; a
blackbird darting across the garden, urgent with song; a bee
worrying the petals; a shuffle or a breath in the garden next to
mine, or simply the sense of someone or something watching
me.

I opened my eyes. My neighbour was in his garden: not
watching me, as it happened. Or, if it wasn't my neighbour,
it was someone burgling his house. A cool way to work: let
yourself in, help yourself to the drinks, stroll around the garden
with your hands in your pockets smelling the flowers. Then
go away again with the silver and the computer, leaving a
note with the telephone messages on it: 'Your mother rang
– coming for the weekend. Courier called with a parcel. Spoke
to your dishy new neighbour: suggest lavish dinner at Ritz
with same. Have taken all the spoons, a few cuff-links,
and your old-fashioned Toshiba. Love from Burglar Bill.'

He moved and saw me and almost nodded in my direction,
and then turned away from me again and strolled down to the
far end of his garden.

No, I thought. Not the makings of a burglar. Very little
promise. Bungler Bill, perhaps.

I turned away from the wall too, and sat on the steps of my
French windows, which open from my very tatty conservatory.
Soon I shall fill it with tomato plants and runner beans and
a kiwi, and eventually a vine. Then I can spend all my time
tending them, and avoiding my book altogether.

I wonder if Wilfred Owen and Siegfried Sassoon felt like
this, nearly a hundred years ago? They described what they
saw, what they knew, what they felt. They painted a field of
poppies and said it was running with blood. Their generation
slaughtered, by their own parents almost. And the poets must
have realised that their 'superiors', their elders and betters,
their parents even, would see them as traitors to freedom
and civilisation and everything else that their education and
upbringing stood for. Only those who came later understood.
And if I describe what I saw, what I knew, what I felt, isn't that
exactly how my parents' contemporaries will see me? If I tell
Poppy's story. If I paint my generation's field of poppies. *Dulce
et decorum est pro matre mori.*

Publication is at the end of the summer. First week of
September. I've given my editor the outline, and the title's
already in the catalogue as if it were a completed book;
jacket design, everything. They know they can make money
out of it: any book which carries our names, Poppy's and
mine, sells well. As does anything which might have a
sinister mystery at the heart of it.

And that's the problem. The heart of it. The summer of 1990.

I've divided the story into two strands. 1990 and After.
The Child and the Growing Up. The two streams of the story
conveniently flow through the two different houses, so I hope
it won't be too confusing. I wondered whether to call the book
The Two Daughters of Time. Then I wondered whether that
would be absurdly pretentious. In the end I simply left it as it
was. Named after that story we wrote together, years ago.

Of course the After, the Growing Up, the second strand,
will be quite easy to write. Childhood after the age of
six; being teenagers; our work together as adults. Recent,
easy to remember. It's the summer of 1990 which I'll be
struggling to recall. Which is why I'm into my routine of

doing anything to avoid work: going into my new garden
and staring at the neighbours; writing my diary; musing
about growing grapes and kiwis.

Not that I was an unhappy child, not at all. Our parents
loved us; they loved each other; good grief, they even lived
together, which is more than most of my friends could say.
We were comfortably off, 'middle-class', in the days when most
middle-class people still expected to work. Before the recession
really set in. More important, before my mother's illness, which
changed everything so much. A trouble-free time, almost a
golden age. So it would come as a genuine shock to anyone
in my family to know that I might have to force myself to
remember what happened that year.

I went to see Abigail in Norfolk at Easter. Almost five
and three-quarters. What a wonderful, fresh, optimistic and
accepting age it is! Truly a Golden Age. An age that believes
all things, hopes all things, endures all things. The age I was
then, all but. I showed her how to feed a horse, and her eyes
shone as though she'd discovered the Meaning of Life. I took
her swimming, and we saw a wasp drowning in the water. I
put a stick in to rescue it, but couldn't reach across the river.
'Never mind,' Abi said. 'He's a very lucky wasp.'

'Why, genius?' I asked her.

'Because Heaven is like having a party all the time,' she
replied.

'Is it? Who told you that?' And I wondered whether Abi
might catch my grandfather's faith, like catching measles,
but posthumously; from beyond the grave. My grandfather
would have believed such things possible, if he prayed
for his unborn progeny – which I wouldn't have put past
him.

'Nobody. I knowed it already, silly!'

'Oh, yes. How did you know? You've got to learn from
somewhere, egghead. People don't just *know* things,
from nowhere.'

'Yes, they do. That's why it's called knowing. From
nowhere. You know when you're cold, and nobody tells you.
I'm cold in this water, Auntie C.'

'Abi, gorgeous, don't call me Auntie – I can't bear it. It
sounds as though I should be knitting something. Just call
me C.'

'Mummy calls you Auntie.'

'Well, for goodness' sake tell her not to.'

'And you know when you love someone, and nobody tells you,' she went on.

'Bet you don't love me as much as I love you, Queen of the World.'

'I love you enough to fill a whole bucket and water the garden,' she insisted.

'Oh, I love you loads more than that. Several buckets.'

'And you know when things are right and wrong,' she mused on. 'And nobody tell you that.'

'No,' I argued. 'Ordinary people only have a very hazy idea of right and wrong. You need prophets for that. And prophetesses.'

'Daddy says we need a profit if we're to go on holiday. A fat one, he said. What are profits and profits'-esses?'

'Prophets – fat or otherwise – are people who know right and wrong.'

'Like children, you mean?' And she was quite serious, her green eyes with splashes of brown in them – 'like peanut butter', a schoolfriend of mine once said of her boyfriend's eyes – staring at me with that heartbreaking trust and honesty that only young children have.

'Children!' I scorned. 'Children – ha!' Enough of this, I thought. 'Children don't know anything! But wizards, like you and me ...' And I picked her up and jumped into the water holding her, her naked flesh clasped against mine, and we splashed and laughed into the spray, and sent the water dancing up into the sun.

My first day of my new house of my new life. Time almost for bed, though it's only nine o'clock, and I rummage in one of my cases for some wine I was sure I had. Garlic crusher; tea-towels; a vase, chipped in transit; an old, battered, Turkish contraption, picked up when I had a rucksack on my back during my year off, to be used for making coffee and consisting of a tiny saucepan, barely four centimetres across, on a tin stick. Put two or three spoonfuls of very strong finely ground coffee, same of sugar, and hold it over cotton wool soaked in meths till it boils up. Remove. Repeat. Three times. Turkish coffee. That daft little machine has been with me to Oxford and back and I haven't used it since I was eighteen. Resume: olive stoner; butter dish; pepper-corn grinder. Ah – Moët et Chandon. Bit over the top. I just wanted a glass of *vin ordinaire* before bed. Doorbell.

Doorbell? I love it when my doorbell goes. Any excuse to stop work, talk. Friends. On impulse I put the champagne in the fridge before going to the door.

Oh. Heart sinks somewhat: Bungler Bill on the doorstep.

'Hello,' he says, with half a smile. 'I'm your new neighbour. I mean, you're my new neighbour.'

'Er, yes,' I said. 'I'd noticed.'

'I wanted to welcome you to the area.'

'Thank you,' I said, 'but I've lived in the area all my life. I've only moved round the corner.' Do I mean to sound as unfriendly as I think I do? Probably.

'Sorry. I won't bother you then. Goodnight.'

'No, no,' I rush on, feeling guilty. 'Do you want to come in?' Not welcoming at all.

'No, thank you...'

'What are you holding?'

'Sheep's cheese.'

'I beg your pardon?'

'Sheep's cheese. Wrapped in nettles. From Scotland. I know it sounds disgusting. Probably *is* disgusting. But I thought I ought to bring you something over: you know, something edible. I mean, that's what one's grandmother used to do, when people moved into the village. And this was the nearest thing I had.'

I started laughing. 'Come in. I'll see if I can find some tea, and the kettle.'

'Thank you. But don't bother with all that. I'll ring for something. The French café is good for coffee and a glass of wine.'

'I know. I've lived here for years, remember. But it's no use: I've no idea where I've put my telephone. Come into the kitchen...'

'Do you always leave your fridge door open?'

'Only when I have unexpected visitors.'

I swung the fridge door to, quickly, so I wouldn't have to share my good wine with a stranger. Then I looked at the half-unpacked case – tea-towels, knives, an empty butter dish – and wondered where on earth I'd find the tea.

The cheese was poisonous. The champagne was good. Bungler Bill left at ten to eleven.

I must say goodbye to the past. I must tell it, remember it, write my book, so that all the world knows what happened.

And then say goodbye, forever, to the dearest friend I ever had.

2 May

I woke again, last night, or rather this morning, in the small
hours of the dawn, and was glad. Just under my bedroom
window, which opens on to the Green, an invisible nightingale
was singing its little heart out into the night. At least,
I assume it was a nightingale. I must confess, I wouldn't
have got first-class honours in ornithology. On and on it
went, beautiful and tireless, pouring its liquid notes into
the deaf, disregarding darkness.
   Jug jug jug jug, tereu, she cries
   And still her woes at midnight rise.
   I wonder if it sounds as lovely to the nightingale herself as
it does to us? Or as senseless?
   Sweet Thames, run softly, for I speak not loud or long.

CHAPTER ONE –
CLANCARTY ROAD, 1990

When we step into the family, by the very act of being born, we do step into a world which is incalculable, into a world which has its own strange laws, into a world which could do without us, into a world that we have not made. In other words, when we step into the family we step into a fairy tale.

G.K. Chesterton

I, a stranger and afraid
In a world I had not made.

A.E. Housman, Last Poems, *1922*. Lancer

Sandy was lying on her tummy. The ground was warm. Her mother had told her to wear her sunhat, but it prickled on the inside so she had put it on the grass beside her. Like that, nearby, only a few centimetres away (it was centimetres because she was at school: if she'd been at home it would have been inches), she felt as if it were nearly on. It wasn't, after all, as if she'd left it on her peg. It was silly anyway, because Mummy said the sun would burn her face and spoil her skin, but Barney had pointed out all the grown-ups in the holiday adverts on the television, sitting in the hot sun, getting burnt, putting oil on their skins like people do when they put things in the oven to cook. And Barney said they paid money to do that; to get burnt like a roast lunch. Sandy had seen them, one summer, ages and ages and ages ago, lying on the beach and cooking in oil like rows of chickens on the sand.

It hadn't been this summer. She thought it might not have been last summer, but even longer ago than that. This summer hadn't really started yet. This summer was only really spring at the moment, even though it was hot enough for Mummy to ask her to wear her sunhat. Sandy knew why it was so hot. It was because the world was turning into a green house. It didn't look like one yet; it only felt like one. Probably it would start to look like one later. In fact it didn't look like a house at all; it was much too big.

Green houses are hotter than red or blue ones.

Even though it was hot, it was only the first week of term. Sandy was wearing her summer uniform, but you do do that before it gets to be summer anyway. The sunhat isn't part of Sandy's uniform. The other people in Sandy's class don't wear sunhats. Mummy got it for Sandy from a friend called Peter Jones because Sandy has such fair skin.

A ladybird wobbled crookedly over the grass in front of her. Sandy put out her hand and helped it climb the vast wall up the side of one of her fingers. It struggled right up on to the end of her fingernail. Now it could see the world from much higher up. It could see where it wanted to go. It opened up the shell of its back, shook out its awkward long black wings, and before Sandy could think of anything to change its mind, it flew away, up into the bright sunshine and the clear blue sky. It was a shame she had put it on her finger. If it hadn't seen the better view, it might have been happy where it was.

She picked at some bits of grass in front of her. There were three different kinds. There was the normal long thin kind that Mummy could put between her thumbs and blow like a whistle. It could scream right across the park. Sandy couldn't do that. It was very loud and startling. Then there was the kind with three leaves called clover. Jack had found one with four leaves once, and he told Sandy that would make him very lucky. Sandy thought Jack was lucky anyway, because he got to have a late night on Fridays, and even went to bed later than Sandy and Barney on the other nights too. After he told her about the clover she always looked out for one with four leaves; if she could find one, perhaps she'd be allowed late nights too. When she explained to Daddy, he laughed and said, 'You mustn't believe that, sweetheart. That's superstition.' And Sandy thought how unfair it was that she'd been laughed at when it was Jack who'd been wrong. Then she remembered Jack's late nights and wondered if it were Daddy who was wrong. It was quite difficult to work it out.

The other kind of grass was feathery. It was like a tiny tiny fern. Sandy knew ferns because they'd been to Scotland last summer and she'd picked lots of them to go with all the flowers she gathered.

They were called wildflowers, but Sandy thought they were quite tame, because they always let her pick them. She picked masses every single day, and put them in cups all over the house, and they looked very, very pretty. After a while Mummy had said she could only go on picking them if she threw away the dead ones. Sandy hadn't realised they were dead: she thought they had simply changed. Mummy helped her collect them all up and throw them out. When Sandy saw how many flowers she'd killed she felt sorry, but Mummy said it was all right. She said she'd buy Sandy a book about wildflowers. But it hadn't come for Christmas, and her next birthday wasn't for ages and ages and weeks and months and hours. Sandy hadn't seen the feathery kind of grass before, but it was her favourite.

She crossed her arms and put them on the ground in front of her, and laid her face on them sideways, so that the grass stretched away for ever and ever before her. She couldn't see the three different kinds of grass any more. She could see some sharp blades in front of her eyes, with the sun shining pale green through them, and beyond them a grassy blur going on for ever. And beyond even that, under the trees, nearly at the end of the world, Mr Peter was sitting on his lawn mower, driving it backwards and forwards, further and further away from her, cutting the grass. Before they'd come out for lunch he'd cut the grass where she was lying now. The smell was comfortable and friendly, and she could remember smelling it before. Nearly as long ago as time went back, maybe even as long ago as last summer, she had smelt cut grass before.

That, she thought, was the Scotland summer. It was the most exciting holiday Sandy had ever known, because she chose it. She really did help to choose it. They had all sat down one Sunday afternoon to decide on their summer holiday, and Sandy had said Scotland because they said there was Heather there, and Heather was a girl at nursery school who was really pretty, and had red curls and freckles. And Mummy and Daddy had said they could go because Sandy had chosen it, and they really had gone. Even Jack had gone, though he wanted to go to Normandy because a friend of his from school had gone there. But Mummy had said he'd have to accept other people's choices sometimes, and couldn't always have life the way he wanted. And Sandy had felt like a queen.

In fact when they got there it had rained a lot and Heather wasn't there. But even Jack enjoyed it in the end.

Sandy froze. Sammy, the school squirrel, had come almost within stroking distance of her. He was very tame, and would sometimes sit in Miss Sylvia's bicycle basket. If she lay very still she might almost be able to touch him.

Suddenly a voice said, 'Hello Sandy,' and Ella flopped down beside her. Ella tended to flop a bit. Sandy thought she was a little fat.

'Oh Ella!' Sandy said in dismay.

'What's the matter?'

With Ella's flop Sammy had turned like a fish and gone. They could just see him, miles away, leaping on to a tree and disappearing round the other side of the trunk. 'You frightened Sammy away,' Sandy explained.

'Sorry,' said Ella, panting. 'What are you doing?'

'Nothing. What are you doing?'

'Max was chasing me,' Ella puffed. 'He kept tying me up and telling me I was in prison and he was going to torture me, so Annie's beating him up.'

'Oh,' said Sandy. She thought for a moment. 'You are a lucky duck,' she said, wishing.

'Why?'

'I'd love to have a sister who beat Max up.'

'You've got brothers and they're bigger.'

'Yeah but they don't go to school here. And they don't play with me. Not much anyway.'

'Why don't they play with you?'

'I don't know really. They say I mess up their things. And anyway, they're not a girl. I'd like to have a sister. Mummy says when you have a sister they pinch your makeup and clothes and boyfriends. I think that must be fun. I'd like to share a bedroom with a sister.'

'Annie's a pig,' Ella said.

'Why?'

'She won't let me get to sleep all night long, and talks to me and tells me there's monsters under the bed.'

'Oh,' said Sandy. She still felt she'd like to have a sister.

'Look,' said Ella. 'I've got a gun. It's a really good one.'

'That's not a gun – that's a stick.'

'Yes, but it looks like one. Look, there's the trigger. Bang-bang-you're-dead-fifty-bullets-in-your-head.'

'My mummy won't let us play guns at home,' Sandy told Ella.

'Gollygosh. Why?'

'She says it's not very nice to kill people and you shouldn't make a game out of it. We can play guns in the garden though.'

'Is it all right to kill people in the garden?'

'I suppose so. We're allowed to make more noise in the garden.'

'Oh,' said Ella. 'What's your mum?'

'What do you mean, what's my mum?'

'My mum's a home-maker what's your mum?'

'Oh,' said Sandy. 'I don't know. She runs a business.'

'What's that mean?'

'She makes telephone calls. What's your dad?'

'He goes to work,' said Ella.

'Mine doesn't.'

'Doesn't he?'

'No,' said Sandy proudly. 'He writes newspapers. He lets me write on his computer. I'm learning to do all the right fingers. Then you print it out and it comes out all neat as if you'd spent hours writing it. And when you make a mistake you don't have to rub it out.'

'What do you do when you make a mistake?'

'You just go back and do it again.'

'Oh,' said Ella.

'Your mummy's nice, isn't she?' said Sandy.

'Yes,' said Ella.

'If I had to have a new mummy, I'd have yours,' said Sandy.

'Why?'

'She makes biscuits.'

'Andrew and Sally's mummy's having a baby,' said Ella.

'Is she? Is she really?' Sandy was impressed. 'You mean their *parents* are having a baby,' she corrected.

'What?'

'The mummy can't have a baby without the daddy. They have the baby together.'

'It's in the mummy's tummy.'

'I know that, silly! It wouldn't be in the daddy's tummy, would it?' They giggled.

'No!' said Ella. 'In the daddy's tummy!' It was very funny, the thought of a baby in a daddy's tummy. Sandy had seen Andrew and Sally's father. He wore a suit, and didn't have hair on the top of his head, and his name was Justin. Sandy tried to think of him with a baby in his tummy, and it was so funny that she couldn't stop laughing. She rolled on to her back and laughed so much that

29

the world wobbled around like a jelly in a picture book. She'd just stopped laughing when Ella said, 'In the daddy's tummy,' again, and they started laughing all over again.

At last all the laughter came out of Sandy and she lay on her back, still, and tired by the laughing, looking at the sky. It was very, very blue, and it was more blue at the top than round the edges. There were a few fluffy little bits of cloud like cotton wool – white cotton wool not the coloured cotton wool her mother had – but not very much. Her granny used to say, 'Enough blue sky to make a sailor's trousers.' But Sandy never understood that quite, because it would depend on how big the trousers were. You could make a pair of trousers out of the tiniest, tiniest piece of sky, if they were small enough; and that would depend on how far away they were. Or how far away the sky was. Or even how small the sailor was. And what would be behind when you'd cut the material out of the sky? She wished she'd talked it over with Granny when she had the chance; and she was surprised how much the wish hurt. Today Granny would certainly have said there was enough sky for the sailor's trousers, even if they were big.

The whistle blew. Sandy and Ella stayed where they were. For the first whistle you have to keep still. It's difficult if you're running or being chased when you hear the whistle, because it's sometimes hard to stop. Yesterday Sandy was being chased by Timmy when the whistle blew, and she stopped but Timmy didn't; he bumped into her and said, 'You're It,' which Sandy thought was really stinky because that meant she was It for all the rest of the day, because they didn't play again. But if you're lying on your back when the first whistle blows it's easy to keep still because you're still already.

When the second whistle blew, Sandy and Ella got up.

'Can I go in with you?' Sandy said.

'Yes.'

'You sometimes go in with Annie,' Sandy reminded her.

'Annie's not in my class.'

'I know.' Sandy was glad Ella had agreed to go in with her. She held her hand ready to get in the line, but Ella held her hand the wrong way at first, back to front, so Sandy had to let go to get Ella to get it right, with the thumb at the top and the fingers underneath so it was comfortable.

They had a story that afternoon, about Hansel and Gretel. Sandy knew it already. She didn't like the story. She didn't understand why the witch was so horrid. She didn't need to eat the children, because her house was made of gingerbread, so she could have eaten that instead, and it would have tasted much nicer. Sandy didn't believe that anyone would be that horrid. People only hurt children like that in newspapers, not in real life. People are kind to children in real life. Though sometimes they don't listen, or tell you off when it's not your fault, or they get tired and lose their temper. But they aren't unkind on purpose: it's usually a mistake. Adults are all right really; except for the kind of strangers you mustn't talk to in the street or take lifts from or go home from school with if they aren't other people's parents. But you never meet that kind of stranger; you just practise in case you do. Ordinary people, parents and teachers and things, don't usually mean to be cruel. Sandy's mummy and daddy never are. Sometimes they're horrid by mistake, but then they usually say sorry or explain why. When they say sorry it means it was their fault for being tired; those times are all right. But when they explain why, it means it was your fault for being naughty; then you sometimes don't get fruit yoghurt for tea.

Sandy wrapped her skirt round her fist, and took her fist out, so it left a bit of her skirt round like a balloon. It was interesting. She did it over and over again. They'd got to the bit of the story where Hansel and Gretel were asleep in the wood. Sandy couldn't remember whether that was after all the other bits or before. She thought about Andrew and Sally having another baby. Of course it was their father's baby too, even though it wasn't in his tummy. Sandy had a book at home about a baby inside its mummy's tummy. It showed you all the sizes of the baby from when it was as small as a pea to when it was as big as a marrow just before it was born. Sandy didn't think she'd ever seen a marrow, but she knew what it was. And it showed you what the baby had and did when it was all the different sizes. It was a very busy baby, that baby in her book. It had fingers and things from when it was tiny. And when it was about the size of a pear it sucked its thumb. And it kicked and swam about until it got too big and then it just sat there kicking. That was when it was about like a pineapple.

Sandy wondered what Andrew's baby brother or sister was doing now. Was it banana-sized? Or tomato-sized? Or avocado-sized? And why was it always the size of fruit or vegetables, not ... oh, the size of a tennis ball, for instance? Perhaps it was sucking its thumb already. She made another balloon out of her skirt before she realised the story was finishing and it was time to go home. It was the best time of day. If Daddy came for her he'd be on his bicycle and she

ANNE ATKINS

could go behind him and hide from the wind and they would go in and out among the traffic and he would never hear what she said because he never did, and she would hold on round his waist and lay her face on his big strong back.

Sandy shook hands with Miss Jenny and said 'Good afternoon, Miss Jenny' and ran outside. And there was Daddy on his bicycle leaning against the little green fence and talking to Alexander's mummy.

'Daddy!' Sandy said, and climbed up on to the seat behind him. He went on chatting for ages, but Sandy didn't mind much because it was comfortable behind him on the bicycle.

They were halfway home, behind a big lorry, when Daddy said, 'Where's your sunhat?'

'I don't know,' said Sandy.

'What?'

'I don't know!' Sandy shouted.

'Hang on, sweetheart,' Daddy replied.

Sandy thought of her sunhat. She remembered lying on her back in the grass, and the blue sky with the sailor's trousers in it, and Ella laughing beside her.

Daddy got to some traffic lights, stopped, and turned in his seat. 'Sorry, sweetie, I couldn't hear what you said. Where's your sunhat?'

'I left it in the garden.'

'Oh dear. Mummy will be pleased,' said Daddy. He says that sort of thing when he doesn't mean it. It doesn't count as lying; it's a kind of joke. Adults are allowed to tell jokes that aren't funny.

'Mmm,' said Sandy, and held Daddy tighter as he started bicycling again.

She'd already decided what she was going to do when she got home. She was going to go straight up to her room and look at the book with the busy baby. She couldn't remember all the things he could do when he was the size of an avocado. Or she, if it was a girl.

10 May, Monday, Parsons Green

Finally grasped the nettle; and, as with so many things when one was a child, it didn't sting nearly as much as I'd feared it would.

I started with South Park again, funnily enough. Strictly speaking, I thought I ought to go back to Knightsbridge. 'Go back to Knightsbridge'! I make it sound as if I haven't been near the Old Brompton Road or Kensington Music Shop or the Science Museum since I was a child! Anyway, I thought I should have hiked to my old school, or the place where my old school used to be, as a starting place. But I didn't. Yes, all right, I admit it: I'm a coward. Or perhaps I'm just lazy, and the house in Clancarty Road is nearer. But I didn't go to the house. I expect it's unrecognisable now anyway. Maybe if I'd rung the doorbell, and explained, and been invited in, and after some obligatory cup of tea and unasked-for biscuit been allowed to go upstairs to my old bedroom; and perhaps if I'd lain on the bed and looked through the window at the huge white chestnut (not so huge now, of course) and remembered what it had looked like as the evening crept into a pale greyness on a summer evening when one couldn't sleep, and the dark leaves and branches against the sky became the head of a lion continually snapping at a little bird every time the wind blew; and perhaps if I'd heard my parents' voices drifting up the stairs after I'd gone to bed, when they had friends to dinner but it was too late for me to stay up, and a sudden wave of grown-up laughter had splashed up the stairwell...

But I didn't. How could I go to someone's house and say, 'Excuse me, but I used to be a child here and please can I come in?' Though I think my family knows the people who bought the house, so I could have arranged to call. If I could bear to explain to my parents why I want to go back. Which I must soon: the book will be on the shelves in four months.

So I simply went to South Park and lay on the grass and tried to remember what it looked like when I was a child. What grass looked like; and sky; and grown-up people. And, sure

33

enough, certain memories began to come back very clearly. Not important memories, it's true; not painful memories. But I have to start somewhere. Then I came back to my desk, and, just like the awful old Joyce Grenfell cliché, it began to write itself. It really did. As if this child were nothing to do with me, at the beginning of that summer all those years ago.

Strange how some things haven't changed at all since then. I saw a Scotty dog – what are they called? Like the picture on the Black and White whisky bottles – dashing across the park, quite illegally, off its lead, chasing some awful chewed-up old tennis ball, and the scene could have been lifted straight out of my childhood. Similarly, as I walked round the park I found myself swimming into different currents of smell; the particularly powerful, early-summer-wedding, sweet smell of something my mother used to call syringa, but I'm not sure that it is. A creamy-white, four-petalled flower with little yellow blobs on the stamens. The sort of flower young girls ought to weave into their hair. And then the hard-hitting, dry smell of the cotoneaster. None of this – the flowers, the smells – has changed since my childhood, or anyone else's for that matter. Though of course I didn't notice such things as a child.

As I walked home along the pavement, a little girl skipped past. She was running in the way that children do; in the way that they always have and always will: not because she was in a hurry or frightened or even trying to get anywhere; not running with any purpose other than to run, because for that brief moment it was more interesting than walking. Then she tripped on a loose paving stone and went flying on to her hands and face. I didn't rush to help her because I knew her mother was close behind with another child and I thought she might resent the intrusion. But as the girl lay on the pavement, crying into the dirty concrete, the woman behind me made no attempt to hurry to her side, or ask if she were all right. It was the other child who ran to help. Or rather, toddled up beside her and bent over, keeping her fat little legs quite straight and looking with great seriousness into her sister's face. She was younger than the other girl, perhaps three or four, and wasn't such a deep, rich, chocolatey colour as the older sister, but more of a dark golden tan. They both had their hair in those beautiful thin plaits and patterns that take hours to do, which had then been tied in bright-coloured ribbons. For some reason it struck me as strange, pathetic, that it was the child who ran

to help the other child while the adult didn't seem to care.
I wanted to go to the little girl and lift her to her feet. But
I glanced behind me and the mother had a look of grim and
bored indifference on her face; and I thought if she took offence
at my interference there could be 'racial discomfort'. So I simply
watched as the woman waddled slowly over to her daughter,
and pulled her up, and released a tide of rebuke over her. But
the extraordinary thing was that it was the little one who was
told off: the one who'd run to help her sister. If the older child
had been nagged for running it would have been stupid, but
at least familiar: we've all seen adults annoyed at children who
ask intelligent questions, or who put their foot in a puddle
to see what it feels like, or who do anything else essential to
learning and growing up. But to nag the younger one? For
what? Loving her sister? Making her mother feel guilty? And
then the younger child was smacked, hard, on the face.

I stared at them, and told myself that there must be some
justification for the way she treated the child. That mothers
know what they're doing. That children survive far worse
treatment. That every culture, every family, behaves in ways
which are incomprehensible to an outsider.

And I turned away, feeling sad and grown-up and alienated
from the little child and her burning humiliation.

And talking of being grown-up, why did nobody tell me about
gardening? Naturally we had a tiny garden in Perrymead
Street, but it meant nothing to me. But now I need no excuse
not to work; I simply wander into my scruffy conservatory
when I'm having my coffee break, and then just keep on
wandering through the French windows and I'm lost for
the next two hours. It's pretty small too, but it's mine, and
it's like a baby. Every fragile thing in it, every shoot that
comes up, every delicate blossom, gives me a ridiculous
little thrill that makes me think, in my saner moments, that
I must be prematurely middle-aged. I mean, this is what my
mother's friends do, you know.

Of course I know nothing about gardening. But, like a real
middle-aged neighbour, I lean on the fence and talk to Bungler
Bill and he tells me what to plant where, or even climbs
over the fence and does it for me.

Had tea with him yesterday (Sunday). Not quite as dreadfully
dull as I thought he was on first meeting. I mean, quite shy and
gentle, you know, but all right.

And, to be totally lyrical and over the top about it, I feel the tentative, painful beginnings of whatever it is that butterflies do when they emerge. The fresh air of spring. The fragile shoots. *April is the cruellest month; mixing memory and desire.* All right, yes, I realise that this is May, but you know what I mean ... I went to Perrymead Street last night, to a cocktail party at an old neighbour's house, and I didn't feel a pang. Not a pang. I didn't walk past the old family house and think, Why don't I live here any more? I didn't agonise over losing her. I didn't even dwell on what had happened.

Nor did I call on my parents, in fact. Not yet: I'm not quite ready to begin all over again with my mother with everything honest, open and good. Besides, I was late, as I seem to be for everything now I've left Poppy's chaotic influence; as if I've taken on her unpunctuality now she's not around.

But soon I will call on them: soon. After all, they were wonderful parents. What do I mean *were*? I do sometimes feel as if I left everything when I moved out, and have no family at all any more.

There are things that need to be said. We need to talk about what happened that summer; the effect it had on all of us; what it did to us as a family. Before that we *were* truthful with each other; we did talk about things. Or have I remembered an Eden that wasn't? But no, I don't think so: I can recall being free with my father about matters which touched me deeply; I can remember him sharing his weaknesses with me; I know that my brothers talked to him openly, as friends. Now they're like any other Englishman with his father. Never mentioning what we all know. Never commenting on the smell on his breath as he comes out of his study looking very steady. Never asking whether my mother's going through a good patch, or whether they've been out of the house for the last month. Nor asking what, or even who, might be missing from his life.

I shall write to B. about it. At least I can be open with him. Surely. And not just make polite platitudes, but say: What happened to us that year? What did we do? We took a joint decision, after all, young as we were, and we must take joint responsibility for it. And we must ask ourselves how, and why, we changed after that, and why we aren't quite the same family. Happy though we are, in many ways.

That's what I shall ask B. the very next time I write, and not sweep it under the carpet any more.

Met a screamingly funny man at said cocktails; specialist

on Pepys, who looks exactly as I've always imagined Pepys himself to look. Flirting with all the pretty women half his age. Took me out to dinner afterwards and regaled me with stories from the diaries themselves, and anecdotes from his own personal life, which I had great difficulty distinguishing from one another. Came home extraordinarily tipsy, and almost fell over Bungler Bill going into his own house. Don't suppose that's done a bundle for my image. As bad as my father after a party. Or before one, come to that.

Winter kept us warm, covering Earth in forgetful snow. (But now) *the flowers appear in the fields, the time of the singing of birds is come, and the voice of the turtle is heard in our land.* (Love that beautiful song of Solomon's 'Catch for us the foxes, the little foxes . . .' etc.) Snow melts. The river pelts, inexorable, down into the sea. Which is a way of saying I hurtle inexorably towards my publisher's deadline, and I'm not sure what flotsam will be left on the beaches of my life when the tide goes down. *Hold me when the tide goes down.*

CHAPTER TWO –
PERRYMEAD STREET

There is nothing that God hath established in a
constant course of nature, and which therefore is
done every day, but would seem a Miracle, and
exercise our imagination, if it were done but once.

John Donne, Easter Day, 1627

I remember the day she was born.

My father had picked me up from school and taken me straight to
the hospital. My brothers weren't there, but I've no idea why not.
Perhaps my father arranged for them to have tea with friends or
something, but didn't have time in my case. Or perhaps my eldest
brother was already at Marlborough. Yes, perhaps he was. Funny
how some of it remains in my mind very clearly, but the rest fades
into the edges of childhood.

I can remember us dashing, hand in hand, along hospital corridors,
dodging the trolleys and the disapproving nurses. I remember my
mother's screams of pain. I think it was the first time I really loved her.
I mean loved her with the agonising pity a child can feel for an adult.
Until then I had simply loved her as one does, because one's mother
provides: but when I heard her terrible cries she became a stranger
to me, vulnerable and mortal, needing me. I can also remember my
father buying a cup of something violently orange for me, out of a
machine, and something lukewarm and grey, for himself. And then I
suppose we waited for a long time. Eventually my mother's screams
turned to groans and howls of such desperate effort that I vaguely
wondered why nobody did anything.

Then, for no apparent reason, the adults changed, became more
alert and attentive, gathered round the bed; the dreadful noise stopped.

Something had happened: there was something on the sheet. I still have a vision in my mind of a creature which bore no resemblance to anything human I'd ever seen. It was a muddy-looking, slimy, wriggling thing. It was very suddenly there. And it was my sister.

By the time of my next memory, which must have been about twenty minutes later, she'd turned into a baby girl. A small bath stood on a table in the hospital. I had on one of those white plastic hospital aprons, which of course was much too big for me and stretched way below my feet, and I was bathing her. The nurse by my side was bathing her too. The water was gently warm. We didn't use soap. We had a blue, artificial sponge, and we sponged and sponged her, avoiding her eyes. Then the nurse showed me how to clean her eyes with sterile cotton wool, using a fresh ball for each eye.

One of the second-hand facts of tired conversational gambits is that a baby duckling will bond with the first thing it sees; that, to extend this rather trite analogy to the human race, the first few minutes of life are very important to the baby herself. I doubt if it's true. I'm sure my sister couldn't have cared less who bathed her, so long as she was warm and comfortable, and had a belly full of milk soon afterwards. But it was very important to me. It was I, not my parents, who first looked after her. It was I who shared the bonding moments. Presumably my mother herself was being bathed, and my father was with her. Quite right and proper. And I was as happy as I'd ever been; happy in a more grown-up way than ever before. Not like a child who has been given an icecream or taken on her favourite treat, but with the wonderful responsibility of loving and caring for someone even more helpless than myself.

We dressed her in a tiny white Babygro which was several sizes too big and far too long in the arms and legs, then we laid her tiny morsel of humanity in a huge grown-up bed, and then we sat either side of her on the bed and looked at her and talked to her and told each other how beautiful she was, while my heart shone, and I still bless that nurse as one of the little islands of adult understanding in my vast child's world.

And that's all I remember of my sister's birth. Presumably my father and I went home that night, leaving her in hospital. Presumably mother and child did well, as they say, and came home soon afterwards. I know I was too tired to go to school the next day, but I think I know that because I was told so years later, not because I can remember it.

*   *   *

For the next few months I have photographs to turn to. Time and again I can be seen cuddling her, cradling her, smiling over an ugly baby and squinting into the sun.

One photograph in particular brings back, with that sharp feeling of loss in the pit of the stomach which we call nostalgia, all the radiance of childhood which one is unaware of at the time. There are two in this picture: my sister is a few days old, and my grandfather is in his seventies. I am holding the camera. My grandfather could obviously see that I was aiming it inaccurately, for he has ducked his head to try and get his face into the frame. He has succeeded. He wears the over-enthusiastic smile which my grandparents thought appropriate for photograph albums. In his effort, however, he has forgotten the baby, who is captured in the middle of sliding off his knee, head first, towards the ground. Her head is arched back, and she gazes seriously at the tree waving above her head. One hand reaches blindly towards the sky. Her fingers look extraordinarily long and graceful, as new-born babies' often do. Even as I look at it now, I can sense the delightful feeling of conspiracy which the three of us shared that afternoon.

It was a Saturday. Grandfather had come all the way to London to see the new baby, and we had picked him up from the Tube station, loaded with presents for us as well as his overnight bag. We all sat round the kitchen table, down in our sunny basement, chattering wildly, forgetting to make him tea, and even forgetting the purpose of his visit, the baby who was asleep in a small cot under the window upstairs in the sitting-room. Eventually, though, after he'd been relieved of books and paintboxes and a kaleidoscope and possibly even a balloon or two, we showed him our exhibit, and he looked suitably impressed and tried to behave as though she didn't look like every other baby he'd ever seen.

'She's lovely,' he said uncertainly, and dithered over her.

Then someone must have said that my eldest brother had a football match at school. (So he couldn't have been at Marlborough? Perhaps not yet anyway.) And someone else must have suggested that we all went to watch. And Grandfather must have explained that he was tired after his journey, and he must have offered to look after the baby while the rest of us went. And I, of course, opted out of the football, which I could never summon any interest for and still can't; and that must have been how Grandfather and I, two of the most unlikely but

ANNE ATKINS

enthusiastic baby-sitters in the world, were left alone with her and in charge, that Saturday afternoon.

'There's sterilised water in that bottle, if she's hungry.' 'Nappies in the bathroom; Sandy knows what to do.' 'Make yourselves at home.' 'She should sleep for an hour or two.'

And so she would have done, if we'd left her alone. But we both kept creeping in, on tiptoe, and checking she was still breathing. And every so often I would touch her cheek, and tell Grandfather how it felt like velvet because that's what I remembered the midwife saying. And Grandfather would go 'Shhh!' very loudly. And in the end she opened her eyes and blinked at us, and with great delight I pulled her blanket off her and picked her up while Grandfather said, 'Oops, careful, shall I take it? I mean her.' And we carried her between us, like Laurel and Hardy carrying a piece of Ming china, across the room and into the pale sunshine where we laid her on a rug on the floor.

I sighed with contentment and sat cross-legged on the floor beside her. Grandfather sat gingerly on the sofa.

'What do we do now?' he said.

'Um,' I said, wanting to sound omniscient. 'Er, we change her nappy. Come on, I'll show you where they are.'

'Can we leave her on her own?'

'Oh, yes,' I said, growing in confidence. I knew more about this than Grandfather, at any rate. At least I knew that she couldn't crawl yet.

'Doesn't it involve pins and things?' Grandfather asked. I wonder now if he was playing a part, to make me feel in charge. But no, I don't think so. His was another generation. It's quite possible that, in those days, he'd never changed a nappy in his life.

'No, of course it doesn't, silly. They have kind of Sellotape on them, you know.'

We found the bag of nappies easily. And the baby was where we'd left her, in the shaft of sunlight on the sheepskin rug, staring intently at the light. And we managed to unpop the poppers on her Babygro. And tear open the nappy. But we hadn't realised what we'd find. I had confidently told my mother I could change nappies, having once been shown by a friend's mother when she changed the nappy of her baby boy, who'd wet himself. That was easy: you took the wet nappy off, threw it away, put the new one on and simply stuck it up like a plaster. This was completely different. When we opened her up we found she was slimy like the bottom of a pond. There wasn't much of a smell, and it was a wholesome, baby smell; but the sight took all our

42

confidence away. It was a dark, dark green, almost black, and it looked as if it would stick to her tiny bottom like dog pooh sticks to a child's shoe. I was squatting, with my feet flat on the ground; Grandfather knelt on the floor. We looked at the dark green bottom, and the white legs happily kicking the air. Then we looked at each other.

'Oh,' I said.

'What now?' Grandfather asked me, the expert.

'Um . . . bath!' I said, remembering the hospital and feeling that my bathing credentials, at least, were unimpeachable.

'Good idea.' So we left her where she was again, and went up to the bathroom. I don't know if we had a baby bath – I suppose we must have done – but Grandfather and I certainly didn't know where to find it. So we started running the water in the bath, and I put in plenty of bubble bath, then Grandfather found something called 'Infabath' for new-born babies so we put lots of that in too, and I put in a squirt of baby oil and a squirt of baby lotion just in case, as we weren't quite sure what else we'd use them for, then Grandfather said, 'I know what we do now,' and he knelt down on the floor and rolled his sleeve up and stuck his elbow in the water.

'What are you doing that for?' I said, intrigued.

'I don't know,' he said, 'but I know you're supposed to do it.'

At last, when the bath had two or three inches of the most inviting water in it that either of us could imagine, with bubbles and oil and little white worms of baby lotion which didn't want to mix in, we went downstairs to fetch her. Halfway down the stairs we could hear her whimpering and crying gently, as if she wasn't quite sure whether she should be upset.

She wasn't yet able to crawl or turn over, but even a new-born baby can move a little by kicking and waving. It was only a few centimetres, but it was enough to shift her bottom off the nappy and on to the sheepskin rug. And it was enough to rub quite a bit of whatever it was into the deep white pile of the wool.

'Help!' said Grandfather, hurrying for the baby and picking her up under her arms. 'Do you think Mummy will mind?' As he lifted her into the air, she kicked the nappy and turned it over, slime side down, on to the rug. At that point Grandfather lost his footing slightly and knelt on it, rubbing it deep into the rug, as well as his trousers.

'Shouldn't think so,' I said uncertainly. 'Daddy's always saying you mustn't mind about that kind of thing. They had to buy this rug because I got green paint on the other one, and in the end Daddy said it didn't matter. In the end.'

'Here, you take the baby and I'll take the rug.'

So we took both up to the bathroom. It would have been more sensible if we had put the baby in the basin and the sheepskin in the bath, as the rug was much the bigger of the two. But we didn't think of it, and even if we had, we wouldn't have wanted to waste all the lovely bubbles.

My sister couldn't sit up, of course, so after Grandfather tried holding her from one angle, and I tried from another, and we both had our sleeves wet, I took off my socks and shoes and stepped in the bath. But I couldn't hold her without squatting down, and I couldn't squat down without dipping my skirt in the bubbles.

'Can you hold her a minute, Grandfather?' I said, and then let go of her head a bit too quickly. The back of her head hit the bath and the bubbles closed over her face.

'Crikey,' Grandfather said, and scooped her up into his arms, along with a great deal of bath water and several angry and desperate yells. At that point I lost my footing and sat down altogether, splashing more water over Grandfather's legs.

'It's all right, Grandfather. You can give her to me now.'

'Sure?' he said, over the cries.

'Yup.'

So I sat in the bath in my clothes, while she played between my legs, and Grandfather sponged the green slimy mess further into his trousers and squeezed corners of the rug into soapy water in the basin.

The photograph was taken some half hour later, after I'd changed my clothes and Grandfather had dried off a little and the rug was still dripping dirty water into the bath.

After the photograph we took her little cot down into the kitchen and made ourselves a cup of tea. Grandfather used to let me have sugar in my tea, if we could find it, which on this occasion we could, so we sat either side of the table, Grandfather bouncing her rather too energetically on his knee and trying to persuade her to drink some of the water in the bottle, and we chatted over our cuppas.

'Well now, what are they going to call her?' he said. 'She can't go on being "the baby".'

'They can't decide,' I said. 'It took them three weeks to decide with me.'

'I know it did. Nobody had any idea what to call you: you were lucky you got a name at all. We ought to call her Polyxena.'

'Polly-What? Oh, yes,' I said, remembering our conversation the previous summer. 'Polyxena. Because she's my sister, you mean.'

We both looked at her, sizing up such a grand name against such a little person.

'Grandfather?' I said, harking back to that sunny afternoon in his garden. 'You know you said those stories are, you know "myth"?' I'd remembered the word myth, by remembering it as 'miss' with a lisp.

'Did I?' he said. 'I can tell this is going to be a tricky one,' he added, smiling.

'What I don't understand is, are myths true?'

'Humph!' he began. 'Well, yes, I would say they are. But they're true in the way a poem is, not in the way that science is. If you said you'd given me a packet of chewing gum today, would that be true or not?'

'N-no,' I said, rather uncertainly.

'Correct. But if you said you'd given me an armful of sunshine, well, would that be true?'

I wrinkled up my nose. 'I don't know,' I said.

'Well, there you are!' he said triumphantly.

I folded my arms and frowned at him.

'I'll tell you what,' he went on. 'Have you heard of Pandora?' I shook my head. 'Well, now.' Grandfather stopped to think. 'Look at the world.' I looked at the wooden cupboards in our kitchen, and then at some crumbs and a biro which had scuttled across the tiled floor. 'No, no, look out of the window.' Our kitchen was in the basement; it had a half-glazed door leading up to the garden, so I obediently looked up through it at the moss and ferns on the stone steps outside. A shaft of sunlight had struggled through the leaves and the lattice fence round our garden and the window itself, and now waltzed tentatively with the motes of dust in front of the glass door. 'It's beautiful, isn't it?' he went on.

'Yes,' I said. My sister looked quizzically up at me. I smiled at her. 'Yes, it is.'

'But it's spoilt. We do all sorts of unkind things to each other, and to the world. We spoil it. The story of Pandora is trying to tell us that in a way we can understand. Pandora was the first woman. She was given all sorts of gifts by the gods. Intelligence, beauty, a lovely singing voice. She was charming. Then she was given to her husband; and he was the happiest man in the world, because he had the loveliest wife who'd ever existed.'

'But Grandfather,' I objected. 'she must have been the only wife who'd ever existed. If she was the first woman.'

'Well, yes, I suppose she was. No flies on you, young lady. Anyway, they lived in a world before there was any selfishness or disease or anything wrong with it. So Pandora and her husband were perfect people, living in a perfect world. Now, all the gods had given Pandora gifts, and the gift Jupiter gave her was a box. But he told her not to open it.'

'Then why did he give it to her?'

'Good question. I don't know. So she didn't. She gave it to her husband.'

'Uh-oh.'

'And Pandora's husband was curious, so he opened it. Can you guess what was in it?'

I had a chilly feeling deep inside my stomach, as if I'd eaten icecream and it had gone right down inside me. 'No,' I said. I didn't want to hear the awful thing that was about to happen. But I did want to hear the story.

'Unkindness. And lies. And sickness. And poverty. And selfishness. And naughtiness. And everything bad you can think of. And death. And they all flew out of the box. And they could never be put back in again.'

'Oh, why didn't they keep it shut!' I cried, and my sister blinked, alarmed.

'Why indeed? But they were only doing what we do every day. We're given a lovely world to live in, and we let those things loose in it every day, and spoil it afresh each day, because we don't do as we're told.'

'But, Grandfather,' I began. I thought the story sounded familiar. I'd heard of someone else who'd done that too, and spoilt the world, but I couldn't remember who it was.

'Yes, dear?'

'Nothing.'

'Well, do you know what was in the bottom of the box?'

'No.'

'When everything else had escaped, and all the worst possible evils had entered the world, and Pandora and her husband were filled with despair at what they'd done, Pandora looked in the box to make sure it was all over and there was no more to come, and one last thing flew out. It looked a bit like those pretty little blue butterflies we saw when you came to stay last summer. "Who are you?" she said. She was frightened to think what else there was to come, that was so bad it had to wait until the end; but she couldn't quite believe that something so lovely could be worse than all the rest. And it said, "I'm Hope. And despite all you've done, I'll always be here. Even though I'm so much smaller than all the other things you've let out today, even though there's only one of me, and so many many of them, they'll never be as strong as I am. And I'll win in the end, if you just trust in me."'

I thought for a moment. 'So it was a good thing in the end?' I said.

'Perhaps it was. Yes, perhaps it was. Because if she hadn't opened the box, she couldn't have let out Hope. After all, without all the evil in the world, there wouldn't be hope would there? There'd be nothing to hope for.'

'And that's a myth?'

'Yes, that's a myth.'

'And Polyxena, and her sister, and everything, was the same?'

'I think so.'

We sat silent for a minute, tipping our tea mugs towards us and looking at the tea leaves. Grandfather always made tea with tea leaves: he thought tea bags tasted of cardboard. Though I'm sure, if you'd blindfolded him, he could never have told the difference.

'What about Polly for short?' he said after a while.

'No,' I said. 'I don't like Polly. Polly's silly. Poppy,' I said. 'Poppy would do for short.'

'Poppy?' he mused. 'A poppy's the symbol of Persephone, I think. She was a young girl who went missing, and her mother searched all the world for her, and couldn't find her.'

'Where was she?'

'She'd been stolen away to the Underworld. And she'd eaten half a pomegranate, which is why we have to spend half the year in winter.'

I couldn't follow the logic of this. 'D'you think it's a good name then?' I said.

'She does look a bit like a poppy: bright red and wrinkly.' At this point we turned to look at her, and found that Grandfather had absent-mindedly put the teat of the bottle in her eye, and water was dribbling on to her clean Babygro. It was remarkable that she hadn't cried much till then. But when we started fussing over her and feeling her clothes and wondering whether she was too wet, she set up a relentless howl which got worse the more we tried to stop it. By the time my parents came back we were nowhere to be found. There was a dirty nappy on the sitting-room floor, my wet clothes on a chair, and the rug still dripping over the bath. We were missing, the baby was missing, and her pram was missing.

We were all three outside South Park talking to a traffic warden about our wonderful new baby.

I was just the right age for a baby. Had I been older, like my brothers, I would have had too many distractions, and music lessons, and after-school clubs, and homework, as they did. Had I been younger, I would have been unable to take any responsibility for her, and perhaps would have found in her more of a rival, and been jealous of my parents' attention. But, aged six, I could feed her, change her, read to her, and carry her on my back or in my arms, or push her in her pushchair.

I recently saw my niece, who is now about the age that I was then, with a baby a few months old. The baby had been left at my brother's house for an hour till her nanny came to fetch her. Everybody was busy, no one had time for her, and when she began to cry various people talked to her in passing, or picked her up for a moment to try and comfort her. Nothing worked, and she was soon put back in her bouncer.

But the next time I looked she was on the floor, lying on her back, with my niece beside her. I don't know how the baby got there. Perhaps my niece picked her up and put her there, or perhaps she persuaded some grown-up to do it for her. Now the baby was completely calm and quiet. My niece didn't talk to her, or play with her, or do anything except sit next to her and look at her, as if she were a beautiful painting or something of exquisite fascination. The baby gazed back. And when I looked again, ten or twenty minutes later, they were both in the same position and both as still, and as quiet, and as content as before. Children of that age are supposed to be continually restless, unable to sit quietly even to watch the television or a computer screen, but this child was as fulfilled as someone who has just fallen in love, and has no need to speak or move or even think, but simply to rest in another person's face.

She kept the baby occupied until her nanny arrived. And in that hour, seeing the contentment which fell into my young niece's afternoon like a ripe fig falling into a lap, I saw the gift which fell into my life when I was that age and gave me such satisfaction.

48

It shouldn't surprise us. Young creatures are irresistible. They have
to be. Nature makes them that way to cope with their vulnerability.
Kittens and puppies compel us to love them and care for them until
they can fend for themselves and afford to lose their charm. Babies are
more vulnerable still. Unless we love them they die. Children know this
instinctively, and instinctively look after them. But most children now,
of course, have no younger brothers or sisters. Those that do seldom
play with their siblings because the children themselves are too busy.

I was lucky. She was born at the right time. It was the right time for
me, and it was a time when families seemed to spend more time with
their children.

I always called her Poppy after that. Soon the rest of the family
did too. Even after she was christened with her real name. I can't
imagine why my parents had her christened; I'm sure my brothers
and I weren't. Presumably they did it to please my grandfather.
It wouldn't have pleased him though. It would have puzzled him
that they went through something they didn't understand. Looking
back on it now, I find it distasteful that we made a mockery of
something that other people still believe in. It's strange; my parents
were people of such integrity, as a rule.

The days of childhood are so long, so indestructible! She was a baby
for ever.

I had my own life, of course. I had school, and friends, and swimming club for a while, and ballet while the fun lasted, and riding
when I got sick of ballet. I had changed schools a few months before
she was born. The academic standard at my new school was much
higher than it had been at the other one, which was why my parents
moved me, and the change was quite a shock. After the first few
weeks the boys in my new class started to bully me. I did nothing
in response, which provoked them even more. At the beginning of
my second term at my new school I was sent home one day with nits,
and after that no one would touch me or hold my hand on outings,
because they said I was diseased.

It was over a year before my parents found out. Funnily enough, it
upsets me more now, looking back on it, than I remember it doing at
the time. In particular I now feel angry that my teacher did nothing.
She must have known, after a few weeks, what was going on. The
children grew bolder, the girls joined in, and soon none of them
would talk to me without unkind jibes and surreptitious kicks on

the shin. I presume the teacher kept quiet because she didn't want to admit failure, to be seen to have lost control. She was rewarded for this canny careerism by being made Head of the Lower School soon afterwards. Which rather confirms a half-hearted view I hold that many of the adults who are considered good with children aren't fit to be allowed near them. Anyway, in the end it was another parent who rang my mother up, late one Sunday night, and told her what had been going on.

We had just come back from a weekend school trip. I suppose I was seven by then. Mrs West, the parent of a classmate of mine, had gone with us to help the teacher. Time and again she noticed me being jabbed from behind as we walked in a crocodile, or prodded by another child who would then run and wash his hands in mock horror, screaming that he had caught my plague. Every time it happened the teacher would turn in another direction, and busy herself with some other pupil's need.

I still have a snapshot of myself on that trip. It's not in very sharp focus, but you can see a bright little blonde child with the school logo emblazoned proudly on her tracksuit, smiling broadly at the camera. If I didn't know the context, I would think it a happy photograph. But knowing what I do about those three miserable days – which, however, were presumably no worse than the rest of my time at school – looking back as an adult watching a seven year old cope with a hostile world, I'm filled with a kind of dread at the bravery of childhood.

It was Mrs West who took that photograph. That night she rang my mother. And the very next day my parents went to see the headmaster, and my eighteen-month failure to fit in at my new school suddenly made sense.

My parents kicked up a fuss, the teacher made a big show of being furious with the class, and for the rest of that term she watched them more carefully. The next year, when I was eight, I had a different teacher, a wonderful woman who was like a saint to me, and the worst of my unhappiness was over. But it had given me a resilience, an independence from my peers, which may have lasted me ever since.

I was already an avid reader. Even if I hadn't been bullied, I might have preferred to sit quietly in the corner of the playground and read, rather than join in some game which made no sense to me. Perhaps that was why they picked on me. Soon I had no choice: there was no social life for me at school, so I spent my playtime devouring the library. And because I was happy at home, it didn't perhaps matter as much as it might.

We got on remarkably well in our family. We used to rag and fight, but we also used to play together. I never argued with my eldest brother; I admired him too much, and he was too distant. My next brother was far closer to me; we shared, and fought, and battled, and spent time together. After my parents uncovered the bullying, I would often catch sight of him at school, at lunch or break time, looking round the corner of a building in my direction and then disappearing again. He was breaking all the rules of schoolboy conduct and keeping a protective eye on me.

But it was with Poppy that I was really close. We almost never disagreed. I was too far above her, I suppose, in the way that my brother or parents were above me. She was much too young to object to any of my plans or instructions, or even to know that she might have been able to.

She was a baby, growing into a toddler, while my classmates were rejecting me. She was always there when I got home. She was always ready to be entertained on Saturdays. She was always happy to be dressed up as the cowboy or the puppy or the captured wild lion just waiting to be tamed. She always made an audience for my shows or an extra for my plays. She was ideal in every way. And I was ideal for her. I taught her, led her, read to her, explained the pictures in her favourite book or showed her where to find ladybirds.

A family of four children was quite large even then, and people often asked my mother how she coped. 'Oh,' she said, 'four really is easier than three. I never would've believed it, but it's true. These two look after each other all day long.' And it probably was true. My father used to observe that parents of large families never seemed to complain about the work, whereas modern mothers with only one often appear exhausted.

We even slept in the same bed most nights. At first, I think I used to creep out of bed and lift her from her cot so that I could read to her. Soon she herself learnt to climb out of it and into my bed. Once or twice I even got into her cot and slept there with her, though it was much too small for me. She always fell asleep before I did, but I would go on reading out loud to her in the light from my little lamp, and then reading in my head, for hours after my parents had left us safely tucked up in the dark. When my father came in to wake me for school he would find two heads on the pillow, and two bodies,

ANNE ATKINS

back to back or in each other's arms or sometimes at different ends
of the bed. Funnily enough, once when we were on holiday we were
asked if we'd share a bed and we refused, or I did. I insisted on the
privacy of my own bed, to the great inconvenience of my parents,
who had to have my sister in theirs. And after one night I was so
lonely I got into their bed too.

It always surprised me when children didn't want to spend time with
their siblings. When I was eight my piano teacher, a close friend of
ours, got engaged and asked me if I would be her bridesmaid. As a
number of her pupils had been auditioning for this part, one of them
even turning up for a lesson in a pink fluffy dress with petticoats, it
was quite an honour to be asked. I was pleased, I suppose, but the
first thing I said was, 'Can Poppy be one too?'

My teacher hugged me, and said I was sweet, and told my parents,
and the adults repeated it in front of one another as a great joke, and
of course Poppy wasn't one too but was quite content to make do
with the smart straw hat and beautiful new lacey gloves my mother
bought her to wear at the wedding instead. But it seemed strange
to me that anything should have been made of it. My brothers and
I tended to share our things quite well with one another too; if one
went to a party which the others weren't invited to, for instance, we
would dish out sticky things from our party bags, and carefully divide
up the crumbs of the birthday cake. And Poppy and I were religious
at it: strictly half each of everything. Which was why, when I won my
first competition, I wanted her to win the next one.

And that, in turn, was why we first started working together.

16 May, Sunday, Parsons Green

Dear Ben,
Fabulous weather. Yes, thanks, I'd love to come and stay for
half term. Though I know farmers are too busy for anything
interesting like sailing or windsurfing or riding or anything. But
no doubt Abi will look after me.
　　I don't remember a summer like this since we were children.
Why is it that childhood summers are always hotter – L.P.
Hartley's or ours? I think the last blisteringly hot summer, like
this, was about 1990, wasn't it? And now suddenly, abracadabra!
Heat wave and it's only May. Bliss. Though I suppose you don't
like it, because Technical Farming, like the Water Board,
doesn't like anything that hasn't been passed by a committee.
　　And yes, thanks, the book's going well, and should be out
on time. What d'you mean, won't it be autobiographical like
all first books are? What kind of a question is that to put to a
well-established writer? Cheek or what!
　　My new house is great. Mine in a way that nothing ever has
been before. My little patch of lawn with daisies on it. My own
clematis opening itself up on the wall. My time, my place, my
life. I feel a kind of peace that I've never known before. Not
since I was tiny, anyway. I can understand now you having your
acres and your contentment and all.
　　And, no, I am *not* in love, thank you very much, and have
no intention of being. Whatever gave you that idea? I shan't
gossip to you again in a hurry!
　　But love to you all, lots and lots. Aching till I see you.
　　　　　　C.

CHAPTER THREE –
CLANCARTY ROAD, 1990

What shall I cry? All flesh is grass, and all the
goodliness thereof is as the flower of the field: The
grass withereth, the flower fadeth . . .

Isaiah 40:6–7

οὐ ταὐτόν, ὦ παῖ, τῷ βλέπειν τὸ κατθανεῖν·
τὸ μὲν γὰρ οὐδέν . . .

No, child. Death and life are not the same,
For one is oblivion . . .

Euripides, Women of Troy, *632–3*

Sandy's granny had been Grandfather's best friend. Grandfather said
she wasn't very old, but she seemed very old to Sandy. She had
tortoiseshell spectacles on a string, and she smiled a lot. She was
always rather smart: she wore pleated woollen skirts, and jumpers,
and brooches, and underneath she wore pink cotton vests with pretty
patterns on them in holes that were there on purpose, and pants that
were more like knitted shorts. Not like Mummy, who wears jeans and
things. And she used to make tea in a cup instead of in a tea pot, using
a funny spoon with a lid covered in holes, with tea leaves inside.
She would put the spoon in the cup and pour water from the kettle
on to it. Grandfather makes tea like that too. And she never used to
walk much because her legs hurt.

Sandy and Barney and Jack used to go and stay at Granny and
Grandfather's house. It's a nice house. It has pink and blue flowers
on the curtains in the bedroom, and a big garden that you can get

55

lost in, and a larder with lots of tins of cake. Grandfather always gave them cake. Granny would tell him off for it. 'George, dear, I really don't think Amanda would want them to have any more.' Amanda is Sandy's mother's name. Sometimes Jack and Barney call her Amanda. If Daddy wants to make Mummy really cross he sometimes calls her Mandy. He's not allowed to call her Mandy.

'Nonsense!' Grandfather would say, and give them all another slice.

In some ways it was stricter being at Granny and Grandfather's. You had to go to the loo before you went out anywhere, even if you didn't need to. And you had to brush your hair every day. But you could stay up late and have dinner with the adults, and go to bed as late as anything, and have breakfast in your nightie.

Last year Granny had gone into hospital. She needed new bits at the tops of her legs because she couldn't walk properly because it hurt her so much. She'd explained it all to Sandy. They were going to take out the bone that she'd been born with.

'Have you got the same bones you had when you were a baby?' Sandy had asked in great surprise.

'Of course!' Granny laughed. 'When did you think I got new ones?'

'When you became an adult. I didn't think your baby ones were big enough.'

'They grew. When I grew, they grew with me. In fact, when I grew it was mostly my bones that were growing.' Then Granny showed Sandy where the doctor would cut her open, and put a plastic and metal bone in instead, and then it wouldn't hurt any more and she'd be able to dance and skip and hop.

'You wait,' Granny said. 'I'll be playing tennis by the end of the summer.'

But she wasn't.

If Sandy had said that, Daddy would have said it was a promise and she must always keep her promises. But adults don't have to keep their promises. Granny didn't.

'Won't it hurt?' Sandy asked.

'It'll hurt much less than it does now.'

'When I cut myself it hurts.'

'Do you mean will it hurt when the surgeon cuts me?'

'Yes. What's a sturgeon.'

'A kind of fish. And a surgeon's a kind of doctor. Yes, when he cuts me it would hurt, a lot. But someone called an anaesthetist will give me a special medicine that'll make me sleep, so I won't even know I'm being cut at all.'

'Won't you wake up when he cuts you? When Mummy tries to take my splinters out in my sleep so it won't hurt, I always wake up when she pricks me.'

'This medicine's so strong that you can't wake up at all, however much you're hurt.'

'But then you won't ever wake up!' said Sandy, horrified.

'Oh, yes, I will. When they've finished I'll wake up. The anaesthetist's very clever, and he gives you just enough to sleep through the operation but not so much that you won't wake up. He has to be highly qualified . . .'

'What does that mean?'

'Good at his job. Because it could be very dangerous if the medicine went wrong.'

'What could happen?'

'I suppose you could die.'

'Will you die, Granny?'

'No, darling, I'll be fine.'

Granny was fine. When she was in hospital Sandy made her a card with a cat coming out of a basket. The cat was saying, 'I've got four new legs and I'm going to catch four mice every day.' Sandy posted it to her, and Granny rang her from a box in the hospital to thank her. When you telephone from hospital you have to get in a box. It must have been a huge box. Sandy had seen some fairly big boxes at J. Sainsbury's, but she didn't think even they were big enough for Granny and a telephone together.

And when they next went to see Granny, she was home again and walking about with a stick. She didn't look any different to Sandy except that she had the stick which she hadn't had before.

They were in Granny and Grandfather's house. Sandy sat in their kitchen, thinking hard, while Grandfather made Granny a coffee, and got tea and things for Mummy and Daddy, and at last asked Sandy if she'd like some orange juice and lots of cake.

'Oh, George!' Granny said.

When she had thought for a long time, Sandy said, 'Granny? I thought you were going to be skipping when you came out of hospital, but you're not skipping at the moment.'

Granny and Grandfather both laughed, and Grandfather went to tell Mummy and Daddy what Sandy had said. Adults are funny like that. You say something perfectly normal and they make a big fuss about it and laugh and tell each other.

'Not yet, darling. I've got to get used to it first. And I've got to have the other one done too.'

'Have you got to go into hospital again? Will you have two sticks when you've got two new legs?' It rather seemed to Sandy as if Granny had been better off before.

'I don't know. But I'll tell you when I will be skipping. Shall I tell you a secret?'

Sandy ran over to her to sit on her knee, then remembered it might be sore, so just put her ear up to Granny's face instead. She loved secrets. She was very good at keeping them. Sandy had never given a secret away, ever.

'You needn't put your face like that, darling, because I'm not going to whisper. It's rude. The others are all in the sitting-room now, so no one will hear anyway. Now then. Grandfather and I are going to have a party this summer.'

'Are you? Are you really?' Sandy was astonished.

'Yes, indeed. And do you know why?' Sandy couldn't possibly know why. Grandparents don't have birthdays. Birthdays are to make you older, and grannies are old already. She shook her head.

'It's our Ruby Wedding Anniversary.'

'What's that?'

'We've been married forty years.'

'Is that a long time?'

'It doesn't seem very long. But it's a good excuse for a party.'

'Gosh,' said Sandy. Then she said, 'Shall I tell you a secret?' Sandy thought this was only fair. 'Our other granny isn't married at all. Do you know our other granny?'

'Yes, I know her a bit. She was married once.'

'Was she really? What happened to her husband?'

'Her husband was David, your other grandfather.'

'Oh,' said Sandy. 'But he's married to Sue,' she protested. She knew David and Sue well. They'd taken her to the zoo for her last birthday once.

'He is now. But he used to be married to the other granny.'

'Why isn't he any more?'

'She got fed up, I think. She decided she'd rather live on her own. I think she didn't like David having other girlfriends. It's not much fun having to share your husband with other people when you want him to be your best friend.'

'Is Grandfather your best friend?'

'Yes,' Granny said, and she smiled her lovely smile.

'Did David make love to his other girlfriends?' Sandy asked.

'Er,' said Granny. 'Yes, I suppose he may have done,' she added rather quickly. 'Do you know what a ruby is?'

'No.'

'George dear,' she called into the other room. 'Sandy darling, run and ask Grandfather if he could please get my jewel case from upstairs. Tell him I want to show you something.'

Then Granny showed Sandy a beautiful old ring, made of gold with red stones in it, and she said that they were rubies and that was the kind of party it was going to be. She told Sandy that all the food, or most of it anyway, was going to be that lovely red colour. She said they would have red cabbage, and beetroot, and red beef, and tomatoes, and kidney bean salad. Sandy didn't know what kidney beans were, and said they didn't sound very nice; but Granny said they were a beautiful colour and tasted very good with oil and garlic on them. She asked Sandy if she liked garlic.

'Yes,' she said. 'What is it?'

'It's like a small white onion, and it keeps vampires away.' Granny showed her a garlic from the vegetable rack. When she smelt it Sandy remembered Mummy sometimes put little bits in their potato and things for tea.

'Yes, I like it,' she said. 'But Jack and Barney don't.'

'Well, it's very good for you,' Granny said. Then she said they'd have raspberries, and strawberries if they could get them, and blackcurrant icecream, and red wine, and Ribena, and Sandy said she thought a ruby party sounded quite a good idea. 'And I think I shall wear a ruby-coloured dress,' said Granny.

'Oh, can I, Granny, can I? Please can I?' Sandy said. She thought how wonderful it would be to have a dress in that dark red colour, made of that soft stuff that was lovely to feel. 'Please may I have a ruby-coloured dress? Will you ask Mummy if I can?'

'I'm sure you can, darling. I won't need to ask Mummy, I'll get you one myself. I'll have one made for me, and I'll ask my dressmaker to make a little one for you, out of the same material. What do you think it should be made of? Silk?'

'That stuff that you stroke.'

'Satin? Velvet?'

'Velvet. Yes, velvet.' Granny was clever, the way she knew these things.

'Well, we'll see. It might be too hot for velvet. I'd better take your measurements, and then ask Eileen to add a bit on in case you grow.'

And Granny took all her measurements, there and then, and wrote them down on a piece of paper for Eileen. And Sandy thought how good it was to have secrets; and how glad she was that she wasn't a boy, because they couldn't have dresses in the same material as Granny's, made by a real dressmaker.

They went back to London after that, and didn't see Granny for a while.

One night Sandy couldn't sleep, and got out of bed to get a drink of water. She came down to the kitchen and heard her mother on the telephone.

'Oh my God. Yes, Daddy, straight away. We'll be with you in an hour.' Mummy didn't often say 'Daddy'; she usually called Grandfather 'George', though Sandy knew he was her daddy really. Then she heard Mummy and Daddy talking.

'We'll have to take the kids. You'd better go and wake them. Or could we get someone to babysit?' Mummy sighed. 'Oh God.' She sounded what adults call harassed.

'Don't worry, Amanda. We'll take them. They'd rather come. It'll be much better for them.'

'Hell, you don't think it's serious, do you?'

'No, darling, no. Come on.' Then Sandy thought she heard her mother cry a little, and her father give her a kiss. She changed her mind about the water. She went back upstairs and waited for someone to come and get her. Daddy came and turned on her light, took her tracksuit from her drawer, and said, 'Wake up, sweetheart. We're going to see Granny. I'll tell you why when we're in the car.'

He never did tell them why; not properly anyway. He said that Granny was in hospital and they were going to visit her. But they knew that already. Why should they go and see her at night? They sat in the car for ages, with their tracksuits over their nightclothes, and nobody asked Sandy if she'd done her safety straps up. To begin with she was really pleased that she was travelling without her straps on. But after a while, when she realised nobody was going to tell her, she put them on anyway. It was no fun getting away with something naughty, if nobody cared. She felt a bit sad as she did them up. She'd always waited to be nagged before putting them on, but now no one seemed to care.

She was asleep when they got to the hospital. Daddy lifted her out of the car and carried her all the way into the hospital and the lift and the ward. When they got inside the ward he stopped.

Sandy looked. At the other end of the long room there was a bed. Granny was asleep in it. Grandfather was next to the bed. But he wasn't standing or sitting. He was kneeling on the floor. He held Granny's hand in both his hands on the bed; their hands were together on the bed; and his face was resting on the hands. Sandy thought she would remember Grandfather like that always.

'Daddy,' she said. 'What's he doing?'

'I don't know,' Daddy said.

'I do,' Jack said. 'He's praying. Priests do that.'

'What's praying?' Sandy asked.

'Being religious,' Jack said.

'Why is he being religious?' Sandy wanted to know.

'Shh,' her mother said. Then she said 'Daddy?' more loudly, and went towards Grandfather.

Sandy thought Grandfather looked much older than before. He was thin and grey, and his face was covered in lines. Granny looked all right, though, asleep on the bed.

After a while Daddy took them to Grandfather's house, while Mummy and Grandfather stayed in the hospital with Granny. Daddy gave them cocoa, and forgot to make them clean their teeth, and put them in the bedrooms they always had. Then he told them they probably wouldn't go to school the next day, and they felt glad but a bit naughty for feeling glad.

And Granny never woke up.

That was what Daddy said when they had breakfast the next morning. He said Grandfather and Mummy were still at the hospital, and Granny hadn't woken up and never would again. He said she'd died peacefully in her sleep. They were all quiet for a while and looked at their spoons. Sandy noticed all the chips and scratches on Granny and Grandfather's kitchen table which she hadn't seen before. Then she thought, I suppose it's only Grandfather's kitchen table now. She wondered how long they ought not to talk. It seemed to last for a long time. In the end Daddy asked them if they'd like orange juice, and got up and went to the fridge.

Then he said, 'Oh. Granny won't have ordered orange juice for you. There's hardly any here. We'd better leave it for Granny and . . . I mean for Grandfather. Who'd like some milk?'

They didn't see Granny again. Sandy would have been interested to have seen her dead, but she didn't think it would have been polite to ask. Grandfather didn't speak to them much that time. They were taken back to London that night, and Mummy said Sandy would be staying at Sophie's house till after the funeral. Sandy and Jack and Barney weren't invited to the funeral.

It was nice at Sophie's house. Sophie's mother took them swimming after school. And Sandy was allowed to eat anything she liked. And they took the little puppy for walks twice a day. And Sophie's parents even said that if Sandy was still with them at the weekend she could come and stay in their country cottage. But in the end she went home on Saturday morning and everything went back to normal.

But Grandfather never had the ruby party.

And Sandy never got her ruby-coloured dress.

27 May, Thursday, Parsons Green

Still blistering weather.

Went to the Chelsea Flower Show today, for the first time in absolute years. In fact I haven't been since I was a child, and then only once.

What a wonder it is! How to create a world in a few days, and then make it disappear again just as quickly, as if it had never been? I remember talking to a cranky Christian when I was at Oxford, who held that the world really is only four thousand years old, or whatever it is they believe. I can still recall him gazing at me intently through his thick, bottle-bottom spectacles, nodding his head repeatedly to emphasise some point or other – I couldn't take in what, I was so transfixed by the sight of his spectacles getting lower and lower on his nose to a point when one thought they absolutely must fall, and then, at the last possible moment, being pushed up again on to the red indentations on the bridge of his nose where they so obviously lived, when the whole process would start all over again.

'How d'you work that out?' I said, to humour him. 'The world looking so old and all?' I can't remember what his immediate answer was, but it probably involved the Bible and Abraham, and no doubt Adam and Eve too. 'And what about fossils that are billions of years old?' I continued.

This time his answer was miraculous in its simplicity. Now I remember, he was a scientist, which makes it all more so, somehow.

'Do you think,' he said, 'that God is incapable of making brand new fossils which simply *look* as though they're billions of years old?'

Now of course you and I can see that this fascinating notion leaves a string of superbly unanswered questions. Like *why* this God would rub his hands in schoolboyish mischief, and go to the trouble, like a trendy divine designer, of distressing fossils to look so much older than they really are. And why the student himself bothered to study science

63

at all, when the God he believed in had made the world so random that many of its certainties are simply His capricious illusions. But his answer thrilled and delighted me. It was like a child's answer. Watertight, logical, and unanswerable. And yet, to an adult, completely implausible: though, infuriatingly, one can't entirely say why.

Well, that's what the Chelsea Flower Show was like: an extravagant, almost divine, illusion. The vans, carefully packed floor to ceiling with prize plants, only arrived last week, but those gardens that we saw today must have been there for years, surely? And will be there for years to come, won't they? Even though the same vans are booked to take them away again the weekend after next.

One of my favourites was the miniature garden. Rose arches twenty centimetres high. Fountains fit for Borrowers. Rose bushes which one could hide under the cup of one's hand. And a knee-high bonsai elm a hundred and fifty years old; the only mature elm I've ever seen. I wanted to shrink to the size and age to fit under its branches, and sit in its shade and climb up it in miniature childish glee.

Then we moved on, and I saw a stall full of terracotta pots, most of which were utterly boring. But there was a strawberry pot which was enormous; or so it seemed after the tiny garden. I could barely reach my arms round it, and I imagined it on the patio outside my tumbledown greenhouse, cascading with strawberries in the summer months, which I would pick and put straight on my muesli in the morning, still warm from the early sun. So I bought it there and then, and gave them my address for delivery. Which made me decide that I must have gardening gloves, and one of those wonderful old-fashioned cane baskets for gathering fruit – trugs, they call them. And then I insisted on a watering can, and said we must go and look for one. So we went round and round the stalls, past water gardens and senior citizens' gardens and gardens for the visually challenged and even a revival Zen garden, and at last we found a stall full of beautifully shiny bright aluminium watering cans with brass roses, of various different shapes and many different sizes, from ten-litre cans right down to plastic child's watering cans that would hardly hold a cupful. And I bought a proper, old-fashioned but brand new 'two-gallon' traditional Haws watering can, and asked them to deliver it to my house as soon as they possibly

could. And I had a wonderful grown-up feeling of having my
own home and it being a real one.

And then I agreed to go and have a glass of Pimms. We
decided to cut through the big marquee. Though 'cutting
through' was of course impossible. Not so much because of the
crowds, but because of the wonderful sights and smells and
creations. Lilies. Rose gardens. Dripping silver birches which
swept the ground. Dipping poppies in the latest colours: lurid
yellow, deep blue, and – horror of horrors – completely black.
Small fir trees in various shapes and greens, like a little Alpine
valley. Then, just as we were about to emerge through the front
opening of the tent, we passed a garden (I think called the
Garden of Romance, or something silly) with an archway, set
diagonally, half hidden by some trees, over a garden bench, and
on the bench there was a hat, and a book left face down and
open as books never should be. And I stopped and smiled and
thought, Wouldn't Poppy love that? and found myself just on
the point of thinking, I must tell her about it.

And then instantly realised what I'd done. I tried to shake
off my mood, like a dog shaking off water, but it wasn't until
I'd been out of the marquee in the sun for some minutes
that I began to warm up again.

We had to queue for the Pimms for fifteen minutes, and when
it came it was in a paper cup and weak and warm and had one
mint leaf in it that was probably alive with aphids, and I sat
down on the dry brittle grass and downed it in one. I dare say
we would have gone straight back and bought several more
if it hadn't been for the queue.

For a while we just sat, on the prickly grass, watching the
people go by. Again, and involuntarily, I thought of Poppy,
and the quick, impressionistic sketch in oils that she would
have made of the bright colours and chattering faces and tired
feet. And we went on saying nothing and just watching, and I
noticed how remarkably comfortable I felt; effortless; quiet and
not bothering to talk. As if I were with an old friend.

By the time we got up to go my hands had stopped shaking
and I was almost calm deep inside. We went out through the
crush and the turnstile and the various faces that Poppy would
have painted, and turned right at the river for Chelsea Bridge,
where we'd moored; and ten minutes upriver later we got
out at the Duke for a half pint.

His real name is Will. I accidentally smiled when he told

me, and I had to explain why. Well, you see it's like this: I
thought you were a burglar at first except that you looked
too incompetent, so I gave you a nickname ... Etcetera.
Fortunately, he was also familiar with Burglar Bill, and smiled
too. That was when I realised we might be friends. Strange
how the random discovery of a shared childhood can do
that. We might have nothing in common except two copies
of *Burglar Bill* on our two different nursery bookshelves, and
yet we instantly felt as if we understood each other, because
of that one thing. Perhaps we felt like brother and sister, as
if we had shared the same nursery itself. And perhaps, again
perhaps, that's why being with him feels almost and just a
tiny bit like being with Poppy.

To exhaust an already beggarly analogy, the friendship
itself is a bit like the exhibits at the Flower Show, or my
Christian friend's fossils: it's only been there a few days
though it feels like years and years.

Oh dear, will I read all this stuff in later years? What
does one do with a diary, other than burn it so one's
great-grandchildren don't get embarrassed? Will I ever look at
it again? If I still know Will in ten, twenty years from now,
will I want to know how the friendship started? Will I want to
know how my friendship with Poppy ended? As if I could have
forgotten that ten or twenty years from now.

So we sat, overlooking the water, with the cool river breeze
washing our bare legs, drinking our drinks in the little yard
overlooking the muddy bank and the houseboats and the
narrow boats, five minutes downriver from Chelsea Wharf.
Once or twice he looked at me in silence, and I thought: He
knows how shaken I was, how upset I was in that tent, and
he is deciding not to ask me about it. Then I found myself
wondering whether I wanted him to, and I realised that I didn't;
that I would in fact be affronted, annoyed, if he did. And I
wondered whether he knew this about me before I did?

And I think he probably did. He observes, and says little.
The silence which I thought, when I first met him, was shyness
or even gaucheness, is in fact a contained reserve: a deliberate
decision to draw to himself information about other people, just
so that he can understand them. I think. I'm still trying to work
it out. Anyway, whatever it is, it made me unwind, quieten
down, open out as if I'd been left in the sun.

So, after saying little and sitting for some time in
companionable silence, we got up to go home. It was

unexpectedly chilly on the river, and the waves rocked our
little boat and splashed spray in our faces as the river bus
overtook us, taking its commuters home after their unnecessary
day in the office. The wake of the bus lapped gently against
us, and a group of female mallards quacked harshly away
into the gathering dusk. The sheets tapped against the masts
of the sailing dinghies moored at the Chelsea Yacht Club,
smack-smack, their friendly little shots saluting us as we went
past. Then, speeding behind the bus, a small but very noisy
motor came snarling along much too fast and much too close
to us, and the water changed from its gentle whispering into a
panicking, frantic imitation of a miniature seaside.

We passed several houseproud boats, with their darkening
geraniums hanging over the side, and their Victorian lettering
boasting genteel names in smart paint on the prow: *Joseph
Conrad*, we read, and then, in smaller letters underneath,
Chelsea. Or *Florence Nightingale*, or even *The Elsie Maud*.
Suddenly, just beyond the spanking *Joseph Conrad, Chelsea*, the
empty hulk of an old, long-dead boat heaved out of the water,
alive with weeds, with its bare bones jutting into the closing
night. It rested on the mud of the Thames, with a vigorous
buddleia sprouting from its rotting carcass, and the baby
skeleton of a little rowing boat sitting on top of it. We were
nearing Cremorne Gardens, where the weeping willows shake
their hair over the pavement. Little jetties overhang the shallow
river bank, supported by thick old wooden beams which
plunge down into the silty brown mud and look as if they have
pretentions to appear in a Dickens novel. Somehow a species
of small yellow rose was scrambling over the top of one of the
jetties, trying to escape from the gardens perhaps, and it leant
down over the rails and waved at us cheerfully.

'Look,' I said, and pointed at the mass of blooms. 'Wouldn't it
be fun to take one home?'

Will looked up to where the flowers wobbled precariously
two or three metres above us.

'I may be some time,' he said.

Getting up the post seemed simple enough. It looked
pretty filthy and full of splinters, but it was rough enough to
offer a grip. But it was set in from the edge of the jetty, so
when he reached the top the flowers were still out of reach,
peeping over the side behind his head. He grabbed a rope
which agreed to take his weight, but by the time he had
chosen a stem and twisted it round and round to make it let

ANNE ATKINS

go of its parent plant, the rope had got fed up and suddenly
announced the end of the contract.

There was a heart-rending cry of something rude, followed by
the sickening sound of wet wood slithering along bare legs, and
then an explosion against muddy water. When Will eventually
stood up again, which he could do quite easily as the water
only came up to his knees, he was black from the waist down.
He did, however, have a rather startled yellow rose in his teeth
which had shed a number of its petals with the shock.

'Madam,' he said with difficulty, as his teeth were still
gripping the stalk, 'I should be honoured, and very surprised, if
you could accept this little tribute without laughing.'

I was not in a fit state to reply.

When he eventually climbed back in, I stood up to steady the
weight in the boat, and then told him what I thought of him. He
presented me with a leaf, a stalk, and a few wet petals, put his
arms around me, and then toppled us both slowly back into the
water.

I lost the rose.

We had a very wet, cold, hilarious and shivering ride back
to Putney Bridge, and a wet, cold, sodden and stared-at walk
back to Parsons Green. When we eventually got outside
both our houses, he said, 'I think the least I can offer
you is a hot bath and a brandy.'

'Yes,' I said. 'The very least.'

He opened his door and we squelched on to his doormat.

I was taken aback. Once, when I was newly arrived in
Isfahan, a friend took me for tea one afternoon to the Shah
Abbas Hotel. We stepped off the hot, noisy, dusty streets of
the town into the cool elegance of a fairytale palace. Entering
Will's house was similar. I felt as if I'd stepped off a London
pavement into a house in the heart of the countryside.

Most of the Victorian family houses in the terraces round
here open on to a little hallway on one side of the house,
leading to a drawing-room at the front, dining-room in the
middle, kitchen at the back, and stairs down to the basement
and up two or three more flights to the bedrooms and former
maids' rooms. They tend to be plush with deep carpets, chintzy
furniture, and very streamlined kitchens.

Will's front door opened straight on to what could have been
the main living-room of a gutted and converted Scottish croft:
the first impression was that this wasn't a town house, but the

68

holiday home of a rather scatty and comfortable large family.
The room seemed very spacious. In the centre of one wall was
a large fireplace – if it had once been the original Victorian
coal fireplace it must have been enlarged – with a big basket
full of logs, a huge pair of bellows and some heavy iron tongs.
The floor was of deep, dark, polished wood, with one rather
worn Chinese-looking rug skew-whiff on it. The far wall
consisted of almost nothing but archway, which led down a
step or two into a kitchen. All I could see of the kitchen was a
tiled floor, an old wooden table, and some cupboards which didn't
match. On the wall opposite the fireplace was an upright piano,
and a rather dirty oil painting of a castle somewhere in Scotland.
The whole of the wall to either side and above the fireplace
was smothered in bookshelves; and the books, which were
of all sorts, tatty paperbacks, leather-bound tomes, dog-eared
old hardbacks, not only filled the shelves but overflowed on
to the mantelpiece, floor, and sofa. I half expected to find a
huge dog sleeping on the armchair.

'D'you live here alone?' I said, and must have conveyed my
astonishment.

'Yes,' he said. 'I know, I know. All my friends comment on
it.'

'What?'

'It looks as if half a dozen children live here too. I'll go and
run you a bath.'

The bathroom, instead of being a carpeted, compact room
with a power-shower and a corner-bath with hidden taps and
jets and a matching bidet, was another large room with a big
window. The loo had a wide wooden seat and a real chain to
pull. There was a wooden horse with a huge white towel on it,
and a dressing-gown that looked as though it had seen better
days and had once belonged to the black sheep of the family
who used to travel in the Orient. The bath had feet. There was
a little wooden bookshelf by the window, full of paperbacks,
with a wicker armchair by it and a copy of Dorothy
Sayers' *Gaudy Night* on the cushion.

The only vaguely modern thing in the whole room, apart
from some of the books, was a portable television-soundcentre,
and a telephone discarded in one corner. There was a collection
of CDs on the floor, including Monteverdi, the Beatles,
Beethoven, Joan Baez, and sketches from *Beyond the Fringe*.

The bathwater was steaming. I put one toe in, yelped, and
turned on the cold tap. I was sitting on the edge trying to get

my feet in when Will came in, wearing a dressing-gown which he hadn't bothered to do up, set down a large glass of brandy by the taps, gathered up my muddy clothes, smiled, and went out again.

It wasn't until I was happily in the bath, leaning back with my brandy, that I heard a squeak from directly beneath me which sounded as though something needed oiling. I leant out of the bath and looked underneath, and saw a wide-eyed ginger kitten with a white face peering up at me and miaowing.

'Good grief,' I said, and lay back in the bath again.

As I sat in front of his fire half an hour later, warm from the inside out, in somebody else's Indian silk dressing-gown with my second glass of brandy and Gibbons purring loudly on my lap, I noticed over the piano a motley collection of photographs.

'Who are they?' I asked lazily.

'Family.'

I lifted the kitten on to the floor and went over to look at them more closely. 'Mother and father?' I asked, picking up a large colour photograph of a couple laughing into the wind, as her veil blew over the car and her hair went into her eyes, and he had to hold on to his grey top hat to stop it blowing away. You could see people in the background, in front of the little village church, grabbing their new hats or trying to keep the hems of their skirts from getting carried away. He was dark and she was fair and they were both full of joy.

'Yes.'

'They look fun.'

'Yes.'

'Who's this? You?' I said, wandering back to the chair by the fire with a framed boy wearing knee-length blue corduroy shorts, a chunky Aran jumper and an uncertain smile. 'Move, feline. Please.'

He nodded. 'My first winter in England. Actually I think it was autumn. Just after my father died. We moved back here from Italy,' he added by way of explanation.

'How old were you?'

'Seven and a half.'

A large log, which had been crumbling for some time as it burned, tripped on the fire, and began to fall out towards the rug. Before it hit the ground he caught it up in the tongs and held it a moment, before placing it back on top of the glowing wood and ash.

I was about to ask him more when his front door started thumping. Our supper had arrived. I put the photograph back and we settled down in our dressing-gowns on the rug in front of the fire, with lamb korma and chicken tandoori and three kinds of rice and a vindaloo and a large pot of tea. One helping of rice was for Gibbons.

It was after two o'clock when I said I must go.

'Do you want a bed for the night?'

'Nice try,' I said. 'Bloody cheek!'

'Win some, lose some. Are you happy to walk home in my dressing-gown?'

'It's probably safer than nothing. And safer than staying here.'

'I'll bring your clothes round when they're dry.'

'I should think so,' I said.

It was as I stood on my doorstep, in his dressing-gown, looking up at the thin moon tangled up in the television aerials opposite, that I thought of the little boy, lost in an England whose language he didn't understand, waiting for a father who would never come home again. I wanted to go and say something to him, and turned back to see him in his doorway too.

'What?' he asked.

'Um,' I hesitated. 'Thanks for the swim.'

CHAPTER FOUR –
CLANCARTY ROAD, 1990

Thou didst knit me together in my mother's womb . . .
my frame was not hidden from thee,
when I was being wrought in secret . . .
Thy eyes beheld my unformed substance;
in thy book were written, every one of them,
the days that were formed for me,
when as yet there was none of them.

Psalm 139:13–16

When Lord Shaftesbury brought in a Bill to forbid
the employment of small children in the coal mines
he was . . . assured by the experts of the time that
these children did not suffer because they were not
able to *feel*.

Dr Margaret White, Two Million Silent Killings

Sandy could keep a secret.

The secret Granny had told her, about the ruby party, she never told anyone even after Granny died. She wondered if she should have done. When Grandfather didn't have the party, she wondered if perhaps Granny hadn't even told him the secret, even though he was her best friend; perhaps she had only told Sandy. Sandy wasn't sure what you were supposed to do about secrets if the person died. But nobody had ever said to her, 'You only keep secrets if the other person doesn't die,' so she thought she'd better not tell.

It was a shame, though, about the party. Sandy felt sure that Grandfather would have had the party if he'd known that Granny had wanted it.

She didn't know where Granny was now. When she asked her parents they said they didn't know. Which was odd, because Ella said her great-grandparents were in Heaven. Why wouldn't Granny have gone to Heaven too? She asked her mummy again, and she said nobody knew; nobody even knew where Ella's great-grandparents were either. But Ella did. Ella went to Sunday School, and her Sunday School teacher had told her; and he must know because that's what he was there for, and Ella said he was going to be a curate one day.

But how could Ella know something that Sandy's own mother didn't know? Why hadn't somebody told Mummy and Daddy? It was very strange, because Sandy thought it was quite important to know where Granny had gone, to know if she was all right, and she couldn't understand why her parents hadn't found out. She wondered if she should tell them about Heaven; but then, she didn't know for certain about heaven either. And even if she had known, adults hardly ever believe you when you tell them really important things.

One day, soon after Ella had told Sandy about Andrew and Sally's new baby that they were going to have soon, Mummy told Sandy a secret too.

It wasn't a school day. It was a weekend day, a Saturday day, so they didn't have to get dressed as quickly as usual. Sometimes on weekend days they were even allowed to have breakfast in their nightclothes, like they used to when they stayed at Granny and Grandfather's house, when it was still Granny's house too. Sandy was trying on some of the makeup Mummy had given her for Christmas. Mummy was on the loo, reading a newspaper.

'That doesn't go on your cheeks, sweetheart,' Mummy said without even looking up. Sandy stared at her. How could she see where Sandy was putting her makeup without even looking up? It was very clever.

'I like it there,' Sandy said.

'Fair enough.' Sandy went on putting it on; it looked good on her forehead too. After a while Mummy got off the loo, and then she said, 'Blast!'

'Blast what?' said Sandy.

'I'm always forgetting these bloody things,' Mummy said.

'What bloody things?' asked Sandy.

'Sandy!' said Mummy. 'What language!'

'You said it.'

'Yes, I know. I'm sorry.'

'What bloody things?'

'These pills.'

'What are they for?' Mummy took little white pills every day, a bit like Sandy and Barney's fluoride pills, except the fluoride pills were pink and Mummy's were white. Jack didn't take fluoride pills any more. His teeth were all right, or grown-up, or something.

'They're to stop us having any more babies. So Si and I can make love without having any more babies.' Si is Daddy's name. Even Jack doesn't often call him Si. His real name is Simon, but Si's his nickname.

'Why don't we want any more babies?' Sandy asked. 'I think it would be nice to have more babies.'

Mummy laughed. 'Yes, in some ways it would be lovely. Babies are gorgeous. But I think three's a good number, don't you?'

'I think four would be nicer,' Sandy said.

'Well, maybe,' said Mummy. 'But it's quite pleasant for me now you're all at school. I can spend more time on my work, which I love. And then I really look forward to you coming home from school, because I've done a good day's work.'

'I like babies,' said Sandy.

'So do I. When I see someone else's baby in a pram I feel quite jealous; and I think how lovely it would be if you were all tiny again; and I think how easy it was when all you needed was a sleep and a bit of bosom.'

'Do you mean breast?'

'All right, breast. But then I think of all the nappies, and not sleeping at night, and how much more fun it is now we can sit down and have a talk, like now; and how much more interesting now you can read, and tell me things I didn't know. And then I'm quite glad that you've grown up a bit.'

'I can't read very well,' said Sandy. 'And I don't want to grow up.'

'Don't you? I didn't either. I remember my eleventh birthday. I thought, how awful to be eleven and never ever ever be ten again; and I hated that. Jack didn't seem to mind. The next bad one was twenty-five. Oh well. It happens to us all. Just think, Granny was your age once.'

It was quite a thought.

It was sometime after that that Mummy told Sandy the secret. The next day, or week, or a long time anyway, Mummy and Sandy were having tea together. Jack was playing something at school, some sport that Sandy didn't do yet, and Barney was staying at school to watch, and Daddy was working in his study. Jack might go away to school soon. To the school that Daddy went to when he was little, where you had your own bed and you took a suitcase with all your things in, and your family came to visit you at weekends with a box of chocolate cakes and pots of jam. Sandy thought it sounded great fun. But Mummy said that Sandy might not go to that kind of school. Mummy wasn't very keen on it. She thought it was nice for all the family to live together, in London, and that the schools in London were all right. But Jack wanted to go very much, and Daddy said he had loved his time at school, and it was supposed to be super dooper to live in the countryside in term time, and have lots of trees and conkers, and foxes at night, and they would all spend more time together in the holidays. So Mummy thought Jack, and Barney too, would probably end up going.

Sandy thought the boys were a lucky duck.

It was a Mummy-tea today. But it wasn't too bad. They had bread and cheese and tomatoes, and Mummy toasted her bread and had black pepper all over the tomatoes. Sandy just had them nice, on their own. And Mummy made a pot of tea in the Peter Rabbit china teapot, and Sandy tried some, but it was horrid. And then they had a pudding. It was green. It was really good. It was bananas and avocados and yoghurt all mixed up together with raisins in it; Sandy had three helpings, but she couldn't eat the third helping very well because the third helping makes you feel sick.

It was good having tea with Mummy. It was quiet, because nobody else was there. And no one was in a hurry to do anything. And when they'd finished they just sat for a while doing nothing. Daddy came and poured himself a cup of tea and went away again without saying anything; and neither of them spoke to him because they could see he was thinking about his work.

'Sandy,' Mummy said, 'do you remember when we went on holiday together, just the two of us? By the seaside, in that little cottage. It was good, wasn't it?'

Sandy remembered. It had been lovely. There was an old dolls' house there, with latticed windows and tiny green curtains. She and Mummy had had to walk to the shops, and it took nearly all day. And they had collected blackberries from the hedges and eaten them for tea and breakfast. Sandy had been very little when they did that.

'I think it's time we went again. You could take some books this time, and we could go round the windmill again. Last time they were putting new sails on. That was exciting.'

That was the thing Sandy remembered the best. They went to see the windmill, and you couldn't go round it like you usually can, because they'd taken down the big arms that go round. And the man who lived in the windmill was in a little basket right up in the sky, which was only held up by a piece of string, attached to a big mechanical crane which lifted him up and down. But when he came down he said to Sandy, 'Hello, li'le miss, what c'n way do fer you then?'

They all spoke a funny way at the seaside, and it was hard to understand them at first.

'Can I go round the windmill?' Sandy had asked him.

''Fraid not, on account of they puttin' em noo sails innit. Do you wanna go up in' barrskit?'

'Oh!' said Sandy, and looked at Mummy.

'Oh, Sandy! How exciting!' Mummy said. 'We'd love to.'

''Spec your'll wan your mummy ter come too willyer?' the man said, as he lifted Sandy in.

'Yes, please,' Sandy and Mummy both said together.

It was frightening in the basket. Sandy was relieved to see, now she was closer, that the piece of string she'd seen from the ground had become a very thick rope. But they swayed and swung about, and it didn't feel very safe at all, and a seagull even came and perched on the edge of the basket. He looked very big, close like that. Mummy showed her the dykes and the rushes, and far out over the marsh the sea, pale and grey and misty, and she said that people came from all over the country just to look at the birds on the marsh, because they were wild and unusual. But Mummy and Sandy didn't know much about birds, so it was a bit wasted on them.

And after they had come down, and thanked the man, they went to a pub in the village and ordered a cider and an orange juice and two Scotch eggs.

'Yes,' Sandy said. 'I'd like to go back there again.'

'You must go up for your bath,' Mummy said. It was then that she said, 'Shall I tell you a secret?'

'Yes, please,' Sandy said.

'You know my pill that I forgot to take a few weeks ago?'

'No,' Sandy said.

'Oh. Well, I did. You know: I take those pills so as not to have more babies? Well, I forgot one. And I think I may be pregnant.'

Sandy's mouth dropped right open. 'Are you?' she said. She couldn't think of anything else to say. She'd never known her mother pregnant. Her mother was looking like Sandy thought she herself must look when she was naughty but didn't mind much.

'Aren't I an ass?' Mummy said.

'No,' said Sandy. 'I think it's fun.'

'Oh, you are sweet,' Mummy said. 'I'm so glad I told you first. But it isn't fun really: it's a disaster.'

'Haven't you told Daddy?' Sandy was astonished.

'Not yet. I told you, it's a secret. Actually I haven't seen him much today. I'll tell him tonight. Come on. Bath time. But don't tell anyone else, will you?'

'Of course not,' Sandy said, and danced all the way upstairs; as best as she could dance on the stairs, which wasn't very well. 'Can I have bubbles in my bath?'

The next day at school Sandy thought and thought about her and Mummy's secret. It was news day, and Jennifer put her hand up and asked if she could tell her news, and stood in the middle of the circle and said she was going to be a bridesmaid at her cousin's wedding and she'd have a blue silk dress with blue flowers on it. And Sandy thought it sounded lovely. But she also thought her news was much more exciting, and if she didn't tell someone she'd burst. But she mustn't tell anyone; she knew that. So instead she just longed and longed for play time, so she could go outside and be on her own and think about her secret instead.

It was cold outside. Sandy didn't mind too much. She had on her Loofy, her winter coat, even though it was really summer and she had her summer school dress on under it. She sat on the bank of grass where it slopes down to the lawn and she hugged her knees and she thought: Good! Now I can think all about my secret and no one will disturb me.

And she was so surprised at not being disturbed that she didn't know what to think about.

She watched Annie and Ella and Antonia looking for something in the grass. They were probably worm hunting. Everyone was worm hunting at the moment, since they'd had a lesson on worms, three of the classes all together, when a man came to talk to them about garden life.

And Sandy thought, We'll do that, my new baby and I, when

she's old enough. And it came over her all of a sudden and like five birthdays all at once, that now she was going to have her very own sister. And if Sandy waited for years and years and years, her sister would be old enough to go to school, and they would be able to go worm hunting together.

A sister! Sandy knew their new baby was a girl. She didn't know how she knew, but she had no doubt at all. Perhaps that was how Ella knew where her grandparents were; she just knew, without anyone having to tell her. But then Sandy remembered that Ella had been told, at church, so it wasn't the same at all.

And Sandy wondered what they would call the new baby. She remembered Grandfather saying that there was once someone called Helen, who was the most beautiful person in the world. Sandy knew her sister would be very, very pretty, but perhaps Helen was a bit too smart for such a very little baby.

Then she remembered that her favourite name in the whole world was Poppy. She remembered, because she was thinking into the distance, her eyes gazing over towards the very end of the garden, and there in all the faraway long grass the red of the poppies was smudging and bleeding into the green. 'Poppy!' It was the prettiest name ever. She said it over and over again. 'Poppy, Poppy, Poppy.' Then she hugged her knees to herself again, and put her face sideways down on them, and shut her eyes, and dreamt.

A little baby. When she was born, she would be tiny. Sandy knew that. Much smaller than the babies you see on television. Much smaller than the babies in pushchairs in the street. Smaller than anything. Sandy wondered if she would be allowed to be there when Poppy was born. Of course she might not be called Poppy because the others might not like the name; Sandy had to be ready for that, so she wouldn't be disappointed.

Antonia had seen her baby brother being born. Her daddy had taken her to the hospital because he hadn't got a baby-sitter, and she had actually seen him coming out of her mummy's tummy. She talked about it for weeks. She told everyone in news time; and she fell asleep in school because she was so tired. And then she had shown everyone her baby brother when he came to pick her up from school and he had been the smallest thing they had ever seen. He had a screwed-up little face, and tiny finger nails, and long red fingers that kept pulling at his blanket, and eyes that blinked and didn't see anything.

And Sandy would be able to bring Poppy to school! Mummy or

Daddy would come and pick her up, and they'd have Poppy with them in a carry-cot in the car, and everyone in school would crowd round and come and see, and Sandy would be able to show her little sister to everyone. Miss Jenny and Miss Sylvia and the other teachers would give them a present for the baby; a little red and yellow rattle made to look like a teddy bear, or a soft ball with a bell inside.

Sandy opened her eyes and looked at the drive where the parents come to pick up their children. Usually it is the mothers, but some fathers come too. Ashley's, and Rachel's, and hers of course. And she thought of her mummy driving up in their big blue car, and everyone calling, 'Sandy! Your mummy's here,' as they always did; and Sandy would say 'Come and see my baby sister.' And Mummy would open the back of the car and there she'd be, with her screwed-up face and long red fingers and tiny finger nails.

Of course, babies are hard work. All the adults say that. So Barney and Jack and she would have to learn to change nappies and things like that. That bit might not be fun. And they might have to wash Poppy's clothes until she was old enough to wash them herself. They had to wash their own clothes at the weekend and in the holidays, in the washing machine. And Poppy would be too little to do that.

Sandy started picking the daisies on the grass in front of her. School would be much more fun when she could share it with a sister.

'Hello, Sandy,' Ella said, and plopped down on the grass beside her. She was holding some dandelions and a poppy, and something blue and a bit broken-looking on a long stalk.

'Hello.'

'Watcha doing?'

'Nothing. You're not supposed to pick the flowers,' Sandy said.

'Mmm,' said Ella, picking some daisies from the grass to add to her bunch. Then she started pulling the petals off one of them, going, 'She loves me, she loves me not, she loves me . . .' Soon she was trying it with the petals of a dandelion. When she still got the wrong result, she did it with the poppy, which was easy because you can see how many petals it has before you start.

'Don't!' Sandy shouted at last, sickened by so much destruction. 'And anyway, it's "*he* loves me" if you're a girl,' she added more quietly.

'Why?'

'Because you're supposed to love a boy if you're a girl.'

'Yuk! I hate boys.'

'So do I. Except Barney and Jack. And then only sometimes.'
'Yes, but why not pull the things off? Off the flowers?' Ella persisted.
'Because you'll kill them, silly.'
'They're dead already, silly. I've picked them.'
'They're not dead already. They go all grey and screwed up when they're dead.'
'Do people go like that?'
'I don't know. I haven't seen dead people. I've got a good game,' Sandy said. 'Look.'

And she put her hands flat along her sides, and lay down along the top of the slope, and rolled over and over down the slope like a roly poly pudding rolling on to the floor. 'It's really good!' she said.

And it was. They played it over and over again, till they were giddy; and then when they stood up they were even more giddy, and fell over again; and then they laughed and laughed and laughed.

'Do you remember when we laughed about Sally's daddy having a baby?' Ella said. 'I got a sore in my side.'

'Yes,' said Sandy. Then she thought, Ella will know my secret soon anyway. The baby will be born and everyone will know. And she thought of Granny's ruby party that hadn't happened because Sandy hadn't told anyone. And she said, 'Ella. Can you keep a secret?'

'Of course I can, silly.'

'No, but really really really. A real secret that you mustn't tell, not even to Annie.'

'Yes,' Ella said very solemnly; and Sandy believed her.

'You mustn't tell anyone, right. My mummy and daddy are going to have another baby.'

'Gosh,' said Ella. And the first whistle blew.

When they got home for tea nobody talked about the baby. Sandy thought perhaps Mummy hadn't told Daddy yet, so she didn't talk about it either.

But when she went to bed she got her book out about the baby inside the mummy's tummy, and she looked at all the pictures. She wished she could read better.

'Barney!' she called out. 'Barney!'
'Yes?' He was in the bathroom.
'Barney, please will you read to me?'
'I'm busy.'

'Please, Barney,' said Sandy. 'Please. If you read to me, I'll marry you when I'm grown up.'

'I don't want you to marry me when you're grown up.'

'All right then. If you read to me I won't marry you when I'm grown up.'

'I don't have to marry you anyway.'

'Please, Barney.'

'All right. Hang on.'

So Barney came and read to her. They sat on the bed and Sandy looked at the pictures and Barney read the words.

'For the first few days the baby is very small indeed. You would hardly be able to see it at all. Even if you could it wouldn't look much like a baby. But it grows very quickly, and when the baby is just four weeks old it is about the size of a pea. Already it has eyes and ears, and a mouth. Inside the baby is a heart, a liver and kidneys. After another four weeks it has fingers and toes, and is as big as a plum. It is now showing family characteristics; like big ears, perhaps, if its parents have big ears. This is rather interesting,' said Barney.

'I know,' said Sandy. 'And it's really true.'

'Have you seen my book about the sky?' he said. 'The one Daddy gave me for my birthday?'

'No. Is it good?'

'It's brilliant. Did you know, stars are absolutely ginormous? And there's millions and billions of them.'

'Will you read it to me after this book, Barney? Please.'

'Oh, golly. It's so much slower reading it to you. I'll see.'

'You sound like Mummy or Daddy.'

By the time Sandy got her cuddle from Mummy, she was nearly asleep. She opened her eyes a little, and found that Mummy was lying on her bed with her arms around Sandy.

'Hello, sweetie,' Mummy said.

'Mmm,' said Sandy. 'Mummy,' she said sleepily.

'Yes, darling.'

'Do you like the name Poppy?'

'Um. Quite. Not much. Why?'

'I wondered if we could call the new baby Poppy.'

'Oh,' Mummy said. Then she didn't say anything for quite a long time. Sandy may have fallen a little bit asleep. Then Mummy said, 'Sandy?'

'Mmm?'

'Look, sweetheart, I shouldn't think too much about the baby. Perhaps I shouldn't have told you. I know we always try and tell each other everything. But, you see, it may not even happen.'

'Oh,' Sandy said, nearly in her sleep. What did her mummy mean, it may not happen? What may not happen? But she wasn't quite sure if she'd dreamt it or if Mummy said it. She snuggled up to her mummy and finally gave herself up for the night.

Outside Sandy's window, the early-summer breezes whispered and danced in the dark shadows of the leaves. In the half light, late birds darted busily about, as if they had urgent things to do before bedtime. Somewhere in a garden a dog yelped; and a woman's high-heeled shoes tap-tapped along the pavement, sounding just like a horse clip-clopping along, as she went on a man's arm to a party, or the theatre, or a restaurant. The diesel of a taxi hummed in a distant road.

After what seemed a long time, Sandy's mummy lifted herself off the bed and stood in the dark bedroom. She bent over Sandy and kissed her. 'Darling girl,' she whispered.

Then she picked up the book that Barney had been reading to her. They had never got on to the one about the stars. Sandy's mummy looked at the pictures of the naked little baby, looking much older and thinner than a clothed and born baby. She looked at the row of naked babies, in different sizes and at different stages of development, above their corresponding size of fruit or vegetable, from a pea to a marrow.

Then she shut the book, put it in the bookcase, and gave a little sigh before going out on to the brightly lit landing.

CHAPTER FIVE –
PERRYMEAD STREET

Forsan et haec olim meminisse iuvabit.

Maybe one day we shall be glad to remember even these things.

Virgil, Aeneid, *I, 203*

It was the sort of thing my grandmother would have done. She was always cutting things out of newspapers and sending them to people. Perhaps that's why my grandfather did it, to try and make up for her loss, to try and compensate in some small way to the rest of us.

It was from his local newspaper, and it was about a competition that Heffer's, the bookshop, was running. You had to write about an endangered species, and there was a prize for the under eights and a prize for the eights and over. I was nine. And I was mad about animals. I had kept all sorts of things, most of which came to a sticky end: Chinese hamsters which were quite untameable and bit everybody and refused to breed; a guinea-pig which was killed by our neighbour's cat; a garter snake which escaped and was last seen slipping through another neighbour's pond, hunting all the frogspawn. I was also very keen on animal rights and Green issues and ecology. In fact almost every child I knew was, at the time. Almost half of the girls in my class were vegetarians, to their parents' despair.

So it was no difficulty for me to write about animals. I'd already written lots of stories. My mother's 'Box of Memories', which is what she called the box in the loft where she put things of ours she thought worth keeping, was full of little four- or eight-page books I'd written: 'Whinnie the Red, the storee of a rud squirel who luved strawbree jam.' (This is going back some time; my spelling was wonderful, and rivalled

Shakespeare's in its inventiveness and inconsistency. By the time of the Heffer's competition it had been straightened out somewhat.) 'The saylor who got seesik.' 'Popeye the runaway pownee.' And so on.

When Grandfather sent me the cutting about the competition I asked my father for guidance about which endangered species I should choose. I knew all about the whale and the panda and the black rhino – which was threatened then – but I thought other competitors would know about those too. He showed me an article in that day's paper about the Venezuelan spectacled bear. It was an ideal choice. The article told me how the bears were trapped when young and taught to dance by being made to stand on hot plates; and how their capture was threatening the existence of the species, as they couldn't or wouldn't breed in captivity.

Looking back on the story now, for I still have it, I can see that it wasn't as good as I've always thought it must have been. There's nothing about it to show that I would necessarily become a writer. But I can see why it won. I had taken the interesting facts from the newspaper article and turned them into a classic story of capture, torture, escape and a happy ending; my bear even grew to have cubs of her own, which must have pleased the ecological sympathies of the judges. And I had sent it in with the newspaper article itself, so they could check it against my sources.

I can remember the day I wrote it. It was a Saturday morning, the same day that my grandfather's letter had come. Saturdays were always lovely lazy days when we were young. My parents made a point of trying not to work on a Saturday, so we would sit downstairs in the kitchen around a late breakfast for hours, often until well past lunchtime. On this particular day I showed my father Grandfather's letter, including the information about the competition. That was when he found me the article in *The Times* for my research. Then he got a pencil and paper for me, and told me to do it by hand before putting it on the computer. My brothers were too old to enter: there was an upper limit of eleven, and my younger brother had just turned twelve.

'But what about Poppy?' I said. 'There isn't a younger limit. She can enter the under eights.'

'But she can't write,' my father objected.

'Yes, but she can draw. And she can make up a story for us to write down.'

'All right. Poppy, do you want to come and do a picture?' he called out. I now appreciate, retrospectively, as many people do, how supportive my father was in those days. I think he saw every childish whim and notion of ours as a sacred commission to him; something he must preserve and nurture in case that one idea became our future. As, of course, in this case, it did.

He carefully explained to Poppy the rules of the competition, told her what an endangered species was, and left the pair of us to finish our work.

A feeling of great contentment settled on us as we worked together. Once or twice my father came in, to make coffee, or check the fridge for supplies for lunch. As he passed us he looked over our shoulders and told us how well we were doing. My mother came in once and said, 'Wow, you look busy,' and disappeared again, and after a while my brother unwittingly wandered in with a book and settled down at the table. This was a fatal move.

'Barney,' I said. 'Poppy needs help with her story.'

'Does she?' he said without looking up.

'Yeah. Can you help her? Please, Barney?'

'Why can't you, brainbox?' he asked pleasantly.

''Cos I'm working, Barney. Please.'

'How d'you know I'm not working?'

'You're just reading.'

'Might be work.' 'Work', in our family, could mean anything, I suppose because my parents both worked from home. With my father being a full-time writer, and my mother running her own business selling stylish and unusual maternity wear, 'work' for them sometimes meant talking on the telephone, posting a letter, or even, for my father, simply thinking in the bath. So we had the freedom, as children, to concentrate on anything, a picture, a story, cricket practice, and be undisturbed because we were working.

'What help do you need, Poppy?' Barney gave in.

'I don't know,' she admitted.

'You need to tell Barney your story,' I explained. 'And he'll write it down.'

'What story?'

'The story that goes with your pictures.'

'Ahh,' said Poppy. '"Once there were dinosaurs and they lived in a hot hot country and it was so hot they had to wear sunglasses and if they wanted to sunbathe . . ."'

'Just a minute,' said Barney. 'I haven't got a pen or anything.'

'Barney,' I said, concerned.

87

'Yup.'
'Are dinosaurs endangered?'
'Pretty terminally, I'd say.'
'Good,' I said, and after sucking my pencil for a minute settled back to work, while Poppy continued: '"... and everything dried in the sun because it was so hot, so the only thing the dinosaurs had to eat all day long was dried potatoes and Coca Cola ..."'

Heffer's Bookshop wrote to me three weeks later. I got home from school one Monday afternoon, and there was a jiffy bag waiting for me with Heffer's stamped on it. My parents had obviously seen this, and, dying with curiosity, had gently prised it open and looked inside before gumming it up again and trying to make it look as though it hadn't been opened. They would never have dreamt of opening a letter from a boyfriend in later years, or unfolding any of the many scraps of paper all over the house which said: 'Top Secret Club. Highly Private. Do Not Open'. They would never have read my diary or spied on my love life. But I can imagine the excitement my father would feel if he thought I'd won a literary competition, and I think it's forgivable.

The envelope was full of posters, and stickers, and balloons with Heffer's all over them, and a beautiful book of *Ronnie the Red-Eyed Bullfrog* as a prize, and best of all a picture postcard of Heffer's saying: 'Congratulations, Sandy! You have won first prize! We were particularly impressed with the way you used a news item in your story. Lots of love from Marcus, at Heffer's Children's Department.'

I whooped around the house, and hugged my father, and showed my family all my prizes, and Poppy clapped and said, 'Sandy's won,' and then said, 'Where are my prizes?'

'Oh Poppy, Sandy.' My mother was looking upset. 'I've done a terrible thing.' She sat down and pulled us both to her with a hug, as adults sometimes do when they are trying to pre-empt a child's justified indignation. 'I never sent yours off.'

'Mummy!' I said, shocked.

'Mummy!' Poppy echoed crossly.

'Now hang on,' my mother said. 'Let's be fair about this. It wasn't my responsibility to make sure they got there. You never asked me to post them, either of you. I just happened to notice, one day when Sandy was at school, that the closing date was the next day and you hadn't posted them. And I wasn't sure whether Barney had helped Poppy, or written the story for her, and none of you were around, and I didn't have time to write a covering letter to the bookshop, and I thought the important thing was to get Sandy's in the post. So I did, and when you came home from school I forgot to ask you about Poppy's, and then the next day I wondered whether to send it anyway, but I must say I looked at it and I thought dinosaurs aren't really an endangered species so I thought there wasn't any point. Sorry. I wish I had now.'

We were only downcast for a moment. As soon as Poppy knew I'd share the prizes with her she didn't care about her story; and I had the thrill of being the one who'd won, after all.

It was less than a week before Marcus wrote to Poppy too. My mother felt so awful at not having sent off Poppy's entry that she'd written to him explaining all about it, enclosing the dinosaurs after all. Marcus replied, 'Dear Poppy, Thank you for your wonderful story about the dinosaurs. It's too late for us to give you the first prize in your category, but we think your story is so good we're sending you a prize anyway. Your illustrations are very interesting. Perhaps you and your sister would like to write more stories, and send them to us. We will always be pleased to hear from you. Lots of love, Marcus in the Children's Department.'

Marcus had sent Poppy a paperback about dinosaurs, and two more balloons, which was just as well as the others had popped or gone down by then.

My happiness was complete.

It wouldn't be true to say that we wrote non-stop after that. We continued in our haphazard way, Poppy drawing and painting as all children do, at nursery school and at home and on my father's papers, when she would get severely told off regardless of Heffer's Bookshop's appreciation of her talents. For myself, I couldn't see what all the fuss was about. I looked hard at her dinosaurs, but still considered I could have done much better. Admittedly she was younger than I; much younger. But her pictures were not as accurate as mine, and the colouring didn't always stay within the lines. And they were not proper, conventional children's pictures. Other four-year-old children drew pin men, and rays coming off the sun. I could accept all that, because it was normal. Poppy's figures, though, had fingernails and toenails and eyelashes, but because of her difficulty in controlling the line the toenails would sometimes end up in completely the wrong place, somewhere near an ear perhaps.

What I failed to see, and what a lot of adults wouldn't have spotted, was that she already drew in proportion, with tiny people or animals on the horizon and slightly larger ones in the middle distance. And that her pictures had concepts behind them, in a rather medieval way, so the sun would shed tears over some sad event on the earth, or fish in the sea would smile because sailors in the sunshine above were being rescued. And her figures had a life, an individual character, that was unique and is hard to describe without the pictures to demonstrate what I mean.

But it takes imagination to notice all this. Most people look at a childish picture and see only its limitations, see only that it was done by a child and think they could do better. I wonder how many children there are like Poppy who draw remarkably well when young but don't grow up to be remarkable artists, either because their talent peters out, or because it was really a talent for something else, perhaps simply observation, or even, most sadly, because it goes unrecognised and unencouraged.

We sent Marcus a story that summer, and he wrote back a most appreciative letter saying it was marvellous and he was displaying it in the shop. He also sent us another poster each, and a pencil saying 'Heffer's Bookshop', and further encouragements to send him our work. The story was about a mother and child, and the conversations they had in the bathroom and loo and bedroom and kitchen. The script was unremarkable; I still have the pictures, though, which I find far more interesting. One, for instance, is a picture of the nursery, with the child lying on a cot and a mobile overhead and a few large flowers on the wall to represent wallpaper. At first the picture simply looks like an adequate, or perhaps fairly accomplished, study of a bedroom by a competent four year old. But as you look at it you begin to realise that the picture is painted from the angle of the floor, as you come into the room. A mouse's eye view from the doorway, or perhaps the view seen by a baby crawling in. And the child in the cot is not depicted with head and body and arms and legs, as you'd expect; all you can see is one foot, waving about, and an arm stretching to reach it. Not very well executed, perhaps, but very accurately observed; what you actually see from below if you watch a young child in a cot.

Another picture was to illustrate the conversation the two of them had while the mother had her bath. This time the picture is taken from between the bath taps. The mother's toes loom enormous; her head is miles away and tiny; she has eyelashes and pubic hair and a tummy-button and dimples on her elbows, and breasts with nipples. A yellow plastic duck plays on the water, which is blue.

But the most extraordinary picture of all is the one of the loo. This takes some looking at. At first you can't quite work it out. You can see the chain ready to be pulled on one side, and the loo paper rolled up and fixed to the wall on the other. In the foreground of the picture, however, is what looks like a woman, but with hair over her face and a bottom occupying the centre of the composition. At last, as you puzzle over it, you realise that it is taken from another low angle. This time the artist's eye has gone down behind the loo, to a point just above the U-bend, and is looking up at the mother, with the back of her feet on either side; and, way up at the top of the picture, her head is covered in brown hair because she is being seen from behind. Poppy can't possibly have experienced this viewpoint. Even she couldn't have fitted behind the loo just above the U-bend. But at the age of four she could envisage what it would have looked like if she could have got there. Her imagination could travel anywhere.

Only a very small part of our lives was occupied with creating books. We had a normal, what I suppose would be called middle-class, upbringing of the time. In the holidays we went to Brittany or Ireland or Norfolk. One year we tried skiing. Once or twice my father went fishing or shooting: one winter I was allowed to accompany him and help the beaters. This didn't go against my Green sympathies at all; under my father's guidance I could see that if we were going to eat meat it was better to eat something which had lived free and died cleanly, and whose diet had never been adulterated with hormones or drugs.

One February half term we spent a week in the Cotswolds. For once we all had the same half term holiday, which was rare. We took a cottage, called Kingfisher Cottage, in a delightful little stone village whose name I can't remember now. Kingfisher Cottage was aptly named. A stream ran through the garden, right under the bathroom window, round the house and under the front door, so we had to step on to a little slate bridge to get away from the garden into the house. I remember sitting in the bath and listening to the running water gurgling outside the window, near enough to touch. The neighbours told us that kingfishers often did come to the stream, and if we watched long enough and quietly enough we were bound to see them.

Poppy and I spent hours in that garden. We got twigs and pretended to fish with them; we took off our socks and shoes and walked along the stream, under all the low branches and through the hidden corners of the garden, despite the freezing February temperature of the water;

we put leaves and little pieces of bark at one end of the garden, upstream, and then raced round to the other end to get there before they came gurgling and tumbling down on the head of the water. My brothers were too old for all this sort of thing, though Barney came out a few times and spent ten minutes with us before getting bored, and I can remember Jack wasting time looking for fish one afternoon when he was supposed to be studying but couldn't face any more of his books. But we never saw a kingfisher, all the time we were there.

At the weekend we drove over to see some friends of ours near Moreton. She was an old school friend of my mother's; an actress, who'd married a successful artist. They had a flat in London, and once or twice we'd seen them there, but they always went to the Cotswolds for the weekend. My mother's friend, Blanche, was great fun and always giggling, and a very easy person for children to relate to even though she had no children of her own. But her husband, Peter, had always terrified me; I suppose for no better reason than that he was rather shy, very tall, and usually hovered in the background somewhere.

Rather incongruously, perhaps, they both rode to hounds with whatever hunt it is which meets in that part of the country. When we went to see them, that Sunday afternoon, Peter asked if we'd like to go and see the horses. Of course we said yes, so he bundled us into the Landrover and drove us to the stables while my mother and Blanche stayed behind in the warm, to get the tea ready and catch up on each other's news, presumably. The horses were the largest horses, other than Shire horses, I'd ever seen in my life. Peter's was called Night. Perhaps he was really Knight, with a K, but because he was pitch black I immediately assumed the name was given him because of his colour. Peter gave us all a carrot to spoil him with, and lifted Poppy up so she could reach him; and then we moved on to see Henry, Blanche's grey.

I had done as much riding as a London girl can, from time to time persuading my parents to take me to a riding school in Cobham on a Sunday, or pay for me to go on a pony weekend with school friends. I loved horses, and was always keen to get up on one. I thought Henry superb. I imagine, looking back, that he was under eighteen hands, probably about seventeen two. He seemed to me then to be near the treetops. Peter led him out of the stable and into a paddock which was obviously used as an outdoor school. He had only a halter on and no saddle, so Jack, who was given the first ride, had to be given a leg up. Jack was fairly competent with horses, but even so Peter didn't let go of the halter.

'He's very gentle as a rule,' he said, 'but you never know. He's a very powerful animal. He'd jump that fence from a standstill.'

Then Barney was led round the paddock, and finally I was, which confirmed my desire to live in the country and get myself a horse as soon as I was able. It wasn't until I dismounted that Poppy said she wanted a turn.

'All right,' Peter said, 'we'll get one of the others back up, and they can hold you.'

'No,' Poppy said. 'I want to get up on my own.'

'Are you sure, sweetheart?' my father said. 'He's very big, and you might slip off without a saddle to hold on to.'

She was adamant. So Peter passed the halter to my father, so that he himself could hold on to her after lifting her up.

A number of times in recent years I've taken the opportunity to watch younger children lifted on to horses for their first ride, and I've noticed that almost always their initial emotion is fear. Even children who love animals and are used to them usually take on a look of barely concealed terror the first time they are put into a saddle and told to hang on. Soon they get used to it, and may become good riders, but there has always been that first frisson of fright when they realise the power of the animal beneath them, and their own incompetence to deal with it.

There was none of that with Poppy. From the moment she sat on Henry she looked as though she'd fallen in love. She had no saddle to hold on to, and he was so big her legs stuck out almost horizontally as though she'd been sketched by Thelwell, but she sat perfectly balanced and perfectly relaxed as if she'd been there all her life. She didn't say a word; she simply held on to his mane and beamed smiles at his ears, while my father led him gently round the paddock and Peter held on to Poppy's hand in case she fell. After a few minutes she was lifted off again. She stretched up to stroke his nose and give him a kiss, and watched him as if in a trance as he walked back to the stables. All the way back in the car she sat in silence. When we arrived at Peter's house again and the car stopped she didn't move. Eventually, when we were all saying, 'Come on, Poppy,' and jumping up and down in our anxiety to get back into the house, she simply said, 'I've forgotten something.'

'What, honeypot?' my father said as he lifted her out.

'I forgot to say thank you.'

'Well, say thank you now. Peter's just there.'

'No. I forgot to say thank you to Henry.' My father smiled, and hugged her, and carried her into the house.

Blanche had a lovely winter tea ready for us. We all tumbled and bundled into their large country kitchen, which was warmed by a smart blue Aga. She and my mother started toasting and buttering crumpets as soon as we arrived, and Blanche poured hot water into a large brown teapot which had been sitting, warm, at the back of the Aga, waiting for us to turn up. We tucked into it all with great relish, dolloping Peter's home-produced honey into the holes on the crumpets, letting melted butter run down our fingers and on to our clothes, and dispatching the crumpets much faster than the toaster could discharge them. After ten minutes or so our greed slowed down a little, and we turned our attention to a large chocolate cake and some biscuits.

'What about you, Poppy?' Blanche said. 'You've got to eat, after your first ride on Henry. I hear you were galloping around the school.'

'Oh, I wasn't,' Poppy said very seriously. 'We weren't at school. And we didn't go fast at all.'

'Very sensible,' Blanche replied. 'What can I get you?'

'Drawing paper,' said Poppy. 'And crayons.'

'Please,' said my mother automatically.

'Please,' Poppy added.

'Don't you want any cake, darling?' Blanche asked. 'If you've had enough crumpets.'

'Yes, please,' Poppy said. 'Can I have it when I do my drawing?'

'If you like. It must be very boring for you children. I'm sorry we've got no toys.'

'Poppy didn't ask for toys,' Peter said. 'She asked for drawing paper and crayons. Where do you want to go, Poppy?' he asked her. 'Do you want to use my studio? You'll have to promise not to touch anything at all.'

'Oh help,' said my father.

The rest of us sat on for a while, continuing to gorge ourselves despite the protests of our exhausted stomachs. After a time I started to fidget, and then Barney asked if he and I could get down. We wandered into their sitting-room vaguely looking for a television or some games or a book. I found a battered old copy of *The Hobbit* and started reading it again. I'd read *The Lord of the Rings* twice through by the time I was nine, so I didn't think I'd enjoy going back to *The Hobbit*, but I had the pleasant sensation of picking up an old friendship and finding it even better than I'd remembered it. Barney said he was going to look at the cows and the beehives, and did I want to come? I shook my head and curled up in the sofa with my find. Later Jack wandered in and asked where Barney was, and then disappeared again while I continued reading. I was several chapters in before I looked out of the window and realised it had been dark for some time. I put my book on a sofa cushion, open and page down as I was always being told not to do, and went to find the others.

The adults were still in the kitchen, sitting round the remains of the tea though now they all had what they would have called 'proper' drinks in their hands. I climbed on to my father's knee and rested my head on his shoulder.

'You're getting a bit big for that. What have you been doing? And where are the others?'

I shrugged, and then said I thought the boys were outside.

'And where's Poppy?' my father said. 'You haven't lost her?'

'She didn't come with me. She got down ages ago.'

'I took her upstairs,' Peter said. 'I told her to come down when she'd finished.

'I hope she hasn't wrecked your studio,' my father said.

'She'll be asleep,' my mother reassured him. 'Head on the table, pencil on the floor.'

We all laughed. A few minutes later Poppy wandered into the kitchen, awake but with the rather rosy-cheeked look that children sometimes get when they're very tired. She helped herself to the last piece of chocolate cake and climbed on to Peter's knee without a word.

'Have you finished?' he asked her. She nodded. 'Can I see them?' he said. She nodded again, and slipped off his knee to leave the room. 'Don't get chocolate cake on your pictures,' he called after her.

We had got to that part of the day when even adults are tired and sit at the table without saying much. So that when Poppy returned and put her pictures down in front of Peter we were all watching and listening, not particularly to be nosy or even because we were specially interested, but simply because we were too full and lethargic to do anything else.

Peter looked at the pictures in silence to begin with. There were three of them. He spent some time on each one. After a while Poppy said, 'That's Henry, looking out of his stable.'

'I can see that,' Peter said. 'I can see what they all are. This is what you could see when you were riding on Henry. These are his ears, here, aren't they? And this is his neck, and these . . .' his voice petered out. 'And this is my studio, isn't it?' Poppy nodded. 'How old are you, Poppy?'

'Five,' she said. 'At least, I was five on my birthday.'

'Good day of the year to be five on,' Peter said. 'You haven't signed these pictures, Poppy. You must sign them.'

'Oh,' she said, and took the proffered pencil and did so. 'Do you like them?' she said. 'They're for you, I think.'

'In that case I shall keep them very carefully indeed. I suspect one day they'll be worth a lot of money.' Poppy looked at him to see why we was teasing her, and wrinkled up her nose. 'If you continue drawing like this, you'll be an exceptional artist one day. These are extraordinary.'

'Oh,' said Poppy. 'Actually they're not for you really. I want to take them home.'

'Oh, Poppy,' my parents said.

'You can't do that,' I said, outraged. 'You've given them.'

'That's all right,' Peter said. 'She didn't know the value of them when she offered them. Did you, Poppy? But will you promise me something instead?' Poppy had the grace to feel guilty enough to promise. 'Are you listening?' Peter went on. 'Never stop drawing. Anything, anytime, anywhere. On the backs of envelopes, on scraps of paper, on the wall if you must . . .'

'Thanks, Peter!' my father said.

'Draw, paint, sketch,' Peter continued. 'Keep looking at everything very carefully. And whenever you feel like drawing a picture, do. Drop anything else to do it. All right?'

Poppy nodded. 'Not very practical,' my mother said. 'We'll get back to you when she's been expelled from school . . .'

'Then send her to a school which won't expel her,' Peter said. 'Or let her stay at home. Seriously, these are good.'

My mother obviously remembered Peter's words. I know that because those three pictures of Poppy's survived in the box, so my mother clearly attached importance to them. And since I now have all Poppy's things, I have those pictures myself. In fact, it was as I looked at them that I remembered that February holiday, and the horses, and the tea. In the first picture Henry looks out of his stable at us; his mouth can't be seen, but he seems to be smiling. The next one shows the rest of us waving at Poppy as she sits proudly on Henry's back; sure enough, you can see his neck and ears, and the back of my father's head as he leads him round the paddock. The last picture is more accurate, because she was drawing what she could see rather than from memory; you can see the rest of the table which she's sitting at, with a jar holding brushes, and a bottle, and pencils, and beyond the table a vase with dried flowers in it, and on an easel a canvas with the same flowers painted on it.

I wonder if Peter was right, and that picture is now valuable. I wouldn't be surprised, though perhaps more on Peter's account than Poppy's; specially now that he's dead. With these three pictures is one more – an exquisite and evocative water-colour of that same Cotswolds countryside which Poppy was painting from her vantage point on Henry. But this picture is by Peter himself.

After that holiday my parents gave Poppy various encouragements. On Saturday mornings my father would arrange some fruit and flowers on the kitchen table and suggest she did a still life, or get a postcard of a famous painting and encourage her to copy it. On one occasion my mother asked her if she'd like to send one of the pictures to Peter. She must have agreed. With Peter's picture is a letter, from Peter to Poppy, thanking her for the picture she sent him, urging her to keep going, and saying very modestly that he hoped she liked his as much as he'd enjoyed hers.

'He sent it through the *post*!' my mother said incredulously. 'In an ordinary envelope. As if it were nothing.'

'Perhaps it is, to him,' my father reasoned.

'It wouldn't be if he sold it,' she replied, easing it out of Poppy's marmaladey fingers. 'I'll get it framed for you, Poppy, and we'll hang it on the wall in your room.'

I could sell it myself, I suppose, since it's mine now. But I won't. I'll keep it for her. And for myself. And for Peter's sake, and Henry's, and that winter afternoon.

6 June, Sunday, Norfolk

Decided to come to Ben's for a week, to escape and think.
Brought diary, of course, to have something sensational to read
on train, etc.

Seemed to have to leave my house at the crack of dawn,
to get here for teatime. I exaggerate somewhat, crack of
dawn being by London Sunday standards, i.e. late morning,
and teatime being by country standards, early afternoon.
Nevertheless, it surely wouldn't take much longer to
nip over and visit James in India?

So I spent much of the journey in a state of hungover city
exhaustion, trying to snatch a bit of sleep before the ticket
collector came round, forgetting that they have those machines
now instead. And every so often I would look out of the
window and see an unbroken sky of blue; and early hay rolled
and waiting patiently in the fields (is it early for hay? I have
no idea of course); and the birds dipping in the sunshine; and
the fields, happily, much smaller than when we were children,
and full of hedgerows again. Once we crossed an old motorway,
crumbling into wildflowers. And a skinny foal staggering
to its feet, on unsteady new legs. And cows munching.
And – would you believe it? – there are still children, after
all these years, who run to the gate and climb on it just
to wave at the train going past.

Funny: I can remember something Grandfather told me once.
I must have been tiny at the time, but it's stayed in my mind, I
don't know why, all this time. When he went on his family
holidays, as a boy, to Norfolk, his father had a car. I think
it went at about twenty miles an hour, and had windscreen
wipers that were operated manually, by the passenger. And my
grandfather's brothers and sisters (there were five of them) and
his mother all travelled in the car with my great-grandfather.
But his nanny and the nursemaid and the cook – or have I
got that wrong? I've a feeling there were only two of them;
perhaps Nanny doubled up as cook for the holidays – and the
luggage all travelled together on the train. Which also went at

about twenty miles an hour. At certain points along the journey the railway crossed the road, or went alongside it; and so all the way to Overstrand my grandfather and his brothers and sisters would be leaning out of the car, shouting and waving at their nanny, who would lean out of the train with her white pocket handkerchief, waving at her children. Strange that I've remembered it all this time.

Suki and Abi met me at the tiny little station. Everybody in the country still has a car, but I'm glad to say Ben's is a proper country car, full of dog hairs and old boots and yellowing newspapers. And they still get newspapers too: I asked Ben once why he didn't save money and get the news on screen, and he said he'd have nothing to line the cat basket with.

Blissful tea. So relaxed compared with London. I can never quite work out why this is. There must be as many things to do in Norfolk as Fulham, there are no more hours in the day. And yet it is a fact: the moment one goes into the country the city stress evaporates. Nor is it simply because one is away from home, and all one's work and commitments. Ben and Suki and Abi are simply more relaxed than London families are.

So after supper I shall go to bed ridiculously early, and sleep and sleep and sleep. I've promised Abi an absurdity of things for the morrow. She's on half term all week, and seems to have planned for the two of us to cover all the entertainments of North Norfolk on the first day.

Feel strangely homesick, don't ask me why or for whom. But it's only for a week and I'm determined to enjoy myself.

7 June, Monday

Just as well I went to bed early. At some unearthly hour,
which felt like five o'clock, looked, from the sun on the fields,
like half-past ten, and turned out to be twenty to eight, Abi
came bounding into my room with a cup of tea. She can't
actually have bounded, or she would have spilt the tea, but
that's certainly what it felt and sounded like. How do people
with children survive this kind of treatment all day, all week,
all year? You'd think they'd be in retreats for the mentally
challenged before their offspring were out of nappies. And Ben
and Suki, being typical farmers, don't even have a help or
anything.

So, tea all down my front, out of bed, and the first task
of the day, apparently, is to warm up the sea. Abi and I are
to go down to the beach, on bicycles, with our swimming
things – ugh – before breakfast. This would be fine, relatively,
if Abi could ride a bicycle, which she can't. We try all
manner of combinations, with cross bars and baskets
and her on the saddle while I stand to pedal, before I
persuade her (and she country born!) that a few hundred
metres can be covered quite easily on foot.

And she's right, the sea is amazing. Bloody cold, but
amazing. And this was another of my grandfather's
principles, I seem to remember: that the sea (and fresh
vegetables) could cure almost any ill, from the common cold
to lovesickness, and would certainly knock on the head a
little spot of city depression. (And hasn't science borne him
out, and advocated Cold Water Treatment for M.E.? Not
that my grandfather would have heard of M.E., but if you'd
described the symptoms to him he would certainly have
suggested sea-bathing and green beans.)

Whether it can cure lovesickness is still up for debate, but I
plunged in as if my life depended on it, and was being thrown
up and down beneath the screaming seagulls before I realised
that Abi had followed me straight in, without armbands or
anything, and her face was under the water and she couldn't

100

swim at all. After I'd pulled her out and thumped her back
and squeezed her dry and shaken all the water out, she
told me she was fine and can swim really but please could
she have a ride on my back first?

And the sky stretched on forever above us, with tiny snags
of translucent cloud on the horizon. The waves lifted us
into the air and threw salt in our faces and on our lips and
on to our eyelashes. And the seagulls protested and dived
and landed on the rotting wooden windbreakers and turned
their heads and ignored us. And the fishermen splashed
and smacked past in their suddenly enormous-looking little
rowing boats, and barked a Norfolk good morning, with
the floors of their boats alive with crabs in the traditional
wooden-and-rope lobster pots, as they went home after a day's
work before eight-thirty in the morning.

And as I waded ashore with Abi, I thought Grandfather was
probably right: if this treatment doesn't cure anything I might
have brought with me, then nothing will; if there's any malaise
that can't be snapped out of after a week of the North Sea and
the sunshine and the country air and the fresh vegetables
and the company of a nearly six year old, then I'll eat my hat,
as he would no doubt have said.

We even collected the eggs for breakfast, and the
honey was off the farm, and I would have been quite
happy to go out gathering mushrooms only we didn't
happen to see any and there were some vacuum-wrapped
from Sainsbury's sitting happily in the fridge so it seemed
sensible to eat them instead. Besides, Abi had never heard
of mushrooms growing in a field instead of being bought
off a shelf, which rather destroyed the pastoral dream I
was trying to weave around myself. In addition she hates
mushrooms, as all self-respecting children do, so she tells
me, and she would never have consented to the expedition
anyway.

And she hates eggs. And bacon. And sausages. But not
honey, a great deal of which went on the white bread she
found for herself, as well as the floor, table, knife, and all
over her body, which she hadn't put any clothes on, just
in case. I had asked her, 'In case what?' but as soon as she
began her breakfast, I realised.

The rest of the day seemed so full, it makes me tired to think
of it now. And again it makes me realise how exhausting it
must be to have children, and I wonder how people with three

or even four, like my parents used to manage at all. And
does that explain, perhaps even excuse, the way they coped
with it? I try and tell myself it does.

After breakfast we went to the riding school. Abi wasn't
going for a ride, you understand, she just wanted me to see the
riding school. And there we saw huge, beautiful Shire horses,
almost as large as elephants it seemed to me, and almost as
strong, with their vastly powerful shoulders, and feet large
enough to step on a puppy by mistake and crush it and not
notice; or so it rather morbidly struck me. And their kind,
gentle faces, and their velvet soft noses. One had a two-day-old
foal, and the foal seemed as large as a mature pony. And then
we saw the ugly, dumpy, ginger Suffolk Punches; and again,
and involuntarily, I thought of Grandfather, and the theory he
had that anyone with red hair had a distinctive smell. That
was exactly what these Suffolk Punches reminded me of:
someone with ginger hair. I think my mother told me once
that she had a boyfriend, for a day or two, whom she thought
deliciously wonderful at the time: tall, freckled, handsome
with auburn hair. The moment he walked into the house, her
father was convinced that he could smell him – not that the
smell was unpleasant; simply that it was there – and she
never went out with him again. Did she really tell me that
herself? It doesn't seem like her, somehow.

When we'd done the rounds of the working horses, and
the pigs and goats, and the ducks, and even completed the
inspection of the guinea-pigs, we finally had a look at the
riding ponies, patiently going round and round the school with
children on their backs who could scarcely have distinguished
between the mane and the tail. This was obviously supposed to
be the high spot of the morning, and Abi showed it to me with
a pride and joy which she could hardly contain.

'Look, look,' she said. 'Look at the little one. She's called
Tiffany. She's the favourite. She has all the disabled children
on her, and the ones who can't ride.' And she pointed out to
me a pony which looked hardly bigger than a large dog, who
nevertheless had a child on her so small that his legs barely
reached the beginnings of the stirrup leathers.

'Wouldn't you like a ride, Abi?' I asked her.

'I can't ride,' she said. 'And it's too expensive. Daddy said so.'

'But if I paid for you. And if you went on Tiffany, who's so
gentle and careful.'

Once she understood what I was actually offering her, Abi

could hardly believe her ears. 'You mean I could have a real
ride, on a real pony, like that one? On Tiffany? Really? Oh,
Auntie Caz...'
'Don't call me Auntie, it's loathsome.'
'Oh, Caz, thank you, thank you, thank you.'
Of course we then discovered that Tiffany, being one of the
most popular ponies, was booked for half the morning; so we
decided to go for a walk along the ditch and through the village
and over towards the cliffs, and come back when Tiffany was
free. But after about ten minutes Abi said she couldn't walk
any more, so we sat down in a field and listened to the lark,
miles away up in the empty sky, spraying her notes down
on to us and all the surrounding countryside and the village,
oblivious as to whether or not anyone heard or cared what
she sang. The field was spattered with wildflowers: that tall
yellow one that isn't a buttercup but ought to be; the purple,
bell-shaped one that you get in London, which grows really tall;
something royal blue and foxglovey. And of course the poppy.
Hundreds of them. Normal, proper, old-fashioned red poppies,
not the garish yellow or dignified blue or chilling black poppies
of the Chelsea Flower Show. Just ordinary, happy poppies.
'D'you have a boyfriend, Auntie Caz? I mean Caz?'
'Of course not. Whatever gave you that idea?'
'I thought all grown-ups had boyfriends.'
'Oh, I see. Daddy has a boyfriend, does he?'
'Don't be silly. All lady grown-ups.'
'What about Granny then, eh?'
'She's got a husband, so that doesn't count.'
'Right. So all lady grown-ups have to have either a boyfriend
or a husband?'
'No. Really old grown-ups have husbands. Normal grown-ups
have boyfriends.'
'Don't normal grown-ups get married?'
'No. None of my friends' parents are married.'
'None of them?'
'Uh-uh.' She shook her head. 'Anyway, he doesn't count,
because he falls over.'
'What?' I said, mystified by the turn in the conversation.
'Who doesn't count?'
'Granny's husband. Grandad.'
'Why not?'
'He drinks whisky and falls over. It's very funny.'
'Is it?' I said. I noticed that the lark had given up, and all

ANNE ATKINS

I could hear now was the remote sound of traffic from time
to time, or a child shouting in the village. The horizon was
beginning to shimmer in the heat. I thought perhaps we should
get up and go.
'Yes. Like this,' she said, and staggered to her feet, and started
tripping over the tufts in the grass, shrieking with laughter.
'Come on, Abi, let's go. Let's see if Tiffany's ready.'
'She won't be ready yet.'
'Come on,' I said, and helped her to her feet.
'Ow, you're hurting me! Let go.' And I had to apologise.

Naturally Tiffany was not ready, and we had to wait for ages
while the previous ride finished. But we filled most of the time
finding a hat to fit, and paying for the ride, and talking about
all the things Abi would do in her first half hour in the saddle.
'Will I trot? Will I canter? I'll canter, won't I, Auntie Caz?'
At last she was lifted the tiny distance it was from the
ground to Tiffany's saddle, I put the reins in her hand, and she
burst into tears.
'Please let me down. Please, please, let me down. Oh,
Auntie Caz, please let me down.'
'Just try for a minute or two. You'll get used to it. She's very
gentle.'
'No, no, no. *Please!*' So I lifted her off, sobbing, into my arms,
and we decided to go home for lunch.

I could have slept all afternoon. Or rather, I would have slept
all afternoon if I could have done. After lunch I found a blanket
and the shade of a tree and a cushion, and was just drifting
off when Abi found me and insisted we go down to the sea
front. Not simply the sea, which we did this morning, but the
real promenade, with the stretches of postcard-golden sand,
and the painfully reddening bodies, and the smell of fish and
chips and the dripping icecreams.
I thought I'd stepped back in time, I really did. There they
were, fat greasy families, sitting on a step on the prom on a
boiling hot day, eating warm and greasy fish and chips out of
oily paper, with genteel little organically disposable wooden
forks. Unbelievable. A few yards away, on hired deck chairs,
sat grannies in white cloth sunhats, knitting things; and fathers
with red faces, sitting in the full sun, for goodness' sake. I
mean, sights like these were dated during my childhood, during
my mother's childhood. It was wonderful.

104

The Lost Child

'Can I have an icecream?' Abi sang, and I realised the point
of our mission.

'Certainly not. For all sorts of reasons,' I added, before she
could ask. 'Not least the fact that you're almost certainly not
allowed them. They usually contain poisonous substances.
I don't want to throw my money away. And if that's the
only reason you woke me from my delicious afternoon nap, I
am seriously annoyed with you.'

'It's not the only reason.' Abi was put out. 'I thought you'd
like to see the beach.'

'Thank you,' I said. 'Why?'

'Why what?'

'Why did you think I'd like to see the beach?'

'Because the people look so funny.'

She was certainly right there. Why do the Anglo-Saxon races
look so white and red, fat and stupid when they're on holiday,
especially if they take their holiday by the seaside?

Then I realised what it was that had been troubling me all
day. Ever since I had arrived in Norfolk, twenty-four hours
before, I hadn't seen a single black, or even brown or yellow
face. I hadn't heard a single voice that wasn't speaking English.
It was odd. This was a little England of years and years ago.

As we sat there, Abi and I, facing the sea, watching all
the people, the white, Anglo-Saxon people, passing in front
of us along the prom, we were overtaken by a couple of
teenagers walking together, in step, in those wonderful
heavy boots that come back into fashion every decade or so.
They were, I think, the opposite sex, and as they passed I
thought, That's what I never had. As a teenager. Abi's right:
grown-ups are supposed to have boyfriends, and I never did.
Because of Poppy? Who knows. And if it was because of
her, is there anything to stop me having a boyfriend now? Or
will I live in her shadow always?

And then, as this teenaged couple passed us, I saw
something which, for some reason, struck me as shockingly
neoteric. She – I think it was she – had her hand in his
trousers, down the back of his trousers, in a way that I
suddenly found totally obscene. Not because the gesture was
erotic or sexy, for it was neither of those. Nor because it was
defiant, or possessive, or rebellious, or even just *young*, as it
might have been when I was a teenager, ten years ago or so.
It was simply absolutely and utterly bored. The gesture said to
the world: This is my sexual partner and I couldn't care less.

105

ANNE ATKINS

Perhaps this isn't new, but it seemed to me that when my grandparents were young sex had to do with romance and love, and babies, and risk, and commitment. For my parents it was none of these, but at least it was for fun, or for growing up, or for independence, or just for friendship. Now it has no connotations but death, and necessity, and it has become a bodily function as monotonous as defecating; or perhaps as eating, which may occasionally be enjoyable but is more often simply a biological need. We've gone back full circle and more, beyond the time when sex could endanger the life of a woman nine months after the act: now more people die of sex than are born of it. Has the magic gone altogether?

I glanced at Abi, and she too looked at the couple, and she too looked bored by it all; and yet when we were children we would have hooted with laughter and derision at anything vaguely sexual.

'What did you say you wanted? An icecream?' I said rather absent-mindedly, before suddenly asking her, 'Do you ever think about sex?' expecting a healthy five year old's response: 'Sex? YUK!'

'No,' she said. And that was all.

This evening I asked Ben, for some reason I don't quite understand, if he remembered a holiday in the Cotswolds years and years ago. Perhaps it was the sight of Abi getting on the horse, or the huge Shires reminding me of those fabulous hunters, or simply the peace and refreshment of being in the country, that reminded me.

'Do you remember? They had a shiny blue Aga, and gave us buttered crumpets, and Peter let us all ride on Henry.'

'Who on earth's Henry?' Ben said, pulling off his boots.

'That beautiful grey hunter.'

'Beautiful grey what?'

'Hunter. As in horse.'

'Wait a minute. You're asking me if I remember a horse, called Henry, that I met once – how many years ago did you say?'

'Er ... About fifteen.'

'Caz dearest, I can't remember human beings I've met last week.'

'He sent us a picture afterwards.'

'Who? The horse?'

'Peter.'

The Lost Child

'Oh, wait a minute, was he that famous artist chap? Yes, I remember: Mother made a great fuss about it afterwards. I bet she's still got that picture. If she hasn't sold it.'

'Neither,' I said. 'I've got it.'

'Oh, well done. I should hang on to it, if I were you. Didn't Father reckon Peter's inspiration accounted for the success of those books of yours? Some of the success. I mean, the success of the illustrations. Or rather, I know the words are good too...'

I smiled at dear Ben, trying to make a compliment and then thinking he was making such a hash of it. I don't mind if people think Poppy's contribution is better than mine, as some reviewers have implied.

'I think so,' I said. 'And what's all this about Daddy getting drunk? In front of Abi?'

Ben was bending over, doing up his shoes. When he straightened up, he said, 'Come on, let's go and have supper. I think it'll be ready.'

CHAPTER SIX –
CLANCARTY ROAD, 1990

οἴμοι, πί δράσω; τοὶ φύγω μητρὸς χέρας;

Alas, what can I do? Where can I escape the hand
of my mother?

Euripides, Medea, 1271

It is now a fact that in the affluent west the most
dangerous place for a child to be is in his mother's
womb.

Dr Margaret White, Two Million Silent Killings

The funny thing was, nobody talked about the new baby at all.

After a while, a day or two, Sandy forgot about her. That is to
say, she forgot to think about her. It was like being five; most of
the time you didn't think about it, but you always knew you'd had
your birthday and you weren't four any more. Sometimes you even
forgot that, and for a moment you thought you were four again. But
then immediately you remembered the birthday, and the fact that the
world was different now, and you were glad. Four was all right but
you'd never go back to that now, and you were glad.

It was the same with the baby. Sometimes she'd forget why she
was suddenly happy. She would skip a step, and pick up a stick and
wave it about, and then remember the baby sister and the reason for
the happiness, and be more happy still. And then not think about
her for a long time, after all.

The days came and went. Reading became easier. Maths was easy-peasy. She became better friends with Rachel, and didn't see Ella so much. Then she spent the weekend with Ella and after that they did everything together. But Annie was horrible. When she stayed at Ella's house, Annie frightened them with true stories about a green ghost, and then turned their light off and shut the door, and Ella's mummy didn't come for hours and hours and they cuddled each other and cried and wished Annie would die, or come and open the door. Sandy didn't know sisters could be so beastly. She wondered if Poppy would grow up to be beastly, and frighten her, and lock her in dark rooms and not come back. And she thought, if so, she'd rather her parents didn't have another baby.

Then it was half term. Sandy just woke up one morning, and there it was: half term. Her mummy said would she like to stencil her room?

'What's stencilyourroom?' said Sandy.

'I bought you some stencils,' said Mummy, 'so we can paint pictures all over your walls.'

'But we're not allowed to paint pictures on our walls,' she objected.

'No, I know, but these are special pictures, 'specially for putting on walls, so you are allowed to. Look.'

And Mummy showed them to her. They were beautiful. They were shapes of a kite and two clouds and a sun, cut out of cardboard; and you put them on the wall and then you put paint everywhere you could think of, and when you took the cardboard away the pictures would be all over the walls. And you could do each shape over and over again. Except the sun, of course, because there's only one sun.

'And can we do them, really, really?'

'Really, really,' said Mummy.

So they did.

Mummy wore jeans and a torn old shirt of Daddy's which wouldn't matter if she got paint on it; and Sandy wore nothing, so that it wouldn't matter if she got paint on that either. And to begin with they took it in turns to hold the cardboard and to spray the paint. They didn't paint the paint on with paint brushes. They had it in tins and just pressed a button and it came out. But you had to be careful which way the tin was looking when you pressed the button. After a while they stopped taking it in turns, because Sandy found it hard to hold the shape right up against the wall so that no paint could get through the cracks; so then Mummy held the shapes always, and Sandy did the spraying. They did different colours for different things.

They did the suns yellow, of course. They did lots of suns in the
end, because Mummy thought they looked great; and Sandy thought
perhaps she was right. They did the clouds blue, which was funny,
but the walls were nearly white so white wouldn't have shown up and
Mummy hadn't been able to find a tin of white paint anyway. And
actually the clouds looked all right blue. The kites were the hardest
because they did each quarter of the kite a different colour, so that
took ages, so they didn't do many kites.

It was the best day Sandy had had for years and years and years,
or at least days. After they'd done two and a half whole walls they
sat down on Sandy's bed and looked at it, and thought how brilliant
it was.

'We'll have to give the stencils a rest anyway,' Mummy said, 'because they're going soggy. So we might as well give ourselves a
rest. It looks good, doesn't it?'

It did. Kites and clouds danced in the breeze round the middle of the
room, and suns shone kindly down on them. The real sun shone too,
through the open window, making moving patterns on the warm shiny
wood of the polished floorboards. Sandy watched the dust skipping up
and down in the sun as it streamed in the window. And the sunshine
skipped up and down too, but it was the leaves outside that made the
sun dance so much. If the leaves would only keep still, the sun would
be allowed to keep still too. Though the dust would still dance.

'I wonder if we should have tried to do them higher up,' Mummy
said. 'You know, just under the ceiling. But it would have been very
hard to get both of us up the step ladder.'

'Oh, can we, Mummy? Please let's.'

'I think on balance it might be better if we didn't.'

'Balance on what?' asked Sandy.

'Good grief!' Mummy said suddenly, looking at Sandy and laughing. 'I'm glad you took your clothes off. Look at you!'

Sandy looked. Her tummy was a wonderful rainbow colour, pre-
dominantly blue, but with a generous spray of yellow, green and red.
She laughed too. It looked very interesting.

'Your hair's the best though.' Sandy couldn't see her hair. She was
just going to go to the bathroom when Mummy said, 'Oh, look. How
fantastic! How did you know?'

Daddy had come in with a tray of things. 'For the workers,' he
said. And on the tray were a cup of coffee, a glass of Seven Up, and
two Yorkie bars.

111

ANNE ATKINS

'Thank you, Daddy.'
'You look stunning,' he replied.
'I know. But Mummy says my hair's the best.'
'Yes. I'd go along with that. Could be greener, perhaps. Well,
I'll leave you to get on with it.'
It took them ages to finish. But it did look good. At last Mummy
said, 'That's it. The last one. Good-oh. Thank you for letting me do
that with you. Now, I've actually got quite a lot to do, and we're
going out tonight, so can I leave you to have a bath on your own?'
'What are you going to do?'
'Oh, paperwork. Make a couple of telephone calls and finish off
some letters. Then have a bath after you, and get ready to go out.
Sabine's coming at seven. It looks smashing, it really does. OK, see
you later, darling. Don't forget that bath.'
Sandy looked at her room and smiled. It was alive. All over the
place, out of sight, people were holding kites which flew up into her
bedroom ceiling. Clouds danced round her cupboards. And always,
any time of the day or night, summer or winter, the suns would shine
on to her bedroom.
It was a shame the kites and clouds and suns stopped when they
got to the cupboards. They should have done those really. They
probably would have done if Mummy hadn't had to rush off. Sandy
thought she might as well do them herself. She fetched the chair her
clothes went on, and put it under the cupboard. She had to take
her clothes off it, and put them on the bed. She got a bit of paint
on them from her hands, but it didn't matter; it would wash off.
After all, it would wash off her tummy. And Mummy had got some
on her shirt and hadn't minded. It was quite difficult, standing on the
chair and trying to hold the shape against the cupboard. She thought
perhaps the chair was too small. In the end she decided she'd have to
go down to the kitchen and fetch a stool. The white one would do. It
wasn't too tall, and didn't wobble.
It was much easier from the stool. She did two clouds and three
suns, and only one kite because they were harder. They weren't as
good as the ones she and Mummy had done together, but they still
looked lovely.
When she got down from the stool Sandy thought how nice it
would be to have them on her rug as well. She had a furry white
rug, a sheepskin rug, on her floor; it was soft and silky to walk on
with bare feet, and Sandy always made a point of stepping on it when

112

The Lost Child

she got out of bed. It was much easier to do the shapes on to the rug, because you didn't have to hold the cardboard up against the wall. But when she'd finished they were even more blurry than the ones on the cupboard. After that Sandy did some shapes on to her duvet cover and her sheet, and one cloud on to her pillow. She started doing her chair, but that really was hard because of all the corners; and anyway the paint was beginning to run out. The only tin with much left in was green. She thought she might as well spray it on to her hair because Daddy had said that would look better. So she stood in the middle of the room and pointed it above her head and held her finger down on the button for as long as she could.

'Bloody hell! Oh, bloody hell. Si. Si! Can you come here?'

Sandy's mummy was standing in the doorway, not looking very helpful.

When she went to bed that night Sandy was the most unhappy person in the whole world. Her parents were really, really cruel, and ought to be put in prison like they put adults in prison who are cruel to their children. Mummy and Daddy had both come to kiss her goodnight, but she didn't care. She didn't kiss them back. They were horrible and she was never going to kiss them again.

She waited until the house was quiet and then she let her tears fall. She didn't make a sound. She felt her pillow getting wet, and after a while she sniffed, but that was all. She could hear Sabine talking to Jack in the kitchen. Jack was in his pyjamas, but he didn't have to go to bed yet. After a long time she heard Sabine come upstairs. Then she heard her crossing the landing to Sandy's room. Sandy turned away from the door and looked at the wall. Her nose was full of tears and runny, so she sniffed again, and wiped her face with her duvet. She felt someone sit down on her bed, but she didn't take any notice. Then Sabine's arms were round her and she felt warm and a bit better, and the air all came rushing into her in gasps, and Sabine smoothed the hair off her face and stroked her over and over again; and after a long time Sabine said, in her funny and familiar Swiss voice, 'Would you like a story?'

And Sandy nodded.

She woke up in the middle of the night, when Mummy and Daddy came in, as she often did. Mummy crept into her room to check that her window was open and her duvet was on straight, and then came and gave her a cuddle.

'I'm sorry, darling. I really am. I was tired and very busy, and you know adults can be selfish and bad-tempered, just like children. I love you very very much. And you did your room beautifully.'

But Sandy couldn't remember what on earth her mother was talking about, so she just snuggled up to her and went back to sleep.

She had days and days of half term. It was hot always. She sat in the garden watching little blue butterflies darting through the leaves. She caught lots of ants and woodlice for her Bug Box; the ants crawled out through the air holes into the kitchen, but the woodlice curled up and went to sleep, and by the time somebody reminded Sandy to let them go again at the end of half term, they wouldn't move at all. And she didn't have to do her piano practice at all any day.

At the weekend, on Friday evening in fact, Mummy said London was lousy in this weather and shouldn't they take a picnic to Richard and Sue? Daddy said brilliant idea. Jack said yeah! And when they rang Richard and Sue they said not to bring the picnic, but to leave London as early in the morning as possible to beat the traffic.

So they did.

Richard and Sue have a swimming pool, and a game called 'dead hens', which Sue says is also called badminton but Richard calls it dead hens because you hit dead hens over a net; and they have cats, and a pond, and real doves which have babies. And a big lawn and trees, and you can only be seen in the swimming pool by a tall man on a large horse on the other side of the road. Sandy never understood what the tall man was doing on the large horse on the other side of the road, but it means you don't have to wear things in the swimming pool because he isn't often there. That didn't matter much to Sandy because she didn't need to wear swimming things anyway.

So they swam and swam as much as they wanted, and when they were sick of swimming they ran round the garden or had a drink by the pool, and when they got hot they just got back in the pool again.

Then they had lunch by the side of the pool, under a big sun umbrella, and Sandy thought it was all so good that she said, to everyone in general but also to Mummy and Daddy, 'Can we bring the new baby here after it's born?'

For a moment nobody said anything and people looked at each other; then for another moment everybody stopped looking at everybody; then in the next moment the adults started talking about something else.

'Mummy!' Sandy said. 'It's rude not to answer questions.'

'Yes, darling,' Mummy said. 'We'll talk about it later.'

'Why?' Sandy said.

'Because some things you talk about just as a family, and some things you talk about with other people. This is a family thing.' Mummy was talking just to Sandy, and the other adults were 'specially not listening.

Sandy remembered again in the car on the way home. 'Why wouldn't you tell me if we could bring the baby?' she asked. 'Would Sue and Richard not invite us with the baby?'

'No, it's not that, sweetheart. Not that at all. I think we'll have a talk about the baby. Tomorrow perhaps. Because it affects us all really.'

'What d'you mean?'

'Like we talked about Scotland. Or any decision we make together. We'll have a chat about it tomorrow.'

Sandy wondered what sort of things they'd decide. She thought it would be rather exciting. She would tell everyone that she wanted the name Poppy. She thought the others might easily agree. After all, it was her idea to go to Scotland, and everyone liked that. So she would say she wanted the name Poppy, and she wanted Poppy to share her room. Jack and Barney didn't share a room, but that was because they didn't want to. Anyway, there weren't any more rooms in the house, so she and Poppy would have to share. Poppy would sleep with Mummy and Daddy to begin with; babies always do that, so their mummies can feed them from their breasts when the babies wake up. But after that she would have to sleep with Sandy.

It was after breakfast that they sat down to discuss the baby. They were sitting down already, in fact, because they sat down to have breakfast; but Daddy called it 'sitting down together', even though they already were. Jack wanted to go and finish a model he was making but Daddy said it would be better if he could leave it for a few minutes, if he didn't mind. That's what adults say when they mean even if you do mind.

'Now then,' Daddy said. 'Mummy's pregnant. She didn't get pregnant on purpose; it wasn't planned; it was an accident. Now then . . .' he said again. 'In the old days, I mean up until this century, people couldn't very easily choose when they had babies, or how many they had. We didn't have much control over pregnancy then. The Victorians often used to have about ten children, or more, and often lots of them would die. Nowadays we have far fewer children and they hardly ever die, which is much better.'

ANNE ATKINS

Jack was already looking bored.

'But now that we've got more choice, we have more responsibility too. In the past people just put up with it, and looked after their children as best they could. But now we have no excuse for ever bringing a child into the world which isn't wanted. So this means we have a decision to make. We have to decide whether to have the baby or not. And because the decision will affect you, we want to know what you think about it. We want to hear your opinions. We won't necessarily do what you want, but we promise to listen to what you say.'

Sandy was listening very carefully, but even so she didn't understand very well. The baby was already there, wasn't it? She was in Mummy's tummy. She was the size of a pear. Though of course she wouldn't look like a pear in other ways. And she was wanted, wasn't she? Sandy could see that there might be other people, bad people perhaps, who didn't like babies. But her parents loved babies. All good people loved babies. That's what babies are for. And her parents loved her and Barney and Jack.

It was her mother talking now. 'You see, with any choice, you have to look at what you'll gain or lose if you make that choice. Obviously we'd gain a baby, which would be lovely. In some ways. But children are a very big commitment to look after. And the more children we have, the less we can spend on each of you. Not just the money. That's not particularly important. But time too. We'd have less time for each of you. And there'd be less space in the house. And one of us would have to give up work for a while, which would be very difficult.

'Do you all understand?'

'Yeah,' said Jack.

'Not really,' said Barney. 'What do you mean?'

'Look at it this way, Barney,' Daddy said. 'At the moment we can afford to go away for holidays, and buy you things you need when you need them, and even send you away to boarding-school if that's what you want. If we have the baby we'll have to cut back. I don't want you to get the wrong idea. Life isn't just about money. But you must count the cost of anything you decide to do, and that includes the financial cost. So, for instance, we wouldn't be able to go for such expensive holidays. We could go and stay with Grandfather instead perhaps.'

'Do you mean I wouldn't get my tennis racquet next birthday?' asked Jack.

'Well, that sort of thing,' Daddy said. 'Perhaps. But you shouldn't see it as a choice between a baby and a tennis racquet, Jack. I'm just trying to give you an example.'

'Well, I don't want a baby,' Jack said simply.

'I see.' Daddy sighed. 'I see, Jack. You don't want to think about it any more than that?' Jack shrugged. He wanted to go and finish his model. 'Barney, what about you?'

'I don't mind,' he said. 'But I'd like to go to boarding-school. And I like our holidays.'

Daddy turned to Sandy. He put his arm round her and kissed her. He seemed to Sandy to be very gentle. 'Sandy? What about you?'

Barney had read the beginning of *Alice in Wonderland* to Sandy once. Alice falls and falls and falls, and for ever and for ever doesn't seem to hit the bottom. Sandy felt as if she were falling and falling too. When she spoke her voice came out all small and squeaky, and it didn't sound like her at all.

'Daddy?'

'Yes, darling?'

'What will happen to the baby?'

'You mean if we don't have it?'

'Mmm,' Sandy said, and the sound hardly came out at all.

'It's called a termination, sweetheart. It means ending. It means you stop the baby growing and don't let it be born and become a person.'

There was a small silence.

'What about you, Si? What do you want?' Mummy asked.

Daddy didn't look at her when he answered. He sighed again. 'It's not quite like our summer holidays, this. It's not a decision where we all have an equal say. You see, there's one person who'll be influenced much more than the rest of us by this decision, isn't there?'

Sandy nodded. She thought of Poppy, the size of a pear, in a little pink bonnet and sucking her thumb.

'Mummy, obviously. For myself, I'd like to have another baby. I think the financial considerations are secondary. We'd make do. But it's Mummy's body, and I really can't ask her to have a baby she doesn't feel she can cope with. No man can make that decision for a woman.

'And Mummy doesn't want to have the baby. At least, in some way she does. In some ways she'd love to. But, being realistic, she doesn't think she can cope.'

They all looked at each other. Jack looked questioningly at his father, asking with his face if he could go. Daddy looked at Sandy. 'What about you, darling?'

Sandy blinked. She would keep the tears down if she had to fight them with all her body. She held her bottom lip with her teeth. Under the table her hidden fists kept seizing the air and letting go again in a quick little rhythm. She knew what she could say. She would save up all her pocket money for all her life for the baby. She would give up school to look after her, so Mummy needn't give up work. She would do her washing: Barney and Jack needn't help. She could even feed her with a bottle like some people did, if Mummy was too busy to feed her properly. But somehow she knew these minute arguments of delicate and fragile logic would be useless against the vast tidal wave of adult feeling. All she had was her vote; her tiny little vote.

She looked at the middle of the table cloth, at a petal that had fallen from the vase. The sweet pink of it had begun to turn brown.

'I want to keep the baby,' she said; and her voice was tiny too.

There was silence for a moment. Then Jack said, 'Please may I get down?'

'Yes, Jack, in a minute. Well, Sandy. You're good at maths. Even with you and me wanting the baby, we don't have a majority, do we? Never mind, sweetheart. There'll be other things to look forward to. We all have disappointments. And it's a very good lesson to learn. We can never have everything we want in life. You're learning that now. That's good, you know, sweetie, because it means you won't have to learn it later. Yes, Jack, you can get down.'

Jack and Barney left the room. Mummy took Sandy's hand and held it in hers.

'Sandy, darling, I'm sorry. You must be very disappointed.' Mummy sighed. 'You see, I got quite depressed when I was pregnant . . . when I was last pregnant. Depressed means sad, but much worse than sad. Sad in a way that sort of destroys you. It wasn't anyone's fault. I love all three of you very much and I'm more pleased than anything that I've got you all. But I was quite ill, and couldn't be a proper mother to anyone, and I had to keep going to the doctor to be cheered up.' She smiled. 'It was beastly. I was horrible to everyone. I really don't think I could go through it again. And I'd much rather have more time with you, than have to worry about a new baby all over again.'

Sandy tried to nod, to pretend she understood. She took her hand out of Mummy's, and after a little while Mummy gave her a kiss and got up and left the room.

Then Daddy got up too. He was only going to put the kettle on to make Mummy a cup of coffee, but Sandy thought he was going to leave the room as well.

'Daddy!' It came out all funny, and for a moment Sandy wondered if it was really she who'd spoken. But Daddy turned and came and sat down next to her. He put his arm round her. It was no good. She couldn't keep them down. They were coming, and there was no controlling them.

'But, Daddy, what about the baby?'

'What about it, love? There won't be a baby now.'

'What about the baby?' And they came. In great heaves and sobs they came, shaking her over and over again in Daddy's arms. He couldn't hear her words, or understand them, she was crying so much. She must make him hear. She must make him understand. Because Daddy was fair and good, and when he understood, he'd know it would make a difference.

She took a huge breath, and shook. She clenched her fists again, and determined to stop crying long enough to say it.

'What about the baby's vote?' Because that would be three against three.

And then she gave in, and let Daddy kiss her, and cover her face with his handkerchief, and hold her tightly for ever.

That night, an age later, when Sandy lay in bed with her cuddly smiling monster, no tears came. She looked out on the empty summer night, and felt nothing at all.

Elsewhere in the house life went on. Jack was still up, finishing his model. It had gone wrong, and he had had to start again, and it had taken him all day. Barney lay in bed reading *Questions and Answers*, and learning what kept a bird in the air. Amanda and Simon sat in the kitchen with some Brie and a bottle of wine, trying to think of an extra special treat for Sandy; while from the next room, on Simon's CD player, Rigoletto mumbled angrily in a beautiful bass as he plotted horrible murders to avenge his violated daughter.

It was the last and smallest member of the family who looked forward to the most blissful sleep. Snug and warm in her mother's womb, she knew nothing of the agonies and worries the others had to endure. She listened to the gurgles made by the supper, and the steady and comforting sound of the voice she already knew so well. She even heard, in the blurred and murky distance, the dip and thrill of another human voice, as Gilda died in her father's arms at the hands of his hired assassin; and the song Dame Kiri sang was as sweet and incomprehensible as a bird's at an open window on a summer's night. The child's eyes, as she listened, were not yet open: most of the time, in any case, there was nothing to see in the warm dark night of her world. Only when her mother was briefly naked in the bathroom, or by her bedroom window, the dim promise of a future dawn seeped through the darkness. Meanwhile the world heaved and pitched around her, lively with noise and movement, and she loved it and turned in delight.

This world around her, she knew without knowing it, was dedicated to her safety. Her mother's body would starve itself sooner than let her go hungry. Her mother's womb would shield her from the cold, and cushion her from violence, and continually keep her protected and nourished.

At last her parents stopped talking: they had decided on her future, and there was little more to be said. Verdi also finished his complaint: the child was dead, and the father mourned, and there was no more to be said there either. The warm red glow that should soon become her gentle daylight was extinguished, and she already half knew to anticipate the relative stillness of a pleasantly turning and rumbling night.

She knew nothing of the plans her sister had for her. How they were to have picked the wildflowers together, and worn matching sunhats, and shared makeup; how Sandy was to have read to her late at night until she could read for herself; how they were to have chosen together next time what pictures to paint on the walls.

She knew none of this. Nor did she know anything of the other, rather different, plan being laid for her.

She turned over again, and settled down for sleep. Suddenly, for the first time in her short life, she found something in her mouth. She sucked it. It felt good. And that was how she fell asleep, with her thumb in her mouth.

She was in the safest place in the world.

CHAPTER SEVEN –
PERRYMEAD STREET

μήκων δ'ὣς ἑτέρωσε κάρη βάλεν, ἥ τ'ἐνὶ κήπῳ,
καρπῷ βριθομένη νοτίῃσί τε εἰαρινῇσιν.

He dropped his head to one side like a poppy in a
garden, weighed down by its seed and the gentle
showers of spring.

Homer, Iliad, *8, 306–7*

Of course there were times when Poppy was a little terror. Being
the youngest by more than six years, she had affection lavished on
her. Even Jack, scrupulously objective and very particular about his
possessions, was seldom cross with Poppy even if she wandered into
his room, which no one else was ever allowed to do without his
permission. Barney was so gentle he seldom argued with any of us
anyway. Funnily enough, I was the one who used to argue with Poppy
more than anyone else, when she drew pictures on my books or wore
my favourite bangles or necklaces and then lost them; but our disagree-
ments never lasted more than a minute or two. Poppy would say, 'I'm
soo sorry,' in her irresistible way, whether or not she'd done anything
wrong, and it was impossible even for another child not to forgive her.

I can see now, with hindsight, that it was my father who really
doted on her. He's a demonstrative man anyway, never economical
with physical affection. When we were younger we often romped in
my parents' bed in the morning, or called my father into our rooms
for a cuddle late at night. My mother loved us dearly, but I think she
could have survived without close physical contact in a way that he
never could.

By the time Poppy was born my brothers had grown out of this sort of thing. Barney would still take a brief hug from his father, but Jack's contact had been reduced to the occasional arm round the shoulders. And then suddenly my father had a baby again, a girl like me who need never grow out of his caresses. I'm sure none of us felt he treated us unfairly, but in my memories I can see him pouring on her even more affection than he'd given the rest of us. From the age of two or three, Poppy often crept out of my bed in the night, when I was asleep, and into my father's or less often my mother's arms, and would be in their bed instead of mine in the morning. At an age when the rest of us would have kissed my parents on the cheek, Poppy kissed my father, and my grandfather, on the lips. While I might give a sparse hug or kiss to an adult visitor and my brothers would shake hands, Poppy would kiss indiscriminately over and over again.

Surprisingly, she was the one who got homesick if she was away, who couldn't cope without my parents, who cried if she was separated from them for any length of time. She and I went to stay with our grandfather for half term once, when I was twelve and she was six. Even though she was with me, she cried and wept when my father left us behind, and after several days wrote my mother a heart-rending letter.

'Dear Amanda,' she wrote, in a very careful and precise hand, with her new fountain pen which she'd just been given, 'I hope you're having a nice time. I'm not. I'm missing you terribly and I want to go home.' (She was a meticulous speller even then; better than I was at twice her age.) 'I heard about the blackbird's nest and babies, Er it was very interesting. Love Poppy.'

That holiday – the half term when she wanted to go home – was when we wrote our first real book together.

Grandfather was nearly eighty by then, and had settled into the lifestyle of a lonely old man. It was obvious even to us that he didn't eat much on his own, but he had made a big effort for our visit, buying in breaded chicken 'bites', and oven chips, and lots of fresh fruit which he knew we liked, and cooked beetroot. I helped him get the meals as best I could, undomesticated as I was, and a kind of frightening sadness came over me as I realised I was looking after someone who was supposed to be looking after me.

His old-fashioned house amused me, and I kept trying to persuade him to make his life easier.

'Why don't you have a microwave, Grandfather? Nobody cooks

on these things any more, except, you know, full-time housewives and professional cooks.'

'Well, that's what I am. A full-time housewife and professional cook.'

'Yes, but Grandfather, you don't know how to cook anything but hamburgers anyway. If you got a little microwave you could get a week's worth of meals from your supermarket and just pop them in. And you can get dishwashers for one person, you know.'

'And then what would I do with my time, young lady? Nobody wants to learn classics any more, so I have time on my hands as it is.'

'I want to learn classics. Will you teach me? My school says I won't do classics at my new school. Everyone has to study modern European languages now.'

'What?' he said, appalled. 'St Paul's won't teach you classics? St Paul's used to be one of the finest girls' schools there was, a few years back.'

'None of them teaches classics any more, not unless you drop half a dozen other subjects to do it. That's what my school says anyway. Latin's not on the curriculum and my school says even universities don't want it any more. Will you teach me?'

'And me,' Poppy said. 'What's classics?'

And then my grandfather sat down at an old round polished table, which we weren't allowed to put hot mugs on in case we took the polish off, and pulled down one or two old, dog-eared school textbooks which looked as if school boys had flicked ink on them in the 'fifties, and started to tell us about Agamemnon and Cassandra, and Clytemnestra and her lover, and Helen and all the trouble she'd caused, and the question of whether or not it was her fault; and all the supper burned while we sat there, and we didn't particularly mind because everything Grandfather served was always over-cooked anyway.

On our second morning there, Grandfather said, 'Heffer's Bookshop was asking after you.'

'What?' we asked him.

'Chap called Marcus. Said he still remembers you. Didn't you win a competition with them, Sandy?'

'That was ages ago,' I said. 'Yonks and yonks.'

'Well, he was talking about it. He's leaving the bookshop in a couple of months to work for a publisher. But he said why don't you write again, because the publisher he's moving to is looking for stories by children. He said write him something and get your sister to draw the pictures.'

'My sister? How did he know I had a sister?' I said, forgetting he'd written to her too.

''Course he knew about me,' Poppy said. 'Who's Marcus?'

'I don't know how he knew. He just did. Anyway, I thought it would give you something to do.'

'I don't write stories any more,' I said, as if I'd grown out of a very childish phase. 'I write poems now. Sonnets, mostly.'

'Well, write him a sonnet then. I'm sure Poppy could illustrate a sonnet, couldn't you, Poppy?'

''Course,' she said. 'What do they look like?'

But I did write a story in the end. I chose one of the stories Grandfather had been teaching us about, and I told it as if for Poppy. It was probably because of this that she was able to illustrate it so well.

It was the story of Philomela and Procne. I can't remember why Grandfather had chosen such an unpleasant story for his granddaughters, but it caught our imagination – I suppose because it focuses on a fierce love between two sisters which endures beyond adulthood and marriage and cruelty and separation. I think we liked to think of ourselves being heroic in similar circumstances. And of course anything which involves people turning into animals, or in this case birds, to escape a horrible end at the eleventh hour always makes a good story.

And I was fascinated by the infanticide. I asked my grandfather innumerable questions about Procne's behaviour.

'But *how* did she kill him?'

'I don't think the story says,' Grandfather replied. 'I'll look it up under one of the other references, but this one we have here doesn't tell us. Except that she must have cut his head off.'

'How old was he?'

'Itylus? He was six, I think.'

'I'm six,' said Poppy.

'But *why*, Grandfather? I don't understand why she did it,' I persisted.

'Well, it was an ancient feminist protest, I suppose. Like *Medea*. Men could be pretty beastly in those days, and what else could she do?'

'But didn't she love him?'

'Her son? Indeed she did: she died of grief afterwards. She and her sister. That's why nightingales and swallows have such sad voices.'

'Then why did she do something which would upset her even more than it would upset her husband?' I wanted to like Procne, as her story was such a romantic one, but she did seem to me to have behaved idiotically.

'Ah, now, some people would say that's what Women's Lib. is all about,' Grandfather said with a bit of a twinkle in his eye. 'Cutting off your nose to spite your face. I wouldn't say that. I wouldn't dare: your mother would give me a frightful ticking off. But it's only a story, darling. You mustn't take it too seriously.'

The children's story which we made out of it – I say we, even though I did all the writing: Poppy's pictures told the story as much as my words did – concentrated on the sisters' lives together. Poppy showed them picking flowers in a meadow, and asleep in the same bed, and even pulling each other's hair. I was Procne, of course, the elder sister. The one who had left home first. Or rather, Procne was drawn to look like me.

One of the most interesting of Poppy's pictures was her depiction of Philomela sewing her tapestry, the piece of work which told in pictures, after she could no longer speak, the terrible thing which had been done to her. Because Poppy couldn't sew and knew nothing about embroidery, she had given Philomela a paintbrush instead of a needle. And there Philomela sat, looking just like Poppy, concentrating over her paper; and in the picture which Philomela painted, the whole story of her abuse and mutilation was told again in miniature.

Poppy's last picture was of the nightingale. The picture was so dark you could hardly make out the little brown bird in the middle. But you could make out the tears because they'd been left unpainted, so they shone white in the darkness.

'But she sang,' I objected. 'She didn't cry, she sang.'

'She couldn't sing, could she, stupid?' Poppy replied. 'She hadn't got a tongue.'

I thought about this for a minute, and couldn't come up with an answer to it. 'But shouldn't the birds be together at the end?' I said, by way of changing the subject. I felt it unfair of Poppy to steal the limelight by featuring in the last picture in the book, even disguised as a dark bird on a pitch black night. 'The sisters should be together at the end. So it's a sort of happy ending.'

'But it wasn't a happy ending, was it? One was a nightingale, and the other was a swallow. They never would have seen each other again. One would've been around at night, and the other one during the day.'

There was no answer to this either. But it made the story far sadder than I'd realised. At least, I thought, the sisters flew off together; with Procne's son, Itylus, as a sand-hopper. I'd imagined them playing together again, but this time all three of them. Singing in a garden together; hopping from branch to twig on the same tree; basking in the sun. But now, I thought, they wouldn't even have Itylus: presumably sand-hoppers live on a beach, whereas nightingales and swallows . . . my bird-lore gave out at this point, but I had a feeling they weren't particularly seaside creatures.

It was ages before I worked out that Poppy had got the last picture wrong. No, the picture wasn't wrong, but her explanation of it was: I was the one crying in the last picture, not Poppy. Because the nightingale was of course Procne, the elder sister, whose tongue hadn't been cut out. It was the younger sister, the swallow, who had no voice.

When we'd finished our story, Grandfather said we must take it to the bookshop. But first we had to choose a title. 'The Lost Poppy,' my sister said immediately.

'What?' I said.

'Lost Poppy. That's the name of the story,' she explained.

'Whatever for?' I said.

'Because the younger sister gets lost.'

'But she wasn't called Poppy!' I protested.

''Course she was,' Poppy said. 'She was the younger sister, wasn't she? And her name begins with a "pe", even though you think it's going to be a "fe".' Poppy was proud of her level of literacy. 'The Lost Poppy,' she repeated.

'No,' I said firmly. 'I'm going to call it Song in the Dark,' I decided.

'You WHAT?!' asked Poppy, as if I'd suggested The Secret Underwear of Boadicea.

'Because,' I said, 'that's what it's about. The older sister has to spend the rest of her life singing about what happened to her younger sister, because her younger sister hasn't got a tongue.'

'So?' said Poppy.

'And she has to sing in the dark, when nobody's listening, because she's a nightingale.'

'So?' she repeated.

126

'So it's a good title. Meaningful.'

Poppy clicked her tongue, which she'd recently learned to do. ''S daft,' she said. 'Nobody'll understand it.'

So we had to appeal to Grandfather. He suggested *Singing a Song in the Dark in a Field Full of Lost Poppies*, which we both thought hadn't got quite the 'shelf shout' we were looking for. Then he suggested *Flower of the Field*, because that is what a poppy is, and he explained that it was a reference to the ephemeral nature of all human existence. I was just getting interested in Grandfather's explanation of the origin of the word 'ephemeral', and excited by the beautiful language in the leather-bound King James Bible which he had opened in front of me, when I realised that this title was also based on the assumption that the younger sister was called Poppy, and – which was worse – suggested that the whole story was about her.

'All right,' Grandfather said. 'Why don't you call it *The Lost Child*, because then it'll be about both sisters. The younger one, because she loses her childhood at the hands of the wicked king. And the older one, because she literally loses her child.'

So *The Lost Child* it was.

Funnily enough, after the conversation I went back to the story and gave the younger sister the nickname 'Poppy' after all, I still don't quite know why.

Then there was the question of writing it up. My grandfather had no computer, which worried me considerably. 'How will we type it up and print it out?'

'Your handwriting's very neat and legible. We can send it like this.'

But I wouldn't have it. Grandfather even rang Marcus, at Heffer's, and asked if a handwritten submission would be acceptable. Marcus said of course it would, but this wasn't good enough for me. In the end Grandfather got down his old Olivetti typewriter which he used for very official letters, and had to type my story out for me. I still wasn't fully satisfied, as it wasn't properly formatted, and right-margin-justified, and all that sort of thing. But Grandfather said it was perfectly all right, and he wouldn't type it out again.

All three of us went into the bookshop to hand it in. We had to go in by bus, as there was no parking in the city centre. This was probably just as well: even I was beginning to see what my father meant about Grandfather's bloody awful driving.

Marcus wasn't at all as I'd expected him. The name had conjured up a tall, very good-looking, dark-haired young man with rather intellectual spectacles. His handwriting, which I now remembered from his letters several years before, had suggested someone young and artistic. But Marcus, to my dismay, was middle-aged, and had no spectacles at all, intellectual or otherwise.

He was thrilled to see us. He took us into a little office at the back of the shop, and offered Grandfather a mug of coffee or tea. Grandfather said he'd like coffee, and perched on one of the two hardbacked wooden chairs that were in there. 'And what about you two?' he asked us. 'Tea or coffee, or, um, orange squash? Please sit down,' he said to me, indicating the only chair left. 'And you must be Poppy. Would you like to sit on my desk, Poppy? Don't mind the books and things. Would you like to be lifted up? Or do you climb, or what?'

Marcus was one of those delightful grown-ups who 'knows nothing about children', and understands them all the better for it. Goodness knows how he came to be in charge of the Children's Department in such an important shop since he must have been a childless bachelor. He was the sort of man his sisters would dismiss as being hopeless because he wouldn't know how to tell children off if they put their fingers in the jam and then spread them all over the walls. But he treated us, not just as normal people, which in itself would have given us dignity enough, but as if we were celebrities already; as if a famous writer and her illustrator had visited his humble office before their public book-signing session at the front of the shop.

He loved our story, or said he did. 'I won't look at it properly now,' he said, 'but these pictures – oh, isn't that lovely? And a classical story, how clever. I'm sure you're going to be very talented, you two. Well, I mean you are already, aren't you? Now there are going to be an awful lot of entries, so you mustn't be disappointed . . . But we'll just keep our fingers crossed. Ooh, I do hope your story gets in.'

I think we were rather discouraged that Marcus wasn't going to be the person choosing the stories. Nevertheless, he gave us each a sticker from the Children's Department, and showed us what new books he'd just had in, and told us to keep writing even if we didn't have any luck this time, and thanked us very much for visiting him. Eventually we said our rather stilted goodbyes, and went to catch the bus home again.

It was nearly six months before we heard that our story had been accepted, and would be one of a dozen stories to be published, written by children for children.

My greatest sadness, then as now, was that my grandfather never knew. He died of a stroke, doing his garden, three weeks before we received the letter.

8 June, Tuesday, Norfolk

Today it was the windmill.

I seem to remember a time when children read, or drew, or slept, or at least sat quietly in front of the television. But no: with Abi we've got to be on the go all the time.

I asked Suki how she and Ben cope, with both of them working flat-out on the farm, and no nanny or anything. She said they don't really: Abi is simply bored much of the time. The Only Child Syndrome, or modern childhood. Though it's better now she's at school, Suki said. At the moment she's happy there because she's just started; but the school only has twenty-four children, aged five to ten, all in the same class with one teacher, so of course her interest may not last. Though Ben says the teacher does very well, and even the older children seem to learn. The authorities have tried to close the school down often enough and make the children go to Fakenham, fifteen miles away or so, but many of the families which use the school can't afford a car, so the government would have to provide a bus, and the parents have managed to make it all sound so complicated that the plans keep getting shelved.

We had to visit Cley windmill today. Funnily enough, I believe my mother took me there when I was little. That is to say, I know she did. I've had the photographs for years to prove it. The two of us went away on holiday on our own. I don't know why. I was only about three, so it can't have been to make up for anything. And there I am, in the photos, in a sweet little pair of bluey-green cotton shorts, with a T-shirt to match, and a big straw hat to keep the sun off, at the beginning of a walk, sniffing the petals of an exquisite dusty-pink wild rose which rambled all over the front of the squat, friendly, fifteenth-century cottage which we'd borrowed for the week – I think it belonged to a friend of my grandfather's: probably a don or somebody. And then there's another one of me, further on during the walk, with an armful of wildflowers, grinning happily into the camera. Of course there are plenty more pictures of that holiday, all bathed in the light of a midsummer sun: of me

in pretty, sprigged-cotton pyjamas, running round a garden
which is beautifully but casually kept, a garden rioting with
colour; then in a simple loose summer pinafore and the same
huge hat, proudly doing the washing-up while still smiling
madly at the camera; and, twenty minutes later, in the same
dress and hat and cool kitchen, asleep at the scrubbed wooden
table with my head on my hands.

But the pictures I'm thinking of now are the ones of that
walk to the mill. It was some walk, for a three year old: a
good mile or so. And the photograph which was my mother's
favourite was also the funniest. I had obviously asked her if
I could take a picture. She must have said yes, and given me
her camera; in order to explain to me how to use it, she had
crouched on her haunches, presumably to be my height, the
better to talk to me, and she had started to demonstrate how
I should hold the camera and look through the viewfinder and
wait until I could see her face before pressing the button. But
by the time she reached this part of the lesson I had obviously
long since pressed it. And the photograph shows a brown
slender squatting leg, and a plimsoll, and one hand holding an
imaginary camera, with a wedding ring on the fourth finger,
for my mother was, is, left-handed. Funny: I never remembered
seeing her with a wedding ring, but there's the proof
that she must have worn it once.

She loved that photograph, and I think I can see why. Even
now I can't think of it without feeling a stab of anger. At what?
The memory of fun and games; what she was once like to be
with?

Abi and I drove round for a while looking for that same
cottage. Then, after going through a ford that I didn't
remember at all, and down a couple of very unlikely-looking
overgrown country lanes, we suddenly came across it. And
nothing had changed at all. Not the village, nor the huge
church built on those long-ago wool profits, nor the pub, nor
the cottage itself, exactly as it is in those photographs, even
down to the very same rose still higgledy-piggledy all over the
whitewashed wall. So we parked on the green and agreed to
walk the mile or so to the mill.

It was hot, just as it must have been when my mother and
I walked there; and every so often we sat on a stone step,
or rested on a verge by the side of the road, or picked some
flowers. Abi picked a couple of poppies, before commenting on

the horrid smell they left on her hands. Once or twice we were passed by bicycles. Never by a car.

The mill is now an hotel, privately owned and full of en suite bathrooms, so we couldn't go round inside it. But Abi was most impressed, as we sat afterwards in the garden of a pub and I drank a boring cappuccino while she had a kiwi and mango juice, when I told her I'd once seen the sails being hung.

Because, of course, having to write it down has brought it all back to me.

And, yes, I have to admit, I'm thinking of London all the time. Thinking of the task I have to go back and finish. Wondering whether I can cancel the book. Knowing I've got to write it, to get Poppy out of my system, and the curse she put on all of us through no fault of her own. We've kept it hidden all these years: why should we shock people now? And the worst of it is that most people of my parents' generation, people who were in their twenties and thirties, or a bit more, at the end of the twentieth century, won't be shocked at all.

But it isn't only that which draws my thoughts back to London. If I can go through with this, if I can go through the painful, cathartic process, then perhaps I can start again. Perhaps I can have friendships I haven't had before. Or one friendship in particular.

Yes, all right, I confess: I'm thinking of him every minute of every day. And no, it's not love, or anything daft like that. It's simply the relief of having a good friend. Someone I can talk to. Someone who understands what I mean almost before I've said it. Someone I can be honest with, and tell about my childhood, and my adolescence, and even Poppy; and he won't ridicule me, or even look at me with puzzlement, but will understand.

So even while I go on these delightful outings with Abi, I think of him, and how well he'd get on with her, and how they'd be instant friends because they're both such good friends of mine. And it hurts, thinking of him hurts like a physical pain; like an ache inside; like a hunger.

So it was partly also my new friendship that I was running away from in London?

11 June, Friday, Norfolk

Went for a last swim yesterday morning before leaving Ben's:
swam out with the current and the wind, all the way along
to where the lifeboat is housed, and where the early-morning
fishing boats come down on to the beach. And the seagulls
perched on those tall posts – goodness knows what they're for
– like bored sentries with nothing better to do, and every so
often one would decide to give way to another, and fly off low
across the sea, dropping a liquid pellet on the waves.
Coming back was much harder because I was into the
wind and into the sun. Once, the low, bright morning sun
went behind a cloud and I could see where I was going for a
minute or two, though the wind still blew spray in my face
and waves over my head. But it didn't last long, and soon I
was fighting again with white flashes when I opened my eyes
and red flashes when I shut them, and even when I turned
on my back and tried backstroke, with the spray kicking the
sunlight, still the wind would flip little waves over my head
and leave me gasping, so that I felt I was dealing with a
naughty child who was getting the better of me. In the end I
waded in to shore and ran back along the sand. As I towelled
my hair and put on a jumper I saw the black, pirate-like
cormorant skimming the water, leaving the inevitable splash
behind him on the sea before swooping up behind a seagull on
his perch, and usurping his place.
Abi and I went for a last walk through the fields, with the
tall grasses tickling our thighs and the sun beating down on us,
and the birds calling and quarrelling and flirting and chuckling.
'I want to show you something,' she said. 'It's a secret and it's
very important and you're not to tell anyone. Do you promise?'
'I'll try.'
She looked at me sideways, as if not sure whether this was
good enough, but eventually seemed to think it would have to
do. 'It's a long way,' she said. 'The other side of the Hundred
Acer Wood.' This wood is in fact a small conservation wood
on my brother's land, not a hundred acres or anything like it.

133

Abi and I simply call it that out of affection for a certain bear. When we got to the other side of it, we climbed over a little fence and Abi said proudly, 'There!' and opened her arms wide as though to embrace the world.

It was quite a sight. I believe this part of Norfolk has a number of these poppy fields; in fact I think the area is sometimes nicknamed 'Poppyfields', so this is presumably only one of many. Nevertheless it looked lovely. Like straw blonde hair threaded with bright scarlet ribbons. Like a cloud of red hovering in the ears of the corn. Like poppies. We held hands and looked at it together.

'It's a beautiful secret,' I said.

'Why have you got to go, Auntie Caz?' she asked after a moment's pause.

'Don't call me Auntie.'

'But why?'

'Well, I don't live here, for a start.'

'But you could, though. You could.'

'And I have my work to do. And my house.'

'You could do your work here. You can do your work anywhere. It's not like being a farmer.'

'Could I heck. You'd have me exhausted all the time.'

'I wouldn't. Really I wouldn't. I'd help.'

'Would you?'

'Yup. I'd turn your computer on for you, and suggest words when you couldn't think of any, and ... you know.'

'Thanks.'

Abi, quite rightly, ignored the irony. 'I wish you'd stay, though.'

'Why?' I was genuinely interested. What was a dreary spinster aunt to a child of Abi's age?

'I'm so lonely.' Suddenly she seemed much older than her nearly-six years. I know children of that age can be bored, even when blessed with masses of things to do. But for a child to be lonely when surrounded by people seemed more shocking, somehow.

'But why? You have Ben and Suki. And school, and all your friends there.'

'I know,' Abi admitted. 'I don't know why. Mummy and Daddy are busy trying to make the farm pay,' she added lamely, as if that helped to explain it. I must say I had been taken aback at how hard-up my brother is. I know farming hasn't paid well for generations, but I hadn't realised, until this summer, quite how devastating the effects of Europe, and the shrinking population, had been for people like Ben. It seems astonishing that anyone outside the Third World bothers to produce food at all, except to feed their immediate families. Perhaps they won't soon, and we'll simply import it all.

'Come on,' I said, and pulled Abi to her feet. 'You wanted a last day at the beach. Let's go and get your things.' We went back home, through the little wood by their house, under the dark cool leaves of the young oaks and beeches, over the stiles, round a stagnant brackish pond and along the clean, rustling stream that runs nearly up to the kitchen door. When we'd got a picnic and Abi's bucket and spade we jumped in the car and headed for the little seaside town, she of the icecreams and fish-and-chips and grannies on their deckchairs.

And we did it all. Made a sandcastle, topped with pebbles instead of flags, with a deep moat around it in the vain and idle hope that the tide would not be able to get beyond the moat and pull the castle down. Sat in the chilly breeze and ate sandwiches with sand in them and drank luke-warm stewed tea from our thermos. Went for a walk up the little hill and watched people in their sixties on the putting-green talking about how much it had all changed. Wondered what the fairy lights along the prom will look like in August when they are all lit up at night. And I gave in and bought Abi a disgusting-looking cerise-coloured icecream which she dribbled all over her jumper.

I had foolishly thought the leisured unwaged went abroad now, to Israel and the Nile and the Black Sea for their holidays. But here they all were, as English as ever, still playing Bingo and eating chips on the prom, and it made me feel very comforted somehow.

Ben and Abi drove me to the station just after lunch. Suki had given me a packet of sandwiches and fruit to eat on the train, and I handed it to Abi in the back of the car to put in my handbag.

'What's this Auntie? I mean, Caz?'

'DON'T touch that.' I said, just like any harassed parent. 'That unlocks my whole house. Have you touched the button?'

'I don't know. Have I unlocked your house?'

'Luckily probably not from this distance, but you never know. Leave it alone.'

'What's this?'

'My computer *put it back* please.'
'Abi don't be a pain,' Ben said, waiting for some cows to cross the road.
'Why haven't you used it? And why hasn't your mobile rung for you?'
'Put it back *please* Abi. Because I've been on holiday, so I diverted my calls to my agent. She would ring in an emergency.'
'Then why did you bring them both, and why haven't you got a videophone?'
'Because I carry them everywhere with me just in case, and because I think they're vile.'
'What's this, Caz?'
'My diary and it's private can I have it please!'
'Abi, are you being a nuisance?' Ben contributed, with his eyes on the road.
'Who's Will?'
'A friend of mine and can I have it back please?'
'He's on nearly every page.'
'Is he, can I have it back please Abi?'
'Is he?' Ben turned into the station.
'Why are you getting cross, Auntie Caz, and going red?'
'Because you're being a blasted little pest! Give it here.'
When they were waving me off, Ben said, 'We're always here. If you need us. Any time.' He doesn't often say that sort of thing.
'And listen ... Caz. Don't be too hard on yourself. Or anyone else for that matter. Bye, old thing.' He hugged me.
'Bye, un-Auntie Caz.'
Bye.

CHAPTER EIGHT –
CLANCARTY ROAD, 1990

Almost all the evil things that have been done in
the world in the last decades, have been done in
the name of justice, equality, and compassion.

Malcolm Muggeridge

All revolutions in ethics are preceded by a revolution in language . . . Beware of people who use
a Latin word when there's a perfectly good Anglo-
Saxon one.

Dr Margaret White, Two Million Silent Killings

The fire started downstairs. Somewhere near the kitchen.

By the time Sandy was aware of it, the staircase was on fire and
the landing outside her bedroom seemed thick with smoke. She was
gripped with terror. She couldn't scream, or cry out, or move. She
simply stared at this awful livid mindless monster which was devouring
their house. As far as she could make out no one else was about. She
seemed to be alone in the house; alone with the fire. Everyone must
be somewhere, doing something; busy.

Somehow she found herself at the window. She was in the open
window, facing safety and fresh air and a sea of faces below her. A
fire engine. A fireman in a big shiny helmet. Her family. Ladders and
onlookers and the night sky. Jump, Sandy, jump! Sandy, you're safe!
Jump! The fire was nearly at her room already. She looked at the
fireman and jumped.

It was when she was in mid-air that she remembered.

She was in the fireman's arms, in Daddy's arms, safe, loved, kissed.
She'd escaped the fire. But she had remembered, and remembered

just too late. She turned and looked at her window. And she saw, framed in the window, sitting on the window sill, a row of dolls and teddies crying real tears. They didn't move. They sat in the window as they always sat; one arm stuck in the air; one teddy half falling over; two of the dolls quite naked, and one with just a bonnet. They had no dignity of their own. But they had been loved, and they had been left behind.

In their eyes were the tears; in their faces was the question: 'You couldn't wait for us? You loved us and you left us behind?'

She turned to the adults. There must be one adult in the whole world who would understand. She didn't know most of them. They were strangers in the street that she'd never seen before. Mummy! There was Mummy. She ran up to her.

'Mummy, Mummy, my dolls. My dolls and teddies!'

'Oh, Sandy, thank goodness you're safe. Join the others, away from the house.'

Perhaps Daddy could help. 'Daddy!'

'Yes? Do whatever Mummy says, darling.'

'Daddy, please help.' He was gone.

Suddenly Sandy felt a terrible terrible despair. She knew there was time to save them. She knew it could be done. She'd just been in her room, and she knew the flames were still only on the landing. If one of the firemen would only put his ladder against her bedroom window, she knew they could be rescued before it was too late.

She felt a wave of horror. She saw, because she was a child. None of the others could see, because they were all adults. They were too busy to see. But because she was a child she couldn't do anything. She could only know and watch. She was too small. It would have been all right if an adult could have heard her. But all she had was her voice, her little child's voice, and nobody could hear it. Nobody would listen. She was right, and they were wrong, and they would never believe her.

The next time she looked up it was already too late. She could see the flames behind them. Not long now. The expression on their faces had changed. The tears had dried in the heat, and now they seemed to be saying, 'You tried, and you couldn't help. Never mind: we still wait. Always we'll wait for you. Always.'

At that moment the bell on the fire engine began to ring, and Daddy put his arms around her, and as Sandy watched her window it was swallowed up by the fire.

She could still feel Daddy's arms. She shivered. Then she snuggled
into him. She heard a bird singing outside her window before she
opened her eyes.

'Come on, sleepy head. Your alarm's gone off.'

'Is it still holiday?'

Daddy laughed. 'No, it isn't. It's Monday morning. Up you get.'

Sandy tried to sit up in bed. She could hardly move. Her arms and
legs felt so heavy that she thought she might have to stay in bed for
ever. Daddy lifted her out of bed and set her feet on the floor. She
rubbed her eyes. Then she saw, with great surprise, that all her dolls
and teddies were where they lived, under the empty toy shelves where
Mummy always put them. They were where they'd been when she went
to bed the night before. Someone had rescued them after all.

She thought she ought to feel great joy and relief. But she didn't.
It was still as if the awful thing had happened. She still felt the dread
weight on her, as she walked slowly into the bathroom; still feeling
as she'd felt when she saw them disappear into the flames.

At school that day Sandy couldn't quite remember what was dream
and what had happened. Had they really talked about not having the
baby? It didn't seem possible.

It was singing that day, and Mrs Janey sat at the piano, playing,
while they sung a song called 'My Bonny Lies Over the Ocean'.
As Sandy sang it, she wondered what a bonny was and why it lay
over the ocean. It sounded a bit like a baby. She imagined a large
and rather fat baby, with no clothes on except a nappy, hovering
over a calm and still blue sea while the seagulls screeched above
it and the little waves lapped. Would the bonny be suspended in
the air like that, or would it be resting on the water? If it rested
on the water, what would stop it drowning? She'd heard that Jesus
walked on the water. Perhaps a bonny was a kind of Jesus, a baby
Jesus?

'Oh, bring back my bonny to me,' they sang.

No, she didn't think the bonny was anything to do with Jesus.
Someone was singing for the bonny to come back, because someone
was worried that the bonny shouldn't stay there, resting on the
waves without being able to swim.

It wasn't possible, what she thought she remembered about the
baby. Sandy knew her parents were very good people; probably
almost the best in the world, she thought. Though Ella's mummy

was jolly nice too. And she knew her parents wouldn't hurt a baby. She'd heard them talking about a woman on the news who'd stolen a baby. The woman hadn't wanted to hurt it; she'd just wanted a baby of her own. But she'd taken somebody else's, and Mummy had said that was a very naughty thing to do.

'Is she a baddy?' Sandy had asked.

'I should think she's a very unhappy and lonely person. She probably needs help,' Mummy had replied. 'A doctor to look after her.'

'But why is it wrong to take the baby, if she wants to love it and look after it?' Sandy had asked.

'It's not very loving towards the baby, is it?' Mummy said. 'If she wants to love the baby, she should think what's best for her; for the baby, not for herself. It's best for the baby to be with her own mother, who's all ready for her and wants to take her home.'

'But the other lady might be ready for her too. She might look after her very well,' Sandy objected.

But when the policemen found the baby, Sandy's mummy said, 'You see, she didn't really want the baby at all. She wanted to get her boyfriend back. She wanted to make him marry her by pretending they'd had a baby together. That's no way to conduct relationships. What kind of a mother would that make?'

This conversation left so many unanswered questions for Sandy that she didn't know where to start, and in the end didn't ask any of them. How could she pretend to the man that he'd had a baby? Sandy knew that men were aware when they made babies, because they had to go to bed with the women first. And if he went to bed with the woman he must be in love with her anyway; she was sure her mother had told her that. So if he was in love with her, he'd want to be with her anyway. And why wouldn't the woman make a good mother? She had wanted the baby very much.

So Sandy was sure she must have dreamt about the conversation round the kitchen table, with her and her brothers and Mummy and Daddy pretending to choose whether or not to have the baby. It was quite a good game, perhaps, but they wouldn't do it for real. They'd always said you mustn't hurt babies. And they wouldn't ever hurt their own.

She went into the playground at lunchtime a little relieved, but still feeling the overwhelming heaviness she had woken up with. Perhaps it was just the bad dream. Bad dreams can make you feel very bad. Perhaps they were both bad dreams; the fire and the baby dream.

'Bang-bang-you're-dead-fifty-bullets-in-your-head!'

Quick as a flash Sandy replied, 'Bang-bang-you're-dead-fifty-bullets-in-your-head.' Then she said, 'Oh, go away, Dominic. I don't want to play. It's stupid to play games of aggression.'

'What are games of aggression?' he asked, rather interested.

'Ah,' said Sandy knowingly. Then she said, 'I'm not sure. Killing people, I think.'

'Why is that stupid?'

'It's wrong to kill people, silly.'

'Not always,' Dominic said, superior and very knowing. 'What about Hitler, eh?'

'Who's Hiltler?' Sandy asked. It seemed a funny kind of name. She was glad her parents hadn't called Jack or Barney Hiltler. She supposed it was a boy's name.

'Hitler was a real real baddy, who killed loads and loads of people. He killed anyone who wore a yellow star because he didn't like yellow. And all the good people there were tried to kill him because he was so bad.'

'And what happened in the end?'

'I don't know. Oh, yes I do. In the end they found out who was the very best person out of the good people in the whole world, and that person killed him. So it can be right to kill someone, if they're very bad.'

'Still doesn't mean you should play games of aggression, clever clogs.'

'Does. Bang-bang-you're-dead-fifty . . .'

'Shut up, Dominic,' said Sandy, and put her hands over her ears.

Her parents knew better what was right and wrong than Dominic did. When she got home, she would ask Daddy about the dream. The first one; the dream about them all sitting round and talking about the baby. It seemed very real, but Daddy would be able to explain it to her.

'Are you all right, Sandy?' Miss Sylvia asked as they went back into school.

'Yes,' said Sandy.

'You're very quiet today.'

'Oh.'

She never got round to asking Daddy after all. She meant to, but she didn't quite know what to say. She wondered whether to ask him if she'd dreamt it; but when she thought about it again it seemed so real that she thought she couldn't have done.

In the end she said, 'Daddy, who's Hilt, um. The man, you know. Hiltum or something. The man who didn't like stars.' Daddy looked unenlightened. Sandy sighed. 'You know. The one who killed the people with the stars.'

'Say his name again?'

'Hiltum?'

'Hitler!'

'Yes, Hitler. Who was he?'

Daddy sighed a big sigh, as he does when you ask him a difficult question. 'He was a man with a great dream.' Then Daddy thought for a moment. 'He wanted work for all his countrymen, and he wanted health and happiness for them all, and he wanted the best nation in the world.'

'So why was it good to kill him?'

'I'm not sure that it was. But he was completely wrong. He was wrong about how to go about it. He thought he could do anything he liked, just so that he could have his dream. He killed millions of people, and attacked other people's countries in order to make his own country better.'

'Is that wrong?'

'Yes, it's very wrong. No dream's worth killing for. You never get freedom that way. You can't build your own liberty on other people's lives.'

'But why did all the good people try to kill him?'

'They didn't. Grandfather didn't. He was nearly sent to prison because he thought it was wrong to kill, even to kill Hitler. You ask him about it. He thinks it's wrong to try and kill anyone ever.'

'Can you be sent to prison for not killing people?' Sandy's mouth was wide open. She was very shocked.

'In wartime you can. Maybe it was wrong to try and kill Hitler,' Daddy went on, thinking it out to himself, 'but not as wrong as letting him kill millions more. I've not expressed that very well.' Sandy wrinkled her forehead up, trying to think harder to help Daddy explain.

'Have you heard of capital punishment?' Daddy asked. Sandy shook her head. 'Capital punishment is when you actually kill people, instead of putting them in prison, when they break the law. It doesn't happen in this country any more. Even in other countries it only happens to people who've done something very bad. If they're murderers, for instance. And the only reason a civilised country would do it would be to save other people's lives. Suppose you've got someone who keeps putting bombs about, and killing lots of people. When you catch him, you might decide to kill him. Then he can't kill people any more, and it may put other people off doing it too.'

'Why not just put him in prison for ever and ever?' asked Sandy.

'Well, yes,' said Daddy. 'I think that's better. I think capital punishment is a mistake. It hardens people; it makes them think death doesn't matter much. And it makes us think we have a right to take people's lives. We never have. Hey! Eat up: I've got a treat for you.'

'What? What, Daddy? Please what?'

'Eat up and I'll tell you.'

'So Daddy can you only kill people if they're really, really bad people?'

'Yes. Come on, don't you want your straw— oops! Your treat?'

Strawberries were the treat. Strawberries and yoghurt. It was only Mummy's boring white yoghurt that she made sometimes, but it didn't matter much because the strawberries made it nice.

It was during bathtime that Sandy asked, 'Daddy. Can babies be bad?'

Daddy laughed. 'Babies are very selfish. But they're not really bad. They have to be selfish in order to survive. They have to cry when they're hungry or we wouldn't know when to feed them. I suppose they can be bad when they're a little older. One, or one and a half.'

'So a baby that hasn't been born yet can't be bad?'

Daddy said nothing for a moment. He was soaping a sponge for Sandy. He ran the tap and soaped the sponge, and for a moment she thought he hadn't heard the question. Then he gave her the sponge.

'Here you are. Don't forget your neck and ears. No,' he said, 'a baby that's not been born can't be bad.'

Then a moment later he said, 'But we don't normally call that a baby. A baby that's not been born is usually called a foetus.'

Soon after that Mummy offered Sandy a treat. She said she was going to the Chelsea Flower Show, and would Sandy like to go? Mummy said it was the first year Sandy had been old enough, because children under five weren't allowed to go.

Sandy was very excited. She said she wanted to wear a hat, so they found the straw hat she'd worn to Beano's wedding, and it still had all its little pink silk flowers on it. She was going to go after school, in her school dress and straw hat. Mummy said she'd pick her up from school by bicycle and they'd go straight to the flower show, because the traffic would be frightful and the parking impossible.

'How can parking be impossible?' Sandy asked. 'Why can't you just get out of the car and leave it?'

'Yes,' said her mother. 'Good idea. But then you'd get a great big yellow clamp stuck on the wheel, and have to spend all night trying to get it off, and pay them £50 for giving you the big yellow clamp, and then be told that you can't pick it up that night anyway because they've all shut down and please could you come back in the morning and spend all the next day travelling back on the tube to pick it up.'

'But it wouldn't matter by then,' said Sandy, 'because we'd be at the flower show so we wouldn't need the car any more.'

'Thanks very much,' said Mummy.

'Do you get to keep the big yellow clamp?'

'No,' said Mummy.

When Mummy came to pick her up from school she had Sandy's straw hat in her bicycle basket, just as she'd said she would. On Mummy's bike you sit behind the handlebars: in some ways this is better than Daddy's bike, because you can talk better; also you can see what's in the basket. So Sandy sat on her little seat in front of Mummy, behind the basket, watching her hat trying to jump up and fly away. She wished it would. She didn't want to lose it for good, but she wanted to see it escape and leap up in the air and sail across the road. But then it might sail into the river and she'd never see it again.

She watched the river dancing in the sun. There was a sailing boat on it, with bright red sails, going out into the low sunshine and sailing away from them, under the bridges and away into the sunset, with the light shining through its sails. And there were the big heavy barges, the houseboats that people live in, lying low in the mud on the side of the river. Sandy could only just see them over the wall. One was bright purple, with white-painted windows, and out of each of the windows a piece of washing had been spread out to dry.

The flower show was big, and crowded, but not noisy at all. It wasn't like a railway station, where all the adults seem to make a noise like children in the playground but of course without being told off for it.

They went in through some really interesting gates. Mummy said they were called turnstiles. They were painted with old green paint, and clicked to let you through after you'd paid. Sandy would have liked to go through them several times, but she thought that might get rather expensive so she didn't suggest it.

'Now,' said Mummy. 'What do you want to do first? The gardens? The marquee? Or a cup of tea?'

'I don't like tea.'

'Well, you know what I mean. Pimms, then.'

'What's Pimms?'

'Pink lemonade.'

'Pimms please.'

'Actually you can't have Pimms. It's alcoholic. You could watch me drinking it.'

'Ohwo, Mummy!'

'Sorry. Tell you what, let's look around a bit first, and then when we're tired of doing that we will go and get a drink. Something that you'd like. Proper lemonade. Well, not proper lemonade but children's lemonade.'

'All right.'

They went into the marquee first. As soon as they went in Sandy noticed a smell of honey. Mummy said it was the flowers. It was very pretty, if a smell can be pretty. But most of the flowers were awful. They were big and ugly and unrealistic. If you had them in your garden you'd never be able to play at all. Sandy and Mummy passed one display, a pile of flowers behind a rope, which Sandy thought looked like plastic flowers for a dolls' house, on plastic grass; only not as much fun. Dolls' house flowers are fun, after all, because they're only pretending to be flowers. But real flowers can't pretend to be flowers. That's just silly. They were silly; they were pink and orange and red all mixed up together and much too bright, and if you wore a dress like that your brothers would say, 'Ehrr! Sandy!'

Sandy got sick of looking at the flowers. She sat down on a little wall and looked at the people instead. They were very funny. Some had cameras, and some had funny hats, and one woman had a bright red pleated skirt that wasn't level all the way round; it was longer at one side. And she had red plimsolls on that weren't quite the same red.

'Very pretty,' said a voice. 'If you had that in the border, Julia . . .' and it moved on. The voice had been right on top of her, looking over her shoulder, as if she weren't there at all. But then, adults often behave as if you don't exist. She watched, beyond some rather pretty little trees and a bush that looked like purple feathers, as a fountain spat water up into the air. She couldn't see the fountain; she could only see the water. So it was a bit as if a naughty boy were lying on his back out of sight with an endless mouthful of water, blowing it up into the air. It was rather fun.

A kind-looking lady with a leg bandaged inside her stocking, and a walking stick, passed her and looked down and smiled. Sandy thought of Granny, and then remembered that she wouldn't see her again. Granny would have liked the flower show. Granny loved flowers.

Right next to her, a few inches along the wall, a woman with dark purple lipstick bent down and looked at a little pink flower. She lifted it up with her programme without touching it, and inspected it lying on the paper, rather as though it had been a wasp or something dangerous. When she'd gone, Sandy reached out and touched it very carefully, to see if it would sting.

'Sandy!' There was Mummy again. 'I thought I'd lost you.'

'Oh. Sorry.'

'Have you had enough of this?'

'Yup.'

'So have I. Come and see one thing, and then we'll go outside.'

Sandy got up reluctantly. She didn't particularly want to see any more, even the one thing, but she followed Mummy to see what it was.

'There. Isn't that lovely?'

Sandy had to admit that it was. There were roses everywhere. Climbing, scrambling, exploring; for ever and ever, reaching into the distance and up into the roof of the tent. They went over the arches, and the arches seemed to stretch for ever too. As Sandy looked down the tunnel of pinks and whites and the soft summer smell, she realised that this was where the honey was; and she also saw, suddenly and with a catch of breath, a garden seat with a hat and a book on it, and a table laid with a teapot and a jug and a blue and white cup and saucer. Before Mummy could say anything she ducked under the rope and ran down the tunnel. She thought if she could only catch the dream at the end of it she might stay young for ever, like Peter Pan; or at least grow up into years of only summer.

'Sandy! Sandy! You're not allowed in there.' She reached the bench and suddenly realised that none of it was for real. The roses were real roses. But they weren't in a real garden. There was no real tea in the teapot. Nobody ever wore the hat and it wasn't anybody's book. It wasn't a real dream at all.

'If you could keep the children to the pathways, madam.'
'Yes, of course. I'm so sorry. Sandy!'
Sandy walked back to the rope. How was she supposed to get out?
Mummy lifted the rope up, and she walked under it again.
'Come on, you,' her mother was laughing. 'What did you go and
do that for?'
'I wanted to see who lived there. And nobody lives there at all.'
'Of course not, silly. Let's find the tea, or icecream, or whatever
they have.'
So they sat in the sun with a cup of tea and a Coca Cola, and
Sandy watched all the different types of shoes go by. There were
men's sandals, with brown socks underneath. And women's sandals,
with bare feet. And men's leather shoes, of course; normal lace-ups.
No high heels at all. And more sandals; blue, and white, and some
which were just leather-coloured. Sandy heard a camera whizzing, and
caught a sudden whiff of strong cigar smoke. There was a cigar-end on
the grass: longer and thinner than a cigarette-end, and the colour of
chocolate. The grass wasn't like grass at all, but like dry grey shreds
of paper on brown earth. There were interesting things on the ground:
a pale green tissue in the shape of a little dog; a box-shaped piece of
cellophane which would hold things if you were really careful, and
which caught the sun and sparkled; and a glitter of silver that once
opened a beer can but now made a beautiful ring.
'Sandy! You mustn't touch things on the ground, they'll be dirty.'
'Oh. Sorry,' said Sandy, remembering.
'I'm going into hospital at the end of July,' Mummy went on.
'Are you? What for?'
'The termination. You know. To stop me having a baby.'
'Oh.' Sandy nodded.
'So will you look after Simon for a couple of days for me?'
'Yup.' It was funny that. Sandy wasn't quite sure how she should
look after Daddy. Perhaps Jack would know.
'Thanks. What would you like to see before we go home?'
'Dunno. What is there?'
'I know. One last thing. You'll love it.'
Mummy was right. It was a little stall that reminded Sandy of all the
summer holidays she'd ever been on. Round the walls were flowers like
you only get on holiday; and then you get them along the sides of the
road, and you're allowed to pick them all the way home. But they don't
grow along the road in London. Inside the wall was a little pond with

flowers growing round it, which made you think you might see a real frog or a bird at any moment. And beyond the stones was a tiny corner of a meadow, with meadow flowers, sky blue cornflowers, and bright red poppies, and something yellow on a stalk which Sandy didn't recognise, waving in the long grass. Sandy wanted to run through it in her bare legs and catch the butterflies. But perhaps if she ran here this dream would die too. Perhaps everything dies. Perhaps it was like the wildflowers in Scotland. Perhaps all you could ever hope to do was not to pick too many flowers.

'. . . and do that for a year, madam, and you should get an area of meadow flowers in your garden, no problem.'

'Sadly,' Mummy said, 'we only have a few feet round a patio in Fulham. But it's lovely. It's the most beautiful display. So how long does it take you to set it up, if a meadow like that takes a year to grow?'

' 'Bout ten days. We bin here a fortnight now.'

'How on earth do you do it?'

'Bring it all down in pots.'

'Oh, what a disappointment! Well, it still looks super.'

'Thank you.'

'Oh, Mummy!' Sandy said. 'I want to go for picnics, and pick blackberries, and run and run.'

'So do I,' said Mummy. 'So do I. But we must hurry now. Daddy's got to go out in twenty minutes, and we'll hardly be home on time.'

'When I are an adult,' Sandy said, 'I'm going to have a garden like that all round my house, and have all my friends to stay.'

Sandy pictured her own little cottage, surrounded by poppies and cornflowers and huge daisies. And as she pictured it, she saw herself coming out of the cottage in a long skirt with a bucket of fresh milk in her hand. With her was a friend. She looked just like Sandy but a little smaller.

Sandy wondered if the friend was Poppy.

12 June, Saturday, Home

All the way home I kept wanting to ring. I got a book out of
my bag, and saw my telephone that Abi had been messing
about with, and thought of it. I started to read, and my
mind kept going back to my bag. I went to the buffet to
get a cup of tea, and when I opened my bag for my money I
immediately saw my mobile again.

This is ridiculous, I told myself, and went and sat down
again with my book and tea and started to read. After fifteen
minutes I'd read five pages and hadn't taken in a word.
All right, I said to myself, if you want to ring, ring. Then I
looked at my fellow passengers, scattered throughout the
compartment, and thought, No, I don't want to ring. I don't
want them overhearing my conversation. Nor do I want to
keep my voice down, particularly.

I stared out of the window at the velvety green fields, and
the corn beginning to turn, and the poppies and cornflowers
flicked like paint all over the landscape, and thought, Ben
is a lucky devil. A lucky duck, as we used to say when we
were children. Even if he is broke. It seems silly that
I should have so much money, and nothing particularly
to spend it on, when Ben and Suki have almost nothing.
Then I had an idea: why shouldn't I pay for Abi to go to
a different school, the school of Ben and Suki's choice?
I'd have to consider carefully. Once started, I'd have to
pay for twelve years or so; fifteen if she wanted to go
to university. And suppose I have a child of my own? I
can't envisage it now, but I ought to anticipate it. Or more
than one? Foolishly, I've always longed for four children
if I ever have any. But I've never met any contemporary
of mine who's wanted more than one, so I can't imagine
ever finding a man who would.

Then it struck me with nausea that my family might think,
if I helped with Abi's education, that I'd done it to 'compensate'
in some way for something. But what? Why should I feel
guilty? Why should they think that I needed peace of mind?

149

ANNE ATKINS

I'm being too complicated here, I thought. No such thing would occur to anyone. Perhaps I'll try and talk to my father about it, fat lot of good that would be.

I had wandered into the corridor and was looking out of the train door. For a moment I wondered what I was doing there; then I realised that I could telephone from the corridor without being overheard. But there was too much coming and going, and noise from the train going over the tracks, to have a proper conversation here. I went into the loo and locked the door. It carried a lingering odour of disinfectant, and took away any desire to talk to anyone. I sat down on the loo and said to myself out loud, 'Now, look. Do you want to make a call or don't you? Because this is getting ridiculous.'

'Yes and no,' I replied. 'I'd quite like to talk to him...'

'"Quite"?'

'Yes. Quite.'

'Not "desperately"?'

'No. Absolutely not. Desperately, no. He's a friend, not a lover.'

'But on the other hand...?'

'But on the other hand, I don't want to make a call from a noisy, crowded train. It's a waste of money. And...'

'And...?'

'And I don't want to make the first move.'

'Why?'

'"Why?"? What do you mean "why?"?'

'Why not? "He's a friend, not a lover." Where do first moves come into it?'

'Ah. Dunno.'

'So, are you going to call or not?'

'No. I'm not. No.'

'Right. Then go and sit down and shut up and get your book out, and stop behaving like a love-sick twelve year old.'

'Right.'

'Right.'

So I did.

I got home about three in the afternoon. And, ah! It was bliss to be back. My own home, with my own honeysuckle just beginning to scramble to its feet in the front garden. My own front door, my own welcoming kitchen. And, unfortunately, my own letters on the mat and my own telephone messages which my agent had sent back to my answering service. But then nothing's perfect.

I dealt with the messages and letters first, because I hate
them all, and had just unpacked and made a cup of tea and
opened my French windows on to the garden when the doorbell
rang. I stood up and knocked over my cup of tea and fell over a
chair and reached the door. I fumbled with the simple latch and
flung open the door, and then stared open-mouthed at the filthy,
greasy messenger who stood there.

'Oh,' I said, and leant against the door post.

'Sorry,' he said, looking very cheerful. 'Didn't mean to
disappoint. Letter for you.'

He handed me the letter, which he'd somehow managed to
keep very clean, jumped on his bike and roared off, turning and
waving at the top of Parsons Green, as he rounded the corner.

'Don't be silly,' I said far too late, as he disappeared out of
view. And then, to myself, 'Blooming cheek.' I went back into
my little conservatory and started mopping up the tea, and then
sat down, still feeling hot and sick and shaky. 'This is pathetic,'
I said to myself. And then I supposed I ought to read my letter.

Dear Ms Sanderson,
I am Anna, cousin to William, from Italy. We go for a picnic
now, and I tell him he must bring a pretty girl, and he says
he doesn't know any but will his next-door neighbour do? I
am sorry he is so rude but please will you come for a picnic
with us? We are at Putney Bridge and waiting for twenty
minutes, if you are back from the countryside. You can tell
the messenger to tell us if we wait.

There are my children coming, I know the English are funny
about this.

I look forward to meet you,

Anna.

I immediately thought: Italians, pretty dress, makeup, look nice.
Then instantly afterwards I thought, How long did I spend
mopping up the tea? How long did the messenger take to get
here? How long will it take me to get to the river? So I grabbed a
straw boater with a ribbon, which was only suitable for picnics,
punting, and proposals, not that I expected all of these, locked
my house, got my bike from the basement by cutting my finger
and taking some skin off my shin, and sped to Putney Bridge.

Halfway across the river, just pulling away from Fulham
Palace, was Will's boat with a couple of women and two
dark-haired children. I couldn't see Will anywhere.

'Hoi,' I shouted. 'Anna!' Nobody took any notice. 'ANNA!' I yelled, much louder this time. Several people on the bridge turned and stared. 'Si!' somebody called back.

I couldn't see who'd said it, but I shouted, 'I'm Caz. Caz Sanderson.' Slowly the boat turned round and headed back for shore.

13 June, Sunday, Parsons Green
(Too tired to write any more yesterday.)

'Will says we're not to call you his girlfriend. Is that right?'
She was very British: comfortable; smiling; kind, one
felt, in a vigorously practical way.
'Absolutely,' I replied, with more emphasis than was
necessary.
'I'm his mother, Elizabeth. How d'you do? It's so difficult to
get everything right nowadays, isn't it?'
'Hasn't it always been?' I said. 'How d'you do.'
'I suppose so. Where is he, Anna?'
'We sent him for wine, the idiot. Fancy saying that his
neighbour isn't pretty. Look at you: you're beautiful. *Eh! Andrai
a finire nell'acqua!*' she shouted at the smaller of the two
children. '*Siediti bene nella barca.*'
'*Ho visto un pesce!*' the girl replied. She was leaning out of
the boat and pointing at something in the water. '*Uno grande,
guarda!*'
The boy joined in. '*È un salmone,*' he said. '*Mamma,
possiamo acchiapparlo?*' Then their Italian got too fast for me to
follow.
Elizabeth looked at me and smiled. It's like a film, I thought:
with these dark-eyed, dark-haired children delivering a gurgling,
nimble libretto over the laughter of the river and their mother
and the sparkling light; while an impeccably Scottish woman
with an impeccably English accent inclines her head politely
at a stranger in her son's boat.
'The children thought they saw a big fish,' Anna explained to
me.
I nodded. 'There are supposed to be salmon in the river,' I
said, 'but nobody ever sees any. The day I see a salmon in the
Thames I shall know a new dawn of civilisation has come.'
'Aha. I shall buy one from the delicatessen and throw it in,'
she said. 'To herald your new dawn.'
'Oh no,' I laughed. 'It must be a living, swimming salmon.
I suppose it wouldn't be a new dawn really, but an old dawn

coming round again. After all, salmon was the poor man's fish in London four hundred years ago. By the way,' I said, 'what did you mean about the English being funny like that?'
'Like what?' Anna said. *'Ehh!'* she added to her son, who was leaning too far out of the boat, and pulled him back in with a string of unbroken Italian without moving from her position at the tiller. 'Like oysters,' she suddenly added.
'What?' I said, mystified.
'Oysters. The poor man's food in Dickens' London. What did I mean about what?'
A wave of pure joy broke over me. I'd known this woman, what, five minutes? and she expected me to follow her dizzying conversation as if we'd been at school together.
'Anna dear,' Elizabeth said, 'I'm not sure Will's friend can keep up. I'm sure I can't, and I'm used to you.'
'Sorry,' Anna said, squeezing my arm and winking.
I tried to collect my scattered thoughts. 'You said your children would be coming and you were sorry the English are funny like that. Or about that. Or something.'
Elizabeth smiled. 'Anna is shocking,' she said.
'Ah, I remember. Well, the English, they hate children.'
'Do we?' I said.
'I don't,' said Elizabeth.
'True,' conceded Anna. 'The grandmothers don't. And you are not English, besides.'
'I'm not a grandmother, either. Or not really,' she added.
'No, but you should be.'
'Yes,' Elizabeth said, and looked out towards the south bank. We were getting near to that bend where the grass runs down to the water, and it doesn't look like London at all any more. 'Where *is* Will?' she added, as if we'd been talking about him.
'He'll join us somewhere along here,' Anna said vaguely.
'What do you mean,' I said, 'that we don't like children?'
'Ha! Look at you!' Anna said with sudden energy. 'You have a party, what do you do? Put your children to bed! You go to the opera, what do you do? Tell your children they wouldn't like it! Though, I admit, you none of you like opera, so that isn't surprising; you go to the opera to be clever or spend money, not to enjoy yourselves.'
'Anna!' Elizabeth said, laughing anyway.
'You have dinner, what do you do? Give your children this "high tea" nonsense. And you all have nannies. So every household has three adults and one child. Absurd! And look

at your pubs! You build them for enjoyment, so what do you
do? Abolish children! So you must build the special rooms
for the children to go in! It is impossible for the English
to enjoy themselves with their children. Why do you have
children? Who knows? To stop the wonderful English dying
out. What a shame. It is better if the English die out. Except
Will. And Elizabeth. And you.'

The boy turned and looked at his mother with a frown for
a moment. He understood the words, but not the humour, and
couldn't see why the foolish grown-ups were laughing. Then
he shrugged, and turned back to his sister and the water and
the far more interesting task of running his fingers through the
ripples.

'It's the EC that did this,' said Elizabeth.

'Did what?' I asked.

'All this xenophobia.'

'I think maybe Anna's got a point. I don't know why half
my friends do have children.'

'Of course I've got a point. Will, he says he wants four
children. This is crazy, of course, but never mind; four children
is crazy, even the Italians, we don't have four children. But he
says he can never find a woman who will have more than one.
Even his wife, Helena, she only wanted one.'

'His wife?' I said.

'Oops,' she said. 'Now I have let the cat out of the can of
worms.'

'Don't be silly,' I said. 'There's no can of worms. Will and I
are just friends.'

'She's not his wife any more,' Elizabeth said quietly.

'There's Will,' Anna shouted. 'Silly boy. He is shaking up
all the wine if he runs along like this. Eh! Guglielmo. Here we
are! On the river! In this boat!'

Wave on wave I plunge in them to meet you.

I lay back in the sun, and thought, I could be happy in this
family always.

We went through Richmond and on to Ham before mooring
on the south side. I hadn't realised how late in the afternoon
it was, nearly early evening, by the time we secured the boat
and jumped on to the bank. The children wanted to explore, so
Will went running off upstream shouting in Italian, while they
laughed and chased him and threw sticks into the water.

'Do you want to go with the children?' Elizabeth asked me.

ANNE ATKINS

'I'll just sit here with Anna, and a glass of wine, and watch the ducks go by.'
'Huh!' said Anna. 'Me? I don't want to sit with the grannies and watch the ducks go by.'
'All right, you join the children too. I'm fine on my own.'
'What! Run up and down like an idiot?' said Anna. 'I'm staying with the wine.'
I smiled. 'I think I will go for a walk,' I said. 'Though I don't think I'll catch up with that lot. I won't be long though.'
Richmond and Kew Undid me. Ham along the towpath was looking great. Last time I came this way was just after Easter, when there was nothing but the fresh green and white of early summer: cow parsley, hawthorn or May, white chestnut, dead-nettle, elder; no colours at all except the grey-white on the green leaf. And the smells then had been light and delicate and very much the smell of the elder. Now, everything was richer. Buttercups, bluebells, dandelions, and a strong smell of river.
Why do I feel so at home with these people I've never met before? Why do I believe, without even talking to them about it, that they will value the valuable things? I had stopped to pick some of the flowers, for Elizabeth I think, and as I continued, walking in step with myself, I felt a peace, a calm and happiness, that should be easy to attain but in fact is quite rare.
I remember feeling it quite distinctly when I was about ten. I had been invited to the birthday party of a friend from school. Her name was Yvonne, and she wasn't, in fact, a close friend. I had nothing against her, but we hadn't got much in common, and I remember feeling, even at that age, rather superior to her. I considered her sweet but not very clever, and I didn't think her birthday party would, frankly, be up to much. Perhaps she was the year below me at school: yes, I think that was it. Her mother was a friend of my parents; perhaps she'd even invited me to be polite, because her mother had asked her to. Anyway, I was expecting a very ordinary afternoon, which I suppose it was. We went to see some soppy Walt Disney film or other; 'The Rescuers', or something equally silly. And suddenly, as I sat in the cinema with the other children waiting for my icecream or popcorn or whatever we were getting, I had an overwhelming feeling of well-being. I thought, This is happiness. Why? I think because nobody was trying to *impress* anyone else, or be clever or daring or showy, which I suppose was beginning to become the thing amongst the children in my own class. It was simply an afternoon

156

that we were supposed to enjoy. That was all that was asked
of us: enjoy yourselves. There was something eminently
good about the event: kind; simple.

And that was how I felt about the picnic. Oh, I don't mean
Anna doesn't like to impress: of course she does. Anna, who
was a model when she was a teenager, and is now a university
tutor in eighteenth-century literature; Anna, who shows off
almost like a child, with a child's delightful and delighting
innocence. But that isn't the point. The point is that she'd
invited a perfect stranger to come on a picnic. Why? Simply
so that stranger would enjoy herself. That was all anyone was
asking of me. That I should have a lovely afternoon.

I sat down by the river bank and watched a pair of swans,
preening themselves and ducking their necks deep under
the water. Last year, slightly further upriver, there had been
a swan's nest in midstream, but the authorities had tried to
encourage the couple to move it this year because they were
worried about disturbances from river traffic. I wondered
whether they had succeeded, and whether there were
any cygnets to show for it yet.

'Guess who?' said one of the children, the boy, in English,
as I was grabbed from behind.

'Look!' I shouted. 'Look, look.'

'That's an old wheeze,' said Will.

'No, really,' I said. 'Didn't you see it? The flash of blue?'

'*Sì*,' said the girl. 'I did.'

A kingfisher.

We had wine and baguettes and goat's cheese and cherry
tomatoes and truffle pâté. And lettuce and gravdlaks and
Bombay prawns. And strawberries and mangoes and Italian
icecream and more wine. And the light was drawing in as we
motored home along the north side of the river and I found
my bicycle and Will pushed it home for me, as we all walked
back to his house. And I declined the invitation for coffee and
went home and slept like a child.

Wave on wave I drown.

CHAPTER NINE –
CLANCARTY ROAD, 1990

ὦ βάρβαρ' ἐξευρόντες Ἕλληνες κακά
τί τόνδε παῖδε κτείνετ' οὐδὲν αἴτιον;

Oh, you Greeks, inventors of barbaric wickedness!
Why kill this innocent child, who has done nothing
wrong?

Euripides, Women of Troy, 764–5.

There is no such thing as an unwanted child. If no
one else in the world wants them, I do: you can
send them all to me.

Mother Theresa of Calcutta.

The day Mummy went into hospital was very hot. It was another
sunhat day.

Daddy picked them all up from school in the car. He had the roof
off, and all the windows down, and was playing music very loudly on
the car radio. The mothers at Sandy's school turned to look at what
was making all the music. The other children's cars had children's
music in them, when they played music at all. There were usually
six or eight children in each car, going over the river to Clapham;
and they had cassettes like 'Fun Shop' or 'Children's Play Time'.
Daddy never played children's music. Sandy had some children's
music in her room, but in the car Daddy played music with cellos
and violins and flutes in it. Sometimes there was a harpsichord. Daddy
had drawn Sandy's attention to it once; at first she couldn't hear it,
but then she noticed a sort of tinkling sound, like lots of soft little
bells, and that was the harpsichord.

So when Daddy drove up the school drive with all the music coming out of the top of the car where there wasn't a roof, everyone knew Sandy's mummy or daddy had come.

'Sandy! Your daddy's here!'

And Sandy ran up to the car and threw all her things in and was able to go in the front because Daddy hadn't picked the boys up yet because Sandy's school finished first.

'Hi, love.'

'Hello, Daddy.'

'We're all going to go and see Mummy in hospital before we go home for tea.'

'Is she in hospital? Is she all right?' Sandy was worried.

'She's fine,' Daddy reassured her. 'Today's the day they take the foetus away so it won't grow into a baby. You remember: we talked about it.'

'Oh. Yes.' For a moment Sandy thought she had forgotten.

She sat in the car listening to the violins dancing and racing against each other, and felt the same smothering kind of panic she remembered from all her fire dreams. If only she could tell them! If only she could explain to the adults, they would be able to do the right thing.

There was a funny little dog going for a walk on the way to the boys' school. It had a white fluffy hairdo, and reminded Sandy of old ladies when they come out of the hairdresser. Sandy sometimes went to Mummy's hairdresser for a 'trim'. She didn't like it much because she always came out looking like someone else, and the hairdresser always said, 'You look smashing now, darling. Real trendy.' She thought the dog probably looked real trendy, and wondered if Mummy's hairdresser would think so too. At first she was sorry for the dog, who probably also felt he looked like someone else. But then she saw the way he was strutting along the pavement, as if he had four high-heeled shoes on, and she thought perhaps he was a silly dog after all. He certainly had a silly woman with him. She had very tight black trousers on, more like tights, and a fluffy blue top like a brushed blue sheep. You could see her bottom wobbling in the tights. Her legs were wobbling on her high heels too.

'Look at that silly person,' she said to Daddy.

'Yes,' he said. Then he looked again. 'She's quite sexy.'

Sandy made a face. She thought she would never understand grown-ups. 'Daddy!' she cried suddenly. 'The lights are red.'

'Ooops,' he said, as two different horns hooted and someone's brakes screeched.

When they got to the boys' school Jack and Barney were fed up because Sandy was in the front. But she had been there first and Daddy said they would have to put up with it.

'It's good to see you're both so chivalrous,' Daddy went on. 'Glad you're learning to put girls first, and so on. You must get it from your father. Talking of which, we're going to visit Amanda before going home for tea.'

'Where is she?' asked Jack.

'Criss Cross Hospital,' said Sandy proudly.

'Aren't we the little Miss Smarty Pants today?' said Jack.

'Don't be bitchy, Jack,' said Daddy.

'You mean Charing Cross Hospital,' Barney said quietly from the back.

They parked the car in a side street and walked to the hospital. It had a funny square pond in front of it, with a statue, and Sandy wanted to stay by the pond to see if she could see any goldfish. She'd seen goldfish in a tank at the Hurlingham Dog Shop, and they were very interesting to watch. She thought it was rather a shame that Daddy kept telling her to hurry up so they could go inside the hospital; it would have been better if they'd just come to see the square pond. But then she remembered it was Mummy they'd come to see, and felt a bit guilty for having forgotten.

Everything about the hospital was very big. The doors were big; the big hall they walked into was big; the staircase was big; the noise was wide and echoey. Sandy saw a shop selling flowers and chocolates, and immediately wanted to buy Mummy a box of chocolates. Daddy said it wouldn't be kind, because Mummy wasn't allowed to eat anything until the next day at lunchtime. Jack said that wouldn't matter because they could eat them for her, and anyway she could look forward to them; but in the end they settled for a purple flower in a pot which Daddy said was called a Rip Off.

Sandy was allowed to carry it up the huge staircase and along all the big corridors and up the lift and into Mummy's room. But when she got to Mummy's bed she didn't know what to do with it, so she gave it to Jack and he said, 'Happy birthday, Amanda.' She called him an idiot, gave him a hug, and said it was nice of them to come.

ANNE ATKINS

The others all sat on Mummy's bed talking to her, but Sandy got a bit bored because Mummy wasn't taking any notice of her so she explored the room. All the people in it were women, and they were all in bed. Sandy expected them to be in bed. In fact, she was a little surprised that Mummy was allowed in the hospital, as she wasn't ill. And she was surprised that Mummy was in bed: she'd heard Daddy say that Amanda will never stay in bed, even when she's really ill. But now she was in bed and she wasn't ill at all. Sandy found she'd started thinking about what they would do to Mummy, so she ran straight over to the window to see what was outside so she could think of that instead.

'Hello.' Sandy looked round to see where the voice came from. It was a friendly voice; warm and round. In the bed nearest the window was a lady with a crooked face and dark hair. She smiled. Sandy smiled back.

'Hello,' she said.

'Have you come to see your mummy?'

Sandy nodded.

'Is she all right?'

Sandy nodded again. 'She was going to have a baby but she's not any more. They're going to take the feet us away.'

This time the lady nodded. 'What's your name?' she said.

'Sandy.'

'What a pretty pretty name. Sandy. I used to have a school friend called Alexandra. I always wished my name was Alexandra too.'

'Oh,' said Sandy, and tried to work this out.

'I'm Sara, which is rather an ordinary name, I'm afraid.'

'It's nice,' Sandy said reassuringly.

'Thank you.' And Sara smiled her lovely, crooked, friendly smile. 'Would you like a grape, Sandy? My husband brought them in for me, but I don't feel like eating them, and they'll only go bad.'

'Yes, please,' said Sandy. Sara held the bowl out to her, and she took as big a handful as she could hold. Then she wondered if that was perhaps rather rude, so she put one back.

'Are you married?' she asked.

Sara smiled. 'Yes.'

'Have you got lots of children?'

'No. I haven't got any children.'

'Why? Don't you like children?'

'Yes, I do. I love children. Do you?'

162

Sandy nodded. It seemed an odd question for an adult to ask a child. Of course Sandy liked children. She had to, because she was one. All her friends were children. But perhaps Sara didn't know what questions adults were supposed to ask children if she didn't have any children of her own.

'Are you going to have lots of children then?'

'No, Sandy. I'll never have any children.'

What a funny person. She said she liked them, but she wasn't going to have any. 'Why not?'

'I can't. I've just had my last chance and it didn't go right. Now my body can't make children any more.'

'Oh.'

'I had a baby inside me. In fact I've had two. But they stopped in the wrong place and had to be taken out.'

'Do you mean feet us's?' Sandy asked. 'Daddy says babies that haven't been born are called feet us's.'

'They were foetuses, yes. But they were also babies. They were babies that weren't allowed to grow up and be born and become children.'

'Like ours.'

'Yes. A bit like yours.'

'So why did they take yours away? They're taking ours away so we can have summer holidays and tennis racquets,' Sandy explained.

'What did you say?'

'Why did they take yours away?'

Sara looked out of the window, and for a moment Sandy thought she was going to cry. But that wasn't possible. She was an adult, and adults didn't cry for no reason. Daddy was often telling her to behave like an adult, and not to cry.

'They took mine away because if they didn't they would have killed me.'

'Who, the doctors?' Sandy gaped.

'No,' Sara smiled her nice kind smile again. 'My babies.'

'But babies can't be bad and kill people,' Sandy objected.

'Perhaps they can't be bad,' Sara said. 'But they can kill their mother if they try and grow in the wrong place in her body.' This made sense. Daddy had said you could sometimes kill people to stop them killing other people. Sara's babies would have killed her, so they had to be taken away. You can't put babies in prison. You'd have to put their mothers in prison too, to feed them.

'So if they hadn't killed your babies, the babies would have killed you?'

'Yes. And then they would have died anyway. They were too young to live without me, so in killing me, they would have died as well.'

'Can't you have another baby? One that won't kill you?' Sandy said encouragingly.

Sara shook her head. 'When they took the babies away, they had to take part of me away as well. Now my body hasn't got all the bits it needs to make a baby.'

'Oh.' Sandy sat for a while looking at the bowl of grapes. She wondered whether Sara would notice that she'd finished her helping.

'And we can't adopt a baby either,' Sara went on.

'What does that mean?'

'When you adopt a baby, you take someone else's baby.'

'What, stealing, you mean?'

'No, not at all. Sometimes people have babies when they don't want them. They've made a mistake; perhaps they're not married, and didn't mean to have a baby, but they're having one anyway.'

'They'd have to make love to someone to have a baby,' Sandy informed her.

'Yes, they would. But that doesn't mean they necessarily want the baby, or feel they can look after it. So someone like me, who wants a baby but can't have one, says, "Don't worry, I'd love to have your baby. I, and my husband, will be its mummy and daddy in every other way. We've got too much energy, too much love just to spend it on ourselves, and perhaps you haven't got enough at the moment. So let's do a swap."'

'So why don't you?' Sandy asked.

'I'm too old. They won't let us adopt any more. There are too many young couples wanting to adopt, and not enough babies to go round. We spent too long hoping to have our own, and now they won't let us have someone else's.'

'But there are too many babies in the world!' Sandy exclaimed.

'Are there?' said Sara. 'I wish there was one more, for me.'

Suddenly Sandy thought of something. A tide of overwhelming joy came over her. She'd got it! The answer to all their problems. She knew she'd find a way for the adults to work it out. Why hadn't she thought of it before? It was so simple that even they, the grown-ups, would understand it. Oh, she wanted to hug the world, she was so relieved. And it wasn't too late. Suppose she had thought of it tomorrow . . .

it didn't bear thinking of. Of course, it wasn't quite as good as having her very own baby sister living in her house, but it was very much better than the ridiculous plan her parents and the doctors had thought of.

She ran straight over to her mother's bed without even saying excuse me to Sara. She was bursting with her idea, but she had to wait until Jack finished saying something.

'Mummy! Mummy!'

'Darling, just a minute, please. Jack's still talking.'

'Excuse me, please. Mummy?'

'Just a moment. Let Jack finish.'

Oh Jack, hurry, hurry! 'Please, Mummy.'

At last, after hours, Jack finished. It hadn't even been interesting. It was about a tennis game at school.

'Mummy! I've got the answer. To everything. I know what we're to do. It's much much better. They needn't take the feet us away. It'll all be all right. You needn't worry. You needn't even stay in the hospital if you don't want to.'

'Calm down, sweetheart. I can't make head or tail of what you're saying. Start again from the beginning.'

'The lady over there, she's called Sara. She's really nice. She gave me some of her grapes, because her husband brought them for her and she didn't feel like eating them and she said they'd only be bad. But they weren't bad. They were very nice.'

'Darling, what are you told over and over again about taking sweets from strangers? Or anything.'

'Oh,' Sandy was completely dashed. 'Oh yes.' Surely Sara wasn't one of those horrible strangers who did nasty things to children? Sandy knew that horrible strangers looked just like normal people. Sara looked like a normal person, except that her nose came out a bit funny. Sandy no longer knew what to say.

'Darling, I'm sure she's a lovely person, and you're quite safe here anyway. But please be careful. You must never, ever ever trust a stranger that you don't know. Though almost all of them are very nice people.'

'She is,' Sandy said. 'She really is. Anyway . . .' Sandy began to wonder whether they really could trust Sara with Poppy. But then she remembered that otherwise there wouldn't be any Poppy anyway, so what did it matter? 'Anyway, she wants a baby and she can't have one, because her body hasn't got the right bits; and she can't have someone else's because they think she's too old. So,

165

so, so . . .' Sandy was so excited, she couldn't think how to say it.

'So why can't she have ours?' Daddy finished up for her.

'Yes!' Sandy knew even the adults would understand, if she could only explain.

They didn't say anything. She looked at Mummy and she looked at Daddy, and they didn't say anything. Mummy looked at the bedclothes, and Daddy looked at Barney and Jack, and in the end Daddy put on his very gentle voice.

'It just doesn't work like that, I'm afraid, sweetheart.'

'What do you mean?'

'It's not as simple as that.'

'But it is! Mummy can have the baby, and we can give her to the nice lady.'

'It just wouldn't work.'

'Why not? Mummy,' Sandy turned to her, 'why not?'

Mummy sighed. 'I don't know. But it wouldn't. Daddy's right. You see, you can't just give babies away like that. As if they were toys you don't want. It's much more complicated.'

'But you're letting the doctors take her away! They're going to kill her! Can't you see? They're going to kill our baby! How can you be so STUPID?'

As far as Sandy remembered, Mummy and Daddy never quite answered. She and Daddy had an awful quarrel that night, and she got a smack before bed. In the end she was so upset that Daddy let her sleep in his bed, and even let her stay all night because Mummy wasn't there.

She dreamt that all her teddies were in the square pond outside the hospital, that they were sinking under the water; that she couldn't reach them and all the adults were rushing by. Somebody was holding her so she couldn't reach them. She struggled and fought, and tried to escape, and woke up in Daddy's arms again and he was saying, 'Shush, shush, sweetheart. It's all right. Were you having a bad dream?'

Sandy nodded unhappily. 'Why is the light on?'

'I was just reading before going to sleep. You go back to sleep again.'

'What's that funny smell?'

'What smell? I had a little drink before bed, that's all. Go to sleep.'

Sandy snuggled on to his chest. It was hairy and a bit prickly, but no worse than her teddies.

'Daddy,' she said. 'Doesn't it hurt when they take the baby away?'

'No,' Daddy said. 'They'll give Mummy an anaesthetic. Like Granny when she had her hips done.'

Sandy frowned. That wasn't what she had meant, quite. And besides, wasn't it that that Granny had died from?

She tucked her arms up under her chin, by Daddy's side. And after that she dreamt no more.

13 June, Sunday, Parsons Green

The sun woke me early, and I sat up and enjoyed one of
the luxuries I will take to Heaven with me, or at least to my
desert island: several hours in bed with a good book and
an endless pot of tea with the light from the morning sun
slanting across the bedclothes.

The doorbell rang at about ten o'clock, so I threw on a
dressing-gown and went downstairs.

'Come in,' I said. 'Where's your family?'

'Gone their separate ways. I came to thank you for coming
on our picnic. Actually the truth is that after any of my Italian
relations go they leave such a vacuum behind them that I feel
lonely for days.'

'Come in,' I repeated. 'Come and have breakfast in the
garden. And,' I said, as I put the kettle on, 'tell me about your
wife. If you want to.'

She was called Helena, she was beautiful ... 'More beautiful
than me? I mean than I?'

'I think it should be me. Usage over pedantry.' He mused
for a moment. '"*Plus beau que* moi"; not "*je*". And yes,' he
continued, deliberately looking at me, '*elle était plus belle que toi.*'

'Fine. Continue, please.'

She was sweet and charming and lovely.

'Why on earth did you leave her?'

'I didn't. She left me.'

'For another?'

'No. For a private grief.'

'Croissant?'

'No, it wasn't for a croissant, but yes please. And coffee.'

'I've changed my mind. You don't have to tell me after all. If
you don't want to.'

'On the contrary, I do.'

'Why?'

'I'll come on to that.'

They met at university, moved in together after Finals, for

168

some inexplicable reason to do with Helena's parents got married two years later, and the following year decided to have a baby.

'I know, I know. Most people would have waited another ten years, but she was a teacher and loved children and thought she could combine the two things easily enough. I'm not sure that she could have done, in fact. I doubt if it was the right choice. But,' he shrugged, 'who knows?'

The pregnancy went well, to begin with. She felt fine, she continued with her work, they were very happy. Then, in the eighth month, at Easter when most of the doctors were on holiday, she caught pneumonia and was rushed into hospital unconscious, with one of her lungs collapsed.

'They did everything they could. They saved Helena; she's now fit and well.'

'But they couldn't save the baby?'

'They thought they could, at first. They did an emergency caesarian of course, and put it in an incubator. But the next day, when Helena was still unconscious, they came and told me that in their medical opinion they considered the foetus "non-viable".'

'And?'

He thought for a minute, as if wondering how to put it. 'Helena never got over it. She was still unconscious, you see, so she never saw it.'

'Oh.' I poured us both another cup of coffee. The weeds that hung on the wall between our two houses were nodding up and down in the breeze. Were they weeds? Or wallflowers? 'Surely she was still young enough to have another?'

'She said that wasn't the point.'

'No. I can see that. But why did she leave you?'

'She blamed me for it. She said I shouldn't have believed the doctors, that I should have questioned everything they said.'

'Even modern doctors can't make every child live.'

There was silence. He was watching a sparrow which was gathering the crumbs under our table. I was going to ask him what he was thinking, but suddenly I didn't want to. After all it was his child too. After a long time I said, 'Will?'

'Mmm?'

'Was it female?'

'Yes.'

The sparrow looked up, cocked its head on one side, and darted off.

ANNE ATKINS

'She wasn't a foetus. She was a baby girl.'
'That was what Helena said too.'

We didn't talk about his child again. But I did return to the
subject of Helena.
'She sounds almost perfect.'
'Nobody's perfect. She was a lovely person. No doubt still is,
though she's been quite ill since then. She won't see me, but my
mother still calls on her. I hope she'll pull through.'
'Would you go back to her if she'd have you?'
'Until a few weeks ago I would have said yes. I could have
lived happily with her for years: but I would have gone back
more for her than for me, I think, because I wouldn't have
wanted to let her down again. I couldn't go back to her now.'
'Why?'
He looked at me and smiled a smile that looked almost sad:
or perhaps he was simply squinting into the sun. A blackbird
dived between us, chucking its noisy call. 'Do you honestly not
know?'
I looked away and changed the subject. Why do women do
that? Emma did it because she thought Mr Knightly was going
to tell her he loved someone else. 'Did you love her?' I asked.
'I thought I did. But now I know what love is, I realise I
simply liked her very much.' He took a deep breath, hesitated,
and then let it out again. 'Look,' he started, picking up my
hand by the tips of my fingers; then he let go and looked
away and stood up. Almost immediately he sat down again. 'I
don't know what you feel about me, so I won't say I can't live
without you, because I might have to. If you see what I mean.
And I won't say I love you because – oh, because it sounds
daft. People say it all the time...'
'Well,' I said, shading my eyes against the sun to look at
him, 'what *are* you going to say?' It was supposed to be a joke,
but it came out rather funny. Rather like a demand, from a
cross headmistress.
'Helena was a fabulous woman, and I thought her smashing.
Whereas you ... You're just part of me. That's all. I don't know
how else to say it.'
'Oh.' I wasn't sure whether or not to be disappointed. He
made me sound rather ordinary. But then, after a paragon
like her, I thought with a touch of very old-fashioned pique,
presumably any normal woman would be.
'And I suppose I can live without you, if I have to. But I'll

170

never be the same again. I'll never be me, on my own again, without you. I mean, you know what Charles Williams said: "Love you..."'

'"I *am* you."' I completed the quotation.

'Thank you. What I'm trying to say is that I love you.'

I felt, and feel, like a child, falling and falling in a dream. Is it Alice that I'm reminded of? I keep waking up with a jerk, and catching myself. Is this real life? Is this what Ben and Suki felt, and feel, for each other. And James? And my parents!? Surely not. This, this feeling, this wild, exhilarant madness, can't be as common as coupling, or ... Or what? Or it would dominate all of life. All our literature would be full of it. Poetry and music would be about little else. Yes, Caz, well spotted. But anybody who had ever felt like this would never take life seriously again.

Hold me. Hold me. *Hold me when the tide goes down.* Can this really be what the troubadours invented in the twelfth century? No, you dolt. What about the Shulammite? *Sustain me with raisins, refresh me with apples, for I am weak with love.*

Oh Will I love you.

Will I?

Calm rock pool on the shores of my security.

Hold me when the tide goes down.

CHAPTER TEN –
PERRYMEAD STREET

Sister, my sister, O sister swallow,
How can thine heart be full of the spring?
A thousand summers are over and dead . . .

Take flight and follow and find the sun.

Swinburne, Itylus

I moved to St Paul's School late, when I was nearly thirteen. Then I asked for my own bedroom.

Jack and Barney were both away at school, and Jack was applying for Oxford and hoping to have a year abroad before going up, so my parents said I could have Jack's room and my brothers could share whenever necessary; meanwhile they would have a roof extension put at the top of the house.

Generally people were moving house far less than they had when I was a small child. As families got smaller, and houses in London continued to go down in value, people stayed in the houses they'd bought when they got their first job; or continued to rent the same house for ten or twenty years, instead of three or four. So we, as a family, stayed at the house in Perrymead Street until I was in my twenties, when my parents moved into the country and Poppy and I kept the house on still.

By and large I was a very happy teenager. At school, though, I was a disaster. I hated the teachers telling me what to study, when I had my own agenda which was far better suited to me than theirs. They wanted me to become competent at computing and geography and chemistry and economics. I wanted to study grammar, and Greek, and Anglo-Saxon history. My careers advisor told me I would need subjects appropriate to the twenty-first century, otherwise I'd find myself unemployable when I came out of university.

'But I know what I'm going to be,' I said. 'I'm going to be a writer. So Latin will be far more important to my future than economics. After all, I'm only asking to study things which will be occupationally relevant, which we're always being told to do.' I didn't add that, if I was heading for unemployment, as over half my contemporaries were predicted to be, I wanted to be able to have an interesting unemployed life, able to read and think and continue my studies even if I wasn't going to be paid for it.

But school didn't encourage that kind of independence. Then, as now, we were expected to learn what we were told, not what interested us or would be useful. So I took no notice of my teachers and learnt what I wanted.

Adolescence was hectic. As well as having my academic studies, I joined a drama club and learned fencing and judo and kept up with my piano. Half my weekends and evenings were spent at parties. During the holidays my brothers' friends from Marlborough or Cambridge invited me to dances and balls and weekend country house parties; during the term my school friends and I went out with day-boys from St Paul's or Westminster. I saw all this as important to my future as a writer too. Some day I would want to turn all my adolescence into books. My parents, wisely, saw I was self-motivated and gave me a free rein.

Poppy and I grew apart. Oddly enough, she did very well at school to begin with. This surprised all of us, because Poppy had such a wicked personality we had all assumed she would spend most of her time in trouble. But it was almost as if school were a game which had very simple rules, and Poppy had decided to abide by them while it amused her to do so. My father's comment, as he received each glowing end-of-term report and enthusiastic assurance that she was a gifted child and a very hard worker, was always: 'She must be keeping under cover till the Revolution comes.'

But she and I no longer had much time to spend together. A sister younger by six years is not much of an asset to a teenager, and for a while we had little in common.

I can remember odd pockets of sunlight through those years when we sat and talked with open hearts despite the difference in our years, but they were rare.

'Do you think Amanda and Simon will get divorced?' she asked me once, when she was about eight and I fourteen. 'And if so, what will Amanda live off? She doesn't earn much.'

'Golly,' I said, shocked. 'Why do you think that? Don't you think they're happy together?'

'Most of the people I know get divorced, that's all,' she said, 'so I thought they probably would too.'

'Poppy, you only get divorced if you're unhappy together. You mustn't worry about that. Lots of people stay married.'

We were on a walk, in a wood somewhere, I think. Perhaps it was a family holiday or something. I can remember Poppy sitting on a huge fallen tree, in the dappled sunlight which broke through the trees. She was wearing an enormous sweatshirt of my father's as she often did. She was one of the most eccentric dressers I ever knew, even at that age. She would wear huge, grown-ups' T-shirts large enough for a big man, and nothing else at all. Or tights and a T-shirt of her own, and no shoes or trousers or skirt. Whenever she could be persuaded into a jumper, it would always be a grown-man's jumper.

'I'm not worried. I just wondered what Amanda was going to live off, that's all. Anyway, my teacher says nobody gets married nowadays.'

On another occasion, a year or two later, she said, 'Do you think Bach is the sexiest composer there's ever been?'

'Sexiest?' I said, astonished at my baby sister asking such a question.

'Yes. You know, most erotic.'

'Why do you think he's sexy?' I was trying to think of explanations from Bach's private life: his twenty children, for instance; his marriages; even his music for Anna Magdelena?

'Oh, I don't know. Sort of controlled, that's all. You know, the romantics are all soppy: splurge everywhere. Bach doesn't.'

'Poppy, you're not thinking of experimenting with anything, or anything, are you?' I wasn't sure how one was supposed to have this kind of conversation. It sounded to me as if she was repeating someone else's ideas, and it worried me.

''Course not,' she said, indignant. 'What d'you think I want to catch?'

But for the most part, during those years, we had our own lives to lead. When I had boyfriends she still had girlfriends, and when she had boyfriends I was up at Oxford.

I left Oxford when I was twenty-two. For a while I had felt my writing style had begun to stagnate, and long before I sat my degree

I was already planning my next move. I had learnt all I could, for the moment at any rate, from the academic disciplines available to me. I needed more to write about, not more examples of how writing has been done in the past. I would travel. I'd been to Africa during one long vac, and Turkey during my year off, and I felt they had given me enough material for years.

I told my parents what I wanted to do, and my mother suggested going overland to India where my eldest brother was working as an engineer. My father thought he himself might be able to get me some freelance journalistic work with a paper he worked for.

So that was what I did. After Finals I went straight home and didn't bother to collect my degree; I got various visas in order, had various injections, and packed a few basics in an otherwise empty rucksack. I took a small first aid kit, a spare pair of pants, a spare shirt for sleeping in, a waterproof sheet and a sleeping bag, a *chador* for the Moslem countries, and a pocket computer with several packets of discs. That was all.

Then I kissed my family at Victoria, got on a bus, promised to ring whenever I found a telephone, and agreed to give everyone's love to Jack.

Geography can change a relationship as easily as birth, or death, or falling in love can. I suppose I'd always found my elder brother rather a distant character. I looked up to him, I never openly argued with him, but I'd never felt particularly close to him, or able to talk to him about things which mattered deeply to me.

But when I came across him, several months later and after a long hot search through a dusty village, squatting on the ground with hardly any clothes on and drawing a diagram with a stick in the dirt to explain something to several elders who squatted with him, I almost felt as if I saw my brother for the first time. He looked up, shielding his eyes from the sun, and frowned at me for a minute. Then he put down his stick, stood up, and said, 'Well, take your rucksack off!'

Then he gave me a long hug before introducing me to the men he was with.

'You look pale,' he said.

'I've got dysentery, I think,' I said. And then I fainted.

I slept for the next day and a half, almost without waking. I'd travelled for two nights and a day in a bus, lying in the aisle in agony, oblivious of the people around me as they were of me. When the bus stopped, as it occasionally did, I got out and emptied my insides anywhere I could, regardless of who was watching me, amazed and thankful that I'd been able to last so long. When I found the village which bore the name I was looking for, I got out and shouldered my rucksack and showed one or two people the scruffy bit of paper with Jack's name and address on it. Then I walked for what seemed like an hour or more in the midday heat along streets and lanes and behind houses which all looked the same, before Jack himself was at last pointed out to me.

When I was next conscious of my surroundings, I found I was in a cool, simple house, with beaten floors and threadbare rugs and a banjo hanging from a nail on the wall. I was in a real, narrow bed, with real, clean sheets, and a mosquito net hanging over me. I smiled, and lay there for a long time, not even attempting to move. When the rays of the sun had moved several hand's-breadths round the walls, a little Indian face looked through the doorway and then disappeared again. Sometime later Jack came in, and smiled, and took my mosquito net off, and sat on the bed.

'Better?'

I nodded.

'Cup of tea?' I nodded again. 'I'll bring you a cup of Indian tea,' he said, 'with boiled milk and sugar in it. Then we'll take a sample over to the hospital and get you some medicine. Looks like amoeba. It's ghastly at the time, but it clears up quicker than some of the other things. I suppose you drank something stupid?' I shrugged, and nodded again. 'OK. You rest, and someone'll bring you something.'

I stayed with Jack for several weeks. I learnt how to cook extraordinary curries out of goat's meat and nuts, how to grind spices between two stones, how to eat with the fingers of my right hand, and how to make a peanut chutney so hot that one mouthful in a plateful of rice would make you break out in a sweat.

And I learnt to love the people he lived with, and the way of life he enjoyed. I wrote several pieces for the paper my father had put me in touch with, and once a week the van which took post to the nearest town would take my disc and deliver it to the telecommunications office there. They didn't buy any of the articles, but after a month they sent me a message asking me if I'd like to return to Iran, to Isfahan, because they needed a woman correspondent based there for several months at least. I accepted, and told Jack I must make my plans to turn around again.

'So I may not see you for a while,' I said. It was about ten o'clock at night. We were sitting in his little sitting-room, just before dinner, drinking a very strange, clear drink, fermented from something very odd: rice, or nettles, or something.

'You never know, I may get home before you,' he replied. 'My contract finishes in ten months.'

'Will you go straight back?'

There was a long silence. Jack swirled his drink round in his cheap tumbler, looked through the window at the gathering dark outside, listening to the water buffalo snuffling under the window, and took a sip, tasting and swallowing it before looking back at me.

'I don't know. I used to think I'd never be able to settle outside England. And I still miss it in all sorts of ways. But when you look at our society, at Europe, from a long way off, from another society and another set of values, you can see how sick the whole thing is.'

'Sick? What d'you mean?'

'What d'you imagine it felt like,' Jack asked me, 'to be living in the Roman Empire at the time of its collapse?'

I was completely stumped. 'Well, I suppose . . . er. What did they have? Orgies and things. I guess if you were rich enough . . .'

'Exactly,' Jack said. 'It probably felt all right. Perhaps quite fun: they might even have argued that that kind of sexual freedom, for instance, was an advance on the strictness they'd had before.'

'I ought to know about this,' I said.

'Yes, you ought really. Anyway, that's what Europe looks like to me now: a society in decline. When I was at school I thought the most important thing in life was to get a steady job with a good income in six figures. Unemployment meant failure. And failure mattered. But I look around the people here and realise they've got something much more important.'

'What's that?'

'I'm not sure, quite. Religion, maybe. Oh, I know there's Islam and Christianity and Hinduism in Europe too, but it doesn't affect society any more back home. In Europe, politics and economics come first; relationships, poetry, matters of conscience, sunsets, all the other things of life, have to fit in round the money. Here, God or the gods come first, and the people next; possessions don't matter. Or do they?' He paused, staring at the floor as if the answer were written on the bare earth. 'Perhaps they matter more: they become genuinely important. After all, if you've only got one cooking-pot, it matters more than a Porsche.' Then he looked up at me and smiled. 'I don't know.'

'But how does it affect things? What d'you mean?' After all, does it matter if society's in decline, if people are fed and warm and comfortable?

'It affects everything. It means children over here are more important than cars or telephones. It means people would rather have a family than an electric oven. It means there's a hierarchy, and people have duties to one another, instead of simply having rights. It means I have to decide whether I want to give up my way of life back home and stay here and marry Shangani; or take her home with me; or give her up. If this were Europe we would have been living together for the last year, and she would have had a child if she wanted one, and wouldn't have if she didn't, and if she wanted a career she'd have a career, and if she didn't she wouldn't; and if I wanted to leave I'd leave, and if I didn't I'd stay for a while.'

'But isn't that sensible, Jack?' I said, as much to argue the point as anything. 'It's much more convenient, after all. We don't want people going around doing something out of a sense of honour, surely?'

'Why not? Oh, Europe's more convenient, certainly. But I'm not sure it's right.'

'You're not becoming religious, are you?'

'I hope not. No, I'm not. I'm just wondering whether I want a child enough to stay here and settle, that's all.'

'You could have a child back home,' I said. I tried to imagine Shangani in the Home Counties, or fitting into the Indian community in London.

'I don't want a child in England,' he said. 'Europe doesn't value children. I think that's what I'm trying to say.'

I arrived in Isfahan in November of that year.

It's a very beautiful country, but a cruel, hard one. I'd had Moslem friends, of course, and thought I knew about Islam, but I'd had no idea how a religion can dominate a country so completely. I wasn't sure that I agreed with Jack, that any religion is better than none.

And behind the doors of my house, when I took off my *chador*, I lived the life of a European woman. I had friends to dinner, drank wine, and telephoned home. I worked as a journalist, with a computer terminal and radio line back to London.

I'd been there nearly eighteen months when my mother wrote and said Poppy was coming to see me.

'She finishes school this June,' she wrote, 'and wants a few months abroad before Art School. Can you put her up? Give her a ring sometime and let her know. We went to Norfolk last week, to visit Barney. He seemed very fit and happy . . .'

I rang and said of course she could, and then forgot all about it. But as the summer came, and the weeks passed, I kept realising I was looking forward to something and I'd forgotten what it was. Then I would remember Poppy was coming, and wonder if that was it. Then I asked myself whether I'd been in Iran too long. Then I looked at what I might miss if I left, and realised there was very little. By the time June came I was longing for some female, English company. I had a close friend who was American, with whom I spent a lot of time with, but I was heartily sick of his harmless Americanisms.

In the middle of June my parents rang and said Poppy had set off. 'When's she planning to arrive?' I said.

'You know Poppy,' my father said. 'She refused to make any plans. I should expect her in a week or two.' So I bought some proper 'English' tea, made a list of things we ought to go and see, and waited.

By the middle of July I was ringing my parents almost every day to say she still hadn't arrived. I was far more worried than they. I was acutely aware how vulnerable and unprotected Western women are when faced with the Moslem male; they were only aware of Poppy's idiosyncratic ability to do daft things and still come out on top.

Then one night, in late July, there was a hammering on my door. I pulled a shirt over my head and went downstairs. Looking through the little security window in my front door, I saw two men with dark hair but pale skin, like Armenian men; one tall and one short.

'What do you want?' I shouted at them in English.

'Your sister,' they replied. 'We will give her to you when she has paid us. She owes us much money.'

My heart sank. 'Show me,' I said. 'Show me my sister.'

At that moment, Poppy sprang into view. Her blonde hair was frizzed out round her face like a cloud, and she pressed her nose against the glass.

'Hi,' she said with a big smile. 'I don't owe them any money. It's a complete con. I hitched a lift from Tehran, and now they're trying to charge me. It took us hours to find your house.'

'Wait there,' I said loudly, as if any of them were likely to do anything else, and fetched a scarf for my hair and about as much money as it would have cost her to come by bus. Then I went back, unlocked the door, and pulled Poppy in. The men tried to push their way in too, but I told them to step outside again or I wouldn't give them anything. Then I showed them the money.

'I don't care how much you're asking for,' I said. 'This is all you're getting. Take it or leave it. And if you're still here in five minutes I call the police.'

They took the money without a word, and I shut the door and locked it again.

'I didn't owe them anything,' Poppy said indignantly. 'I told them when I got in the car that I didn't have any money, and I was hitching. I explained it to them very carefully.'

'Poppy!' I was nearly shouting, confused by my own feelings of fury and relief and incredulity, and even an idea that I would soon find this amusing. 'How can you be so pig-ignorant about a country you come and visit? Women here are quite well protected provided they obey certain conventions. But if you flout those conventions you're likely to be raped, beaten up or murdered. You're bloody lucky to be here.' I stopped for a moment, to draw breath and stare at her clothes. Then I shook my head and said quietly, 'What on earth were you doing hitching?'

'There wasn't a bus for forty-eight hours,' she said simply, 'and I wanted to get here.'

To my utter astonishment I burst into tears. 'God, I hate this country,' I said. 'I've never been so lonely in my life.' Then I laughed, and blew my nose, and cried, and we hugged, and I blew my nose again, and said, 'Why don't we have an English cup of tea?'

It was like rediscovering a long-lost friend and making a new one, all in one. It was like finding Jack in India, and suddenly knowing I loved him far more than I'd ever realised. It was like meeting a lover you know you can talk to about everything, and yet having all our childhood memories in common. It was like finding a younger version of myself in an alien and hostile culture.

And yet Poppy and I were very different. Where I was cautious, she was reckless. Where I was thoughtful and observant, she was instinctive and quick. Where I would stop and think, she would jump in with both feet first right up to her waist.

That summer we went everywhere and did everything. I had work to do, but did it to my own schedule; and when I was busy she sat and sketched and drew and painted. Whenever we left the house I made her wear a *chador*. We visited mosques and palaces and bazaars and shops. We went to see the copper-smiths and silver-smiths and dyers and weavers and carpet-makers. Most of all Poppy liked to sit and watch craftsmen whose work hadn't changed in hundreds of years. We spent a whole afternoon watching a man beating and tapping out an intricate pattern on a vast silver dish. There were no pictures, of course, for this was Islam; but the swirls and dots and shapes were exquisite. Poppy loved it.

One morning I took her to see how they make the patterned frames around the miniatures which used to be painted on ivory and are now on bone or plastic. A little frame can take several hours to make. They bind together tiny wooden sticks of different colours, and copper threads, and then slice through it all to get the pattern, which they then smooth and polish.

'Why don't we take this much trouble over beautiful things?' Poppy asked me.

'Because it's not commercial.'

Sometimes we hired a car and drove hundreds of miles into the desert. Then we sat under the craggy, bare rocks and drank cool water which we'd brought in a thermos, or Coca Cola.

'I wish I were a geographer,' Poppy said. 'I'd love to know how all these different rock formations were made, and how old they are.' Once we saw a black cloud of Bedouin women in the distance, walking along with the dust hovering around them. They seemed miles from anything which could have sustained life.

Halfway through August Poppy said to me, 'How much longer are you staying here?'

'I've handed in my notice,' I said. 'I might come home with you.'

'Oh. When did you decide that?'

'The other day. You've made me realise how homesick I am. I've been chronically lonely for nearly two years, and didn't realise it. I may be able to finish in time to travel back with you.' I felt such relief as I said this that I marvelled that I hadn't decided it before.

'But I thought I'd go on and see Jack,' Poppy said. 'I don't have to be in London until October.'

'Well then, you go on and see Jack. I'll stay and wind everything up here, and make my own way back.' I looked out of my window at the colourful streets below me, and heard a wild shout from a man, selling something perhaps, or chasing someone. 'I've no idea what I shall do when I get home.'

'Amanda and Simon are moving into the country,' Poppy told me, 'and I'm staying in the house in Perrymead Street. Why don't you come and live there with me?'

I turned and looked at her, and thought about it. I could probably do freelance journalism. I might even start work on a book. I thought of that short story, long ago, which, with Poppy's pictures, had won the Heffer's competition and been the beginning of my professional writing career. Perhaps we could even work together again, if Poppy could discipline herself for five minutes. In any case, she'd be out at college most of the time. I thought Poppy's friends would probably be a nightmare, but at least I'd get peace and quiet during the day.

'All right,' I said. 'I will.'

14 June, Monday, Parsons Green

Dear Abi,
All right, you win. I have fallen in love. Yesterday at about, um,
ten to one I think it was; after a very late breakfast, certainly
before lunch, just there, under that sweet-smelling pink
flowery thing in my back garden.
   And that's all I'm going to tell you, so don't pester me. And
don't be too beastly and teasy, will you? Because, you see,
we grown-ups can't really help it. Or I certainly couldn't help
it. Want it? It was the last thing I wanted. Getting on quite
happily on my own, thank you very much. When, wham,
bam, just like the measles. Not that you horrid children catch
measles any more, because you have inoculations and things;
but, in my good old grandmother's day, or in your granny's day
come to think of it, all decent children got measles once in a
while and half of them died of it.
   Which is probably what'll happen to me. What nonsense am I
talking? *Men have died, and worms have eaten them, but not for
love.* Yes, but that's men, isn't it? Women, on the other hand ...
You won't know that side-splittingly funny play *Rosencranz and
Guildenstern Are Dead*: 'the toenails, on the other hand ...'
   Of course you won't. But your daft father, who is reading
this letter to you at this very moment on the extremely flimsy
grounds that you can't yet read, does, because we went to see
it together when he was up at a very mouldy secondary-modern
institution called Cambridge. So he can explain the reference.
   Anyway, you are *not* to tell him or Suki about my misfortune
under any circs. And whatever you do, don't let him go using
that oldest trick in the book that just because he's reading
my extremely private matters out loud to you he can't help
hearing them himself, because I've been around longer than that
one and I can see through it, see.
   And no, to answer your next few questions, I have not had
a baby yet. No, our houses are right next to each other so we
don't need to move in together and I quite like still having my
own kitchen not to mention garden, thank you very much. No,

because I loathe weddings. So therefore, no, you cannot be a bridesmaid. But perhaps next time you come and visit us you can dress up as one to make up for it.

Happy?

How is that disgusting slobbery dog of yours? Or was it a cat? Difficult to tell with your animals. Perhaps it was just a very dirty rug.

And tell your absurd parents that if they ever decide you'd be happier at a different educational establishment, I shall be dippy enough to sponsor you for an absolute maximum of sixteen years *and not a day more*. Got it?

Come and see me – I mean us – soon.

Your extravagantly affectionate auntie but don't you dare call me that yourself.

C.

CHAPTER ELEVEN –
CLANCARTY ROAD 1990

οὐκ οἶδ᾽ ὅπως σοι ῥᾳδίως εἴπω κακά.

I do not know how I can easily tell you such evil
things.

Euripides, Women of Troy, 717

Sandy's and Jack's birthdays were in the same week. Sandy's was
always first. Jack had been born first, so Jack's very first birthday
had been first, and some of his others too. But nowadays Sandy
always had her birthday first.

Nevertheless they usually shared a birthday tea. Not a birthday
party, when they had their friends and things, and Sandy had party
games and balloons, and Jack had loud music and noisy boys and
Barney was allowed to come but Sandy wasn't really. Their family
birthday tea was shared. That was when they had scrummy tea and
presents.

So on Friday they had scrummy tea, with Lilt, and crisps, and
Hoola Hoops, and Twiglets which actually make your lips hurt and
aren't that nice, and lots of sandwiches and cold sausages. The egg
sandwiches were the best. Mummy had just learnt to make bacon
and avocado sandwiches with garlic mayonnaise, and kept saying
how brilliant they were. But they were a bit too clever really: the
lettuce fell out. And egg is still the best.

They weren't allowed their presents till after tea. Sandy knew
Mummy and Daddy had got her something pretty exciting. She'd
asked for a donkey but she thought that was a bit of a long shot
really. There wasn't much room in their garden, and they did have

ANNE ATKINS

some rather posh flowers which a donkey might eat. So she didn't
hold out much hope for the donkey. But Barney kept saying, 'You're
going to love it, Sandy; you're going to so love it,' till Sandy thought
she might burst.

But first they got the presents that weren't from Mummy and
Daddy. Sandy wanted to give hers first. She'd bought Jack a tiny
tiny little paint set. It was sweet. It had cost her a whole week's pocket
money. In fact it should have cost her a bit more: it had really been
fifty-five pee, but Daddy had lent her the extra five, and she thought
he might not make her pay it back. It was so small Daddy could fit it
inside his hand without it showing, and it had six real colours which
worked, and a real paintbrush. Sandy wasn't sure that Jack did much
painting, but it was still super to look at even if you never used it.

Then Barney and Jack gave Sandy her presents from them. Jack
had got her a doll, and Barney had bought the doll's clothes. They
were very smart. They were real teenaged clothes, not baby clothes
like dolls usually have. Sandy thought the doll was beautiful. She had
real blonde hair that could get longer and shorter, like a real person's.
Well, no, not like a real person's. Better than a real person's, because
it could grow really fast and ungrow again.

Then Sandy was given a little present from Mummy, which wasn't
her proper present. It was a book all about wildflowers. It had
pictures of all the different wildflowers, and their names, and if you
took it on a walk you could tell what all the flowers were on your
walk.

'I promised it to you,' Mummy said. 'Do you remember?'

'No,' Sandy said.

Then Sandy had to decide whether she wanted her big birthday
present, from Mummy and Daddy, before Jack had his, or afterwards.
The problem was if she had it after Jack she'd have to wait and if
she had to wait she thought she might explode; but if she had it
first she wouldn't have it to look forward to while Jack had his. In
the end she decided to have it afterwards. She was so excited, she
couldn't bear the thought of having it straight away. So Mummy
went to get Jack's present. As soon as he saw it he knew what it
was, by the way it was wrapped up. It was a real, adult's tennis
racquet. Jack didn't say anything. Sandy could see his face was
shining and he was really pleased. It seemed to be a lovely tennis
racquet. Sandy didn't know anything about tennis, but as far as she
could tell, it was pretty good.

188

In the end Jack spoke. All he said was, 'Wicked.' That meant he was very, very happy. He didn't say 'wicked' about many things, and when he did they were pretty good.

Sandy was pleased that Jack was so pleased. At first, when she'd seen the tennis racquet, she had felt uncomfortable, sad; she didn't know why. Something in her wanted to cry. She didn't feel the tears coming; it wasn't like when you hurt your finger and cry straight away. But deep inside her something seemed to be crying. But when she saw Jack's face she knew it must be all right.

'In time for tomorrow's tournament,' Mummy said. 'We thought we'd all come and watch, if you want us to. Not if it'll put you off. Have a think, and tell us whether or not you want us to come.'

'Thanks, Mum,' Jack said. 'Thanks Si.'

'Pleasure,' Daddy said. 'Now. Sandy's turn.'

Sandy thought her insides felt like the sea, rising and falling like waves. She wondered how big it was, and whether it would be wrapped in red paper.

'You've got to come into the garden,' Daddy said.

'Sandy, you're going to love it,' Barney said for the tenth time.

'Why have I got to come into the garden?' she said.

'Elephants don't fit in the house, silly,' said Daddy.

'It's not an elephant,' Sandy said. 'It's an electric sausage. Daddy told me so.'

'A what?' said Mummy.

'Daddy promised me an electric sausage.'

'Simon you are such an ass.'

'He promised.'

'Sandy, it's much nicer than an electric sausage. What on earth would you use an electric sausage for?'

'Um,' said Sandy. 'Lots of things.'

'I can't see anything wrong with a good old-fashioned manual sausage,' Mummy went on. 'It's just Simon's mania for gadgets.'

'You're all mad,' said Jack.

They were at the French windows.

'Shut your eyes,' Daddy said.

'Why?'

'I don't know. It seems the appropriate thing to do. Don't then. Come on.' And Daddy took her by the hand and she stepped on to the patio. Then he pointed. Sandy saw a green wooden box, with a door on it, and chicken wire at the front.

ANNE ATKINS

'Is that it?' Sandy said. She felt a little disappointed.
'Not quite. Sit down.' Daddy opened the door of the box, put his
hands in, and then pulled out the most gorgeous creature Sandy had
ever seen in her life. It was a soft browny-grey colour, with dark brown
wide-awake eyes, and fur as fluffy as a summer cloud. One of its ears
fell down and one pointed up.
Sandy couldn't speak. Daddy put the animal down on her lap and
showed her how to hold it, and as she stroked it she looked up
and saw all of them watching her, and thought perhaps she was
the proudest person in the world.
In the end Mummy said, 'Do you like her?' Sandy simply nodded.
'What will you call her?'
Sandy shrugged. In the end she said, 'Is she really for me?' And
then, 'What is it? Is it a rabbit?' and Mummy nodded.
'She's a dwarf lop-eared cashmere. That means she's a kind of
rabbit.'
'We'll have her for Sunday lunch when she's a big bigger.'
'Oh Simon belt up.'
'Yes, shut up Daddy,' the boys said.
'Yes,' Sandy said crossly. 'Shut up.'
'Sorry,' said Daddy.
'What will you call her?' Mummy said.
'Poppy,' Sandy said without thinking.
'What a lovely name,' Mummy said.
'You said you didn't like it, before,' Sandy reminded her.
Mummy looked at her oddly for a moment. 'Did I?' she said.
'Yes. When I asked you before.'
'Oh,' said Mummy. 'Well, it's a lovely name for a rabbit.'

She was the best present Sandy had ever had in her life. She was
allowed to hop around the garden, as long as Sandy kept an eye on
her to make sure she didn't eat the best plants. She was easy to watch
and soft to hold. And she belonged only to Sandy.
The next day was Jack's tennis tournament, but Sandy didn't want
to go. She wanted to stay at home all day and play with Poppy. Daddy
offered to stay at home with her. He said he had some work to do, and,
if Jack didn't mind, it would be better if he stayed at home.
It was a wonderful day. Daddy finished work by lunchtime. He made
lunch and put it on a tray and they ate it in the garden. They had paw
paw pies and tomatoes and cider. They're really pork pies, but they're

called paw paw pies because when Sandy first used to take one in her lunchbox to nursery school she called it a poor poor pie, and it had been like that ever since. Sandy was even allowed a tin of cider just like Daddy, because it was cider without the stuff in it that makes you drunk. And she was allowed to give a bit of her tomato to Poppy. She tried a bit of her paw paw pie too, but Poppy wouldn't eat that.

Daddy said, 'Just as well. She'd probably get spongy whatnot encopholis and turn into a mad cow.' That was just one of the things adults say sometimes that you don't take any notice of.

'You ought to have your sunhat on,' Daddy said.

'So ought you,' Sandy replied.

'I haven't got one, cheeky. And I'm so old and wrinkled anyway that there wouldn't be much point. And I'm a man.'

'Don't be sexy.'

'Do you mean sexist?'

'No.'

'It's nice, isn't it? Sitting in the sun, on a quiet Saturday, having finished work; just sitting around eating lunch watching your rabbit hop about.' Sandy nodded. 'Oi, bunny! Get off Amanda's azaleas! Go on, shoo!' Daddy settled down again and shut his eyes in the sun. 'Where shall we go for our summer holiday, gorgeous?'

'Dunno,' Sandy said.

'Oh, of course. Those boys are going off on some camp or other, aren't they?'

'Dunno.'

'I've got an idea. Would you like to go and stay with Grandfather for a holiday?'

'Yeah!' Sandy said with gusto.

'Grandfather could do with cheering up. He gets jolly lonely these days. We could ask if you could go there while the boys are away, and I could take Mummy away for a quiet holiday, just the two of us. I think Mummy needs a bit of a break, without children or responsibility or anything.'

'I'd like to go with you,' Sandy said.

'Well, that's a possibility. But you can see us any time. You haven't seen Grandfather properly for over a year.'

'A year!' It sounded like almost for ever.

'More than a year. I mean seen him properly, you know; for more than just Christmas dinner. And anyway, sometimes Mummy and I need a bit of time just to ourselves, without anyone else around at

ANNE ATKINS

all. You see, when you get married it's a special kind of relationship. It's not like having brothers and sisters, or mothers and children. It's even more special than that. Sometimes you need to be on your own together. Think about it: when you're married, you won't want Amanda and me around all the time.'

It sounded a bit silly to Sandy. After all, as Daddy said, he and Mummy weren't brother and sister or anything like that. Your family must be more special than anyone you got married to. Dominic said he was going to marry Sandy, and she didn't think he was very special. And she wouldn't mind Mummy and Daddy being around always. As long as they didn't make her tidy her room.

'Anyway,' Daddy went on, 'if you went to Grandfather's he'd feed you icecream and take you to the park and let you stay in bed in the mornings.'

'Yeah,' Sandy said again.

'So would you like me to ask if you can?'

'Yes please,' said Sandy.

So they rang him there and then, and Grandfather said that would be super, and he told Sandy to pack her swimming things and they'd go in his neighbour's swimming pool every morning before breakfast.

'Can I bring Poppy?' Sandy asked.

'Who, darling?' Grandfather said.

'No,' Daddy said. He was standing next to her. 'She wouldn't like to be moved. She'll be much better off here, with us looking after her.'

Only of course Daddy had forgotten that nobody would be at home. They were all going away, and Poppy would be left behind.

There were only two more days of term. When Sandy got to school on Monday morning she was dying to tell everyone about Poppy. It wasn't a news day. If it had been a news day, she would have asked if she could stand in the middle of the circle and tell the whole class her news. She would have told them about Poppy, and her one floppy ear, and her dark brown twitchy face.

Instead she decided to tell Ella at playtime.

Ella and Annie were playing a game with Rosie. Sandy watched them for a while. It was a skipping game, and you had to run in when the rope was going round and jump over it, singing a song. It looked quite tricky. It also looked great fun. Rosie was in the middle, and Ella and Annie were at each end making the rope go round. Rosie was very good, but after a while she jumped

192

at the wrong place and tripped over the rope and made it stop going round, so then she had to stop and swap with Annie and take Annie's end of the rope.

Sandy longed for them to ask her to join in. She thought it was the best game she'd ever seen. And then, when they'd finished, she'd tell them about Poppy and they'd be very excited and ask if they could come to tea, and then she'd have them all to tea in the holidays and they'd all play with Poppy. She moved a little nearer the rope, waiting for them to ask her if she'd like a go.

At that moment Annie's foot hit the rope and it was the end of her go.

'Oh, Sandy!' she said very crossly. Sandy was a little afraid of Annie. 'Why did you do that? That wasn't fair,' she said to the others. 'Sandy made me go wrong. It's still my go.' Sandy knew she hadn't touched the rope. She wasn't even near it.

'No it isn't,' said Ella.

'Yes it is,' said Annie.

' 'Tisn't.'

' 'Tis.'

' 'Tisn't.'

'Oh, I don't care anyway. It wasn't my fault. Oh Sandy, go AWAY! Who asked you to play?'

'I wasn't playing anyway,' Sandy said, not moving.

Ella started her go.

'Why can't I play?' Sandy said.

' 'Cos you can't,' said Annie. 'Go away.'

'No.'

Ella tripped over the rope. 'Oh, look what you've done now, Sandy,' Ella said hopelessly. 'Now I've lost my go too.'

'My go,' said Rosie.

'It's my go,' said Sandy.

'No it isn't,' said Annie. 'You're not playing, so go away.'

'That's right. It's my go,' said Rosie. 'Go away.'

'Go away, Sandy,' said Ella.

'No. Anyway it's not your rope; it's a school rope. And I want my go.' And Sandy took hold of the rope.

Rosie had just started skipping. When Sandy took the rope, it jerked into her hands unexpectedly. She wasn't quite sure what happened next, but Rosie was on the ground screaming, and she had a red mark where the rope had pulled against her leg. Sandy hadn't meant to hurt Rosie at all, but Annie said, 'You bully!' and pushed Sandy hard in the middle of her back so that she fell over.

Sandy got up. Her back was really sore, and she'd scraped the skin off her hands, but she didn't cry; not yet. She turned to Ella. 'Anyway, I hate you. I was going to tell you my best secret ever, but I won't now. I won't tell you ever. I hate you and your sister.'

Ella said, 'I don't care. Your secrets aren't true anyway. You said your mummy was going to have a baby and she's not. I know, because she's not getting fatter and when ladies have babies they get fatter. So I don't want your secrets, liar.'

Sandy ran.

She couldn't put her hands over her ears because they were too sore, so she just ran. She didn't stop till she got to the other end of the playground, where there was the grassy bank that she had sometimes sat on with Ella. She'd never sit on it with Ella again. She hated Ella so much she wanted to go up to a tree and hit it. But she didn't because it would have hurt. She lay down on her tummy and started pulling out the grass. It looked different now. It was mostly a pale brown colour. The fern-like bits of grass were still a dark green, but when you looked across the lawn you saw a sandy desert colour, and no daisies in the grass, or wildflowers at the end of the garden. And it was less comfortable lying on her tummy now, because all the grass was dry and prickly against her legs.

She could hear other children screaming and playing behind her. Sandy thought of Ella and Annie going home for their tea together, and sharing a room at night when it was dark, and standing up for each other in fights. Then she thought of the fights they had with each other sometimes, when they were at home; Ella had told her about them. They must be very horrid children, to be fighting all the time.

She started pulling out the ferny grass and laying it down in front of her in a row. Then, as she watched it, it became a watery blur. She saw bits of brown and green, and her own pink fingers, all mixed together in a wash of muddle in front of her eyes. She felt the warm splashes on her hands. Then she laid her face on her arms and sobbed and sobbed on to the dry ground.

When Sandy got home she went up to her room. She didn't go and see Poppy. She got out her new doll and the dolls' clothes Barney had given her. She had put them in the basket with her other dolls' clothes. When she tipped them out of the basket she found an old nappy pin that had been hers when she was little. Babies didn't wear those kind of nappies any more. Nowadays babies wore nappies that even brothers and sisters could put on and take off when the babies wet themselves. Sandy opened and shut the nappy pin several times. They were supposed to be made so that you couldn't do that to them; so that you couldn't open them unless you were supposed to. But in fact they were easy to do up and undo.

She decided to give her new doll a nappy. She had a handkerchief in her dolls' basket that she used for a nappy; she took it out and folded it like a nappy, and laid the new doll on it.

Then she clicked her tongue. 'It's not supposed to have a nappy. It's an adult doll.' She looked at the doll lying on the ground with no clothes, and realised how like an adult she looked; how like a real person; how like a mummy. She picked up the open nappy pin and jabbed it into her. She jabbed it into her tummy, really hard, over and over again. She went on jabbing her until she realised that her new birthday present, the beautiful, expensive one Jack and Barney had given her, the one they'd saved up for for weeks, was covered in great big holes and was completely spoiled. And then she cried and cried.

At last Sandy rubbed her eyes and hid her ruined doll and came downstairs. Mummy was making tea. Everyone was in the kitchen. She could hear voices. She went into the sitting-room to go through into the garden, and there she saw Jack's brand new tennis racquet, standing proudly in the corner, after its one and only triumphant match.

Sandy thought, If it weren't for Jack's tennis racquet we'd still have Poppy. The real Poppy. The baby. She suddenly hated it. She picked it up. She didn't want to spoil it, because it was such a lovely tennis racquet and Jack loved it so much, but she couldn't help feeling that it was all the tennis racquet's fault; or something the tennis racquet stood for. In the end she simply hid it under the sofa cushions. Justice was satisfied, and she hadn't done any harm. Someone would find it soon.

Then she went out and picked Poppy out of her hutch and held her silky fur against her face.

'But I left it here!' Jack said. 'Here in the corner, I know I did.'

'Jack, you are hopeless,' said Mummy.

'Sandy, have you seen it?'

Sandy looked at him miserably. He didn't even wait for an answer. Perhaps if he had she would have told him. He was bound to find it soon. Surely somebody would think of looking under the cushions. Things were always getting lost under there, and Maria always found them when she came to clean on Fridays.

But today was only Monday. And Jack had his last match of the term tomorrow!

Sandy had never prayed before. But she went up to the bathroom and prayed, 'Our father in heaven, please can Jack find his tennis racquet? Before tomorrow. Please, please.'

It half occurred to Sandy, at the back of her mind, that she could go down and take the racquet out of its hiding place and put it back where it was. But some rather big and hidden reason seemed to stop her. She never asked herself what it was. No doubt if she had, she would have seen that there was no good reason at all. Perhaps then she would have gone down and showed everyone where it was, and been called a silly ass, and nothing else would have happened. Nevertheless the tennis racquet had taken the place of the baby sister she'd never have, and she had had to do something.

Jack hadn't found it by bedtime. Sandy told herself that she would go down at breakfast and take it out again. Before breakfast. As soon as she woke up. So that when Jack came down he'd see it there. Perhaps she wouldn't go to sleep. Perhaps as soon as Mummy and Daddy had gone to bed she would creep downstairs again. That was it. As soon as the lights were out, she would be really brave and turn on the lights again and go back into the sitting-room.

But Sandy didn't know that Mummy and Daddy were having friends for supper. Not a proper dinner, like they sometimes had, with adult voices floating up the stairs all night, and the chink of glasses, and sometimes even the smell of smoke. Just a couple for supper.

Sandy didn't see them come. She heard the front doorbell and the knocker, as if one or the other wasn't enough, and she stole out to the landing to see them come in. She'd seen them once before. The man was the biggest, fattest man she knew. Sandy didn't like him much because he was also noisy, and laughed at his own jokes. His wife was small and pretty, and like a bird. She had curly brown hair, and chirruped and hopped by his side. Sandy saw them come in and walk towards the sitting-room. The voices quietened to a muffled burble. She went back to bed and prepared for a long wait before she could come downstairs again and go and rescue the tennis racquet.

She heard Daddy going into Jack's room first. His room was above hers. Daddy had to walk past her room to go up the next flight of stairs. She couldn't see him, but she could hear him, and she knew it was Daddy. She heard him talking to Jack, in a low, steady voice, as if he were explaining something. Then she heard Jack go, 'What?!' really loudly. Then she felt a dreadful sinking in her stomach, and her legs went cold. She was glad she was lying down in bed, because she felt as if she were falling down and down through the bedclothes. She knew something awful had happened, and she knew it was her fault. She had never before not wanted to see Daddy; but as she heard him coming down the top stairs again she longed for him to walk past her door and not come in. She wondered whether he would find her if she hid under her duvet. But she didn't move.

Her light went on. She looked up and saw Daddy. In his hand was the handle of the tennis racquet. The head of the racquet flopped down like a dead flower. Daddy's knuckles, where he held the handle, were white.

'Is this anything to do with you?'

Sandy stared dumbly. She thought her head moved a little bit, but she wasn't sure that it looked quite like a nod.

'Did you hide this under the sofa cushions?'

This time Sandy nodded properly.

'Well then, let me tell you something, young lady. A joke is only a joke if it's funny. And it's not funny if it upsets somebody else. It's not funny if it means other people wasting a lot of time. And it's not funny when it involves other people's property. When were you going to tell him where it was? Eh? He has a match tomorrow.' For a long and awful moment Daddy looked at Sandy and said nothing. Then he tossed the racquet down on to the floor. 'You can't even pay for it. You wouldn't have enough if you saved up all year.'

Sandy looked at the broken racquet. She didn't dare move her eyes. She didn't know whether she most wanted Daddy to go or stay. Both would be awful beyond words.

'I'm going downstairs to look after our guests. You can apologise to Jack in the morning.'

He was gone. He was gone, and he had left her in the dreadful empty hollow of her own guilt and shame. Her eyes were still fixed on the gut of the racquet. She watched, fascinated, as the pattern changed. One moment it seemed to be going away from her, and the next moment it was moving towards her. Her eyes were very wide open and hurting. An awful thought was dawning on her, and she'd never be able to tell it to anyone. She would live with it all her life, it was so evil.

Suddenly she said to God, 'That was cheating. You know it was. You knew I didn't mean that.' But she wasn't sure whether God had to keep the same rules as everyone else.

She started. Daddy had come back in. He came and knelt by her bed and took her in his arms and she knew he was going to be kind. Her eyes smarted even more.

'I know you didn't mean to break it, sweetheart. I daresay you didn't mean to be naughty. And I'm sorry I was so angry. But you do know that you mustn't touch other people's things unless you've asked them. And you must know that Jack spent a long time looking for it. Never mind. It's over now.'

But it wasn't over. Jack had no racquet. And Daddy obviously hadn't yet realised what Sandy had realised. At last the tears escaped from Sandy's eyes and ran down her nose and her cheeks, and into her ear because she was lying on her side. Daddy wiped them away, but they only came faster.

'Hey, hey, that's enough. What does a tennis racquet matter? You know what my father used to say to my sisters whenever they broke anything? "As long as you don't break a heart." That's what he used to say. Isn't it silly?'

He hadn't worked it out. But he would one day. And then what would he think of her? Because what Sandy had realised, with such dawning and frightful horror, was that now Jack hadn't got his racquet they could have had the baby after all. They hadn't had the baby so that they could afford a racquet for Jack. Now they had neither, so they could have had Poppy after all.

The tears poured down her face. Her nose was running, and Daddy had no handkerchief. He held her closer, and then he said the strangest thing Sandy had ever heard.

'It doesn't matter, poppet. Come on, dry your eyes. After all, we can always buy him another one.'

28 June, Friday, Parsons Green

I had no idea life could be as important and trivial as this. I am awake, alive, present, perhaps simply myself, for the first time ever.

And yet everything goes on just as before. I wake, go for a morning swim at the unspeakable Hurlingham, which I reluctantly admit breathtakingly beautiful in the morning mist, come back for breakfast, read my letters. Then I spend the morning in my study. Sometimes, the break I take at mid-morning coincides with the break he takes, and we have coffee together; usually not, as it would then stretch to an hour off. Occasionally we have lunch together, but not often: he works away from home far more than I do. I do some work in the afternoon, then at about teatime I stop for the day and go into the garden with a pot of tea and a piece of cake and a book, perhaps welcome Gibbons on to my lap if he's chosen to grace my garden, and start to enter Heaven very slowly. Because sooner or later, eventually, before the shadows have lengthened far into the evening, he's there in my garden too, and we're having a drink, and putting something on the barbecue, or ordering a meal or a film, or just talking talking talking.

What do couples do when they've found out everything there is to know about each other? After all, there must be a finite amount we can find out about ourselves. And is that why marriages become boring? But no, because when we've finished talking about each other, we talk about the decline of democracy, or how to read a figured bass, or D.H. Lawrence and the death of eroticism, or how children understand space and time, or why icecream doesn't taste as good as it used to. And when we've finished talking about all these things, we sit and watch the sunset going down over Chiswick, and hear the birdsong slowing down for the night.

Is this what life is like for married people? Why did they never tell me? The perfect contentment of finding yourself at last, as if you'd been lost all your life.

I understand now all the fairy tales which mystified me as a

199

child. The prince who freed the princess from her paralysing sleep. The beast who becomes lovable once he is loved. The girl who kisses a frog who then turns into a handsome young man. I was trapped in a tree, like Ariel by Sycorax, and Prospero came across me almost by mistake.

The curse has gone out of my book, as if by magic. I can sit down and write it without shivering, without the aches across my temples, without the dreadful painful tears, most of the time. I can write about Poppy without that terrible pang of loss. I love her as much, and I miss her as much, and I regret as much. But now I've found what it was she was always substituting for in my life; the voice of which she was the echo.

And then as well as all this there is You Know What! Oh no, here we go, the private revelations to one's diary about ess ee ex and bee ee dee and the bruising tender kisses against the trembling lips...

But suddenly sex isn't cheap, or unimportant, or silly any more. A couple of months ago I thought it boring and irrelevant. And so it was. But that was sex. This is lovemaking, and to call them both by the same name is to allow Ba Ba Black Sheep and Mozart both to go by the name of music. And I don't know if it is the act itself, or the passion which inspires it, but now I can go without sleep for three days and run five miles and work all night and sing all day, and never get tired at all. Though of course I can't sing. But I feel as if I could write a symphony now, without any of the technique to do it, and paint a picture which would be priceless, and write poetry to shake the world. And I go around the next day with a spring of energy welling up inside me, and a memory of the night before or the morning itself, and I laugh out loud.

I suppose, to be utterly practical about it, these feelings have to be part of erotic love, since eroticism gives us babies. And rearing a child is, by all accounts, more demanding and difficult than anything Shakespeare or Aeschylus achieved. We'll need all this extra adrenalin and creativity just to survive the next twenty years.

And when I ask myself, which I never do, how do I know that Will is the right man for me, then the simplest of answers comes to hand. I have never liked the idea of a man in my bed. The precautions always seemed so tedious, and the practicalities exceedingly dull. And I like to wake up in my own house, knowing it belongs to me, without someone else's socks scattered on the carpet. But now I wake up – how do I explain this? In the arms of a man, yes; but that's not what I mean. Now I wake up in the curve of someone else's body, as if we were made as one; as if we were designed to fit together, like a ball and socket. I think what I'm trying to say is that his limbs don't get in the way, as I'd always dreaded they would.

And the other thing of course is guilt; or rather the lack of it. I've been frightened all my life that someone would find out about me, the real me. Nobody can love me when they know everything about me, surely. I know, I talk to Poppy about most things, or used to, but that was different. Your sister loves you anyway, and knows your past before you mention it, because she was part of it herself. The shadows of my childhood that I'm most ashamed of all enveloped her too.

But now, for the first time, I feel I can tell an adult, a stranger – and despite our intimacy, our feeling that we've known each other all our lives, we are strangers too, who know very little about each other. And though I feel nervous, apprehensive, sick at the thought of telling him, I am also convinced that it won't shake his love for me at all. I honestly think he will hold me. When the tide really does go down.

I went to see my parents the other day, for the first time properly since they moved back to London. Which is dreadful, I know, but there you are.

They invited me to supper and at first I said no, I was expected somewhere. Then I thought, How mean can I get? and said of course I would love to stay, and should I ring for a meal?

'Ring for a meal? Certainly not!' my father said. 'How long is it since my little girl stayed for supper? I shall cook something.' His voice wasn't too slurred, no doubt because it was still early in the evening.

'Daddy,' I said, perhaps because he'd called me his little girl, 'you haven't cooked for years, have you?'

'On the contrary. When we were living in the country I cooked nearly every night. Everyone cooks there you know. Big Agas and everything.'

'Oh, darling, what nonsense,' my mother said. 'Everyone uses the Mongolian on the High Street. Or the Casse-Croûte. Sunday brunch is about all most people manage. In the microwave.'

'Oh, all right,' he admitted. 'Beautiful Romanticism sacrificed to the tedious grind of truth yet again. Nobody cooks in the

country. But I'm going to cook now. What about spaghetti
carbonara?'
'Dad!' I laughed. 'You've been cooking that for twenty years.'
'Exactly. Come into the kitchen, my pretty little flower, and
talk to me while I cook. 'Nother drink, old boot?' he asked my
mother.
'No thanks.'
'And neither will I. Never touch a drop. Come on, Caz.'
So we went down into the kitchen, where he fumbled with
the spaghetti packet, and dribbled olive oil on the work top, and
had great difficulty getting the rind off the bacon and the skin
off the garlic, and I thought, Isn't it funny how one's parents
always cook food of the generation before? So that when we
used to visit my grandfather he would cook hamburgers and
cabbage, never touched yoghurt, and hardly knew what garlic
was; and here was my father, resolutely cooking food of the
nineties. My father, getting old like Grandfather? So he was.
'Dad, d'you mind if I ring a friend who was half expecting
me?'
'Not at all, not at all. Bring him along.'
'No, just to say I won't be home.'
'Whatever you like. Use our telephone.'
'It's all right, I've got mine here.'
'Use ours, I tell you,' he said loudly. 'It's right on the wall.'
'I know where it is, old thing. I've lived here.'
''Course you have.'
After I'd rung, he said, 'Boyfriend, is it?'
'Sort of,' I said. 'Yes, he is.'
'Mmm. Ben said something. No, not Ben, Abi.' Then he put
down his knife and looked at me. After a minute he wiped his
hands on his big, old-fashioned blue and white striped apron,
and came and put his arms around me. 'Tell you what, Caz.
Invite him over. Your mother'd be bloody chuffed. Oh, I know
I'm a drunken old fool; but I won't drink any more tonight, how
about that? It's been hard in the country – Mummy not well. I
don't cope with her very well. Get irritated. But oh, it's good to
see you! I've waited every night for you to call. Anyway, don't
bring him over if you don't want to,' he said, breaking away
and getting back to his chopping-board. 'Jolly embarrassing,
sometimes, to have to exhibit your parents!'
I waited for a minute before going back to the telephone.
I looked at my father's back, and wiped my face with my
fingers pretending I was just scratching an itch, and then

looked at a piece of garlic skin which had just fallen on to
the floor. I want Will to accept me as I am, and this is part
of me: my family, my past, the kitchen table where I wrote
my first story. As I dialled I tried to see it through his eyes.
The low evening sun coming through the garden door which
my parents put in when we moved, before my mother's
business started to go wrong. The cool, Spanish tiles that my
mother had chosen with her immaculately good taste. The
attractive, blond limed-oak cupboards which had been very
fashionable then, and are beginning to come back in again. It's
so familiar to me that it's hard to look at it afresh, but it is a
lovely house: my mother made it so.

And it's still brimming with memories for me. The afternoon
Grandfather and I had tea together when the others had
gone to James's football match; the Saturday morning I
wrote the piece about the spectacled bear; the stories about
Ariel all devised at that table. All, all here. Will has got
to love it; it's important to me.

And what about my parents? Will he love them too? My
mother, once beautiful, vivacious and lovely; now drooping
upstairs in the drawing-room. My father, still intelligent and
witty, surely; red-eyed in the kitchen. Well, they are my
parents: he must love them too, if he wants to love me.

I put down the telephone and said he was on his way.

''Manda!' my father shouted in the direction of the stairs
without looking up from his chopping-board. 'She's bringing a
boyfriend home. I've told her she must be in bed by ten-thirty,
and no snogging on the doorstep.'

When my mother finally registered what he'd said she
was thrilled like a child being told she's going to a party. I
could see she wanted to hug me, but didn't in case I didn't
like it. There were tears in the corners of her eyes, and she
went out into the garden to pick some flowers. Then she
came in and started fussing round my father. 'I hope that
supper'll be good. Have you got any decent wine? Look at
you, you've been drinking all day.'

'I have not been drinking all day. And I've told Caz I won't
drink any more.'

'What, ever?'

'I meant tonight, actually. Though if Caz came round every
day I probably could do it for ever. Sorry darling, that wasn't
designed to blackmail you, I should never have said such a
thing. Forget it.' Then he turned to her again. 'And anyway, if

you start getting decent wine out my resolution will crumble, so
I should stick to plonk and count your blessings.'
'He's Italian,' I said, suddenly sounding shy; then
immediately smiled at myself. So perhaps it did matter to me
what they thought of him, after all.
'Oh bugger, my Italian's lousy. Oops, 'scuse the French.
Perhaps I do need another drink,' he said, picking up three
more cloves of garlic instead. 'I would have chosen spaghetti,
wouldn't I? He'll know how to cook it properly.'
'He's only half Italian and speaks perfect English. And you
forget that none of my friends can cook at all.'
'Thank goodness for that,' he said. 'Right. I think we need
to take a break from all this *vieille cuisine* and go out and sit
in the garden, don't you?' Then, as he wiped his face with
his apron and put it down in the kitchen, he said to me, as if
involuntarily, 'Oh my darling, it's lovely to see you.'

They got on perfectly. Funnily enough, my father quizzed
Will about something which I'd never thought to talk to him
about. He asked him about his work.
'Basically, we're redesigning London,' Will replied. 'That's the
aim, anyway.'
'Oh?' my father said. 'London looks just the same to
me.'
'It is. We're not going to be building for years. When
the economy's fully recovered ...'
'"When"?' said my father, with raised eyebrows and
the cynicism of all his generation.
'Yes, when,' Will confirmed. 'Look at the improvement in
other areas over the last five or ten years.'
'Such as?'
'Education,' Will said. 'Morals. Even the population is
creeping back up.'
'Could've fooled me. Whole of civilisation looks a complete
mess to me. Whole kaboodle crumbling.'
'No,' Will said, smiling and shaking his head. 'Anyway,
civilisations don't crumble for ever. Something always comes to
take its place.'
'They can crumble for a bloody long time,' my father
objected. 'Look at the Roman Empire,' he said, and I wondered
where he got that idea. 'Look at Greece: it's not half the
nation it was two and a half thousand years ago. Egypt was
never the same again, either, after that miscalculation of their

weathermen regarding the Red Sea. They don't put up a lot of
pyramids these days, do they?'
'Well, you may be right, in which case my job is a waste of
time. But I have to believe in something, and believing in the
past is depressing, so I'm believing in the future.'
'So when you've got some money, what then?'
'Then we can start to rebuild. It won't all be government
money. We're looking at private ventures too. And my job is to
draw up the plans so that we're ready to do it.'
'Where would you start?'
'Obsolete office blocks; derelict buildings which need pulling
down anyway; one or two edifices which have been bombed or
destroyed and not yet rebuilt. It's a plan for generations, this:
it won't all be done in my lifetime, or even my grandchildren's.
It's an architect's dream of the City, made available for the
future. So that whenever we put up a building, we build to a
masterplan. Instead of at random.'
'Wait a minute.' My father looked at Will. Then he shook his
head.
'What?' Will said, to fill the silence.
'When you say an architect's dream . . .' My father stopped
again. 'This plan doesn't have St Paul's Cathedral at the heart
of it, by any chance?'
Will smiled. 'That's right,' he said. 'That was the architect.
The best.'
'Wren's London!' my father said, and jumped up from
the table, nearly knocking his chair over as he did so.
'You remember I was reading about this the other day?' he
said all in a rush to my mother.
'No,' she replied.
'Or the other week, other month . . . I don't know. In the
papers. I mean, you know, on the news. And I went out and
bought a real paper, I was so excited.' He was rummaging in
a drawer. 'Was it after we moved back here, or was it in the
country?'
'There was an article in *The Times* three or four weeks ago,'
Will said.
'That's it,' he exclaimed. 'Caz, why did you never tell
me!'
'I didn't know,' I said.
'What? You share the man's bed – at least I presume
you share the man's bed, I don't know what you chaps do
nowadays, but you're clearly head over heels in love with the

fellow – and you haven't found out the most fascinating thing about him? What interest do you take in him?'

'I knew he was an architect,' I said lamely.

'Architect! But what kind of architect. God is an architect, and so is the idiot who built Chelsea Harbour. But they're hardly in the same category.'

'Some people think it's very fine,' Will put in quietly.

'Yes, and they should be drowned like surplus kittens,' he said. 'Here we are, here we are, here we are,' he shouted triumphantly, and laid the wrinkled page of newspaper in front of my mother. 'Wren's London, designed after the Great Fire; would have been the most beautiful city in the world if England hadn't been full of penny-pinching Thatcherite bureaucrats who couldn't see the value of anything except money. Then as now.'

'I've seen this!' my mother said.

'´Course you have, you daft thing. I showed it to you.'

'There's Will,' I said.

'So there is,' my father agreed. 'Only I didn't know him then, so I've torn off his face halfway down.'

There, indeed, was the top of Will's face, under Wren's plan for the most beautiful city in the world: where wide pavements reserved solely for pedestrians ambled gently along the river bank as far as the eye could see; where avenues full of trees fanned out from St Paul's with symmetrical dignity; where bollards rose in the streets to stop traffic careering down it; where everything was spacious and graceful and civilised.

'And you're building this?' I said, amazed.

'Oh, not all of it, sadly. It would take centuries, or a major war to destroy the City first. And it'll never look as good as this. But at least we've established the principle: that when rebuilding is done, it's done along these lines. My job is to convert these plans to fit in with the London we've got now, and of course with modern life.'

'Will, it's wonderful.'

'Yes,' he said, and his eyes were shining like a child's. 'I think it will be.'

As we walked home, I said, 'Will?'

'Mmm?'

'I'm sorry I took so little interest in you.'

'How d'you mean?'

'Well, not finding out anything about your work, or anything. My parents may be awful, but they do do some things properly.

Conversation, and finding out about people, and things.'
'What did you say?'
'You know, they ask the right questions, and find out interesting things about people.'
'No, before that. Your parents may be *what?*'
'Awful.'
'What on earth gives you the right to think your parents are awful?'
'Gives me the right? I dunno. Observation.'
'Even if they were, you'd have no business saying it.'
'Whyever not?' I hadn't come across this attitude before. All my friends think their parents are awful.
'D'you want your children to grow up thinking their grandparents are awful? Child,' he corrected himself.
'Children,' I corrected him back. 'I certainly want them to grow up being critical about the world around them.'
'Well, perhaps you shouldn't,' he said. 'Children are not designed to be critical. Or not about some things, grandparents included. Anyway,' he went on, 'your parents are absolutely delightful. Why are you so hard on them?'
'Funny,' I said. 'That's exactly what my dad asked.'
We were going up to the drawing-room after supper. The meal had been fun: lots of spaghetti, stringy with bacon and cream and Emmental; a huge bowl of green salad; masses of fresh water and a bottle of *vin ordinaire*. My father kept to his word and didn't drink. My mother was relaxed and happy. And I got the impression that in some ways Will got on with my parents better than I did; or certainly understood them better. My father had made a jug of fresh coffee and taken us up to the drawing-room, where the French windows were open on to their little, well-kept garden.
Moths flew in and out, or perhaps just in, to the lights, and outside the crickets hummed and whirred as if we were in India.
'Caz says you can hear nightingales out here,' my father told Will, as if it were the silliest thing in the world.
'I heard a nightingale the first night I moved to Parsons Green,' I protested, rising to the bait.
'Are you sure?' Will looked at me carefully.
'Positive.' Is this the way men work to put women down, I thought crossly. Gang up with each other over trivia?
'There's a blackbird that sings in the night,' Will went on.

ANNE ATKINS

'I can tell the difference,' I said, though of course I couldn't to save my life.

'And a robin,' he continued, 'who sits in the magnolia under the streetlight. He likes to sing in the lamplight. The other night he went on for nearly half an hour.'

'And there's the nightingale in my garden,' I said with some stubbornness, since all conviction and credibility were gone.

'And you wrote down every word she said,' my father said, turning to Will with what looked dangerously like a wink.

I gave up.

'And how's the book?' he continued.

'All right,' I said reluctantly.

'Nearly finished?'

'Yup.'

'Autobiographical?'

'Why on earth do you say that?' I asked.

'Hey, Caz, calm down,' Will said, and put his hand on mine.

'Sorry,' my father said, looking comically contrite. 'Just, first novels are supposed to be, that's all.'

'It's not a novel. It's a book about...' what is it about? '...how I write my children's books. And why.'

'Autobiographical,' he nodded.

'Then what about yours?' I said quickly.

'Ah. I'm writing it,' he said. 'I'm writing it.'

'He says the country's too quiet and the town's too noisy,' my mother chipped in. 'So he can't get it done.'

'Quite right,' he agreed. 'Well, old thing, when you write your unautobiographical un-novel, that's not about any of us, don't be too hard on us, will you?'

'Why are you so hard on them?' Will asked again, as we turned into Parsons Green.

'I'll tell you one day,' I said.

'Tell me now.'

I shook my head. 'I'm too tired.'

'All right. The East Wing or the West tonight, my lady? Your house or mine? That is, if I may. Tomorrow being Saturday, if that makes any difference to your mood.'

'Mine,' I said. I always prefer my house.

'Then tomorrow morning I will bring you an endless pot of tea, so that you can read in bed till mid-morning with the sun slanting across the bedclothes; then I shall bring you orange juice and croissants and unsalted butter and a dressing-gown, and we shall go into the garden. Then, when you're ready, you can tell me.'

'And you'll always love me?' I said, turning to look at him.

'I believe I always will,' he said, letting go of my hand and opening the door to my house.

CHAPTER TWELVE –
CLANCARTY ROAD, 1990

τὸ μὴ γενέσθαι τῷ θανεῖν ἴσον λέγω . . .
κείνη δ', ὁμοίως ὥσπερ οὐκ ἰδοῦσα φῶς,
τέθνηκε κοὐδὲν οἶδε των αὐτῆς κακῶν.

I tell you, death is the same as never having been
  born . . .
For her, it is as if she died never having seen the
  light of day,
For she knows nothing now of what she suffered.

Euripides, Women of Troy, 636, 641–2

When they arrived at Grandfather's house he ran out to meet them.
He always used to do that, even when Granny was alive. He would
hear the car coming up the drive, and would run out, saying over his
shoulder, 'Gillian! They're here!'
    This time he didn't say Gillian they're here. This time he had a
trunk on his nose. A long grey elephant's trunk, made of rubber,
held on with elastic. He was waving his arms, and calling, 'Hello,
I'm an elephant. Snuffle snuffle.'
    Sandy laughed. 'Look at Grandfather. Elephants don't go snuffle
snuffle!'
    'Snuffle snuffle,' Grandfather said again, as he opened the car door
on Sandy's side. Sandy put him right.
    'Oh,' he said. 'How do they go then?'
    'They go roar roar.'
    'Even when they're happy?'
    'Yes. Of course.'
    'I see. Roar roar. Oh dear! I must take this thing off; it's all

211

hot and itchy. I expect you'd like a cup of tea, wouldn't you?'
'I don't drink tea. Children don't drink tea.'
'Well then, I expect you'd like some orange juice. And I expect your
daddy would like a cup of tea.'
'Yes, please, George. That would be great. I'll just bring madam's
luggage in.'
'Well now, young lady, the milkman has brought lots of orange
juice just for you, so you can drink as much as you like.'
'Yippee.'
'Within reason.'
When they went into the house, Sandy noticed something. At first
she wasn't sure what it was. Something was different since Granny
had died. Everything looked the same. Grandfather hadn't moved
anything, as far she could see. The sun still came slanting in the
window and fell on the red pattern of the carpet, and on the funny
parquet floor, and on the cleaned-out empty grate, as if Granny were
just upstairs brushing her hair ready to come down and greet them.
The kitchen was still clean and warm, with a tray laid for tea on the
kitchen table; with a cake on it, and a teapot, and a jug of milk, and
a glass for Sandy's juice. And only two teacups, of course, because
only Daddy and Grandfather were having tea.
Then Sandy realised what it was. The smell was different. Grandfather's house smelt like an old man's house now. Although it looked
clean, although Grandfather always kept all the windows open, his
house smelt of age and the indoors of houses. It made Sandy rather
sad. It made her realise how lonely he must be.
Grandfather switched on the kettle. It seemed to boil straight away.
He made the tea and picked the tray up and went straight into the
garden.
'Come on, Miss. I've put the swing up for you, so I want you to
swing a hundred times before tea.'
'Why do you take the swing down, Grandfather?'
'Well, I don't do much swinging on my own when you chaps aren't
here.'
Sandy giggled. 'Grandfathers can't go on swings.'
'They jolly well can.'
'No they can't. But why don't you leave it up always, for when we
come?'
'The metal bits would go rusty, and the wooden seat would get
waterlogged and warped, and the rope would go rotten and not last

so long. It only takes me two minutes to put up and take down.'

'Oh.' Sandy ran to the swing, which hung from a pink-chestnut tree; then she put a rope over one arm and climbed Grandfather's neighbour's fence to get a better swing. She settled herself on the seat.

'Do I really have to swing a hundred times?' she asked, but then let go half by mistake and never heard the answer because the wind was rushing much too fast past her face and in her hair.

The garden rose and sank, and Grandfather's house swooshed up and down; and when she went up she could see the fields and trees and waving corn beyond Grandfather's house on one side, and his neighbours' gardens stretching one after another getting smaller and smaller on the other; and when she went down all she could see was the garden and the patio by the kitchen and Daddy and Grandfather settling down to a cup of tea. As long as they were just drinking tea she went on swinging, but when she saw Grandfather cutting the cake she gave herself an extra swing, jumped as far as she could, landed on the grass and rolled over and over, and ran to join them.

'I hope that was at least a hundred.'

'I don't know,' Sandy admitted.

'Oh dear. Well now, I know you're on a diet, Sandy, and you won't want cake. Would you like some raw celery?'

'No I'm not, Grandfather!' Sandy said. Grandfather said this every time.

'Aren't you? Oh. That's all right them. But of course you don't like this kind of cake, do you?'

'Yes I do.'

'Do you?'

'Yes.'

'What kind of cake is it?'

'I don't know.'

'Then how do you know you like it?'

'Um. I do know what kind of cake it is. It's yellow. Anyway,' Sandy said, suddenly seeing her way out of the situation, 'I like all cake.'

'Ah, well then. Pancake?'

'Yes,' Sandy said.

'Fruit-cake?'

'Yes.'

'Stomach-ache?'

'That's cheating.' But Sandy laughed.

'Here you are. Lemon madeira,' Grandfather said, looking at the label on the packet. 'Courtesy of the W.I. I hope that's not too small a slice.' It was huge.

'Um. No.' Sandy had to admit it. 'It's not really too small. What's the W.I.?'

'A group of people who formed themselves into a club so they could bake cakes for grandfathers when they had little girls to stay.'

'Oh. Don't they mind?'

'They love it. Is the swing all right?'

'Yes thanks.'

'Was the journey all right?'

'It was great. We had the roof down all the way, and Daddy let me go in the front, and we stopped at a pub for lunch and I had crisps.'

'Is that safe?' Grandfather turned to Daddy.

'What, the crisps? I shouldn't think so. Nothing is these days.'

'No. Going in the front.'

'Well, it's perfectly legal, as long as she's properly strapped in. Contrary to popular belief and police folklore.'

'Is it?' Grandfather looked as if he wasn't sure, but didn't want to argue with Daddy. If it had been Mummy he probably would have done. But then that was all right, because he's Mummy's daddy, and you can argue in your own family.

Eventually Daddy got up to go. 'She's brought her piano music. And swimming things. And lots of books. And probably not nearly enough clothes.'

'I have, I have. I packed my tracksuit and I've got these shorts and top and a spare pair of pants and my nightie.'

'Just one change of pants? Oh, Sandy! And didn't you put in a dress for church?'

'Oh. I meant to. Will we go to church, Grandfather?'

'You usually go when you're here. I shall be going, and you don't want to be left behind, do you? But you won't need a dress. Wear what you like. Wear your nightie if you like.' Sandy giggled. 'The choir does.'

'Does it really?'

'Yes. And the vicar.'

'Oh yes, I remember now,' said Sandy. 'Is that really his nightie?'

After Daddy had gone, she said, 'Why don't people go to church in London?'

'They do, darling.'

'Mummy and Daddy don't.'

'That's not because they live in London; that's because they don't go to church.'
'Why not?'
'I don't know.'
'Grandfather?'
'Yes, dear.'
'Do you have to do what your mummy and daddy tell you?'
'Yes.'
'Does everyone?'
'Yes.'
'Oh.'
'Why do you ask?'
'I was just thinking.'
'Right. What would you like to do? Play on the swing? Read? Play the piano?'
'Er. Um.'
'Why don't you come and talk to me while I wash up the tea.'
'All right. Do you want me to wash up too?'

It was a bit funny at Grandfather's without Granny there. Once or twice Grandfather got cross with her.

One night he asked her to get ready for bed, as usual. They'd been watching television together. It was a programme with lots of jokes in. Sandy loved the jokes. She didn't understand any of them, but she laughed much louder than Grandfather, even though he did understand them. It was a funny programme about politics. Sandy wasn't sure what politics were, but she didn't think they made very good jokes.

Then the news came on, and she was asked to get ready for bed. She went up to her bedroom and sat on the bed. It was late and she was tired and she started to look at the books in her bedroom. She was too tired to get undressed really. She remembered how Granny used to read lots of the books to her. Grandfather read them too. He did all the voices, and it was funnier, but Granny used to take longer and read more. Sandy wasn't up there that long, she'd only looked at five or six books, but when Grandfather came upstairs he asked her why she hadn't done anything.

'I was tired,' Sandy said.
'Then you need to go to bed.'
'I was too tired to go to bed.'

'Well, I get tired too, you know. I'm too tired to keep coming and nagging you to get undressed. You shouldn't need to be told, Sandy. I let you stay up as a treat, because you promised to get ready for bed afterwards. And now you've broken your promise.'

Sandy didn't know what to say. She hadn't wanted to break her promise. She didn't dare say sorry in case Grandfather got more annoyed with her. She stood there, not saying anything, and not looking at Grandfather.

'The least you could do is get undressed now.'

She wanted Grandfather to go away. She didn't want to get undressed with him there. She muttered, 'Go away,' under her breath, so Grandfather couldn't hear her.

'What?'

'Go away.'

'All right. I will. But you could say please.'

Sandy sat down on the bed again. She wished she were back home. It was horrid when Grandfather was cross. She suddenly thought it was no fun, being in his house, at all. Outside it was nearly dark. The trees made frightening shapes against the sky, like dark giants looming against the window to look in on her. She wished the curtains were shut. One of the trees was shaped like a head, with a huge hand to one side, waving in the dark.

She shuddered.

'Oh, Sandy! You are a very naughty girl. You haven't done anything since I was here a minute ago. I won't let you stay up late again.' And Grandfather came into the room and started to take off her top, rather roughly.

'No. Don't pull! Don't.'

'Then do it yourself. Come on.'

Sandy began to take her top off, very slowly. 'Go away,' she said again.

'You said that last time. I did go away, and you didn't do anything.'

'I will. Go away again.'

'This is your last chance.'

Grandfather went away again, and this time Sandy did get undressed. She kept her pants on, and put her nightie over the top. She didn't go and do her teeth or her face or go to the loo. She got into bed and hid everything except the top of her head, and her face. When Grandfather came back again, she was tucked up and quite still.

'Good girl,' he said. 'Have you done your teeth and face?'

Sandy nodded.

'Really? Are you sure?' Sandy said nothing. 'Sandy, you mustn't lie. You really mustn't. If you lie, I won't be able to trust you any more. I'll have to test anything you ever say, and I'll never know whether to believe you. I won't make you get up again, but have you really?'

This time Sandy shook her head.

'Well, thank you for telling me. Please don't lie to me again. Because we're friends, and friends always trust each other.'

'Then why did you get cross with me?'

'Did I, darling? I'm sorry. Friends often get cross with each other. But friends always make sure they say sorry and make up. So I'm sorry. Please will you forgive me? I do get a bit bad-tempered without Granny. I miss her dreadfully. She used to keep me in a good mood, and she's not here any more.'

'How did she?'

'What, keep me in a good mood? Goodness gracious me, what a question!' Grandfather took a deep breath. 'Well, Granny was a wonderful person. She was very unselfish. When we were young it wasn't quite like today: women used to give up work when they got married. So she spent all her time looking after me. And when we had children, she spent her time looking after them too.'

'Have you got children?' said Sandy, a bit surprised.

'Yes, you loony. Your mummy; and Uncle Robert and Uncle James.'

'Oh yes,' said Sandy. 'Of course. I knew that really.'

'Then when they left home, I suppose Gillian, Granny, started taking care of me again.'

'She used to take care of me too.'

'Yes. She took care of everybody. Shall we say your prayers?'

Sandy nodded. She never had prayers at home. She didn't understand the prayers, but they were soothing, and made her feel warm and happy; she didn't know why.

'Our Father,' Grandfather began, 'which art in heaven, hallowed be thy name; they kingdom come . . .' Grandfather was kneeling on the floor by her bed, like he always did; he had his hands held together, and his face down and his eyes shut. When he'd finished the prayer that he always said, he said, 'Thank you for Granny, and all that she did for us. Thank you that she's with you now, for ever and ever, amen.'

'Amen,' Sandy said, because that's what you do. Grandfather smiled.

'Please may I have a story? What's that funny-smelling drink?'
'Of course you may. That's my glass of sherry.'
'Mummy drinks sherry. She has it before supper. It's horrible.'
'Yes, I suppose it is.'
'Daddy smelt like that when . . .'
'When what?'
'I don't know,' Sandy said. 'Why d'you drink it?' she added quickly.
'Oh, well. It helps me relax after a long day. It helps me sleep too.'
'Grandfather, I didn't lie. I just didn't tell you . . .' Sandy stopped.
'The truth. That's the same as lying.'
'Must you always tell people the truth?'
'Yes, of course you must. Now then . . .'
'Grandfather?'
'Yes.'
'If you take a baby away before it's born, does it die?'
'Away from where?'
'Away from its mummy.'
'Um. It might live. If you look after it very carefully, and it hasn't been taken away much too early, a baby can sometimes live.'
'But if you didn't look after it?'
'Oh, no. It couldn't live on its own.'
'So if you took it away from its mummy much too early and didn't look after it, would it die?'
'Yes, it would. You're a bit gloomy this evening.'
'So you've killed it then, haven't you?'
'Um. Gracious. Yes, I suppose you have. Now. Are you ready?'
Sandy thought for a moment. Then she said, 'What? Oh yes,' and nodded hard to prove her point.
'Thank goodness for that. Now then. Listening? "Once upon a time, a very long time ago, about last Friday . . ."'
'Ooh,' she said, curling up in the bed, 'I like this one.'
'So do I. It's my favourite.'
'Mmm,' said Sandy. She had lots of other things to ask Grandfather. About Granny, for instance. She would ask him after the story. But before Winnie the Pooh had got halfway up the tree she was already fast asleep.

She didn't remember again until they were walking in the fields behind Grandfather's house. They had taken Sandy's Bug Box, which

Grandfather had given her for her birthday before last, and they were trying to catch ladybirds. They'd only got one, which was what had given them the idea for the expedition in the first place. But they'd seen some beautiful little blue butterflies dancing ahead of them, and they'd caught a whole leaf full of greenfly.

Sandy wanted to catch the butterflies, but Grandfather wouldn't let her.

'For one thing we'd never catch up with them,' he said. And for another, they'd have such a short life anyway that it would be a great shame to lock them away.

'They'd be able to see out,' said Sandy.

'How would you like to be put in a glass bottle and told you could see out for fifty years?'

'Fifty!'

'About that.'

'I wouldn't keep them for fifty years.'

'No, but you might keep them for a day. And as they only live for two or three, you'd be keeping them for the equivalent of forty or fifty years.'

'What's equivaler?'

Sandy gave Grandfather her Bug Box. She was hot and a bit tired. She took Grandfather's hand and skipped a bit by his side, and then slowed down to an amble. For a while they didn't speak. Along the side of the field they saw some tall waving poppies, like a pillar box that had been cut up for a collage and scattered by an untidy child all the way along the edge of the path. They went in the direction of the poppies, and walked along the path. It was washed in shade, and it was pleasant to walk along with Grandfather, with the long grass tickling her legs. She didn't wish she were at home any more.

'By the way, who's Poppy?'

Sandy felt a hot wave flood over her. How did Grandfather know about Poppy? 'What?' she said.

'Poppy. You said could you bring Poppy. Who is she?'

Sandy felt panic. What could she say? Poppy . . . Poppy. Poppy was a secret now. Then suddenly she realised, and breathed again, and smiled. Oh. Poppy. 'She's my rabbit.'

'Goodness me. Have you got a rabbit?' Sandy nodded. 'What a lucky girl. When you get home, will you draw her for me?' And Sandy nodded again.

They walked again in silence. Sandy saw a tree with a white bark and cracked skin, and leaves like green petals shivering all over it in the breeze. A man passed them with green gumboots and two browny-black dogs with cages over their noses. 'See those?' Grandfather said. 'Never ever touch a dog like that. Look at the colour and shape carefully. And don't go near them.'

'Why?'

'They're not safe.'

'What do they do?'

'They can kill you.'

'Gosh,' Sandy said. Then she said, 'Grandfather. Where's Granny?'

Grandfather looked a bit surprised. 'What do you mean, darling?'

'Where is she?'

'She's dead. You know that.'

'Yes, but . . .' Sandy took a breath. 'Where did she go when she died?'

'Oh, I see. She's in Heaven. She's with Jesus now, in a much better place even than this, with the sunshine and the birds – look, look! A skylark. You can hardly see it, but listen to the song! "Hail to thee, blithe spirit. Bird thou never wert." I'll read that to you when we get in. Better even than this world, with all these lovely flowers, and the ripe corn, and you and me walking along hand in hand. Can you imagine that?'

'No.'

Grandfather shook his head. 'No. Neither can I.'

'Will you ever see her again?'

'Oh, yes. Not long now, I hope.'

'What d'you mean?'

'I mean, I hope I don't live too much longer. I love being here with you. I love to watch you growing up and getting older. But I'm tired and lonely, and there really is a much better world to go to.'

'Are you sure, Grandfather?'

'Yes. Quite sure.'

'Daddy says you can't be sure about that kind of thing.'

'Does he indeed? Well, what does he know, eh? Suppose I said I thought you hadn't got a rabbit and you said you were sure you had, who'd be right?'

'I would.'

'Why?'

'Because I have.'

'Yes, but how do you know?'

'Because she's mine. I've got her.'

'You've seen her?'

'Of course I've seen her! You're being silly.'

'But I say you can't be sure.'

'Then you're daft.'

Grandfather laughed. 'You know you've got a rabbit, and you're sure; I don't know, so I say you can't be sure. Granny's gone to Heaven, and I'm sure; Daddy doesn't know, so he says I can't be sure.'

'I don't understand. Or I sort of do.'

'Never mind. You'll have to decide for yourself. Whether to believe me or your daddy.'

They had reached the road. Even though they'd been in the field that was right next to Grandfather's garden, they had to go the long way round to get back home again. The next bit of the way was along a busy, noisy road, with heavy lorries that bullied past, and Grandfather held her hand too tightly and they didn't talk much.

It was when they were back in the garden having tea that Sandy spoke again. She wasn't having tea to drink; she was having icecream and strawberries and a glass of water, and Grandfather was having a cup of tea.

'Will Granny wait for you?' she said.

'What, darling?'

'Will Granny wait for you?'

'What do you mean?'

'She'll wait for you? She won't go away? She'll still be there when you get there?'

A smile overtook Grandfather's face, and if he hadn't been an adult Sandy would almost have thought he was nearly crying. Sometimes adults have tears in their eyes from the wind and things, and they aren't really crying like children are when they have tears.

'She'll be there.' He laughed a little. 'After all, there's nowhere better to go. Is there?'

'Isn't there?'

'No.'

'Doesn't it matter when people die, then?'

'It matters a lot to us, because we miss them. But it's much better for Granny. So when I die, darling, you needn't be sad for me.'

'I'll be sad for me.'

'Well, I suppose in a way I'm glad of that.'

'And I'll be sad for Mummy. I'd be jolly upset if my daddy died. Please can I have more strawberries?'

'There aren't any more. You've eaten two whole punnets. There's more icecream if you like.'

When he came back with the icecream Sandy said, 'But would she wait for a long time? I mean, like a really long time?'

'I don't think time is the same there. She'll have lots of other things to do, but she'll always wait for me. And for you. She'll welcome you when you get there.'

'Even if it's years and years and years?'

'Even if it's years and years and years.'

When she heard this, Sandy was very pleased indeed.

10 July, My Parents' Wedding Anniversary, Parsons Green

Oh, I could fly the world and sing the Queen of the Nights aria and jump over Everest! I used to think the important things in life were writing a book that would change society or chiselling Michaelangelo's David or designing a building to bring tears to the eyes like King's Chapel Cambridge. But those things are of no importance compared to this. Loving and living and procreating; animals do it too, and yet humans do nothing more divine.

I've nearly finished my book. Four more chapters to go. Already it hurts less than it did.

I did talk to Will about it, and it was just as he said. He brought me tea in the morning and we sat up in bed drinking it. Then, at about half-past ten, he rang for breakfast, from the French caff, and we went down into the garden in our dressing-gowns. The sun was shining, and we sat at the far end of the garden where the warmth collects on the corner of the old wall, and after we had started breakfast he said, 'Now, come on.'

'Come on what?' I said, fiddling with my napkin.

'Tell me what happened.'

'What happened when?'

'You know perfectly well what I mean. What happened when you were five, and what happened to your sister?'

I looked at him in surprise. A tiny part of me felt relief, which I tried not to show. 'How do you know about that?'

'I talked to your father a little last night, when you went up to the loo. I know something's upsetting you, and I want to know what it is. And I know it's to do with your book, but so far you haven't told me anything.'

'My father knows nothing about it!' I said vehemently, stabbing the butter with my knife.

'Of course he does, you simpleton. Why do you think he drinks so much?'

'That's got nothing to do with me! If he's got a guilty conscience, it's not my fault.' I sounded like a petulant child.

'Caz, my love, you judge everyone so harshly. No wonder he feels bad. He loves you, he dotes on you, and you've been blaming him for something all your life and he doesn't know what it is.'

I sighed. 'No, I don't know what it is either,' I said sadly. 'But I don't judge him,' I continued, shaking my head. 'I just see things as they are. I can't help it.'

'Perhaps that's true too,' Will said. 'Even if it is arrogant. And a cop-out. Come here, you big baby. Sit on my lap, and tell me all about it.'

And I did. I told him everything I could remember, just as I've told the book everything I can remember, all through that summer of 1990. And then I told him everything after that, everything about Poppy, from my memory of her birth right up until this year, till I moved out of Perrymead Street and said goodbye to her, I believe for ever.

And he listened to it all, and didn't judge me. And he didn't judge anyone else either. He seemed to understand perfectly the way I had seen it all. But he also seemed to understand my parents, and sympathise with them.

'But you can't understand it from both points of view,' I said. 'You can't! You can't! If you do that, you're saying there are no absolutes, and that nothing's right or wrong.'

'Society's been saying that for fifty years,' he said.

'And look at the mess!' I was almost shouting. 'Everyone lives in a moral pig-sty.'

'All right, all right,' he said; 'it was a flippant comment. A foolish attempt at satire. I agree: in an ultimate sense I can't see both points of view. If I were the judge of the world I'd have to divine right from wrong. But I'm not. I'm your friend. I love you and I love your parents. And I can *sympathise* with what happened. Perhaps, at the end of the day, you do see things clearer than the rest of us. Maybe, in that sense, you were right. But in the meantime, you have parents who have loved you, and I mean all of you, as best they knew how. And it's about time you started loving them back in return.'

I picked at the frayed edges of his shorts, stark white against his bare legs, Persil-brilliant in the sun. 'And what about my book?' I said. 'Do you think I should cancel it?' Ghastly thought. Would my publishers ever forgive me?

'No,' he said. 'Because I think your parents understand much better than you think. And probably rather better than you understand them. I think you should change the names. And

I think you should let them read it before it comes out. And I
think you should start talking to them. If you feel angry with
people you love, you don't write them off: you tell them, idiot.'
   So that was that.
   We finished breakfast. Then he carried me upstairs, barely
midday as it was. And I wondered, as we lay in the cool of
the house in the early afternoon and the dappled sunlight
danced on our limbs, how I had managed to find a man
who was so definite and so right and so decided, and yet
so gentle and peaceful and all.
   Calm rock pool on the shore of my security.
   'Bungler Bill,' I said out loud, as I thought of my first
impression, which had been of someone so awkward and shy
that he had barely a word to say.
   But he was asleep so he didn't hear me.

So I went through the book changing Ben's name to Barney
throughout, and James's name to Jack. But I haven't changed
Simon and Amanda's names yet, because I can't think of them
as anything else. I shall pluck two names out of a hat as I
finish, and ask the computer to change them for me.
   So what was I worried about? I don't know. I suppose I
thought he would think I was mad, like Cassandra was thought
mad by all her family (though not, I suppose, by Agamemnon).
Perhaps it's true that love conquers all things; that if you really
love someone, you can accept everything about him. I wonder,
is this true? Being realistic, how would I react if I found I loved
someone who'd committed a murder?
   But wait till you hear this. Last Wednesday, for my
birthday ... yes, I know it wasn't my birthday. Don't be
difficult. It nearly was. He said we were going for a treat, and
we were to set off at nine o'clock.
   Nine a.m., on the dot, doorbell. Down I come, glamorous as
ever, grubby shorts, white T-shirt, haven't had time to put on
any makeup, just about managed to brush my hair.
   'Hi. Good grief!' I said. 'Where the heck did you get that?'
I'm not very good with cars but I think it was a Morgan, racing
green, hood off, looked about a hundred years old.
   'A friend.'
   'Gosh,' was all I managed.
   'Get in.'
   Now, I know cars are provincial and not at all with it
and only for the kind of fogies in their sixties who still get

themselves a suntan and all that; but I must say, once in a
blue moon, on a sunny day in July, with the hood off ... Well,
I felt like Harriet Vane with Lord Peter Wimsey going bowling
along the country lanes, even though we were only passing
Putney Bridge. And it was not at all like a ride in Ben and
Suki's dog-hair-ridden machine.
'Wow,' I said.
He smiled. 'Good?'
'Well, I feel terribly guilty. As if I were smoking a cigarette
or something.'
'One cigarette a year doesn't do much harm.'
'OK,' I said. 'All right. OK. Seriously, how did you ... ?'
'Don't ask. Just belt up and enjoy yourself.'
We drove out through the suburbs, into Kent, and then on
and on, for about an hour and a half. All the time we listened
to baroque music, and the wind blew our hair all over the place,
and the sun danced in the trees along the road.
'Bach,' he said suddenly. 'The most erotic composer.'
'What did you say?'
'Very sexy music. All that energy under control.'
'I thought that's what you said. D'you think we knew each
other in another life?'
'Definitely.' Snorting, in the *seven sleepers' den*?
Eventually we turned into a little lane, and he said, 'Here we
are!'
'Pub?' I said.
'No,' he said. 'Wait and see.'
So we parked the car, got out, and walked for about ten
minutes to some large gates, behind which was a big open
field, apparently barren, with those funny socks on poles that
they used to have in children's books, to test the wind for
aeroplanes.
'Just a minute,' I said. 'What ...'
'Shut up,' he said.
'It's very windy,' I replied meekly.
'Wait here a minute,' he said, and disappeared into a little
hut, and talked to a little man, for what seemed an age. Then
he came out, said, 'Follow me,' and we walked on for another
five minutes.
'What!!' I said eventually, as we stood there looking at it.
'Treat,' he said. 'France, for lunch.'
'But it looks pre-war!' I said. 'Probably First War.'
'Well, it isn't,' he said. 'Jump in.'

'Can you fly it?' I said, incredulous.
'Yup,' he said. 'More or less.'
'How much more and how much less?'

I think it was probably the most wonderful experience ever. Though I'm aware that sounds even more wet than being in love. As we set off, we went along a runway that was going downhill. At the bottom of the hill was a wall. As always with aeroplanes taking off, even the biggest, it seemed very rickety and precarious, as if it might fall to bits at any moment. As we gathered speed, Will said, 'I've never done this before.'
'What?' I said. 'Taken off?'
'Taken off downhill. Facing a wall.'
'Fine,' I said. 'What happens if we don't get off the ground in time?'
'We hit it.'
'Oh,' I said. 'And then?'
'We die.'
'Oh.'
At that moment we lifted off.
We didn't go to France in the end, but circled north and went back over London. We went right over Fulham, and saw our houses, and I saw at one glance all the three houses I've lived in, just as clearly as I saw the nannies with the prams going round South Park. Then we went over Knightsbridge, and I saw the school I was at in the summer of 1990, tiny, in the gardens behind the Brompton Oratory and Holy Trinity Brompton; and it brought back a very strange feeling, because most of my childhood haunts have remained familiar and with me ever since, but I haven't seen those gardens for over twenty years.
'Is this allowed?' I said.
'What?' he said.
'Going this low over London?'
'Not really,' he replied. 'But something this small doesn't matter much. Anything else you want to see?' I shook my head. So we soared up into the air and took off further north.
After a few minutes he told me to take the controls. It was unnerving at first, because you go up and down as well as side to side; but once you realise you're unlikely to hit anything it becomes much more relaxing than driving a car. A bit like driving those pretend racing cars in amusement arcades, when it looks terrifying but you know you can't kill anyone really.

'What happens if you pass out?' I said.
'What?'
'How do I land?'
'With difficulty. Keep going round in circles till I come round.'
'What happens if you die?'
'You're on your own.'
'Thanks.'
'You and the radio.'
'Ta.'
'For the rest of your life.'
In an astonishingly short time we were flying over Norfolk. 'Can we go over Ben's place?' I said. And soon we were over Abi's field, her poppy field, dotted red all over, but funnily enough not looking nearly as red as it does from the ground.

'There isn't an airfield very near,' Will said. 'Otherwise we could call and see them. Would they be busy?'

'They always are,' I said. 'They're farmers. But they'd make time for us.'

'Next time we'll let them know, land at Norwich, and they can pick us up.'

'You mean we can do this again?'

'I have the use of it every two months or so. I was in the RAF at school. And university.'

We went back over Cambridge. Over Ben's beloved college, sitting squat and lonely in the sun, deserted by undergraduates but swarming with Japanese. And the Cam was covered in tiny, incompetent tourists, swinging their matchstick-sized punts from one side of the river to another, just as they used to when I went to visit Ben for a May Ball after his exams, and some of his friends took me on the river and we laughed at the tourists trying to use a punt pole. Suddenly one of them fell in, and there was a tiny little white splash in the middle of the Cam. We both laughed, the sun in our eyes.

And then we went over Grandfather's old house, sold long ago to another family, on the edge of the fields where Amanda used to play as a child. And I saw the swing still in the garden, and a strange child on the lawn, and the path near the house where he had taken me for a picnic once and many times, and suddenly I burst into tears.

'Caz, whatever's the matter?'

'Sorry. I don't know. I knew such a good person once, only he died when I was little. And I've just realised that all my life

228

I've been trying to be like him; and it hasn't worked at all. And I think if he'd lived...' My throat hurt, and my face was wet, and I was aware that I must look frightful. 'I'm sorry. But I loved him so much, and I never really realised how much. And he used to give me strawberries, and far too much icecream, and stale chocolate cake even though my granny told him not to, and orange squash, and he used to say the Lord's Prayer at bedtime, and once he got cross with me.'

'Only once?'

I shrugged. 'I dunno. I feel like Dante, as if I've been taken back through all my life in pictures. Have you got a hankie?' I smiled through my wet face. I blew my nose, and wiped my eyes, and stared stupidly through the window. We'd passed his house now, and there was nothing to see but the black soil of the Fens, and an empty railway track.

'You see,' I blew my nose again. 'He was, oh, I don't know. He had something. Faith and hope and charity, I suppose. And that made him,' I sniffed hard, and wiped my face on my sleeve, '...good, I think. Moral, even. And it seemed such a definite thing to me, so positive; so I tried to copy it. But now I don't think his morality was important, really. The other things were: the faith, the rest. The kindness. The morality was just a spin-off. So I copied completely the wrong thing, and it's made me bigoted and hard and judgemental and horrid to my family.' I started to cry again, and blew my nose again, and turned and tried to smile at him. 'I'm sorry. I must look hideous.'

'Caz,' he said, 'I didn't deliberately bring you up here in order to say this, but will you marry me?'

I tried to laugh. 'I don't believe in marriage.'

'Neither do I. Will you marry me?'

I wiped my eyes with his wet handkerchief, and blew my nose for the umpteenth time. 'All right,' I said. 'I will. Will.'

At that he turned to kiss me, and the plane took a bit of a dive.

That was Wednesday. We planned to tell my parents tonight. In a funny sort of way, I think it might have more significance for them than it does for us. I mean I know I'll always be part of Will now, whether I marry him or not, so it doesn't matter much to me; but marriage is important to parents, you know. Or so they say.

We sat in the garden talking over a late breakfast this

morning, with Gibbons rubbing our legs, as we always do now at the weekend when he isn't being invaded by relations. He has a far keener sense of family than I do, even with distant Italian second cousins that he hasn't seen, sometimes, since he was a child. And he seems to know how to relate to my parents better than I do. I wonder if the English really don't like their families?

'Two letters,' he said. 'Pass the mango juice. One from Norfolk, from your brother?'

'Read it to me,' I said lazily from the garden sofa.

'Yes, m'lady. Pass me the juice.' He settled and opened it. 'Lots of nice things about me.'

'Give,' I said. 'He doesn't know you.'

'No, I won't,' he said. 'You said I could read it. Abi knows me, though.'

'No, she doesn't.'

'By reputation.' He read on. 'Caz, is it your parents' wedding anniversary today?'

'Oh, blimey, yes it is. Why, what does he say?'

' "Very rushed letter. Harvest time. Great idea of yours about ruby wedding party for the wrinklies, though I hate beetroot and am not mad about Ribena, though Abi likes it. But I think they're only up to about 38 or 9. Did you mean for next year? Give them lots of love and do go round and see them, won't you, on Saturday? In haste, B." '

'Is that all?' I said, trying to grab the letter.

'Yes. The rest's from Abi, and all about me. And tonight, madam, we go to your parents, with some very decent champagne.'

On the way there that night, he said, 'Will anyone else from your family be there?'

'Don't think so. Too far to come. They'll come for the ruby, though, if it is next year.'

'No Ben?'

'No Ben.'

'No James?'

'No James.

'And no Poppy?' he said, looking at me rather carefully. 'Definitely not Poppy. Much too far to come.'

Will put his arm round me, and turned to ring the bell.

CHAPTER THIRTEEN –
CLANCARTY ROAD, 1990

αἰαῖ, τέκνον, σῶν ἀνοσίων προσφαγμάτων·
αἰᾶῖ μαλ' αὖθις, ὡς κακῶς διόλλυσαι.

Alas, child, poor wretched child, for your unholy
murder.
Alas again, how wickedly you have been utterly
destroyed.

Euripides, Women of Troy, 628–9

Sandy lay in bed listening to the sounds. These were mostly of
birds, but sometimes she heard a dog, and once she heard a big
car or a lorry in the distance.

She had one more day at Grandfather's. She was dying to get home
to see her rabbit; but apart from that she would have liked to stay at
Grandfather's for much longer. If she could have brought Poppy with
her, she would have liked to stay for ever almost, except that she'd
miss everybody. She wasn't quite sure why she couldn't have brought
her. Poppy would have had a much bigger garden to run around in,
and she and Grandfather would have had great fun with her. It was
probably just one of those adult things.

From where she lay, in her bed at Grandfather's house, she couldn't
see trees through her window, as she could at home. She could if she
got up and stood in the middle of the room. But from the bed she could
only see very very blue sky, and a bird wheeling through it. And leaves
framing the window like transparent green tissue-paper, with the sun
shining through. The sun shone on to her bed, and danced through the
shadows of the leaves, picking out the lions and the circus clowns and

ANNE ATKINS

the performing seals on her bed. Granny used to sit on her bed pointing them all out to her, and telling her that when Mummy had the same eiderdown she used to make up different stories about each one.

There was a knock on her door.

'Here's your early-morning juice, madam. Are you getting up for our swim?'

It was the same every morning.

Sandy had only just learnt to swim without armbands, so she had to make her arms and legs go very fast, which made them splash a lot. Grandfather took long slow strokes, with his face in the water. He just swam up and down, up and down, not getting bored, while Sandy did all sorts of different things. One morning she rescued thirty-two drowning animals. They were mostly little insects, but she still thought it was quite good to have saved thirty-two lives before breakfast. Sometimes she held her nose and went under the water, and then opened her eyes and saw blue patterns of sunshine dancing wildly about, becoming a mad and frenzied storm of broken light when Grandfather suddenly dived in. Then she got out of the water and explored the banks beyond the paving stones, while Grandfather continued to swim up and down.

'Are you cold, Sandy?' She nodded. Her teeth were chattering. Grandfather heaved himself out of the water, bringing a lot of the swimming pool with him. He wrapped her towel around her, put on his tattered old plimsolls, put his own little towel round his shoulders, and started to jog back through the Robinsons' garden. They always ran there and ran back. Grandfather said it helped the blood to go round. Sandy imagined it like a drink inside her, while she was a bottle that someone was shaking up.

It was church day. Grandfather put on a jacket instead of a jumper, and they had boiled eggs on the table in the garden. Boiled eggs always went with church. On other days they had muesli and fruit, and yoghurt just for Sandy because Grandfather never ate yoghurt. But on church days it was always boiled eggs.

Church was quite nice, really, because you got to play with other children that you didn't normally see at Grandfather's house. You had songs, and a story, and did colouring and cutting out, and then you joined the adults again for orange squash and biscuits, and you could run around the church hall.

When they got home again, Grandfather asked Sandy whether she'd like to go out for a picnic, or stay at home and have one.

232

The Lost Child

'A picnic! Wow! What d'you mean, go out or stay at home?'

'When we've made the picnic and put it in a basket, we can either get in the car and drive somewhere and get out of the car and eat it. Or we can just carry it into the garden and eat it. We can't really walk far with it, because I've got this stupid elbow.'

'What stupid elbow?' Sandy tried to imagine an elbow being hopeless at maths or French.

'This one. It's tennis elbow or something, and it means I can't carry the picnic basket very far.'

'Let's have the picnic here.'

'Good idea. That means we can still eat icecream.' Sandy was extremely relieved she had made the right choice. She had very nearly said let's go out. 'Come and help me get it ready.'

Grandfather had half a cold chicken, and some ham, and tomatoes and cucumber, and watercress which Sandy didn't like, and mayonnaise in a bottle, and two brown rolls with butter in. They never had white bread at Grandfather's house. It was a shame, but there you are. She almost never had it at home either. You only got white bread at places like Rachel's house. They put it all in a basket, and Grandfather got a rug for them to sit on, and they carried it out into the garden.

'Here we are. Let's put it down here. Just like the old days.' Grandfather gave her some chicken and a roll, and a paper napkin.

'What old days?'

'When Amanda was little.' They sat in silence for a while. Sandy tried to imagine her mother as a girl. It was difficult. Grandfather sat eating his chicken. He crunched the end bits where the bone was. It was a horrible noise. It made Sandy feel a bit sick. 'She looked just like you,' Grandfather said.

'Who?'

'Mummy.'

'Did she? Did she really? Did she have hair like mine?'

'Yes, rather like. Long and blonde and curly. She was very pretty.'

'Her hair isn't long now.'

'No. But it's still pretty.'

'Was she like me, though?'

Grandfather smiled. 'Yes. Yes, she was actually. Very like you. She was quite naughty sometimes.'

'Was she? What did she do?'

'Oh dear. Well, I can remember her climbing a tree, over there somewhere, beyond those fields. Can you see that huge oak tree?'

'No. What's an oak tree?'

'Dear, oh dear, you London girls. An oak tree is that big one there, which spreads all its branches out like a mother hen; that lovely round shape.'

'Can you lift me up? Oh, yes, I see. I think.'

'Beyond that there's a little spinney. It's near where we were yesterday. And Sandy, I mean Amanda, went there with a boy who'd come to stay, and they climbed right up to the top of a dead tree. It was completely rotten. Nobody should have touched it. And she made this poor boy go ahead of her all the way. They were missing for hours. When we found them, we had to get the fire brigade to get them down, because the tree was so dangerous.'

'Golly. Did Mummy have the fire brigade just for her?'

'Yes.' Grandfather laughed. 'They cut the tree down the very next day.'

'Why didn't they cut the tree down before Mummy climbed up it, instead of after?'

'Hah. Good question. I suppose they should have done.'

'So it wasn't really Mummy's fault. It was their fault for leaving the tree there.'

'Well, she didn't mean to be naughty. She wasn't much older than you. Have a tomato. Do you want me to cut it up, so it doesn't squirt all over your top? I can remember her better as a teenager, really. She always had boys after her, all the time. There was always a stream of them in and out of here. I never knew any of their names. They were always ringing up, and taking her to things. She used to be at dances all night. She never did any work at school. But she was a clever little thing. She did a lot of work when you weren't watching her. In the holidays and things. And she jolly well got to the university she wanted, just as she said she would. The school said she'd never get anywhere. She was very pretty – beautiful really.'

Sandy looked out towards the oak tree. She found it hard to imagine Mummy with all those boyfriends. She'd only ever known her with Daddy. But then, once you become a mummy and a daddy you're not supposed to have boyfriends any more. Dominic's daddy did. Have girlfriends. She knew that, because Dominic's mummy and Dominic had left him because of that. Like David, Daddy's daddy. She felt rather sorry for David, even though he'd been naughty. He must feel lonely sometimes.

'Do you know what she wanted more than anything else, though?'

'What? Who?'

'Amanda. Mummy. She had everything. Brains, looks, boyfriends.
Two brothers. But she always wanted a sister. She always used to say
to us, "Why couldn't you have had a sister for me?"'

'Why didn't you?'

'It just never happened. We always wanted four, actually. Two boys
and two girls. But we were never given another one. Perhaps Granny
was too old by then. Perhaps her body had had enough, with three.
We didn't mind. But Amanda did. She longed for a sister.'

'Why?'

'When she was little, it was for someone to play with. She said the
boys played stupid games, and never included her anyway.' Sandy
nodded. 'She said she wanted a girl to play dolls with, and someone
else who dressed up in pretty frocks with her, to have parties with.
In fact, even before that, she wanted to have a baby to look after.
She used to look at the other mothers with their prams, and summer
babies with their funny little suncaps, and parasols on the pushchairs,
and she would ask Granny if we could have another baby so she could
bath her and put her to bed.

'When she was about ten or eleven she forgot about it. She was
quite a little tomboy then, and most of her friends seemed to be boys
anyway.'

'What's a tomboy?'

'Well, she wore jeans all the time, and played cricket; and she
even carried a knife in a sort of leather thing round her belt at
one stage. But then when she got older she started talking about it
again. I don't know why it was so important to her. I'm sure she's
forgotten all about it now. But she used to say it would have been
such fun to have gone out with a sister. They could have gone out
in a foursome, with two boys. And they could have shared clothes
and lipstick and a car. Mind you, I expect it wouldn't have been
like that at all, really. They probably would have argued no end.
If someone had pinched Amanda's lipstick I'm sure she wouldn't
have been pleased. I don't think she would have minded losing a
boyfriend or two, though; she had far more than she needed. You're
very quiet.'

Sandy looked at the pattern on the rug. She had almost forgotten.
She recognised the rug. She'd had it over her bed once, when she
was little; she'd made a huge fluffy ball of red wool by pulling
out the little hairs on the rug. Granny had come in later and said,

'Hello. Are you pulling my rug to bits?' She hadn't been really. She'd just been making a fluffy ball.

'I think it's time for raspberries and icecream, don't you? We haven't had any icecream for over twelve hours. Have you had enough chicken? Oh, we haven't eaten the ham. You have some ham while I go and get the pudding.'

While Sandy was waiting for Grandfather to come back, she saw a bird washing in the birdbath beside Grandfather's flower bed. She crept closer to have a look. It was a female blackbird. Grandfather had told her that the brown blackbirds were the female ones. He had a stone birdbath, like a shell, on the ground at the edge of the lawn. The bird put her head under the water again and again, scooping it on to her wings and then shaking them out, so the drops of water and the feathers all fluffed and splashed out together. It seemed as if she was having great fun. For a moment she stopped, and looked at Sandy. Then she continued as if to say she didn't care. She didn't care if Sandy wanted to be nosy.

At last she finished, took another long hard stare at Sandy, and flew away, low over the garden, singing on a chucking note as she went.

There were more nettles in Grandfather's garden than there had been before. Nettles with purple flowers, hiding among the real flowers. As Sandy sat there, a little bee flew unsteadily in front of her, waving about a bit before settling on a mauve flower, round like a tiny soft round hedgehog on a green stalk. She tasted the flower, buzzing happily, moving her legs up and down. Sandy wondered if she would sting her. They only sting you if you're bad to them; but if you are bad to them they don't hear you say sorry. A big reddish-brown ant crossed a yellow leaf in front of Sandy. Perhaps it wasn't an ant. It looked a bit like a spider. It had something on its nose, like a tiny black tongue that kept going up and down, but too small for Sandy to see what it was. She wasn't sure if ants, or even spiders for that matter, had noses. She knew they had tongues. She thought she'd seen a picture of an insect's tongue like a coiled-up spring. Of course, spiders weren't insects; even Sandy knew that.

There were lots of real ants on the grass. Once you started looking, you could see them everywhere, hurrying over the dry brown grass in every direction. The grass smelt of hay. Sandy wasn't sure when she'd seen hay, but she knew that was what it smelt like. Daddy had said they'd buy hay for her rabbit.

'Sandy. Pudding! Hurry before it gets warm.'

As Sandy chased her raspberries round the melting icecream with her spoon, and wondered whether she'd get away with using her fingers, she said, 'Daddy, I mean Grandfather, who was Cassandra?'

'Once upon a time there was a little girl called Cassandra who was very very pretty, and lived in a house with her family, and a rabbit called – what's it called?'

'No, really. Who was the real Cassandra?'

'The real Cassandra? What a question!' Grandfather pronounced it like 'sand', to rhyme with 'Amanda'; not like 'marge', to rhyme with 'Sandra'. 'Professors and scholars can't answer that. But I suppose Grandfathers ought to be able to. Cassandra was the daughter of Priam and Hecuba, the King and Queen of Troy. She must have been a very attractive girl. She was very sensitive. She felt things deeply, I think, which is what makes it all so sad. All sorts of people fell in love with her. One of them was the god Apollo. The god of the sun. He promised her anything she liked, if she'd let him love her. Now, if you'd been that Cassandra, what would you have chosen?'

Sandy looked at the sun smiling on the garden, and the wide blue of the sky, and a giddy white butterfly as it curtsied and dipped in front of the sleepy flowers, and wondered what she would ask the sun to give her if she could. The sun, which could see everything. The sun, which could wave at her family in London at the same time as warming her in Grandfather's garden. It could tell her what Poppy was doing, and what her mother had done when she was little, and even what Sandy herself would do one day, when she had her own garden. The sun could tell everything, if it wanted to.

'I don't know,' said Sandy.

'Very good answer,' said Grandfather. 'And that's no doubt what Cassandra said. But in the end she had to decide, or he might have changed his mind and given her nothing. Do you remember what Solomon chose, when God asked him what he'd like?'

'Who's Solomon?' asked Sandy.

'Oh. Solomon was a king. Never mind. Forget Solomon. Well, d'you think she chose riches?'

'Um,' said Sandy. 'No,' she said. 'Because she was a princess, so she was rich already.' And anyway, riches would be a silly thing to choose: Sandy knew that.

'D'you think she chose beauty?'

'Er,' she said this time. 'No, because the god was in love with her, so she must have been beautiful too.'

'D'you think she chose wisdom?'

'What's wisdom?' asked Sandy.

'A bit like being clever only more so.'

'Yes!' said Sandy. 'She chose to be clever only more so. She asked the sun to tell her everything.'

'Yes,' said Grandfather. 'She did. She asked for the gift of prophecy. Imagine that. Being able to see all sorts of things that nobody else could see. Being able to see like a god. Wouldn't that be wonderful? Wouldn't it be exciting to have a friend like that?'

'Yes,' said Sandy. 'It would.' She looked at two birds squabbling so much that they had fallen out of a tree, tumbling over each other as they argued their way to the ground, and wondered what it would be like to understand what they were saying. 'But you said it was a sad story, Grandfather.'

'It is. It's a very sad story. After Apollo had given her the gift, so that she could see everything, she changed her mind. She couldn't bear to go to bed with him after all.'

'Why?'

'She was just that kind of girl, I suppose. I don't know. Apollo was furious. But he couldn't take back his gift. You can't take back a present. So he wet her lips with his tongue and said that no one would ever believe her. All her life Cassandra was condemned to speak the truth, and never be believed. What an awful thing. Can you imagine it?'

Sandy nodded. It would be like being a child, always.

'Suppose,' Grandfather went on, 'you knew the house was going to burn down tonight. Suppose you told me and I didn't believe you. What would you do? You'd have to go to bed and wait for the house to catch fire. That was what Cassandra had to do. She kept telling everyone what would happen, and they all thought she was mad. Even when all the things she said came true, people still thought she was mad.'

'Did they never believe her, ever?' Sandy asked. At last they must have seen that everything she said came true. Even adults couldn't have been that stupid.

'Yes. In the end she was believed.' Thank goodness for that, Sandy thought. 'But that was worse than ever. You see, Cassandra had been told that she would be believed one day, but it would only happen once. And that would be just before she died. So when she was believed, she knew she was. about to die. She knew she'd been believed for the first and last time.'

'And then she died?'

'And then she died.'

Sandy thought about this. It was difficult to know which was worse: never to be believed, or be believed and die. She thought of Cassandra sitting in her house, telling her parents it would catch fire, and then waiting for it to happen, waiting for her bedroom to start burning. And then, suppose your parents did believe you ... What would you do then? What could you do? Nothing. There was nothing you could do. You would die.

They sat in silence. Grandfather was clever, the way he understood things. Suddenly, despite the warmth of the sun, she shuddered.

'Is it true?' she asked at last.

'Did Cassandra exist, you mean? Dear, oh dear, now you're asking. There may have been someone called Cassandra, who lived in Troy at the time of the great siege. There may have been a princess. The rest may not be exactly true. It's not like history, which happens more or less in the way it's told us, with various interpretations of course. It's myth.'

'What's myth?'

'Myth? Myth is a way of teaching. It's telling us something in a poetic way. Just think: real prophets usually aren't believed, are they? And Cassandra may be a symbol for them. That means she's a picture of them; she helps us realise that we don't believe people either. The ones who say we should stop killing whales or dropping bombs. We don't listen to them. Not until it's too late anyway.'

'And what's it called again? That kind of story?'

'Myth.'

'Myth,' Sandy repeated. It was a funny word.

She ate her last raspberry and started to lick her plate. She thought about Grandfather's words. *Not until it's too late.*

'Sandy! It's not very polite to lick your plate.'

'Oh. Sorry.'

Suddenly she said, 'Did she have brothers and sisters?'

'Who?'

'Cassandra.'

'Ah. Yes. Yes, she did. I think Priam had a hundred children.'

'What were their names?'

'Goodness gracious me! Hector, Paris ... oh dear.'

'What were her sisters' names?'

'Well, there was one called Polyxena. She was sacrificed to the gods, I think. Her mother was very upset. As a mother would be.' Grandfather sighed, then smiled. 'But I don't think I can remember any more.'

It had been a great picnic. They decided to go for a walk, and Grandfather would have his cup of tea when they got back. It wasn't until much later, when they'd had high tea and watched television and Sandy had got changed for bed and was sitting on Grandfather's knee and had had two stories, that she decided to ask him the question she'd been wanting to ask for a while.

At first she had thought that the baby, the feet us, was a secret from Grandfather. But then she remembered that Mummy said she told Sandy everything, and Sandy thought she told Mummy nearly everything, and she knew Mummy liked having no secrets from her family. So she realised she must have told Grandfather, because Grandfather was her daddy after all.

'Grandfather?'

'Yes darling?'

'You know you said you have to do what your parents tell you?'

'Yes.'

'Everything?'

'Yes, I think so.'

'And everyone does? Have to, I mean?'

'Yes.'

'And you're Mummy's daddy, aren't you?'

'Yes.'

Sandy paused for a moment, wondering how to ask him. He still had his worn old jacket on. Sandy turned the button round and round. It was made of comfortable brown leather, and had four quarters.

'You'll pull that off,' he said.

'Grandfather. Why didn't you ask Mummy to keep the baby?'

'What, darling?'

Suddenly it all came out. 'Why didn't you tell her to let the baby grow up, so I could have a sister? I want a sister too. I've always wanted a sister. If you'd told her she would have had to do it because you're her daddy. You could have told her to stay at home and not go into hospital. Why didn't you tell her not to let them take the feet us away?'

She looked up at Grandfather's face. It looked different. It seemed grey, like uncooked pastry. He didn't say anything. He pulled his arms close around her, and stared at the empty fire. Suddenly he laid his cheek against her, and stroked her hair, rocking her against himself.

The Lost Child

'Oh my God.' Sandy had never heard Grandfather say that before. 'The poor child. The poor poor child.'

Then Sandy knew. It wasn't a feet us at all. It was a child. Grandfather said so. She had heard him, and she knew that sometimes Grandfather was right and Mummy and Daddy didn't know the answers yet. After all, Grandfather knew where Granny was. Grandfather knew all the important things. They had only called her sister a feet us because you mustn't kill children, so they'd called her something else.

'Grandfather,' Sandy said, and she wiped the drop off her nose with her nightie sleeve. 'Grandfather. Are you crying?'

Grandfather nodded his head, and Sandy thought then that he no longer tried to pretend he wasn't crying. She didn't know whether he was crying for Granny, or for the little baby. But they sat together, for ever it seemed to Sandy, and no time at all, rocking each other and looking at the dead summer fire while the tears fell down their faces and onto their laps. They held each other very tightly, and neither of them minded at all that the other one was crying.

In the end, Grandfather got out a large white handkerchief from his jacket pocket, and tried to laugh a little.

'Well, well. This'll never do. What will your mummy and daddy say when they hear I've been making you cry?' And he wiped her face with his clean handkerchief, and then he wiped his own.

'You didn't make me cry, Grandfather.'

'No. Well. There we are. Let's get you a nice warm drink and take you up to bed. This is your last night. You mustn't go to bed in tears.'

'I wish I were staying longer.'

'Ah. Do you, poppet? I wish you were too. You've made me feel so much better.'

'Have you ever cried before, Grandfather?'

'Goodness me. Yes, indeed. After Granny died I cried every night for six months. But after that I started to find things to do so I wouldn't think of her so much.'

'Do you still miss her?'

'Terribly.'

'Will you miss her always?'

'I don't know. They say you get over things; forget a little. But I don't think so. I think I will always miss her, yes.'

When Grandfather had made her some cocoa and helped her with

241

ANNE ATKINS

her teeth and was tucking her up in bed, Sandy said, 'Will I always miss the baby?'

Grandfather stroked the hair out of her eyes and put his arms round her. 'I doubt it, darling. You've never known her. So you won't know how she would have done things, or what she would have looked like, or what her voice would have sounded like, so you'll never miss those things.'

'But when I'm a teenager, I'll wish she was there to share things with, and go to dances with, and wear the same clothes. And when I'm alone in my bedroom, I wish she was there to talk to and play with. And when I'm at school I want her there so I can stand up for her to all the bullies.'

'Do you? Well then, I don't know. Perhaps part of you will miss her always. But it is easier with someone you've never known. Or perhaps it's harder, because you've nothing to hold on to at all. I'm glad I knew Granny, anyway. Now then, close your eyes. Our Father, which art in Heaven . . .'

This time, when Grandfather got to the end, he said, 'Thank you for Granny, and thank you that she's with you now. Lord Jesus, thank you for Sandy's little sister, and thank you that she's with you too, in a much better place than this. Keep her with you, and may she and Granny be best friends, and . . .'

Grandfather stopped. Sandy opened her eyes. He was crying again and couldn't stop. Sandy realised she must finish the prayers now.

'And Jesus Lord Father, please can they both wait for us. Amen.'

'Amen.'

'Grandfather. They will wait for us, won't they?'

'Yes, darling, I'm sure they will. I'm sure they'll wait for us.'

'And Grandfather?'

'Yes, darling?'

'What does feet us really mean?'

'"Foetus"? I believe it means "the little one".'

CHAPTER FOURTEEN –
PERRYMEAD STREET

ὦ τέκν', ἐρημόπολις μάτηρ ἀπολείπεται ὑμῶν,
οἷος ἰάλεμος, οἷά τε πένθη
δάκρυά τε ἐκ δακρύων καταλείβεται
ἁμετέροισι δόμοις· ὁ θανὼν δε ἐπι-
λάθειται ἀλγέων ἀδάκρυτος.

Children lost, city lost, all lost.
Lamentation and sorrow.
Tears following on tears are poured down in our house;
But those who are dead forget tears,
And can cry no more.

Euripides, Women of Troy, 603–607

Poppy was eighteen and I was twenty-four when we started living together again.

We got on remarkably well. After all, it's a family house, with plenty of space, so we weren't on top of each other. Sometimes we had lodgers to stay, to boost our income – an old school friend of mine, and later a college chum of Poppy's – but by and large it was just the two of us.

I was quite envious of Poppy, for the first few months at any rate. I had loved my time at university, with no worries or responsibilities, and nothing to do but study and enjoy myself. Now that I was struggling to find work for myself it was sometimes hard to watch Poppy loving her studies as much as I ever had, without a care in the world.

Her work was very good. I used to go, with my parents, or my brother, or sometimes just with Poppy, to see the end of term exhibits of all the students' work. Much of the work was very derivative, and

ANNE ATKINS

very similar: you could tell, from one year to the next, who were the
famous contemporary artists in vogue at any one time. But a few of
the students had their own characteristic stamp. The moment you
walked in the hall, you could see that there were three pieces by
so-and-so: the student who used that particular orange-red colour,
or the one who was good at portraits. Poppy was one of those;
once you knew her work, you couldn't miss it. It wasn't strident,
like some of the others, but it had a certain haunting quality, like
Monet: as if she painted a world of summers, or childhoods, which
exist in the memory, which happened last year or the year before,
but might never happen again.

I think it was this quality of Poppy's which may have given me the
idea for our first book. I was scraping a living by journalism, as I'd
thought I would, but I really wanted to write seriously, as it were. I'd
been to see a couple of publishers, but without a definite idea there
wasn't much they could offer me.

The catalyst was a letter from a friend of mine. She was a Swede
who'd been at Oxford with me. For a term or two we'd been very
close. She was a stunning girl: brilliantly clever, and always interesting.
She had thick, long, deep red hair which she could all but sit on, and
her father was a professor in Nordic Studies, back in Oslo, I think.
I was studying Anglo-Saxon at the time – it was our first year –
and I loved to listen to some of the stories she told me. We burnt
lots of candles and emptied lots of bottles of wine together, and
I assumed at the time, without really thinking about it, that we
would be friends all our lives.

She went home at Christmas to see her family and her boyfriend,
and by February realised she was pregnant. She had her pregnancy
ended, of course: a baby in one's second year at Oxford would have
been a nightmare, and her degree was very important to her; she
intended to go on and be an academic like her father. She went into
the Radcliffe Hospital one windy, wild February afternoon, came out
the next morning, and resumed life as usual.

Soon afterwards our friendship, like many an Oxford affair, fizzled
out without comment; we found ourselves amongst different friends
almost without noticing it. By the end of Trinity Term we hardly
saw each other. Of course one can't help bumping into someone in
Oxford. But we didn't sit up over our gas fires and *Beowulf* and a
bottle of cheap red wine any more. We no longer wrote each other
poetry in Anglo-Saxon metre to distract one another in the Camera;

or dived into the Nosebag for a coffee and wholemeal biscuit in the mid-morning sun; or scraped together enough money to go for a cheap kebab somewhere. We grew older. We progressed into our second, then third year; then went down leaving many of our ideals and dreams intact behind us, for other undergraduates to discover anew for themselves before growing out of them too. Occasionally one of us would write the other a polite card around Christmas time. That was all. I never expected to hear from her again.

It was a wonderful letter; bracing like a walk in the wind. She gave me news of her family, and the thesis she was writing, and another friend from Oxford who had gone to live in France. She was more than halfway through the letter before she gave her reason for writing.

I write to you because I like to think of myself as an academic, and an academic values truth before everything. So I write to you to tell you the truth.

Caz, when we first arrived at Oxford together, we were best friends and loved each other very much. We saw eye to eye on everything, and had many happy evenings together. Then, in the spring, I took a decision about my future which was personal to me. You criticised me, and made me very angry, and our friendship was broken. I still have some hurt in me because of this. I tell myself I try to understand why you were so passionate about it, but I still feel it was a moral issue which was my business and my business alone. I say this to explain to you why I have never replied to your correspondence.

But I also want to tell you that some of the things you said then were true, and I now see this. You observed some things that were deeper than my own situation. You talked about the importance of the child to society. You likened me – or was it all of modern Europe by then? – to the base Indian, who threw a pearl away richer than all his tribe. You said we were disposing of our children, and soon there would be nothing left. I didn't hear you well at the time, the larger thing that you were saying, because you also said that a baby should be more important to me than my studies, with which I very strongly disagree: our grandmothers and great-grandmothers worked very hard to allow us to put our minds before our bodies.

But now that I have lived in Sweden again for nearly three years, I see a society robbed of its most beautiful people. Here,

ANNE ATKINS

the middle-class members value their salaries, and their careers, and their fine homes and materials. And they have one child, perhaps, or sometimes none. It is not like China, where they felt they were not allowed to have children. Here, they do not want children. Perhaps you say I shouldn't criticise, as I didn't want a child in that time or place. I don't criticise: I merely observe. And the streets are empty and cold. And the mountains are climbed by old people who have taken early retirement. And more than half the desks in the schools are empty. And what the government does not tell us is that the recession which has been eating our society for many years will soon cause it to collapse unless something can be made to change. The proletariat don't have the assets their parents had. The professional classes, like us, it doesn't matter so much. But there is no investment in industry. And on another level there is no investment in the future.

There is an old, old myth, which country people and gypsies still tell, in different forms. There are traces of this myth through the Norse traditions, and in Sanskrit also (though I don't read Sanskrit, but some of my research is in this tradition). You will know this story, through your poet Browning, as 'The Pied Piper of Hamlyn'. Earlier versions of the tale do not have the rats; the basic element of the story is simply that the town gets rid of its children. Sometimes there are some disfigured, poor children left behind. The beautiful ones always disappear. Perhaps this story is based on true events: the last time such a thing happened was in your Welsh town, Aberfan, in the 1960s. Usually, the society which loses its children is to blame in some way.

This story is happening now in Sweden. I think it is happening in England too, but more slowly. And I think you were trying to tell me that this would happen, when we had our quarrel those years ago.

I must say that I cannot regret my decision that I made then. It was right for me. But something has happened recently which made me see it in a wider context, and prompted my letter to you. A friend of my sister's has committed suicide because the doctors told her she could never have children. It has been impossible to adopt children in Sweden for many years now, and it is not usually legal to adopt from another country. So she kills herself. I find it tragic, too, that even in our advanced society a woman can find nothing to do with her life but have babies.

246

I have seen some of your writings sometimes. You write very well. Please, drink to me in a glass of wine. If I would be welcome, I shall visit you next time I have to fly to London. If so, send me your address, as I send this letter via college.
I still love you, dear Caz,

Katerina

I started to write a reply to Katerina's letter before I had time to think about it.

Dear Katerina,
Thank you for your letter, and for having the extraordinary grace to say the things you did. I must have been very pompous and irritating. I'm sorry. Perhaps some day I'll be able to tell you why . . .

I got up and wandered out into our little London garden. One of Poppy's long-standing eccentricities was keeping doves. As a schoolgirl, she had allowed them to breed one summer on the top of a wardrobe in her bedroom: everything else in her room had to be covered with dust-sheets so the furniture wouldn't be ruined by droppings. She would come in from a party at three a.m. and wake her doves, who would squawk and natter in complaint. An hour later, they would rise with the dawn and wake Poppy in ignorant revenge.

Now she'd found a space above the bathroom and turned it into a pigeon loft, where they could come and go through a hole in the brickwork, and were safe from cats. So that, lying in the bath, one could hear a gentle cooing sound which I found very restful, but which one friend told me was like the distant sound of muffled vomiting.

I watched them that morning as they waddled round the garden, pecking at the grass. Although it was autumn, it was a warm day and they were enjoying the sun. I went to an old bread bin in the garden which Poppy kept full of grain for them, and took a handful. For her, they would flock round and settle on her arm to eat from her hand; but I didn't have the patience for this, and threw the grain on the ground. Some of them had huge, proud fantails which made them strut like peacocks; others were a much more sensible shape, just like white town pigeons.

I thought of Katerina again. Yes, I would tell her she was welcome to visit; of course I would. But, being ruthlessly objective, I realised I hadn't missed her as much as I thought I had when I first opened the letter. Perhaps if we'd been friends for years, rather than months, our quarrel would have mattered more. But then perhaps we would have overcome it better.

I went back inside to get myself some breakfast.

As soon as Poppy came in at teatime that day I said, 'How would you like to illustrate a modern "Pied Piper of Hamlyn"?'

'Tell me more,' she said. And that's how our first children's book started.

Its great success was the combination of words and illustrations together. If one of us had tried it without the other I doubt if it would have worked.

We called it *The City of the Lost Children*. It began, 'Once upon a time there was a beautiful city, full of children . . .' It was a true Londoner's book, full of all a London child's favourite places, which were gradually being denuded of children. London Zoo, full of senior citizens who couldn't ride the camels; Kensington Gardens, where Peter Pan had grown old and withered; the Serpentine, with nobody in the boats under the age of forty-five. Policemen with no one to talk to. Toy shops with no one to buy. Empty parks. Deserted schools. Closed-down maternity wards.

And elsewhere, in another world, all the missing children were re-forming into a dream City of London, where there were no cars and no dangerous strangers; where policemen gave rides to the children, on horseback, because they had nothing else to do; and where everyone travelled free on public transport because everyone was under-age. It was a dream city, a fairytale. And sometimes I still dream that it could come true.

It was a lovely book to write. We sat at the old kitchen table together, talking over mugs of tea, inspiring each other and working in complete harmony. We never expected it to do well, I suppose because it was an 'anti-adult' book and everyone had grown out of Roald Dahl years before. Perhaps that's why it did succeed, because today's young parents remembered their Dahl days so clearly.

It was in light, comic verse, with pen and watercolour drawings. And we dedicated it to our parents, and our unborn children.

*   *   *

It was wonderful to begin to feel like a real writer. Many of my friends from Oxford were still unemployed. There was a sense of frantic and precarious good fortune in any who managed to work for a living. Poppy and I both began to feel as if we might be among the lucky ones.

Our book sold well, considering it was a first work by unknowns. Our publisher asked us to think about another; other publishers took us out to lunch; an agent took us on. Poppy was barely nineteen and she was a commercial artist. And the whole thing had only taken us a few idle afternoons to write.

So we did begin to think of others. When Poppy came in from college, in the late afternoon, I would brew tea and make hot buttered toast or buy a chocolate cake, and we would sketch out ideas and themes and plots for stories which we thought might appeal to children. We came out with weird science-fiction and naughty schoolboys and flea-ridden hedgehogs. None of the ideas was right. Sometimes Poppy sketched characters, to see if they sparked off an idea in me; sometimes I wrote a description of something or someone and gave it to her to see if it would trigger off a recognisable personality in her mind.

When we looked back to the books of our childhood, the classics which had lasted our parents' and grandparents' generations, it seemed as if the great children's literature of the past always featured a character, or a group of characters, who would live and live.

'And that's how we'll make money,' I said. 'On the rights sold on the plates and T-shirts and cartoons and pens.'

'That's no way to think!' Poppy exclaimed indignantly. And added, 'You're absolutely right . . .'

In the end we went back to the first book, *The City of Lost Children*. Inspired perhaps by Browning, we had left one child behind in the dead city. She had been nameless and fairly characterless, but we decided to try and see whether she would take us anywhere.

'An only child,' Poppy suggested.

'Very lonely,' I agreed.

'I said *only*.'

'That too.'

So that's how Ariel was born. Poppy made some sketches, and I wrote some poems, and then I wrote down the beginnings of the story, and Poppy did one or two paintings, and we both felt absolutely at home with Ariel. She had all the qualities of both of us. Poppy's garrulousness and my quietness; Poppy's charm and my stubbornness; Poppy's inquisitiveness and my thoughtfulness. She was a five-year-old version of both of us.

But the most characteristic thing about her was her loneliness. She was an only child in a world of grown-ups; a left-behind child in a childless society; the only person in her world who saw life from her viewpoint.

Our agent didn't like her, but we went ahead anyway. Our publisher didn't like her, so we went to another. The seventh publisher we tried said yes. She said it was a financial risk, but she'd do it on the strength of our last book, because she'd liked it. It would be expensive, because of the colourwork. She wasn't confident the European market would like it, and had no hopes at all for the non-English-speaking home market. Nevertheless, she cautiously produced five thousand copies, and they came out during Poppy's last term at art school.

They sold out in barely eight weeks. The book was reprinted three times by Christmas, and by the new year almost every child in the country knew who Ariel was.

Her success was a testimony to the loneliness of the modern child. We had no illusions about this. When Jack read stories of Ariel to his children in India, they were loyal to her because they knew their aunts had created her, but they didn't really understand her appeal. They had brothers and sisters. They didn't need another companion. Many of Ariel's fans had her as their best and only friend.

They were very happy years for Poppy and me.

Ariel was the easiest literary character in the world to live with. We wrote six more Ariel books, and each one, astonishingly enough, took only a matter of hours to create. We would think about her for some months, at the back of our minds, until one of us would suddenly create a new adventure for her. Then the other would fill it out a bit, or modify it, or confirm it, and sketch out a bit of the story. Within a few days the book was taking shape. Within a few weeks it was finished.

And the rest of the time we were both doing our serious work. I still wrote some journalism, if something interested me enough for me to want to take it up. I was also experimenting with a collection of poems, and meanwhile writing several radio plays and then a stage play.

Poppy mounted an exhibition, and tried a bit of portraiture, and painted her series of London scenes.

And Ariel's loneliness, which touched such a chord in all the lonely children around us, freed us to work on the things we cared about better than if she'd been a rich benefactress who had given us both a private income: she established our names in the publishing world and gave us both the opening that a household name has.

Meanwhile Poppy and I lived together as the best of friends. In some ways we were happier than the happiest of cohabiting couples. We never quarrelled, as couples inevitably do because they have so much invested in each other. We were never jealous, because we had no rights to each other. If we found each other irritating we could ignore each other for a few days. If either of us needed a change, we could go on holiday with someone else, or simply travel, for a couple of weeks or more. If one of us had a new boyfriend, as I did seldom and Poppy did frequently, the other would simply take a delighted interest in the progress of the affair. Sometimes other members of the family would come and stay for a night to visit the theatre, or for a weekend to do some shopping.

We shopped for each other, ordered meals for each other, sat up late at night with each other over a bottle of claret, or lazed around all morning over newspapers and coffee in the garden together. We were never lonely, because we could always find each other; we never felt on top of each other, because we could always find space.

My story is nearing the present day. We lived and worked together for nearly four years. For the last few months we wrote no more Ariel books. It wasn't that we took a decision not to: rather that she didn't suggest herself to us any more. We had no financial necessity to write more, and we saw no need to make an effort to write about her when we didn't feel like it.

One of the strangest factors of Ariel's success, to our agent and publisher at least, was the way in which she survived despite our consistent refusal to have anything to do with the normal selling techniques of writers and illustrators. We never appeared on chat shows or interviews to promote the books; we never turned up together to sign them; we didn't do promotional tours or visits to the States. Although I've done some of that with work that I've written on my own, Poppy and I never made a public appearance together.

Over and over again we were approached by bookshops and writers' clubs and universities to talk about our creative process, or how we worked together, or whether Ariel was the autobiographical result of

ANNE ATKINS

our joint childhood. And, constantly, we were asked why Poppy never appeared.

That's what this book is about. Our story. I have no great hopes that it will change the world. The world will change anyway. The tide turns. It always does. Moral fashions mutate almost as quickly as clothes and music. I doubt if the little breakwater of my book will make much difference to the shape of the sea. So why did I agree to write it? Well, perhaps I simply thought the time had come for my sister and me to part anyway.

But in the end I think it was humanity, pity, compassion, which compelled me to answer the question that so many people ask me: 'What happened to Poppy?'

CHAPTER FIFTEEN –
CLANCARTY ROAD, 1990

The small slain body, the flower-like face,
Can I remember if thou forget? . . .

Thou hast forgotten, O summer swallow,
But the world shall end when I forget.

Swinburne, Itylus

No man is an Island, entire of itself; every man
is a piece of the Continent, a part of the main;
if a clod be washed away by the sea, Europe is
the less, as well as if a promontory were . . . any
man's death diminishes me, because I am involved
in Mankind; And therefore never send to know for
whom the bell tolls; It tolls for thee.

John Donne, Meditation XVII

Daddy came to pick her up the next morning. She was all packed and
ready for him when he came. The first thing she said was, 'How's my
rabbit?'
'Fine, love. Hello George! Has she behaved?'
Daddy had a cup of tea with Grandfather, and some toast, and when
Grandfather went out of the room to get some more milk from outside
the front door, he said, 'Have you had a lovely time?'
'Yes, thanks.' It was brilliant to see Daddy again. She wanted to
climb on to his lap, but he said he'd get marmalade all over her. 'Is
she really all right?'
'Mummy? She's fine.'
'No, silly. My rabbit.'

'Oh. Yes, I'm sure it is.'

'Haven't you seen her?'

Grandfather came back into the house and started talking to Daddy before he was even in the kitchen, and Daddy listened to him without answering Sandy's question at all, in the way that adults do. And Sandy waited for ages while Daddy and Grandfather talked again, and then said, 'Excuse me, please,' very politely a few times, and Daddy said, 'Just a minute Sandy, *please*,' and she waited some more, and then Daddy got up to go without asking her what she wanted.

'Daddy!' she said, stung by the injustice of the situation and the bad manners of all adults.

'Sandy!' he said. 'Don't get cross. What can I do for you?'

'Haven't you seen my rabbit?'

'I'll tell you in the car,' he said. 'Now what do you say to Grandfather?'

Sandy knew to say thank you to Grandfather, so it was very annoying that Daddy told her to.

It wasn't until Daddy had put Sandy's things in the car, and she had strapped herself in on the front seat, and they had turned round in the drive, and she had kissed Grandfather goodbye and watched him wave to them with his big white handkerchief and run after them right out into the road still waving, that Daddy said, 'Now, what was it you wanted, sweetheart?'

'How's Poppy?'

'Oh yes. Fine. I'm sure she's fine. I haven't seen her yet.'

'Oh Daddy! Why?'

'Why what?'

'Why haven't you seen her?'

'Because I came straight here to pick you up, that's why. I just dropped Mummy off home and got straight back in the car again to come here. They'll fetch her from Sue's house and she'll probably be home when we get there.'

'I thought Sue was going to look after her at our house.'

'Oh, was she? I don't know. Anyway she'll be there when we get back, and very pleased to see you.'

It's odd, the number of things adults are allowed to say without knowing them. It's not lying, really; it's just what adults do.

The drive back wasn't quite as much fun as the drive to Grandfather's had been. They didn't stop for lunch, because it wasn't lunchtime yet and Mummy would have it ready for them when they got in. And they had to put the roof back on the car after a while, because it wasn't sunny any more and Daddy thought it was going to rain. It didn't in the end, so they could have kept the roof down, so Daddy could certainly be wrong about some things.

When they'd been going for ages, and the things they could see outside the car started to look more and more like bits of London, Sandy said, 'Are we nearly home?'

'Hammersmith,' Daddy said. 'Hammersmith Roundabout. Count to a hundred and we'll be home.'

Sandy could count to a hundred if she thought quite hard. After thirty-nine she seemed to miss a bit, and at fifty-nine it seemed very hard work indeed, but Daddy put her straight, and she was just wondering what to do after eighty-nine when she saw their road.

'Here we are,' Daddy said.

'Not quite,' Sandy said. They weren't outside their house. Their house is at the other end of the park. 'What comes after eighty-nine?'

'Ninety.'

'. . . ninety-eight, ninety-nine, what comes next?'

'We're here. What? After ninety-nine? A hundred.'

'A hundred! We're here! Daddy, can you let me out? Can you let me out, Daddy? Daddy? Daddy please.'

'Just a minute. Give me a chance. I'm not out myself yet.'

'Please, Daddy. I want to go and see Poppy.'

'Take some of your luggage in. Sandy! Come back here. Please will you take your things in?'

And Sandy had to come all the way back from the front door and take ages getting her bag and her coat out of the car, and then wait for Daddy because he was in the way trying to unlock the front door so she couldn't get round him to get in; but as soon as he got the door open, she rushed past him and dropped her things in the hall and ran out into the garden.

'Sandy,' somebody said. She didn't take any notice.

Poppy's cage was open. She must be in the garden. The others didn't usually let her out, but they must have thought she needed it, after being cooped up so much.

'Poppy!' she called. 'Poppy!'

'Sandy! Sandy!'

'Poppy!'

Her mother was at the French window.

'Sandy darling.'

'Hello,' she said, not looking round.

'Sandy, it's lovely to have you home. Have you had a super time?'

'Yes thanks. Poppy!'

'Sandy darling, we've got some bad news. Something very sad has happened.'

'What?' It was tricky when adults said that. Sometimes things they thought were sad, or bad news, didn't matter much. Like when they said the car had broken down. Or a 'line' that Mummy had ordered hadn't sold at all. Sandy never saw the line that Mummy couldn't sell. They didn't have a line in their garden for drying clothes, like some people did. They had a machine for drying clothes.

'Come over here, darling, so I can tell you.'

'I can hear you,' Sandy reassured her. 'I'm looking for Poppy.'

'I know you are. It's about Poppy.'

Sandy knew it. She had known it all along. She knew in the car when Daddy had told her he hadn't seen Poppy. She had known as she saw the empty hutch. She knew even before it all happened, when she had left Poppy on her own and all the family were going to be away. She shouldn't have agreed to go to Grandfather's. But then what would have happened? She would have gone on holiday with Mummy and Daddy anyway. She should have said she must take Poppy to Grandfather's house. But she had said that, and nobody had listened. Nobody ever listens to a child; not when it is about something important.

Even though she knew now, she still went to her mother saying to herself, They haven't picked her up yet. Perhaps Sue was out, and I can't see Poppy till this afternoon. Perhaps that's what the bad news is. Or perhaps she's hurt her paw, and she's gone to the vet. Or perhaps. Or perhaps or perhaps.

Mummy sat down on the step of the French windows. Sandy sat beside her. Mummy put her arms around Sandy and told her that Poppy was dead.

She also told her why and how, and that nobody could have helped it, and that it would have happened even if Sandy had been at home looking after her, and that these things happen to small animals and one can't do anything about it, and that Sue just came over one day and Poppy was dead on the floor of her hutch.

And all Sandy said was, 'Where is she?'

'Where's who, sweetheart?'

'Where's Poppy?'

'Um. I don't know, sweetie. I don't know. Sue said she'd come over and talk to you about it if you wanted her to; tell you what happened. Would you like that?'

'Yes.'

Her mother didn't tell her to say 'Yes, please'.

Sandy stayed in the garden. She picked one of Mummy's flowers, which she wasn't allowed to do. It was purple, and it had a hairy stem, and it didn't smell very nice. She took the petals off slowly, one by one, and then she shredded them very carefully, and thought they would make good clothes for fairies. She would leave them out that night for the fairies to collect when all the humans were in bed, and then they could make purple jackets and dresses to dance in.

Nobody could kill the fairies. Fairies are too quick and clever. Perhaps babies are stupid. Perhaps it's stupid to lie waiting for people to feed you milk. If they don't want to feed you milk, you die. Fairies don't lie and wait. Fairies sneak under the wall by moonlight, and adults can't see them, and that's why they'll always be safe.

The adults couldn't see her baby sister, but she hadn't been safe.

'Hello, Sandy.' It was Barney. 'Sorry about the old bunny. Rotten luck.'

'Thanks, Barney,' Sandy said, and looked away again.

Sandy found a little round pebble, and began to draw on the paving stones. You couldn't draw with it properly; it was too difficult. But she did squiggles and scribbles, and managed to scratch the paving stone quite white. Then she wondered if Mummy would be cross with her. She threw the stone away to the other side of the garden, where it rolled until it hit the little wall Mummy had put round the flower bed, and there it rested.

'Sandy?' Mummy was back at the French windows. 'I've rung Sue, and she'll come round as soon as she can. Probably in about half an hour. Come inside and let me get you a nice drink.'

Sandy shook her head.

She wondered whether to build a little house with the stones in the garden. She gathered a few together. She'd missed her garden, and was glad to be back. Then she remembered the reason she had wanted to come back so badly, and dropped the stones again, and stared at the ground and forgot her little house. There was no point, after all. There was no point in anything. She could have taken Poppy to Grandfather's house, and everything would be all right now. Adults were stupid. Adults are more stupid than anything else in the world. She had told them about Poppy, and they hadn't listened. She had tried to tell them about the other Poppy, and they hadn't listened about her either. They spoil everything. They make things, and then spoil them again. They can make the most beautiful things. They can give the best presents in the world. They can even make new people inside them. In some ways they're very clever. But then they spoil all the beautiful things they've made. Children are more clever really. If children could make those things, they wouldn't spoil them afterwards; they'd look after them.

'You're daft,' Sandy said to herself. 'You'll be an adult one day.' 'No I won't,' she replied. 'I won't be stupid like adults are. I'll remember. I'll remember all the things I know now. All the things that adults are too stupid to see. And when I've grown up I'll remember what it's like to be a child, and I won't kill things.'

But deep down Sandy recognised the impossibility of the task she had set herself. No one can remember. No one has ever done it yet, and why should she be different? It's too long to remember. It'll be so many long long years before she'll be an adult, that no one can stay sensible for all that time. She'll be just the same. When she becomes an adult, she'll be stupid too.

But there was one thing she could do. She could remember just one thing. If she decided now that it was the most important thing to remember, she thought she would still be able to remember it even when she was thirty-eight, like Mummy. She thought perhaps if she made a vow it might stay in her head even better. She wasn't sure how you made vows. Jack said Red Indians cut themselves and mixed their blood with each other, and promised to be brothers for ever. She didn't want to cut herself. And she didn't want to be anyone's brother.

But then she remembered that she was a sister. And that she'd had a sister, once. Whatever anyone said, Sandy knew she had had a sister. No one would talk about her, and no one would give her a name, and no one would ever agree that Sandy had had a sister. But she had been alive, and that counted, and nobody could take that away from her.

Once Sandy had overheard two of her teachers talking about her parents; about Daddy and Mummy, Simon and Amanda, Sandy's parents. It was after the class about garden life, which made everyone start worm hunting. The man who had come to tell them about it asked if anyone knew how worms had babies. Sandy just happened to know, because her daddy had told her the other day in the bath that worms are bisexual. Then he said, 'Oh, no; that's ballet dancers, isn't it? I mean asexual.' And when Sandy asked him what that meant he said they were male one end and female the other, almost as if they had a willie one end and a vagina (that's a lady's bottom) the other; and that they lay side by side but head to toe, and that was how they made love. He also said that if you see a worm making itself into a circle you chuck a bucket of cold water over it and tell it to pull itself together – or rather, apart – but Sandy thought he was probably being silly when he said that. So she had put her hand up to answer the question, and explained all this to her class, and when Rachel asked: 'What's making love?' she had explained that too, and she was very pleased she and Daddy had just happened to talk about it in the bath earlier, because the term before she hadn't known and couldn't have put her hand up.

But that day she was late going out for playtime because they were eating lunch inside because it was cold, and Mummy had put too much in her lunchbox and it took her ages to eat it, so she was clearing away when she heard Miss Jenny and Miss Nicola, the headmistress, saying that they thought Sandy's parents possibly told the child too much. They were laughing about it, but then Miss Jenny got serious, and said it could lead to children being upset if you weren't careful. That was what Miss Jenny thought. Which is just typical of adults. They tell you not to tell lies, and they tell you that also means telling the truth when you need to, but they think it doesn't matter if they don't tell children all sorts of things.

And they think you won't be upset just because you don't know, which is stupid. Suppose Mummy hadn't told her that her rabbit was dead? Would that have been kind? Or suppose, even worse, Mummy and Daddy hadn't told her about the baby? Some people might think that was better: that if Sandy hadn't known she wouldn't have been upset. Well, that was true, Sandy supposed, but she wanted to know about the baby. It makes a difference to know that you are a person with a sister. Most people, Sandy realised, would never know that she'd ever had a baby sister, and nobody would ever talk about her. Except possibly Grandfather, who is more truthful than most adults. But Sandy would know. All her life she would know. And all her life she would think of what she and Poppy would have been doing together if Poppy were still alive. And that, to Sandy, was important.

ANNE ATKINS

Now, for instance. Poppy wouldn't be born yet. But their mummy would be getting a little fatter, and their daddy would be looking after her and making her put her feet up and bringing her nice cups of tea when she didn't feel well. And Sandy and Mummy would go to the hospital together, as Rachel and her mummy had done, and see the moving photograph of their baby while the doctor looked inside Mummy's tummy, and they would see her arms and legs and her head in black and white. Rachel had told her.

Poppy would have been her best friend. They wouldn't have argued all the time, like Ella and Annie. They might have argued sometimes, like she and Grandfather nearly did, but it wouldn't have mattered because they would have loved each other so much.

And when they were adults, they would have stayed best friends, and their children would have played together and might have become friends too. When she was an adult, Sandy would still remember Poppy, and know how old she would have been, and guess at what kind of things she would have liked, and when she would have got married and had children too. And then she would remember her promise. She was going to make a promise, now. And Poppy would remind her, as if she were still alive, and Sandy's living friend; she would say, 'Don't ever forget your promise; don't forget what you promised me when you were five and I hadn't been born.'

'I won't forget,' Sandy said out loud. Then she dropped her voice to a tiny whisper, in case someone heard her. 'Poppy, I know you wouldn't have been born yet. Perhaps you can hear me better now you're dead than you could have done in Mummy's tummy. She's only Amanda really; she didn't want to be your mummy. She still is your mummy, but she didn't want to be. I'll try not to forget. You mustn't let me forget. I'm going to make the promise but I'm not going to cut myself to mix blood, because it would hurt and anyway I've got no one to mix blood with because you're not here. So I'm making my promise now anyway. Are you listening?'

The normal sounds of the garden drowned out the silence. The birds sang. The distant traffic rumbled on. An aeroplane was passing on its way to Heathrow. She could hear the sounds of voices from time to time in the house. Poppy didn't answer of course. But if she loved Sandy she'd be listening, if she wasn't too busy in Heaven at the moment. Grandfather said time was different in Heaven, so perhaps she could leave what she was doing and listen to Sandy even if she was a bit busy.

'This is my promise.' Sandy took a deep breath. Then she had an idea. 'Jesus, if Poppy's not listening, can you tell her later? She may be in the middle of something at the moment, so can you pass on the message. You know; like a telephone message? Here goes. Ready?' She took a deep breath. 'Poppy,' she said, 'I promise I won't forget you. I mean, I won't forget what they did to you. How bad it was. At least, I'll try not to forget. And to help me try, I promise that if I do forget, I'll . . .' What? Cut herself with a penknife to make it hurt? Give away all her pocket money? What was the most important thing she could say? 'If I forget you, I'll kill myself.'

After a minute she wanted to add something. She said, 'You mustn't blame Simon and Amanda. You know, our mummy and daddy. I don't think they realise. I don't think the doctors told them. Because they're a lovely mummy and daddy really.' She sighed. 'But when I tell them, they don't believe me.'

Sandy sat in the garden, listening to the various sounds, smelling the smells and watching the gay dancing flowers. There was no answer from Poppy. There never would be. But she could talk to her; she could talk to her all her life. And then one day, if Grandfather was right . . .

'Sandy! Sue's here. Will you thank her for coming over?' The adults came clattering into the garden.

'Thank you,' Sandy said quietly.

'Not at all,' Sue said. 'It was the least I could do. Sandy, I am so, so sorry about what happened. I came in every day with food and water for her. Yesterday I came as usual. I was a bit late, because it was Sunday. And there she was, on the floor of the hutch. I'm so sorry, love. She'd been fine the day before. There was nothing I could do. I called a vet first thing this morning, and he said it was probably one of those freak things. They just happen, and if you don't know beforehand there's nothing you can do. But he assured me I hadn't done anything wrong. He couldn't tell exactly what it was without seeing her, and I didn't think there was much point in that.'

Sandy nodded. 'Thank you,' she said again.

'I'm sorry, love,' Sue said again. Sandy shook her head. It wasn't Sue's fault. Perhaps it was Daddy's fault for not listening to her. But then he couldn't help that either. Perhaps it was nobody's fault.

'Where is she?' Sandy asked.

'What, the rabbit? Oh, I took her away. I didn't want you to come home and find her without me telling you, so I wrapped her up and took her to my house.'

261

'Please may I have her back?'

'What, *dead*, darling?' Sandy frowned. Adults are funny the way they can ask such stupid questions. 'Well, yes, if that's all right with Mummy. Is that all right, Amanda?'

Sue looked at Mummy. 'Yes, of course,' Mummy said. But Sandy could tell by the way Mummy looked at her that she didn't really understand. 'Do you want to bury her, Sandy?'

'Yes,' Sandy said. She hadn't thought of it before. Now she knew, with a certainty she hadn't dreamt of, that that was what she wanted to do. 'Yes, I do. In the garden. And I want to invite Grandfather to the funeral.'

'I think it'll be too far for him. But let's go to Sue's house and get her anyway.'

Sue had put her in the dustbin. She tried not to let Sandy see, by asking her to wait in the house. But Sandy looked out of the window and saw Sue getting a plastic bag out of her dustbin. She came back into the house and gave it to Sandy, and all Sandy could see was a bundle of newspaper in it.

Mummy was helpful. She found a corner of the garden, and moved the plants from on top of it, and dug a hole much deeper and bigger than Sandy would have thought was possible, and helped Sandy put the bundle in it. She had opened the newspaper, and seen nothing but a stiff brown rabbit with its eyes sunken in, and wrapped it up again, and Mummy had said she must be sure to wash her hands. After they had put her in the large hole, Mummy put the earth back, then she suggested she should put the flowers back to make the grave pretty, then she asked Sandy if she'd like a carved headstone.

'What's that?' Sandy said.

And Mummy showed her. She found a piece of wood, and wrote on it with a pencil, and then got a sharp kitchen knife and carved the words out, and then she showed Sandy what it said. 'Poppy, 1990–1990' ('That's when she lived and died,' Mummy said), 'Beloved of Sandy'. ('That means you loved her.')

'She didn't live long, did she?' Daddy said, who had just walked into the kitchen and seen what they were doing.

'Thank you Simon. No, she didn't. Now you can go and put that on the grave,' Mummy said.

'Thank you,' Sandy said.

'Listen,' Mummy said, as Sandy was about to go, 'you've still got the hutch. It's a very nice hutch. Would you like me to ring the pet shop and see if they've got any more? I'd love to buy you another one.'

Sandy stared at her mother. She felt her fists clenching and unclenching. Her eyes widened and started to hurt. She felt herself go cold. She picked the wooden gravestone off the kitchen table and turned to go.

'I hate you, Amanda,' she said very quietly, and walked out of the room.

But not before she heard Simon say, 'Well, that went down well, didn't it?'

'Oh belt up Si.'

The grave looked beautiful.

Sandy sat in the flower bed, looking at the mound of earth with the flowers on it, and the piece of wood: 'Poppy, 1990–1990, Beloved of Sandy'. It had been kind of her mother to do it. She hadn't meant to be so horrid to her.

'I hadn't meant to,' she said out loud. Perhaps her mother would cry. She would go back inside and say sorry.

'Isn't it odd,' she continued, 'that they let a rabbit have a grave? Simon says people are more important than animals. But they didn't let you have a grave.'

She wondered what Granny's grave looked like. She had never been allowed to see it. She wondered whether Grandfather sat on Granny's grave, talking to her. She thought of Grandfather, so kind and so lonely, crying for Granny every night and nobody ever knowing. She knew he hadn't told anybody except her. And she would certainly never tell. Perhaps he was sitting on Granny's grave, talking and never getting an answer, just like her. Waiting to join Granny. Waiting all his life. Sandy didn't want him to die; but she didn't want him to be lonely either, and she thought that was probably more important. 'So in that way,' she said, 'I think it would be good if he didn't live too long.'

For a long time she sat by the grave. She looked at the little bright red flowers. She was glad they were red. She thought red would probably be her favourite colour now. She saw a white butterfly skipping almost, in her sunny corner of the garden, near the grave. And then she saw a ladybird climb on to one of the red flowers.

In the end she got up to go. 'I must go now,' she said. 'To Amanda. I don't know when I'll come back. And after all, you're not here really, so it doesn't matter.'

263

As she stood up, she looked at the little grave hidden in the corner of the garden, and thought she might not bother to come back. But something was still lacking. She hadn't managed to say everything she meant. She felt acutely the danger of her growing into a normal adult, and forgetting, just as adults always do. Forgetting to see clearly. Forgetting to know right from wrong. She wanted to promise something more. And she wanted to do it now, because she wouldn't return to the grave in the same way. Tomorrow it would be just another flower in the garden.

'Poppy,' she said, 'when I'm an adult, when I'm grown up and a mummy, I'll never ever ever kill my children. I mean, a baby in my tummy. You know.' That was all. That was her promise. It seemed very insignificant now, but it was the best she could think of. Would she remember it? She didn't know.

Then Sandy went back inside the house and found her mother. She found her in the kitchen having lunch with the others. She was glad they hadn't bothered her for lunch.

'Amanda,' she said, 'I'm sorry I hurt your feelings. I would like another rabbit, please, but I'm not going to call it Poppy.'

CHAPTER SIXTEEN –
CONCLUSION

She, she is dead; she's dead; when thou know'st this,
Thou know'st how dry a cinder this world is.

John Donne, An Anatomy of the World, First Anniversary

I realise now, as I come to finish, that I have no way to say what I set out to say. I faced the truth so long, and told myself the facts so often, that I have no idea how anyone else will react to a story which has made me numb.

There is nothing else for it, then, but to use the plain Anglo-Saxon which is adequate for the best and worst of news. 'Always,' I was told at school, 'use clear, simple prose. Never use a Latin word where an English one would do.' Even now, you see, I am putting off saying what I have to say by talking about something else.

Have at you, then; I shall say it. Know what you've already worked out. Poppy is dead. I shall never see her no more. I have mourned and grieved, and as they say of bereavement, I shall never get over her loss though I hope to learn to live with it.

What more can I say? That I see her death in terms of tabloid headlines? Terrified Child Torn Limb from Limb. Callous Cold-blooded Killing. It's not very tasteful, is it, and no one will listen if I tell it like that. But then no one will listen anyway, even if I tell it in its social context. Anonymous Three Millionth Victim.

My sister was killed, by her parents and doctors, before she ever saw the light of day. At the time, as a child, I thought my world had gone mad, when I found that those who were my greatest security, those I was supposed to turn to in times of most desperate trouble, were monsters of grotesque proportions, perpetrating violence against the innocent.

265

ANNE ATKINS

This is, I gather, an adjustmental flaw. Most children can absorb new, even shocking facts about the universe, and modify their worldview to accommodate them. I could not. I still cannot. My only comfort is that I trust, and believe, that future generations will look back on the society I live in now, and shake their heads at the incomprehensible madness and depravity of such a holocaust against the defenceless.

By the standards of contemporary society I am mad. Or perhaps, some would kindly say, 'unbalanced', 'emotionally unstable', or 'maladjusted'. For in order to cope with such a terrible burden of grief, thrust on me at such an age, I used an extreme form of consolation which is not uncommon amongst the bereaved.

I know a couple who still talk of their three-year-old child. The boy had a bad cold, so the parents put his cot in their own bedroom that night to keep an eye on him. The child's father was a doctor, so he couldn't have been better equipped to keep his child alive. At two in the morning he jumped out of bed and ran to the cot, alerted and suddenly woken by the deafening silence. His child had stopped breathing. The father rang a neighbouring doctor and asked him to come to the house immediately to be a witness while he tried to save his child's life. Then he carried him down to the kitchen table and cut his throat with a kitchen knife to try and get air into the trachea to save him. It sounds desperate, but is, I gather, acceptable medical practice. It failed. The boy's sister, a contemporary of mine, remembers coming down in the morning, at the age of five, to see her brother, dead and with his throat cut on the kitchen table.

The reason I mention this story is because I observed, over the years, how the mother coped with the loss. 'People never want me to talk about him,' she said, 'but I long to. I loved him, and I miss him, and I want to tell people about him. I like to imagine what he'd be doing at school, now; and now he'd be going to university; and perhaps now he'd be getting married. It helps me to cope.'

It helped me to cope too. I imagined Poppy's birth, and her childhood, and our friendship and love. I imagined her work, and her boyfriends, and even the times when I wished I didn't have a sister because those times were part of her too. I imagined she lived with me, and worked with me; and I even produced her work for her, and published it in my children's books along with the name I'd given her. I imagined her relaxing with me, by my fire which I always imagined was her fire too, drinking a bottle of wine with me. And no, in answer

266

to your unasked question, I didn't pour a glass of wine out for her: I wasn't completely bonkers. I simply imagined that I had.

It was a way of not going mad, you see, whatever people may say. It was a way of coping with the terrible outrage against her: worse even than her murder. It was my way of coping with the fact that no one would even acknowledge she had ever been. This was what made it all so hard to bear. Even the mother who lost her son could talk about him, however reluctantly people listened. She had a coffin and a grave and a stone with his name on it. Those who lose their families in war and famine and concentration camps, or simply in the local hospital, can tell their story. I could talk to no one. In law, my sister had no rights at all, no name, no existence. In law, she had never been.

There was only one other person who knew, and believed, what had happened. He understood, and felt the loss, as I did. But he had a faith which took him on its back like an eagle, which could soar above such horrors and give him confidence that wrongs would eventually be righted and the broken-hearted would be comforted and that my sister was safe, beyond any more suffering and pain. I had no such faith, and no such confidence, and after he was gone I had no one to wipe the tears from my eyes.

So I had to stop crying, and I had to survive, and I had to learn to live with my agonising loneliness. And the baby sister I'd never known became an invisible companion to me, so that I could celebrate her lost life.

But how could I celebrate her life? Rationalists will protest that I knew nothing about her. How could I know she would have been an artist? Or have fair hair? Or enjoy an outgoing personality? I don't. I don't even know she was a girl. Perhaps it was a baby brother that was stolen from me. All I knew was that this child deserved my love, and that I had to picture the child if I was to love it. And if, Poppy, you were a dark-haired, shy boy-child, with no artistic talent and nothing else that I have imagined on you, if you had Down's Syndrome or other Special Needs – even if you were not a lovable child – I still love you and recognise that you were. Even if I can't, as our grandfather could, believe that you still are.

I think it was the idea of her artwork which kept me going. For some reason, as a child, I consistently puzzled grown-ups by producing paintings and drawings which had the style, superficially at any rate, of a child many years my junior. No doubt a psychologist would come up with some good reason for this: I was trying to be my lost sister,

ANNE ATKINS

or something. My teachers at school assumed I was very backward at art, not taking the trouble to look at the technique behind it or compare my work with a genuine child of the age I imitated. It took a real artist and very sensitive man – Peter – to spot that there was something unique, and in a strange way mature, about those pictures. I don't know what explanation he gave himself as to why I chose to work like that. But he realised it was a choice; he saw that they were childlike only in the way that a trained artist might draw childlike pictures in order to illustrate a child's book, for instance.

For my own part, I think I took to drawing because Poppy was too painful for me to write about. Like Philomela, sewing the story of her tragedy into a tapestry because her tongue had been cut out, over and over again I drew the story because I couldn't speak. The many many pictures that my mother didn't keep were full of the deaths of children.

And Ariel? Ariel was a way of sharing my loneliness with other children. I had no idea so many others were lonely too. I think if I'd realised she would be such a commercial success, I would have had scruples and kept her to myself. I suppose it was a good thing I didn't. I suppose, if so many children have responded to her, they must, in their loneliness, have needed her too.

The time has come when I want to say that I don't blame my parents, because I know that they will read my book and the last thing I want is to cause them any more pain.

When I was studying the Second World War at school, I couldn't understand why such a civilised country, which produced Beethoven and Bach and Mozart and Goethe, and some of the most interesting and gentle people I'd ever met, could have allowed six million people to be murdered without a protest. Had they all gone collectively mad? My teacher explained it to me by saying that many didn't know, and more didn't believe what they knew. And those who both knew and believed did what they could before they were arrested and hanged themselves.

But what will posterity say of us? That we all knew, we all believed, and those that condemned did so politely in the newspapers.

Strangely enough, I think that on a subconscious level, emotionally not rationally, without questioning why, as a child I blamed my father not my mother. This was totally unfair of me. I believe he would have liked another child. But he is a gentleman and a scholar, and would never have dreamt of compelling my mother to do something against her will. Indeed, such an idea is unthinkable as well as repellent. The man must be a monster who would force his wife to carry a child she didn't want, even if the law allowed him to, which it didn't. I have no desire whatsoever to return to a so-called 'Christian' society, or emigrate to an 'Islamic' state, where a man has powers over his wife and can tell her what to do.

But at this point something atavistic and childlike deep within me cries out in protest against the civilised times we live in. Why can't a man have some say over his child's life? And is a woman's body so precious, I want to ask, that it is worth more, for a few months, than my sister's whole three score years and ten?

But of course my father bears no responsibility for what happened. The law, now as then, gives a man no rights over his unborn child. Perhaps I blamed him for not buying a little coffin, and burying her, and putting flowers on her grave: I wanted him to behave as I did when I had pets which died, because that was what I understood. Perhaps I simply blamed him for not being broken-hearted. Perhaps I blamed him for not crying, like me, and rocking her tiny memory in his arms.

But then, perhaps he did. Perhaps he understood everything I was going through, but there was no contemporary vocabulary for him to tell me that he knew.

It'll be said, by those who want to say it, that I had problems because of my upbringing. That I suffered a trauma, at the age of five, because of well-meaning parents who were too liberal, who told me too much, who allowed me to know something that a five year old can't cope with. That I suffered from too much truth. Say that if you must. I'll never believe it. The truth, in itself, can't be harmful. I hope I shall follow my parents' example, and always tell my own children the truth, however unpleasant it is. If they ask me where we go when we die I shall answer, quite truthfully, that for all I know some godless hell awaits us.

So what now?

Now, I am happy to say, I am building a new life. It's taken me more than twenty years to say goodbye to Poppy, but I have said goodbye to her at last. Not that I won't continue to mourn her. But now I've finally buried her, in my heart if not in a cemetery; and told the world about her, in this book if not face to face; and now she is simply a sister who died rather than a lovely but ghostly friend to haunt me.

This book, for me at any rate, has been a tragedy in the Aristotelian sense: I've tried to convey the pity and the terror, and in doing so I've been cleansed. It has been cathartic.

So now, as I end my book, I find I'm looking forward to a friendship with someone who'll be even more true to me than Poppy; to having my very own baby instead of a baby sister; to bringing up my own family, and making my own mistakes instead of dwelling on other people's.

There is, they say, a season for every purpose under heaven. *A time to weep and a time to laugh; a time to mourn, and a time to dance.*

I've done my weeping and mourning for the past: now I'm going to laugh and dance for the future.

26 August, Thursday, Parsons Green

Howle, howle, howle
Olivier. Lord Olivier. Played Oedipus. Gave a howl which
went down in theatre history. Those who heard it in the flesh
say it was the most harrowing thing ... He researched it: when
they trap minks, they put salt down on the road. Mink licks
salt. Tongue freezes to road. Mink trapped. Mink cries. Howl.
How did I come to lick the salt?

Oh, horror horror horror
Tongue nor Heart cannot conceive nor name thee

Oh, Caz, can't you even watch your heart break without
quoting effing literature?
All right, start again.
I have been told something, last night. I want to howl again.
My body feels as if it's been beaten all night by the Japs.
Why the Japs? God knows. Something in Grandfather's distant
memory. They didn't like 'conchies'; nobody does. I can't move
without pain. I woke up this morning and couldn't get out of
bed. I lay for hours. World grey, like an old black and white
telly. Eventually got up, very very slowly, and went downstairs
to get the letters: every step a spasm of pain through my
body. Had to do everything very slowly, like walking in thick
porridge, or on the moon. Still have to. Oh, if only I could cry.
Right. I really will start again. I will explain it, as if to Abi.
Perhaps Abi will read this one day, and want to know why.
Yes, perhaps she will. I shall write it for her.
Abi, dearest Abigail, I want you to understand what
happened to your aunt, because I love you very much. I'm
leaving you enough for your education; the rest's going into a
fund I support – but none of that matters. I'm going to tell it to
you as a story, because that's how it makes most sense.
Once upon a time there was a girl called Cassandra. Yes,
that's right; just like me. In many ways she was a very
happy girl: she had lovely parents (a king and a queen)

271

and a very happy (and very big!) family. But she had one
misfortune. A god had put a curse on her. And her curse
was that nobody would ever believe a word she said. In fact,
they all thought she was mad.

But there was one exception to her curse, and you must
remember this very carefully. The gods told her that one day
she would be believed. Just once. And in that moment she
would know she was about to die.

Well, she had quite a turbulent life, as princesses often did
in those days. There was a war, and lots of unpleasant things
happened, as they do during wars, and one of the things that
happened was that her sister was sacrificed to the gods. Killed.
Yes, horrid, isn't it? But they did beastly things in those days,
and often thought they were doing the right thing. We do
equally unkind things, and we think nothing of them either.

Then Cassandra was carried off by the conquering king
as a 'trophy of war'. That means he thought she was rather
gorgeous, and decided to take her home as his wife. Or
mistress; I can't remember quite, and I'm not sure that it
matters. He had a wife at home already, but that didn't worry
him much. Now, many people might have thought Cassandra
lucky at this point: a nice, handsome, strong king, who'd just
won a battle, was going to take her home to his palace.

But do you know what we find out in the story, when
Cassandra gets to his palace?

Oh, Ben, you remember this bit of the story, don't you? I
know you read agricultural economics at Cambridge, but you
must remember this bit ... Think, Ben, think!

So that he could win the battle, Agamemnon had done a
terrible thing. In order to gain the favour of some god or other
– I forget which one. A right sod of a god, even as gods go.
I'm afraid this bit isn't very nice ... Where was I? Oh, yes, in
order to gain the god's good opinion and get the right wind
on his boat, Agamemnon had killed his own child, his own
daughter, before setting off for battle.

There.

There's a play about it, you see; and we, the audience,
see Cassandra, years later this is now, talking to the chorus,
after she gets to the palace. They say she's like a gabbling
swallow talking nonsense; like a nightingale, crying in
the night for the death of a child.

She tells them that she's going to die and her husband's
going to die and awful things are going to happen and families

will murder each other and fathers will kill their own children,
and in the end ... can you guess what happens? What's
the worst thing that could happen to Cassandra? What's
she been waiting for all her life?
   That's right. The chorus believes her.
   So you see, you can guess what happens after that.
   Ben, help. Please help. Can you come?
   Oh no, of course you can't you've got harvest. Or have you? I
wish I knew more about farming.
   This is ridiculous. I didn't sit down to talk to you about
farming.
   Ben, I can't say it in a letter. I can't say it on the telephone.
But I need you. Something's happened. *Please.*
   Oh God, I can't send this. Ben has his own child and his own
wife and his farm to worry about.
   Ben, I'm not waving but drowning. I swam out to the wrong
rock.

All right, let me start again, and tell it properly. Dear Ben. I've
had some rather bad news. Can I tell you about it?
   The reviews of my book were due to come out yesterday.
So Will bought all the papers and a bottle of champagne
(on the assumption that the reviews would be good!) and
came round last night to celebrate.
   Now it just so happens that by this time he had also read the
book. In proof: the finished hardback is only just ready. And
when he came to see me last night he said he wanted to tell me
something. About his wife. He'd told me about it before, but he
wanted to tell me again; to spell something out.
   This is the hard bit. I don't quite know where to start.
   Who are the modern gods? Success. Intelligence.
Achievement. Not money any more, not since post-Thatcherism
and all that. But the perfect human being. What does
every parent want? Not just a *nice* kid, no. But a perfect little
genius of a child, with bags of talent and a beautiful body and
acceptably high IQ. And because we all only have one child, if
we have any at all, the one has got to be 'it'.
   Will's wife had a difficult labour. She had a caesarian while
she was unconscious. The baby was delivered safely. Well,
safely enough. It was put on a life-support machine.
   The next morning, however, while the mother was recovering
but still unconscious, the doctors came to Will and said that
the probability existed that the foetus might have been starved

of oxygen for a time, either pre-natally or during the delivery itself, and there was a considerable possibility of brain-damage to a greater or lesser extent. Their medical opinion was that the continuance of life-support for the foetus was strongly contra-indicated. They wanted to switch off the machine. And as there was no knowing how long the machine would be needed ... well, suffice it to say that Will would have to make up his mind while there was still the choice.

The consultant said he would be on the ward for another three-quarters of an hour, and he would come back and ask what Will wanted him to do after he and his colleagues had finished their rounds.

Why are you men such bloody idiots?

He told me about it. He still remembers every detail of the next forty minutes, etched on his mind for the rest of his life. How he wasted precious minutes trying to get through to his wife's parents, but they were away on their Easter holiday and he didn't know where to find them: no one had expected the baby for another six weeks. How he tried his mother, but she was travelling down from Scotland to the hospital, and doesn't carry a telephone with her, as people of her generation don't, though don't ask me why. How he thought of the child herself, and whether he was being selfish in wanting her to live. How he even tried going into the hospital chapel and praying about it, to some antiquated God he's never given a thought to before. How in the end he gave up on all these things and simply went and sat by Helena's bedside, and looked at the two vivid spots of red on her white white cheeks, and asked her over and over again, as she slept the sleep of the dead, what she wanted him to do.

And he simply didn't know what she wanted him to do. But the modern gods, now, he did know what they wanted, and the demands they make on our lives. Exams; university; success. And how his child would have none of these. And how we must please the gods if we want the wind to blow our ship from the shore. And what a complicated and capricious set of gods we have, just as the Greeks had too.

So in the end, with five minutes to spare, Will went and found the priests in their crisp white coats, and he told them his decision. He said he would be ruled by them.

Ben, my lover murdered his child.

His child? His little girl.

Why *are* men such idiots? And why on earth do they believe
the gods? You can't see Sarah, can you, going up the hillside
with Isaac and the firelighters and a box of matches, telling
her son not to worry, they'd find a handy lamb stuck in
the snow ha ha. Would she heck. The child of her old age?
Isaac, whose name means laughter? Not for any god. But
then no god would be fool enough to ask a mother to do
it. Except Mary's, I suppose: but at least her god had the
grace to be the victim himself.

    Ben, I can't send you this but I love you.

                    C.

I won't send this letter. Of course.

    So what do I do? I honestly don't think I know anyone who'd
understand. I once knew a man who would have done. But then
he had a future and a city with a crystal river to look forward
to, where the sun never sets. He would have known what to do.
But this, all this futility, wasn't the end for him.

    I don't have his future or his faith, and my point of reference
isn't the Bible but the classics – which he understood well
enough too – so I'll have to look for my answers there.

    Well, it's clear enough, isn't it? Procne took her beloved
son, her Itylus, and killed him out of vengeance for her
sister. Cassandra died the moment she'd been believed; with
the truth, as always, on her lips.

Oh yes, there are two things I forgot to mention. The two
things we were celebrating.

    Will and I are having a child. A boy. Our Itylus.

    And the reviews were very good. My book has been hailed as
prophetic, the catalyst to change the law. 'The tide of morality
is turning (I quote), and soon the law will protect the unborn
child again, as it has throughout most of history until 1967.'

    Oh yes, they believe me now.

    They believe me now.

27 August, Friday, Parsons Green

I've never known what it is to be alone before. No Poppy. No
one else. Nobody. Why does my body ache so?
   It took me three hours to get up. What am I talking about?
Simple arithmetic. Four hours. Half-past five this morning. The
light seemed suffused with mud. There isn't even any radio at
half-past five in the morning. I lay with my knees to my chin.
What now? Nothing. Do nothing. To do anything will hurt.
   Ten to six. I turn over. Try to sleep again. Still no radio.
Will this nothingness never end?
   Is there any point in doing anything? I tell myself I must
finish my book before I go. Then I realise I'm thinking as if I've
got to pack and tidy the house before going on some trip; and
the thought is so ludicrous I almost laugh.
   Then it comes to me that I've finished my book, and, instead
of making me happy, the thought appals me. Why? Oh yes. I
remember it now. Two minutes to six.
   Is this what it's like? Is this what it's like to lose someone?
This sense of feeling cold on a hot day; this tightening of
the stomach as if I were very frightened; this fluttering, this
breathlessness, this sweating although I'm cold.
   And I see that losing Poppy was nothing to this. Because she
didn't know me, she didn't love me, she didn't mean anything to
me in that sense.
   Can I really mean that? That Poppy meant nothing to me?
Not compared with this.
   Take my body, for instance. Because he loved it, loved me, in
the very real and active sense that the Hebrew word 'love'
in the Song of Songs means to love bodily, to know, to enter
into, because he did this my body woke up, became beautiful,
became mine because his. Alive. My skin felt the air on it for
the first time; my nose smelt things it never knew were there.
Because he loved me, I became, I existed at last.
   Now I live in a corpse. There's no point to my body any
more. Discarded, like a husk. Grey. Withered.
   The sun stares through the thick sky, as I lie in bed, like

a blind, idiot Cyclops; bored with the horror of the world.

I think of asking myself whether it's the right thing to do.
Pointless question. It's the only thing to do.
    You see, how can I love a man who did that? And how
can I not love him? I wish I had someone to talk to. I wish
I had Poppy. But I can't go back to that. It's not true; it's not
honest any more. I chose him instead. And now it's too late to
unchoose.

Right. Enough speculation. Practicalities. How the hell can it be
midday already? And today seems such a long time to endure.
How did I get out of bed. I don't know. Perhaps I should go to
the river now, and get it over. Get it over? What on earth
for? You 'get things over' so you can get them out of the way,
so you can get on with the important things in life. You dolt. So
what are you planning on afterwards, eh?
    There is only one thing I must do, and that is ... What is it?
I can't be bothered to do that either, to think about what it
is. Yes, Caz, remember. Abi's birthday. Suddenly I want to cry.
For Abi's birthday? Yes: because it's the only real thing in my
life any more. The other, the so-called events in my life, things
too ordinary, too commonplace to name, my love, my baby,
these are simply aspects of a horror story, a rather exaggerated
tragedy which must come to an end soon. Mustn't it?
    Abi's birthday. I will send her something. Something I value,
because I value her. You don't value her: if you valued her, you
wouldn't think of disappearing out of her life so violently, so
grotesquely.

I think it must be nearly teatime.
    Numb. Pain all over my body, but otherwise numb. I'm sure
that's what I feel. I think it is, isn't it? A nothingness, a dull
nothingness.
    Then suddenly, unaccountably, like a red-hot poker of desire,
I see him turn in the sunshine, his profile caught in the light as
it was when he last looked at me, like that, with his half smile
on his face, before our quarrel that wasn't even a quarrel, and
I want to yelp aloud like a dog, like a dog whose foot is caught
in the wheel of a cart, a cart which keeps turning.
    Does it go on feeling like this? For days, for years? This

sharp, stabbing pain? Or does it sink into a persistent ache of endless hunger?

Or, worse, far worse, does one, after years and years and ever, eventually get bored into feeling almost nothing, into forgetting what one feels; so one would simply become a mother with a spotty, teenaged son, bored with each other; perhaps even with another man in one's life?

Anything, anything would be better than that. I will not sink into that. Into existence for the sake of it. Into an awful prolonging.

And besides, all else besides, I know time can do extraordinary things, turn people into other people, but I never could forget him. Never.

You see, I love him.

I think he's a monster. My mind says he must be. A man who did that. And I still love him.

5 o'clock

I heard the door, the flap on the door, the letter box, the little
hinged thing where the letters come in through my front door.
It was like the sound of a thunderclap inside my house. I ran
to it as if it were the only ship that had passed my desert island
in ten years. It was, it was his writing. I could hear him still at
the gate, closing my gate behind him. And I couldn't open the
door. I couldn't call out. Everything in me screams for him, I
know. But I will not open the door. I don't want him. Not a man
like that. Not a man who destroys everything I've ever lived for.

Friday

Dearest Caz,
You're right, of course.

I was angry last night, because I didn't think you were giving me a fair trial. And because I'd been looking forward to our little celebration, and I was upset, and so on and so forth.

But you are right. I can't apologise to you, because I haven't wronged you, but I will go back to Helena, somehow, and apologise to her at last. Yes, I see now I should have done it years ago. And yes, I know what you're thinking: I ought to apologise to the person who was most wronged of all. But I can't. She has no memorial. To be utterly pitiless, she went out with the hospital waste years ago. And no, I'm not just being coarse: I'm admitting the horror.

You may find this hard to believe, but I feel relieved. Relieved that you know. Perhaps I've always felt guilty about it. I wouldn't acknowledge it to Helena, because I felt so defensive. But I can't lie to you. Though you'll say I seem to have been able to lie to myself. I know guilt is supposed to be bad for one's health, but it feels better to admit I've done something wrong than to go on pretending I haven't. And it's a relief that you know the worst that there is about me, so that if, when – I can't accept, can't believe, that it isn't a when – we are together again, you will have taken me at my worst. No, I don't think I deserve you: not at all. But I don't think desert has anything to do with love.

What will Helena say? Would she agree to have me back, I wonder? If so, would the correct thing be to return to her, to 'make amends' for what I did? We're so ignorant nowadays, aren't we, as to how the traditional morality is supposed to work? What would your grandfather have done if he had killed his own child and then fallen in love with another woman? Absurd question! He would never have got into the mess in the first place. But why not? I don't know.

But you see, dearest dearest Caz, I've tried hard not to

280

say it, but it's true that I can't live without you. I know, I know: you've told me I'm never to see you again, and here I am talking as if nothing had happened. More male arrogance? Or simply the invincible optimism of love?

I have to stop myself, every second of every minute, coming round to your house and simply folding you into my arms. I won't let myself look out of the window. I will have to ask someone else to take this letter to your front door, because I don't think I could make myself turn away again.

And I know you would accept me if I came. I know we can't resist each other. This isn't arrogance, but simple fact. If I appeared at your door I know you couldn't send me away. As they say in those awful clichés, this thing they call Luv is stronger than either of us. But you see I do believe you when you tell me I am not to come. I believe you in every way. And I also now believe what you've been trying to say all your life: that tiny and helpless children have a right to live. You're going to have to face it, my love. Some people are going to believe you.

But now look, you silly thing, that does not mean you go and do something stupid, out of some absurd idea that you are a Greek tragic heroine or something. Come on, look at yourself: laugh. Besides, Cassandra was bumped off by another woman, or I've remembered my school classics remarkably wrong. She was far too wonderful to top herself. Seriously, Caz, I know what you're feeling, or I think I do. I'm experiencing a bit of it myself. But too many children have died in this story already, one in your family and one in mine – not to mention, as you pointed out, all the millions of others lying in unmarked graves – so don't go doing anything daft with mine. Yes, mine. You're always talking about fathers neglecting their rights, or their children, is it? I'm not sure which.

I love you to bits.

Look at Wren. He made plans for a brighter dawn. Just in case. So shall I. I shall buy you some Moët for Sunday night, just like the first bottle we had (but no sheep's cheese!), and I shall actually cook for you myself, and I shall wait for you. Second by agonising second. Yes, just in case.

Love you.

Your Will

I stare at it on the table. I want to tear the letter up, as a gesture. To whom? But, being a writer, I never tear anything up. I always keep it in case it will make good copy later. In case, in ten years' time, I am writing a novel about a broken love affair, and I want to know ... In ten years' time? What am I talking about?

So I straighten it out instead, with careful, shaking fingers, and besides, I notice the sheet of paper is filling up with tears.

So at last I find I can throw my rage and fear and grief out of my horrible, ugly body, and I bawl, very loudly, into my kitchen – surely he'll hear me from his house? do I want him to? – and I know that I want to throw a plate on the floor, but don't because my mother gave them to me and she spent a long time choosing them and wasn't sure if I'd like them and I do feel some pity left in my heart, after all.

But just one plate? I say to myself, and then wipe my eyes.

28 August, Saturday, Day Two

How is it possible for the sun to shine, on a day like this? How is it possible for me to wake so late, half-past eight? And how is it possible for life to drag on, in this leaden, moribund way, for a creature to continue to live (I do appear to be alive) so reluctantly? Perhaps hell means continuing to exist after all life has gone, not being allowed to die.

Today is Saturday. I get out of bed, and tell myself that it isn't any easier than it was yesterday; it's just that the weather's different.

Downstairs. Another letter on the door mat. I don't want to feel this nausea; I don't want to stop, like this, and swallow bile, as if I'd just seen a disgusting accident in the street. This feeling, like fear again, like the moment before battle. And when I see it's my mother's writing, not his, the disappointment hurts like a kick in the ribs, like losing him all over again.

Darling,
Will came to see us yesterday, and told us a bit of what's happened, and I'm so sorry. So very sorry for what you must be going through. He didn't really tell me what it's about, except that you've asked not to see him for a while, and he rather thought it was his fault. Dear Will! I think he came to see us as a sort of way of being near you.

I know in these situations you think your parents can't possibly understand what you're going through. But I'll try and call later and perhaps take you out for lunch, if you'll let me. It's rather early in the morning at the moment and I don't want to wake you if you're sleeping, so I'll just drop this quietly through your letter box.

I know you'll think this is silly, but my father said something to me once, when I was in a similar situation, and I've always remembered it. I was devastated at the time, as you must be now, and he said, 'Don't cry too much. After all, nobody's lost a leg or anything.' I was really shocked at first, because at the time it seemed so much worse than just losing a leg. But then

283

the more I thought about it, the more I could see what he meant. It really wasn't nearly as bad.

So there we are. Nobody's lost a leg or anything. This is probably the wrong time to say it, but we like Will an awful lot.

And we love you very very much, of course! And we're thinking of you. Give us a ring or call round any time of the day or night.

Hope to see you later today.

    Lots of love,
      Mummy

Afternoon

Went out midday. To buy a stamp for Abi. Before the post
office shuts at lunchtime. And all right, yes, perhaps to avoid
my mother.

How can parents be so stupid? 'Not lost a leg or anything'!
Only my life in ruins.

Went round the corner to the post office, saw the back of his
head in the queue. I've seen his face in everyone I pass, seen
the back of his head in everyone who walks away from me,
so it took me the flash of a second to realise that this time it
was. I have no idea whether he saw me. Got home, somehow,
with my pulse thumping and my head pounding and my breath
coming and going, and my letters dropped on the pavement
somewhere and the skin off one of my knees and someone's
voice in my ears, 'Why the eff can't you blank blank look
where you're bleeding going, you silly cow!'

Knee stings. Can't breathe. Shaking. He must have seen me.
He didn't turn round, but he must have known I was there. I
saw the back of his neck, and it seemed much thicker, much
more brutal than I remembered it. He didn't turn round.

And suddenly I see an easy way out, which I would never
have thought possible. I could hate him. What a perfect, simple
solution! I see the back of his neck, masculine, unbending,
hard, and I realise that with a flick of my fingers I could loathe
him. It seems almost the same, now, as loving him: the same
passion, the same energy. But not the same pain, you see. It
would hardly hurt at all. That unspeakable man, who did that
awful thing. I don't ever want to hear him mentioned again.

But I do, every moment of every minute of every day of the
rest of my life of the next twenty-four hours. It would never be
true. I could pretend I hate him, and it would be easier, so much
easier than admitting that I'm never going to have the only man
I've ever loved. But dishonest. And what's the point of anything
if it isn't true? I'd rather die than live that sort of lie.

And I sit in the kitchen and imagine, and dream dreams, as I

285

always have. I'm still shivering, but less violently. And I think of what would have happened if he'd turned, and we would have run to each other, as if in slow motion, like the end of a beautiful and romantic U-certificate film. Or next time I go out, go down to the river, he just happens to be there. And as soon as we see each other – and he's right, this is not imagination, but fact – there's no choice any more. I can't say no. Neither can he. And we find each other in an involuntary and endless hug. And after an everlastingness I say, 'Why didn't you come? Why did you leave me alone, on my own? I've never been alone before and I didn't know how to live.'

'Alone? But you aren't alone. You've never been less alone. Don't you know, you won't be alone even for a second, for the whole of the next seven months?'

'But why did you leave me?'

'You told me to.' Simple. Of course.

'But didn't you know?' I am indignant, aghast. 'I felt like killing myself! If you hadn't arrived...' And I am cross with him, aggrieved, enjoying the delicious luxury of our lovers' tiff. And genuinely frightened, but now in retrospect, of what would have happened if he hadn't arrived.

But he isn't here. He didn't turn round. He'll sit at home tomorrow night, and wait for a very long time.

A letter came from Abi by the afternoon post. I shall write to her now, and send the birthday present I have for her. I'll send it by courier. It'll cost a bloody fortune, but at least it'll arrive on the right day; and what I'm sending her is far too precious to go by post. Besides, I couldn't go into the post office again.

I'm sending her the original copy of my first ever story, the most valued thing I have. I hope one day she'll understand it, and understand me, and forgive.

And tomorrow I shall go down to the river again, and say goodbye to my poppies, and wave at the waves, and there's an end.

And then?

The rest is silence.

27 August, Norfolk

Dear Auntie – oops! – Caz,
My birthday on Sunday. Have you remembered? Too late if you haven't 'cos the post will have gone. Unless you send by messenger but Mummy says don't be ridiculous, that's much too expensive.

This is being written for me by Rebecca, she's the oldest girl in my school and she can spell, and I can't write very well yet, and by the way, Daddy says he can't read my letters without listening and that's just your aunt being silly. Well, don't blame me, that's what he said.

Listen, I had a dream last night, Caz, and I have to tell you. You know you told me that you told Grandad – I mean Daddy to you, Simon – your nasty dream about him killing himself with a drink and now he's stopped drinking, you said, for ever you said, so even nasty dreams can do good, can't they? Um. No, Rebecca, you're not supposed to write um. No, stop it. Oh dear. Sorry about Rebecca. Um.

Anyway this was a really nice dream. We went swimming in that river again. Together. You remember? And it was, what do you call it when the sun comes up? Sunrise, that's right. And it was great. And you said, if you ever go out on your own, you said, 'specially swimming you said, you must be VERY careful – write that last bit in big letters with a line under.

That's all.

Oh, and you know you have all these interesting stories about gods? My teacher told us about Krishna last week and this week we're doing a god called Jesus. He says you have to forgive people and love yourself as much as you love them. Have I got that right, Rebecca? So I told my teacher your story about your grandfather – was he my grandfather too? How do you know, Rebecca? Look, you're not supposed to write down everything! About your grandfather trying to help people, even though they were fighting, by giving them medicines. But then some other people – Chinese or Japanese or something – came along and stopped him, and were horrid

to him and killed the people he'd been trying to help. But he still didn't hate them at all, you said.

And do you remember the story about the butterfly coming out of the box? That was your grandfather's story too, wasn't it? Was she a god too, the lady who opened the box? I can't remember her name. Please write and tell me because I'd like to tell that story in my class too.

And don't forget my birthday, Auntie Caz. I mean Caz.

Lots of love.

ABIGAIL (Her own writing. She told me to put that. Rebecca.)

28 August, Parsons Green

Dearest Abi,

Here's your birthday present. Six, eh? Wow.

Hope you like it. It's a story I wrote when I was younger. I won a competition with it, which is extraordinary because I didn't even make up the story. So there you are. It just goes to show.

Poppy, the illustrator, is an imaginary friend of mine, like your friend Scoops that you made up because you were so lonely, who goes with you to school.

No, sorry, that's not quite accurate. Poppy *was* a real person who died some years before I wrote this story, before I even knew her, before she even had a name, and I imagined that she was still alive and illustrated the story for me. I also did this because I, too, was lonely when I was your age. It's a good idea, isn't it, because then you have a friend who's with you all the time.

Only, of course, when you find a real friend, an alive friend, who really does stick with you all the time, then you must hang on to them like anything. Because that's better really; even if it is more difficult than your imaginary friend, 'cos you can't just make them up the way you want them.

Thank you for showing me your beautiful poppy field. Funnily enough, it reminded me of a very sad thing. Almost a hundred years ago now, in a horrid war, nearly a whole generation of young people was killed, wiped out, because of the stupidity of their elders. A lot of them fell in a beautiful field of poppies. And that's what poppies make me think of: a whole generation wiped out by the stupidity of their elders.

Perhaps we're more sensible now. But I doubt it. We spot one mistake, and then immediately fall into another. I wonder what it will be next?

I love you lots and lots.

Your auntie – oops! – C.

THE LOST CHILD

by Cassandra Sanderson, aged 12

Illustrated by Poppy Sanderson

Once upon a time there were two sisters who loved each other very much. They had a beautiful garden, full of birds, and they played there all day long. They grew flowers, and strawberries, and a tree with crisp juicy apples on it. They climbed trees, and swung on branches, and together were as happy as happy could be.

One of them, the older one, used to write stories about the birds that came to their garden. 'Tell me a story, sister,' the younger sister used to say to her. And the older sister would look at the birds in the garden, and say, 'Look at the birds, sister. Do you suppose that swallow was once a princess, and used to play in a garden just like ours? And do you suppose that nightingale we heard last night was a princess too, and used to play with her?' And then she would make up a story for her.

And then the younger sister would fetch her sketchpad, and her pencils, and draw the birds her sister talked about. They were difficult to draw, because they flitted and danced about so quickly, but as she practised she got better and better, and soon she was fetching her paintbox and giving them colours too.

But most of all, the sisters liked to sing together. As they skipped and ran round their garden, throwing a ball to each other, or playing hide and seek, or looking for frogs and toads, one of them would start a song, and the other one would join in. Usually they sang the same song together, but sometimes they sang in a round, which sounded really pretty. But almost always, when they finished, they would sit down on the grass with a plop, and pick at the bright red poppies which grew round their garden, and one of them would say, pulling the petals off, and wrinkling her nose up at the funny smell, 'I wish we could sing like the birds. I wish we had voices as beautiful as theirs.' And then the other one might say, 'Yes, but the birds always sound so sad. They always sound as if they've lost something.'

And sometimes the younger one would say to the older one, 'You remind me of those big Michaelmas daisies. I'm going to call you Daisy!' And the older one said to the younger one, 'You remind me of those funny poppies. You should be nicknamed Poppy!'

Sometimes the sisters would quarrel, and one or other of them would go off to be on her own. Sometimes they said unkind things to each other, like 'I hate you', or 'I wish I didn't have a sister', or even 'I wish you were dead'. They didn't mean these things. They're the sort of things people can say to each other if they love each other very much, but don't feel as if they do at the moment. Soon afterwards they would forget what they'd said, and then they'd be friends again.

Year by year the sisters grew up. They changed, and they grew, and they grew, and they changed, but they were still best friends. And when the eldest, the one nicknamed Daisy, was completely grown up, it became time for her to get married. She was pleased to get married, because a king was going to marry her, so everyone was happy and laughing.

They prepared for the wedding and the party, and the sisters had beautiful dresses made, and picked beautiful flowers for their hair, and lay in the bath all morning. And teams of cooks made wonderful food, and teams of musicians played wonderful music, and the gardens which the girls had always played in were looking more beautiful than ever.

So they ate all day, and danced all night, and everyone was pleased for the older sister. And when the time came, at midnight, for the king to take her away, the older sister went to find the younger sister, the one nicknamed Poppy, to bid her goodbye.

She found her, under their favourite tree in the garden, listening to a bird singing.

'Will you come and visit me?' she asked.

'Of course,' said the younger one, 'if you wait for me. Listen,' she went on. 'It's the nightingale. Doesn't she sing beautifully? I wonder if I'd be happy if I couldn't say anything, but could only sing a song like that?'

'It's not a real song,' said the older sister. 'It hasn't got any words.'

'Oh, it has,' said the younger sister. 'But we can't hear what they are.'

Then the younger sister smiled, and hugged her sister, and wished her well for her marriage.

The older sister and her husband went away to a far-off land. For a while the older sister was happy. She had a baby, and she loved him very much. And she had everything that money could buy. She had another lovely garden, and her own lovely palace, and servants to do everything she wanted.

But one day, she told her husband she wanted to take her little boy for a walk outside the palace.

'Whyever do you want to do that, my dear?' he said. 'We have everything here.'

'I don't know,' she answered, 'but something is calling me out of the palace.' So her husband asked the cooks to make her a delicious picnic, and they packed it in a basket and gave it to her to carry, and she and her little boy set out for a walk to the meadows.

When they reached a cornfield, the little boy pointed to some bright red flowers, and asked his mother what they were. He'd never seen them before, because there were no wildflowers in the palace gardens, but only flowers which the gardeners had put there.

'They're poppies,' she said, and suddenly realised how much she missed her younger sister.

That night, as she went to bed, she stood by her window and thought she heard a nightingale. She wondered if there really were words to the bird's song, if she really was trying to say something, and if so what it was. Then she thought of her sister, and how wonderful it would be if they could still play in the garden together, and make up stories together, and sing together like the birds did. And she asked her husband if he would go and fetch her sister, and he agreed.

While he was away, the older sister often thought of the younger sister, and how happy they would be when they were together again. Whenever she heard the nightingale at night, or saw the poppies in the fields if she went for a walk by day, she would think of her sister, and tell her little boy about the aunt he'd never seen.

At last, after many weeks and days and a long, long wait, a servant came running up to the palace to tell the queen that he'd seen her husband in the distance. How happy she was! Soon she would see her sister again.

She ran out of the palace to meet them, and strained her eyes to

ANNE ATKINS

look at the horizon. Soon she could make out figures on horseback,
coming towards her. Then she could see which one was her husband.
But however hard she looked, she couldn't work out which one was
her sister. They got nearer and nearer, and at last the older sister had
to admit to herself that none of the riders were women. Her sister
wasn't there at all. Something had happened.

By the time her husband explained to her that her sister had died
on the way, she was so unhappy she didn't listen to him properly. She
went up to her room, and thought of all the times she had listened
to the nightingale singing her sad, lonely song, and wished she could
sing like her. And she remembered her sister's promise, that she would
come if the older sister waited.

Over the next few weeks and months the older sister grew sadder
and sadder. Her women were pleased she had her son to talk to,
otherwise they thought she might have died of grief.

One day, the postman brought her a little package. She didn't take
much interest in it, because there was no one to write to her that she
cared about any more. Nevertheless she opened it, and inside found a
picture just like the pictures her sister used to paint. She wondered
if someone at her old home had sent it to her, to remind her of her
younger sister, but there was no letter or any kind of explanation with
it.

The picture told a story, and the story was like one she had made
up for her sister when they were children. A swallow was flying away
from a huntsman, and the huntsman was chasing her with a spear. A
little further on in the story, the huntsman had caught the swallow,
and pinned her to the ground with his spear. Further on again, he
put her in a cage, and pulled her tongue out, so she couldn't sing,
but could only cry and cry. And the strangest thing of all about the
picture was that the huntsman looked like the king her husband, and
the swallow looked like her sister.

The very next day, when the postman came, the queen asked him
up to her room. 'Where did you get the package which you brought
me yesterday?' she asked him.

'Someone gave it to me, Your Majesty, when I was walking through
the forest.'

'Will you take me to this person?' she asked him. 'If I come with
you tomorrow? But don't tell anyone,' she added. 'I want it to be a
secret.'

So the queen told her husband she was going to a religious festival, and would be back as soon as she had paid her respects to the gods. Her husband told her to take plenty of provisions, and look after herself, and he would look forward to her coming home again.

After many days, and asking many people, the queen found out who had given the postman the package. An old man led her to a strong castle, and inside the castle an old woman led her to the top of the stairs, and in a room all on her own the older sister found the younger sister, looking out of the window and feeding the birds.

'Sister,' she said, 'what's happened? Why didn't you come to my home?'

The sister simply turned to look at her, then shook her head and opened her mouth. She had no tongue.

The older sister felt quite sick, and sat down on the little bed. After a while she looked up at her sister, and said, 'Did my husband do that to you?'

Her younger sister nodded.

The older sister could hardly believe that her husband, the man who was supposed to love her and had been so kind to her, could have done this dreadful thing.

She took her sister out of the castle and they went back towards the palace. 'I must hide you,' she said. 'My husband mustn't know that I know.'

So she smuggled her back by night, and didn't tell anyone about her sister, and took her upstairs. On the way to her bedroom she took her sister into her little boy's room to show him to her. He was sleeping, very peacefully, and the sisters watched him for a while, either side of his bed.

'He looks like the king, doesn't he?' the older sister said. The younger one nodded. And she was so crazed with grief that suddenly, without thinking what she was doing, the older sister seized a knife from the wall and plunged it through her son and killed him before he woke up. Then she picked him up and held him and cried till her heart should break, before carrying him up to her room.

The next day, at supper, the older sister pretended that nothing had happened. Her husband asked her if she'd had a nice time away, and she pretended she had. Then he said, 'Where's my boy, my son? He usually says good night to me before he goes to bed, but I haven't seen him all day.'

So the queen told him that his little boy had been cooked in the pie he had eaten. Then, from under her napkin, she took out her son's head, with his eyes still open and his face covered in blood, and showed it to her husband.

He jumped to his feet and drew his sword. The queen was quicker than he was, and ran up the stairs to her bedroom. She won't escape me in there, the king thought, and flung open the door. He stared in amazement. There was nobody there. A swallow stood perched on a chair, and a sand-hopper looked at him from the floor, with his head on one side. On the window sill a nightingale hopped, just as his wife had hopped out of the dining hall.

'Where are you?' he shouted. And at that, the three birds opened their wings, and disappeared out of the window. Too late, the king realised they had been his wife and her son and sister. He turned to tell the servants to catch the birds which had flown out of the window, but no words came out. He had turned into a hoopoe.

And the cruellest thing of all was that the gods had divided them, so that the swallow flies high in the sky, and travels all the way to Africa every year to look for her nephew and sister, and never finds them there, and flies all the way home again. And the sand-hopper cries on his own, for his mother, into the lonely sea air. And the nightingale sings her song in the dark, and we all love to listen to her. But nobody understands the awful tale she tells, and none of us would believe her if we could.

CHORUS (to Cassandra)

Χο φρενομανής τις εἶ θεόφορητος, ἀμ-
φὶ δ' αὐτᾶς θροεῖς
νόμον ἄνομον, οἷά τις ξουθὰ
ἀκόρετος βοᾶς, φεῦ,
ταλαίναις φρεσιν
Ἴτυν Ἴτυν στένουσ' ἀμφιθαλῆ κακοις
ἀηδὼν βίον.

You are a brain-sick sort of creature, inspired by a god;
And about yourself you utter aloud a song that is no song,
    (Or a song which is unmusical, or lawless.)
Like the brown-yellow nightingale, which can't stop lamenting its
    woes,
Crying, 'Itys, Itys . . .'

Aeschylus, Agamemnon, 1135–1141.

29 August, Sunday, Parsons Green, Early Morning

London abandoned for the Bank Holiday weekend. It feels as if
the city's almost empty.

Felt a bit better when I woke up. Not cheerful: far from it.
But as if I could put one foot in front of the other. Got dressed
carefully and wandered through the dead, deserted streets,
down to the river.

Strange, standing on the bridge. When I was at prep school
I used to go over the river every morning and afternoon
and there were no restrictions on private motor traffic at all.
Extraordinary to think of it now. Fat stinking lorries, weighing
tons, belching and snorting over the bridge, farting muck all
over London; armies of impatient, restless Volvos poised to
mow down or maim the first careless child who stepped out of
line off the pavement; wild motor bikes, roaring and charging
down the middle of the road, blind to a mother with a double
buggy pushing her toddlers in front of her halfway over the
crossing. Hundreds of children killed every year on the roads.
Stupefied by lead poisoning. Brought up in cities, and even in
the country, with the constant growl and whine and stress of
ceaseless traffic on motorways and streets alike.

And today? Peace. Quietude. Rest, even in the middle of
London. A lone bus ambles past. People, even senior citizens,
dare to ride bicycles over the bridge. A late Sunday milk float
wanders home to bed. The Shires from Young's Brewery plod
handsomely over the river as they have for the last 150 years.
Not the same Shires, I presume.

I turn and look out across the water. Behind me someone
whistles sharply, and a taxi screams to a halt, going much too
fast. The driver shouts at a boy who was skate-boarding across
the road. Well, nothing's perfect.

The sun hasn't been up long and is still brilliant orange
and pink over Sands End. I cross to the other side of the
bridge and look out towards Barnes, remembering the freezing
Saturday in March, every year, when my father would push
his way through the crowd, with me on his shoulders, to see

the start of the Boat Race; and as the two skinny boats, like
stick-insects, disappeared round the bend with all the motor
boats and megaphones and helicopters in their wake we would
elbow our way back out again, and jump on his bike, and be
home in time to watch the end of the race on television.

The bank beyond the boathouses is covered now in
Michaelmas daisies, buttercups, foxgloves, cow parsley; and,
yes, there's a stretch by a rugby field that was dug up last
year which now sports hundreds and hundreds of poppies.
It is, indeed, a goodbye: in a few weeks, perhaps a few days,
there'll be none left here any more. Not till another spring. And
I imagine Abi's field again, full of them, thousands of them,
waving their bright happy heads, generation after generation,
no matter what pollutants and poisons and pavements
and pesticides we put down. They will come up again,
long after we've gone. They will.

And Will? I think of him now, and wonder what he's doing.
Is he awake yet? Yes, surely. What is he thinking of cooking
tonight? I picture him, waiting hour after hour, the lonely
bottle of Moët in the fridge, the endless longing for someone to
come, the jumping at every sound in case it might be her. It
seems another world, another timescale, another existence that,
for a short while, ran side by side with mine. A wonderfully
happy, comfortable place that I once knew. So long ago. So
briefly. Impossible, unbelievable, that I could step back into it
again and be there this very day.

I look down at the bright water. A burst of laughter emerges
from under the bridge, going downstream, heading for Chelsea.
A boat full of young girls, barely more than teenagers. They
remind me of a hen party I went to last summer, about this
time of year. It was a few days before one of us was due to be
married, and we met up on the Saturday night to go out for
a meal. But someone, I forget who, had found out where the
groom's party was going to be, so we raided his restaurant
dressed in fish-nets and hot-pants and tap shoes, and sang him
a kissogram and danced a hastily choreographed dance, and
then one of us started to take her clothes off while the rest of
us tried to stop her, and eventually we bundled her out into the
street where we disappeared before the men could take their
revenge. So we ate late, went to a nightclub, danced all night,
then at about five-thirty in the morning went to get a boat
from the river. But there was nobody there to hire from, so we
ended up pinching one in Putney which we took down as far

as Chelsea. We didn't feel like taking it back, of course; but we did, and left it just where we found it.

The memory of it made me laugh. The girls below me were laughing. Perhaps theirs was a bridal party too. The boat was full of flowers – yesterday's bouquets, perhaps? – and one or two of them had flowers stuck in their hair. They were shrieking and giggling, and it sounded loud in the stillness of the early morning. Suddenly they noticed something in the river. I couldn't see what it was, but they laughed and pointed, and as they leant out to get a better look I waited for one of them to fall in. But in the end they simply dropped an oar, which they then made a great business of paddling after with their hands.

After they'd moved on I gazed again into the clear water. It was so clean I could see fish, even from that distance. One or two; more perhaps, and quite large: perhaps almost half a metre long. And while I looked, a little blue butterfly danced and wobbled beneath me, above the light sparkling on the waves, as if it were a little tipsy. Presumably one of the last of summer.

And of course! I suddenly remember that Juliet did wake on her wedding day, the day of her real wedding, to Romeo. The other could never have been her wedding day, because she was married already. And the thought makes me run my fingers through my hair and look up at the sun and laugh out loud.

Against my bridal day, which is not long,
Sweet Thames run softly. For I sing nor loud nor long.

For some extraordinary reason I wondered when it is that you first feel the baby moving. Is it sixteen weeks?

And then suddenly, like a song at dawn, like a great leap of joy, like Elizabeth I dancing before breakfast, a flash of silver jumped out of the river, and was gone. I shut my eyes and could still see the streak on my eyelids, like the bright sweep of a knife. I'd seen it at last – a salmon, jumping in the Thames!

Well, I thought as I turned away, who ever said you couldn't have Moët for breakfast?

NOTE ABOUT THE STORY OF PROCNE AND PHILOMELA

Lemprière's *Classical Dictionary*, Routledge & Kegan Paul, 1788 (third edition 1984), says that it was Philomela, the unmarried sister, who was changed into a nightingale, while Procne, the married one, became a swallow. This was how Poppy illustrated the story, depicting herself as the nightingale.

Sandy, however, follows Aeschylus, who seems to have understood it to have been the married sister, Procne, who was turned into a nightingale. Aeschylus refers to the nightingale who cries, 'Itys, Itys' (or Itylus): presumably it would be the mother (Procne), not the aunt (Philomela), who would cry so piteously for her child.

Also, the nightingale is the one with the beautiful – and sorrowful – song. As Philomela lost her tongue, it's more credible that Procne would be the song-bird, and Philomela the pretty little swallow.